CULVER CITY

CULVER CITY

Brant Vickers

atmosphere press

To Zachary, with sincerest love, for whom I started this story years ago and hope one day might pass it on to Jethro and together grasp a gleam of what it was like.

And for Sam, whose father lived it with me and will hopefully also enjoy our memories.

"Brant remembers Culver City the same way Mark Twain remembered Hannibal."
     -Scott Aronchick, in conversation

In that place, the sun always shone, but it was the essence of things old, dilapidated, devoid of color, beautiful, and disquieting. Not being there caused restlessness in their hearts that couldn't be restrained. Its backdrops ran through their subconscious like a whispered scream. Its buildings became their refuge, its landscape their haven, its memories their reality.
     -Everett G. Brown

PROLOGUE

Cassady and Kyle sat in the limbs of the oak tree, in the dark, over Elenda Street without talking for a minute or two, catching their breath.

"What was that?" Cassady finally asked. He was still panting. "What do you think?"

"I don't know," Kyle answered between breaths. "We'll figure it out in the morning."

"Did you see what happened to Lucas?" Cassady asked.

"I don't know, but I'm sure he got away."

Cassady didn't cease with his questions. "Did John and Davie keep up with Lucas? Could they keep up? Did they see what we saw?"

"I don't know," Kyle said for the third time. He didn't want to talk about it right now. The air weighed heavily on both of them, trying to make sense of what they had witnessed.

"This should have been a simple night sneaking into the Backlot," Cassady said.

"We won't be able to find the brothers or Lucas right now. Let's go home and end this night," Kyle said. "I'll go first," Kyle said before Cassady could respond with more questions.

Cassady was sure they could handle climbing out farther

on the limb. They'd done this kind of thing a million times before. As long as you rolled with the fall and didn't twist an ankle, you'd be fine. Kyle climbed out on the branch, looked Cassady in the eyes, nodded, and dropped.

The instant he hit the ground, the lights on an unmarked police car about a half-block away exploded with red and blue flashing lights, and the car peeled rubber driving straight toward Kyle. While sprinting toward Marietta Avenue, Kyle furtively glanced back over his shoulder as Cassady watched in dread while the cop car flew by, squealing its tires while rounding the corner Kyle had run up seconds before.

Now alone in the tree, Cassady couldn't believe a cop was right there. He was by himself in the monster tree at the far end of the Backlot. He had to think fast. Drop down now that the cop was after Kyle, or wait and watch for a while, or the one thing he didn't want to contemplate—go back through the Backlot by himself. The cops could be anywhere and any car on the dark streets could be another cop; he couldn't compel himself to take the chance. The situation was crazy. If the cops caught Kyle and called his mom, she would call Cassady's mom. She would then have to check the bedroom and realize Lucas was missing, and he didn't even want to think about the brothers; the whole thing had him babbling in his own head. They had always debated the likelihood that the authorities couldn't do much to a couple of kids only fourteen and fifteen years old, for sneaking into one of MGM's Backlots.

He could circle back home down Washington Boulevard. He knew plenty of places to duck and hide from cops along the way. What was usually incredible fun, comfortable, and familiar territory turned sinister and strange. It looked like the best choice was going back through the place that had sent the five of them running, terrified, a short time ago. Contemplating this suddenly gave him chills.

Cassady looked up and down the street one last time. He couldn't see or hear anything except the rustling trees. He

4

climbed back down the oak tree into the Backlot and dropped to the ground. The cottonwood trees towered ominously over him. Usually shielding, now they seemed suffocating. He stopped to listen and couldn't hear a sound in the night. Out toward the sets, it was complete darkness. Cassady knew the Backlot reflected no lights from the surrounding city. The cottonwoods, elms, eucalyptus, and oaks hugged the inside of the fence and blanketed the Backlot from the outside world. Cassady was panicky even though this place had become like a second home to him and Kyle.

He had no choice but to cross through the graveyard and circle back through the European Village, then climb the fence back out to Arizona Street and make it to Washington Boulevard. It was the only way to go and not cross the open field in front of the Southern mansion, and that's where he didn't want to be alone. He couldn't think about what had happened to Kyle, Lucas, and the brothers. Kyle's arrest was a nightmare looming over whatever else had happened. He knew he was alone.

It only took a couple of minutes to get to the graveyard. He moved quickly, staying as near to the ground as he could without crawling. At the arched stone entrance to the graveyard, he stopped. The breeze had died down. He thought about those first days, remembering the discovery of the cemetery, and how he and Kyle were so scared and walked so slow it took what seemed like hours to go even a short distance. The other mansions, towers, manors, and castles loomed in the distance. They were different from the Southern mansion. They had run across the broken-down horror movie set on the second or third day of exploring along with the graveyard. It looked like it should have been haunted; three stories high, with spirals, shutters, and huge, shadowy, gothic windows. Its overgrown yard sloped down to a dirty abandoned swimming pool that edged up to the cemetery.

The graveyard sat on half an acre of land with tall tomb-stones and headstones complete with names and dates. Most went back to the turn of the century or earlier. The graveyard was large and spooky. It seemed so real to the boys that they had argued whether this wasn't, in fact, a real cemetery they had stumbled onto in the MGM Backlot. Kyle was especially superstitious about stepping on the graves as they walked through. They had snuck into other real cemeteries at night around Culver City, like the humongous Hillside and Holy Cross, and ridden their bikes up and down the hills and walked around the graves, and Kyle felt no different about this one.

"Don't step there, man. It's uncool. Don't, really!" Kyle had pleaded, hopping around the graves.

"Okay, okay, I won't. Sorry," Cassady always answered, inwardly smiling to himself. He loved that about Kyle.

The combination of events during this night and the idea of crossing the cemetery made Cassady almost opt to go back and take his chances with the police. He took a deep breath, pushed the gate open, and started running under the archway of the graveyard. He involuntarily closed his eyes and ran, but had to almost immediately open them again so he wouldn't trip. One path led to another, all overgrown with grass and weeds. Cassady was quiet and fast. Nothing registered in his brain as he darted between the headstones and gravestones and ran down one path, then another, heading vaguely in what he thought was the right direction to the other side of the Backlot. He darted down three cobblestone streets and made his way behind the Southern mansion, skirting the open field in front of it. Cassady never turned his head to look toward the field all five boys had been running from minutes ago.

Soon Cassady was at the place they normally climbed in and out of the Backlot on Arizona Avenue. He stopped and proudly looked around once more. *At least I didn't totally panic and freeze,* he thought. The breeze had picked up again and the line of towering trees around the mansion was swaying and making the familiar swishing noise. Cassady climbed up over the steel fence with its braces on the inside, moved over a foot, and started down the chain-link fence on the other side. He thought about Kyle and hoped he was home and safe with Lucas, waiting for him. As he was hanging on the fence ready to drop down to the street, he hesitated. As forbidding as this night was, Cassady couldn't believe their time in the Backlot was entirely over. His thoughts leapt from one thing to another. He knew deep within himself he was still drawn to this place, but they had seen what they had seen, both Cassady and Kyle. Cassady wanted to know more about what it was they saw, what that meant, and possibly come back.

Because they had seen a girl floating through a blue mist.

He willed the thought to vanish as soon as he hit the ground running. He couldn't think about it now.

Cassady was out on Washington Boulevard in about two minutes, and then he cut back into an alley that ran parallel to it. He alternately ran and walked, so he wouldn't draw attention to himself. A few cars passed, but none of the drivers slowed down or seemed to care. When Cassady got to Kyle's house, his heart stopped. Unbelievably at this time of night, lights were on all over the house except in Kyle and Lucas's bedroom. He waited in the alley on the other side of the wall that ran along the length of the house. He noticed several bricks had loosened, and that made him smile in the darkness. He kept watching until the lights in the kitchen went out, and then a second later the lights in the living room. Through a window, Cassady saw the shadow of Kyle's mom walk into her bedroom. He climbed the wall down from the loose bricks and slowly crept up to Lucas and Kyle's bedroom window. He knew it was always cracked open an inch or two; they were both fresh air freaks.

Cassady put his face up close and meowed. That was their signal. They ripped it off from Huck Finn. They knew no one would think it was a cat, but thought it was cool anyway. Lucas's face immediately appeared at the screen.

"What's up?" he whispered.

"Is Kyle here yet?" Cassady asked back quietly.

"No, what happened to you guys?" Lucas asked.

"We got split up. Let me in. Does your mom know anything?"

"No, I'll tell you when you get in. Be quiet. She thinks you guys are in bed, but she's still up."

Cassady walked around to the back of the house. He couldn't climb through any windows because they only rolled open about six inches. When he got to the back door, Lucas was there in his underwear and told him to wait. He put his finger to his lips, ran out to the far corner of the backyard, picked up a pile of clothes, and they both went quietly through the pantry to his back bedroom. When they got to the bedroom and closed the door, Lucas told Cassady what had happened.

"When we took off running I thought you guys were behind us, so I ran ahead of John and Davie. By the time I realized you weren't with us, it was too late to do anything about it. So we went to the fence and climbed out."

"How were the brothers?" Cassady asked.

"Those guys were so freaked out they never said two words the rest of the night. So anyway, we went down Washington Boulevard, thinking it might be safer, and the next thing you know a cop pulled up. He asked us where we had come from..."

"Did you tell him anything?" Cassady interrupted.

"No, no, I did all the talking and told him they were my cousins from out of town and I was taking them window shopping in Culver Center."

"He believed that?" Cassady asked incredulously. "In the middle of the night?"

"Yeah, I know, but it was all I could think of. He must have got another call. I don't know why, but he let us go," Lucas said. Cassady smiled.

"When I got home," Lucas continued, "Mom was up, so I stood outside for a minute and didn't know what to do."

"What happened?"

"So right about then I thought of something. I stripped off all my clothes except my underwear and came in the back door. She jumped a mile and screeched. Then all I did was shake my head and say, 'Those darn cats, they wake me up every night.' She heard them too, but then she told me not to throw rocks at them. We said goodnight and I went into the bedroom."

"Genius, pure genius," Cassady said. He thought Lucas could be amazing at times. He was always coming up with cool ideas like that.

"Let me ask you something, Lucas. What did you see in the field?" He didn't know if he was ready for the answer. If he didn't see what they saw, for some reason he thought it best to keep it a secret. He couldn't explain why he was anxious about telling Lucas what he and Kyle had seen.

"What are you talking about? I thought the only guy was in the window of the farmhouse or whatever on the edge of the European Village," Lucas answered.

Cassady thought for a second, *There was no guy.* But, then said slowly, "You mean that open window we were all walking by, and the light flashed or something?"

"Yeah, I looked back at you as we were walking by in single file, and then I looked in the window and saw that guy, probably a bum, sleeping in there, looking at us. He looked weird."

"What did he look like?" Cassady asked.

"I don't know, strange. It happened so fast I took off running and I thought everybody did then too. I didn't know you and Kyle weren't with us until we were already gone, man."

"When Kyle and I got split off from you three did you or

the brothers see anything else?" Cassady asked, and then held his breath waiting for Lucas's answer. He was confused and didn't know how to move this conversation forward with Lucas. He'd wait and let Kyle decide if he wanted anyone else to know what *they* had seen. They needed time to talk, per usual. He wasn't sure why, but he felt certain of that.

"No, I don't think so. John and Davie didn't say anything then, and I was running too hard to see anything else," Lucas answered. "After we got back, they said they never wanted to go in there again. They split and went home."

Cassady breathed a sigh of relief and felt at ease. Again, he wasn't sure why, but realized Lucas and the brothers didn't see what he and Kyle saw. He remembered Kyle was still missing. He detailed where Kyle went and what he thought had happened.

"If the cops caught him we would have heard something by now," Lucas said. "I don't think they would hold him for simply sneaking into MGM at night."

"We haven't done anything else, so we should be okay. It shouldn't be too bad. We need to wait this one out until he shows up," Cassady said.

Right then they heard something outside the bedroom window: that magnificent *meow* sound. Before they could react Kyle was already coming through the kitchen pantry and into the bedroom. He immediately plopped down on his bed and let out a long sigh.

Straight away Lucas and Kyle both began to pelt him with questions from both sides of the room.

"Did the cops catch you?"

"What took so long?"

"Did you talk to the cops or something?"

Kyle smirked, waiting for them to finish their onslaught of questions.

"As soon as I hit the street," Kyle finally started. "I saw the cop car burning rubber in my direction, so I ran up that cross street—I think it's Marietta or something? I ended up on Milton, and I barely made it to a crawl space underneath a house when the lights hit above me, but they didn't see me. They knew I was close, though, and they parked about three houses down and waited. I couldn't go anywhere or really move much. I was afraid they might get out and walk around, but they didn't. They sat there in the car and flashed the spotlight around every once in awhile.

"It must have been uncomfortably crazy squeezed in there?" Cassady said. They knew crawl spaces in Southern California bungalow homes were barely big enough for a person, preferably smaller than Kyle, to fit in under the house.

"Yeah, it was. As soon as they pulled away, I waited a few more minutes and then left. What's been happening here?"

Lucas related the story about the cat and their mom. Kyle listened to Lucas but kept glancing over at Cassady. When it was over, he smiled and had the same reaction to Lucas's ingenuity as Cassady did. When Cassady told him about going through the Backlot again alone, Kyle burst out with a question.

"Did you see anything?"

"No," Cassady said. "That guy we all saw must have left or something. I don't know what happened."

"What guy?" Kyle asked.

"That guy that Cassady and I saw in the window," Lucas said.

"Yeah, the guy in the window, he caused them to run," Cassady jumped in nodding vigorously at Kyle, hoping he understood not to bring up the girl or mist.

Kyle got it. He understood that Lucas thought the whole thing was about some guy in a window. Cassady could tell he had the same reservation Cassady did about sharing what they had seen. Like Cassady, he wasn't sure why. Both knew it had been such an intense experience and everyone would remember what they thought they had seen. Everyone's experience would be different no matter that they had all seen the same thing. Or maybe, Cassady uneasily thought, they were meant to see what nobody else was meant to see.

The boys got ready for bed. That usually consisted of stripping down to their shorts and lying on top of the covers. In the dead of the summer, it was still too hot for anything else. Kyle and Lucas's beds were across from each other and Cassady usually slept on a foldout at the end of Kyle's bed. After a while, Lucas, on his back, started to fall asleep and soon his breathing was a soft snore.

"Is he asleep?" Cassady asked quietly.

"Yeah, I think so. Wait a second," Kyle answered. "Lucas?" he whispered. No answer. "Lucas?" he whispered again. They both knew Lucas was a sound sleeper and rarely woke up without being prodded.

"He's out," Cassady said. "He said the goon brothers didn't see anything or think about anything other than they wanted to get out of there and never go back again."

"Makes sense," Kyle said. "They didn't see what we saw."

"Yeah, I know... Was that real, Kyle? What *was* that?" Cassady whispered.

"I truly don't have any idea, Cassady. When we split up from the others and started across that field, it didn't look right. But I didn't see anything right then, did you?"

"No, not until we stopped and looked back. It was too dark. But you know it felt weird. It even, you know, it didn't seem or feel, I guess, natural. I felt it more than saw it at first, but I couldn't place it in my mind. I don't know what I'm trying to say, man. The big Southern house looked fresh or new or something. It was shimmering when I saw them."

"What was that? It was a bluish haze, right?" Kyle sat up in bed looking at Cassady.

"I didn't really grasp what was going on, but it was like people, but not modern-day people, do you think? They were like from another time. It was way too bizarre."

"We should have waited and watched some more,"

Cassady said. "It was like I saw them, but not really either. But I didn't feel like I could have handled it another second, but now I feel we should've stayed. At least until we found out what was happening with *her*?"

"Cassady, she was floating by us!" Kyle said loudly. They both looked over at Lucas and waited for a second to see if they had woken him up.

When they saw Lucas's breathing hadn't changed. Cassady said, "She went right by us. She must have come up from the European Village. It looked like... like... she was glowing."

"I don't know, but I wasn't going to stay after that, and we took off so fast I don't remember anything until we climbed the tree," Kyle said, smiling nervously. "I don't know if I want to know. That was way too freaky."

Exhaustion overtook them, and they reluctantly faded off to sleep. In the darkness, Cassady whispered one more thing, the thing that was on their minds from the moment they were back together, but unspoken until the last possible second. Kyle was about to fall asleep and he barely heard Cassady whisper it, but he was too tired to argue or deny the truth in what Cassady said.

Cassady slowly, deliberately, almost imperceptibly said, "We have to go back another night. Kyle, she was so incredibly beautiful..."

CHAPTER 1

Over a year earlier, Cassady was feeling good. He and his friends got stoned at Abilene's house regularly. Almost every Friday night they had been converging in his garage and getting ruinously loaded on pot and acid. A couple of them dropped mescaline every couple of weeks on Friday morning to see who could maintain by lasting the longest in school that day. Cassady didn't think of himself or his friends as bad kids; they simply didn't fit in anywhere else and had found each other by default. Today in Abilene's house, with his mom at work, there were about eight friends ditching school and leisurely meandering in and out that Tuesday morning, which had casually slid into early afternoon. It was about one o'clock in the afternoon when Regis opened the front door, jumped back, slammed the door, and screamed, "Cops, cops everywhere!"

"Lock the door, shithead," Abilene said, as he calmly walked over, locked the door himself, and looked through the curtain of the front window. "Three cars on Culver Boulevard," he acknowledged evenly. "Quick, lock the kitchen door."

Immediately, several cops were pounding on the front door while Abilene steadily kept up a running commentary. "A couple are heading around to the side. Lock it, lock it, lock it!"

Everyone in the house jumped up screaming, yelling, running around, and ricocheting off each other like cue balls. Cassady presumed it looked like a Three Stooges routine. Music had been blasting louder and louder, until eventually some neighbor had grown weary of seeing these young, longhaired, 1969 neophyte hippies come and go and called the police.

Cassady saw Regis trying to crawl out a side window, and then shriek for help as a cop started to pull him through from outside. Johnny Stiles grabbed his legs and started a tug-of-war with Regis's body half in and half out. Several guys stood there looking through the back door window while two cops demanded for them to open the door, and then began bouncing around the kitchen shrieking, "Noooooo!"

Cassady stood transfixed in the middle of the living room with this raucous combustion erupting around him, wanting to cry, and thinking about getting busted for ditching school, smoking pot, underage drinking, and who knows what else. All Cassady had wanted was to have a good time. And Cassady *had* been having one, so far.

Cassady flashed on what had brought him here. He was on tenuous ground with his family. His cousin had a successful year or two and an uncle was still well-known for being a star football player at Culver City High years before. Cassady had played two years of Pop Warner and hated every single minute of it. He hated the game, he hated the seemingly purposeless false aggression, and Cassady especially hated the herd mentality of most of the players. That didn't sit well with his generally fruitless search for an identity. The first week of ninth-grade summer school and early JV practice, he showed up and was relegated to playing a defensive line position, probably based on his height. Several players mentioned to Coach Flat Ass that Cassady might be better suited to playing a wide receiver position.

"He has good hands," one said.

"I'll decide where people play on my team," Coach Flat Ass said. "I want you to shut up about that."

Cassady stood around feeling awkward, thinking maybe it was that his hair was getting longer. It didn't fit in with the current stereotype of football players.

Cassady's dad loved the fact that he had and was continuing to play football. They were searching for something at some level to relate to each other, and Cassady felt quitting would let him down.

Everyone was up for football except Cassady. Coach Flat Ass was again muttering how he was the coach and how he would decide what position his players would play and no one would tell him where they wanted to play...

"Can I use the restroom?" Cassady asked.

Coach Flat Ass looked disgusted, spit on the ground, and grudgingly said, "Yeah, go ahead."

Cassady walked into the locker room, sat down on a bench, and felt sick to his stomach. He slammed his fist into the locker in front of him and almost started to cry in frustration.

"Shit!" he said out loud as he stood up, tore the partial practice uniform off, changed into his clothes, walked out the back of the gym building unseen from the practice field, climbed over the fence, dropped down, and began the mile walk back home to Commonwealth Avenue. But first, he stopped at Abilene's garage.

"Hey," a couple of guys sitting around on old couches and throwaway pillows said as Cassady walked in and sat down. He wondered if they had forgotten about his commitment to play football.

"Hey," he said back. They listened to some music, Savoy Brown's "Train to Nowhere," while one of them lit a joint. Finally, Abilene looked over at Cassady and said, "Hey, weren't you going to play football or something?"

"Or something," he said and smiled. He realized it was likely every one of his friends had a similar story of struggling to live up to someone else's expectations, be it in school, with parents, or in Cassady's case, playing football.

Cassady had started thinking about what his deepest feelings were and how his fear of never being good enough should have already disappeared. The aching he always carried around and thought he deserved because he wasn't good-looking enough, or smart enough, or nice enough, or talented enough, or able to get through school or college, or was ever going to make enough money to live; or eventually, like his cousin, already worried about being drafted and fighting in the Vietnam War, or worse—never lose his virginity.

Fast forward to Abilene's living room where things seemed to be going from bad to worse. Kyle was there with Cassady, as it seemed he was when things were close to being regretful, but luck, again, seemed to play a part. Smoking pot until there was a haze in the room you could hardly see through. Blind Faith's album blazing on the stereo over and over again. Laughing until your sides were going to split and then settling down and doing it all over again.

Cops swarming all over the place signaled an immediate nuance of change, though. The cops had quit pounding on the front door for a second as Smitty had the bright idea of opening another back window on the other side of the house, crawling out, and then having a wrestling match in Abilene's rear courtyard with a couple of Culver City's finest. Cassady noticed for the first time Kyle was back in the living room with him. They seemed to be alone. The screaming had faded for a second, although Johnny Stiles was still having the tug-of-war with Regis's body a few feet away, muttering he'd never let go, but everything else apparently had shifted to another part of the house for the time being. Kyle and Cassady looked at each other without saying a word, walked to the front door, opened it, and walked out on the porch into the blinding sunlight. They glanced around, and seeing not a single cop, walked down the steps out onto the sidewalk, casually sauntered down the street to the corner, and turned up Center Street to freedom. Several neighbors standing on their lawns talking gawked at them, but nobody said anything or raised the alarm.

"Keep walking, man," Kyle said.

This was the beginning of Kyle and Cassady's feeling that they must have special dispensation for some reason. Even outside influences like drugs, crazy friends, and bad experiences couldn't shake the trust, loyalty, and compassion that had bonded them.

Cassady and Kyle had met one summer day months earlier. Cassady and his friend Gram had been walking up the alley a few nights previously, in the dark, to Center Street. Gram lived about halfway down Center and Cassady lived on the next street over. It was late summer and school was fast approaching. The alleys were how they traveled around their neighborhood.

"I can't believe you didn't like that movie," Cassady said.

"It was okay," Gram replied.

"It was great!" Cassady said. "Didn't you love the scenes where he asked about a million times, 'Who are those guys?'" He and Gram didn't always see eye to eye on things, it appeared, some of the time. They were friends since second grade mostly because they lived near each other, and it was convenient. Cassady liked Gram, but there was something that kept them from always getting really close. Cassady wanted that and always felt a little forlorn with it missing from the bond between them. They did have fun and Gram's house was a gas to hang out in. They were coming back from the Meralta Theatre way up in downtown Culver City.

"Man, *Butch Cassidy and the Sundance Kid* is one of the

best movies I've seen in a long time," Cassady said. He wished he had someone to enjoy it with instead of Gram, who acted like he was bored with it. At least talk with someone else about it, more than it's "okay."

"I'm sure as hell not going to see *True Grit* again or *Romeo and Juliet,* either. I'm not into those movies," Gram insisted. Cassady always neglected to tell Gram that he wanted to see those two because of Kim Darby and Olivia Hussey. He had a major crush on both those actresses even though they were as different from each other as humanly possible. He knew he'd be judged for not having crushes on the current hot actresses like Raquel Welch and any of the James Bond women he'd heard Gram exclaim over in the past.

They stopped to talk and make plans for the next day. The corner house had a descending brick wall down to the street. It went from about six feet tall at its highest point to waist high. Large bushes hid the duplex from the alley and street. Gram leaned against the wall and a brick that was loose almost fell off the ledge.

"Hey, check it out. All of these are loose," noticed Gram.

They pushed and pulled and separated them from the top of the wall.

"Someone new lives here, don't they?" Cassady asked.

"Yeah, I haven't seen them yet. Here, help me get these loose."

Cassady and Gram weren't vandals—well, Cassady wasn't— but the temptation proved far too great to resist. The top bricks broke free easily from the timeworn mortar and in the dark the two boys laid about a dozen of the bricks around the yard. They formed a sloppy circular pattern and ran away laughing. About a week later, they found themselves walking late along the same alley again and totally unintentionally they laid a zigzag pattern. They came back again two nights later and did it again. Three nights later, one more time. A couple of days after that last time, Cassady was riding his bike down the street and saw two tall boys with an older man in the front yard cementing the bricks to the top of the wall. He continued riding over to Gram's house, told him what he saw, and they cracked up.

A week later Cassady was riding his bike by again and saw one of the tall boys out in front of his house throwing a football up in the air by himself. He rode up to the curb, got off his bike, walked to the other end of the yard, put his hands up as if to catch an imaginary ball thrown at him, and smiled.

The boy threw the ball hard at Cassady and as he easily caught it said, "I'm Kyle. Nice catch. What's your name?"

"I'm Cassady. Nice throw."

Both boys were wiry and strong from playing sports. Kyle was a year older than Cassady, a tad taller. All angles, bones, and sinew smiled back at Cassady. They both wore their blond hair long and were wearing t-shirts and Levi's with tennis shoes. Kyle and his brother Lucas had moved into Culver City from another part of Los Angeles. After his stepdad knocked down a wall inside the duplex, the boys shared the whole double house with their parents and little stepsister. Cassady couldn't remember or explain what made him stop that day, but the connection was immediate. It was that simple. Kyle was instantaneously Cassady's best friend, and not only a neighborhood friend, or an acquaintance, but the kind of friend that only comes along once in a lifetime. They shared all their thoughts; discussed books, sports, movies, music, what politics they knew; and always endless discussions about girls. It was a friendship Cassady would measure all other friendships by for the rest of his life.

That first weekend, Kyle went with Cassady to see *Butch Cassidy and the Sundance Kid* twice. It was well over a year before Cassady told Kyle that it was he and Gram who were the ones who had put the bricks in the patterns on his front yard. He had almost completely forgotten about it.

"You guys did that! My stepdad went nuts. He thought it was some kind of conspiracy, that someone didn't want us in the neighborhood," Kyle said.

"We didn't mean anything by it. I can't even tell you why," Cassady said.

"He had us hide in the bushes for a couple of nights, waiting to catch whoever was doing it. It drove him crazy."

Kyle often pretended to hold Cassady hostage to the threat of telling his stepdad who put the bricks in the patterns. That would usually get Cassady to concede to whatever demand was being made.

One day Cassady asked Kyle if he thought they would still be friends when they were thirty-five. It was an impossible age for him to imagine.

"Sure," Kyle answered. "Why not?"

CHAPTER 2

Meeting Kyle changed everything for Cassady. They always had an amazing amount of freedom. Since Cassady was about nine he had the run of at least two blocks and now, as long as he was home by dinner, he could hang out with friends all day long. They spent time down on the boardwalk in Venice Beach watching all the strange people—crazies, gypsies, wannabe rock stars strumming guitars, and hippies—wandering around. Since the summer of 1967, the place was packed every day with interesting freaks and of course, girls. Mostly the boys could only manage looking. At night they would tell their parents that they were spending the night at one or the other's house. Usually, the plan was to spend the night at Cassady's house because his parents let them sleep in the garage. There, they had built a room out of old sheetrock and found two-by-fours and pieces of wood. They called it the Shack. His parents always went to bed early, so they could sneak out to do whatever they wanted, and this allowed them the freedom to roam wide and far in their world. Other friends fell by the wayside—only to provide occasional enhanced distractions as a group during the days and nights. Cassady liked Gram, Abilene, George, and the others, but they were there to augment the adventures he and Kyle were collectively enjoying.

One long summer day they rode their bikes up into Bel Air, following a map a guy on the beach had given them. It was a couple hours of riding, but they finally found what they were looking for coming around a bend in the maze of tight streets. Tall walls, trees, and shrubbery hid most of the mansions. They parked their bikes and walked up to the garish gate. Off to the side, a small hut sat out of sight from the street. A uniformed guard immediately stepped out.

"I'm going to have to ask you to leave," he said.

"We're just looking. We weren't doing anything," Kyle said.

"This is a private residence, and the occupants don't want to be bothered," he said.

"Well, we know the family, and we want to know if Elly May can come out and play?" Cassady asked sarcastically in a hillbilly accent.

"Yeah, like I've never heard that before," the security guard muttered.

"We want to know if we can go swimming naked with her in the cement pond and maybe make some lye soap with Granny," Kyle said as they jumped back on their bikes and rode away laughing. They had discovered the real house *The Beverly Hillbillies* used in the opening of the TV show.

There was always something going on at the beach. One day early in the summer break, Kyle and Cassady listened as a guy, with long unkempt hair in a ponytail, was talking about sneaking into MGM's Backlot 3 studio on the other side of Culver City. They both knew the Backlot closest to them down on Culver Boulevard was Backlot 2 and Backlot 1 was connected across Overland Avenue. All the kids in the neighborhood at one time or another had looked through gaps in the old fence to catch glimpses of the trees and buildings on the sets used for TV and movies.

"Can you climb the fence?" Cassady asked after listening for a few minutes.

"Yeah," he answered, brushing the hair out of his eyes. "You have to be real careful because they're filming almost daily on #3 and the workers are all over the place. But you can see through the old wooden fence. Pick out a place when it doesn't look like anyone is around, climb over, and you can cruise inside for a while. It's a gas, man."

"How about Backlot 2 on Culver?" Kyle asked.

"Naw, it's a bummer in the summer. Nothing in there except old abandoned sets, nothing cool. Real spooky place, though, man..." he answered. "Bad vibes. And you can't climb the new twelve-foot steel fence they've put in with that razor-sharp edge on the top at all. You'd end up shredding your hands."

"What does that mean?" Cassady asked. "Spooky how?"

"Nothing, man, never mind, I'm never going back there again, end of story. I'd suggest you do the same. Listen to me man, the Backlot on Culver is a bummer."

Cassady and Kyle walked away discussing what he said and what it could be like.

"If they can sneak into Backlot 3 then we can sneak into Backlot 2 near us," Kyle said.

"Really! It's only a few blocks from our houses."

"We have to find a place to do it. He's right, though, Backlot 2 has that wicked high steel fence all around it," Kyle said.

"Maybe that's a good thing, considering what that freak said," Cassady added. "I wonder what he meant by all that *bummer* stuff?"

Early the next day, Kyle and Cassady found themselves walking along the tall steel fence bordering Backlot 2. Elenda Street was the western border and a couple of other streets cut in on the north end. The first street off Elenda, all the way down, was Arizona Avenue, and it offered a perfect hidden place to climb the fence. A broken-down, dark, and foreboding two-story house sat on the corner of Elenda and Arizona surrounded by its own twelve-foot chain-link fence that connected to the high steel MGM fence. This was a gloomy old two-story house with shuttered windows that seemed deserted from the outside and had a dozen huge oak trees that constricted views from all angles on Elenda Street. Directly across from the MGM fence was a deserted lot. They waited several minutes and saw no cars or people coming or going.

"You go," Cassady said.

"No, you go first," answered Kyle.

"I'll keep watch," Cassady shot back.

"Jeez, you chickenshit," Kyle said, laughing as he climbed up the chain-link fence and crossed over to the steel fence. Cassady followed right behind him. They hoisted themselves up the rest of the way over the steel fence and jumped down into waist-high weeds on the other side. They hit the ground, squatted, and froze. Immediately to their left was a building that looked like a greenhouse with huge windows and a peaked glass roof, dirty and discolored.

"This looks like some kind of old nursery," Cassady said.

"It hasn't been taken care of in years," Kyle agreed.

In front of them, across a dirt road, there was a line of trees and bushes with the faint outline of buildings running as far as they could see. After about five minutes, letting their panic settle and catching their breath, Kyle motioned for Cassady to follow him out across the dirt road and through the chest-high bushes and weeds.

Several buildings were standing on the other side of the dirt road, but as the boys got closer, they realized they weren't really buildings. The largest was a three-story structure, but old two-by-fours supported walls, landings, and platforms running in several directions. The walls were aged and weather-beaten.

The boys ran over and jumped up on one platform. Weeds grew up between the floorboards. It was fifty feet wide, with walls on three sides. They waited again without saying a word. Directly in front of them was the back of what looked like a huge double door. Cassady walked over and looked back at Kyle.

"Go ahead Cassady, open it," he said.

No one was in sight and they hadn't heard a sound except their own breathing, so Cassady pushed it open slowly. They peeked out, then squeezed their heads and bodies out and slowly walked through the door.

"Wow, whoa," Cassady and Kyle both exhaled.

They walked out on a huge porch that ran the length of the building with three whitewashed square columns spaced evenly along its span. Stairs dropped down on all three sides. Plants and ivy grew up the sides of the house and the pillars. The roof slanted down, giving it a regal look. An old path ran up to the front of the stairs with tall, beautiful oak trees running down along each side of the lane. The trees were so spacious and the branches grew together over the lane like a tunnel. On either side of what looked like overgrown gardens were other buildings in the distant background, mostly hidden by still more trees. They cautiously stepped out farther onto the porch, down the stairs, and looked back behind them. What they saw was what they could only describe as a huge Southern mansion. Two stories high, with walls made of false brick, two monster chimneys on each end, a slanting roof, and at least eight full-sized picture windows. It was old and decrepit but had a stately beauty and majesty that took their breath away. They had never seen houses like this in Southern California.

"I've seen this before," Kyle said.

"Maybe," Cassady answered. "But I can't remember where."

"Yeah, I can't place it either, but it sure looks familiar," Kyle said.

"Maybe it looks familiar from movies in general," Cassady suggested.

They looked around, on guard for a vehicle or any noise, but all they heard was the wind faintly blowing through the towering trees.

"What can happen to us if we get caught in here? Cassady asked.

"Escorted out at the least. Maybe parents called, and probably forbidden to come back," Kyle said.

"How about breaking and entering?" Cassady asked.

"Maybe, probably not, but let's not have it happen."

The sun was shining bright and clear, and the outside world seemed remote and far away. Time seemed to stand still. The boys skirted the path and walked in the tall grass and weeds. They came upon another mansion, not nearly as big or stately as the first, but with an old, dilapidated horse stable attached to the side. Over at the tree-lined path down the middle of the open area, the sun reflected off the surface of a lake where four paths converged on the far side.

"This place is huge, man. Check it out!" Kyle said. "It goes on forever."

"It's immense," Cassady answered. "It's like we're in another world."

They turned the corner from the second mansion, and off from the south was a fully constructed train station with railroad tracks running out and ending about fifty feet from the entrance. They actually found two separate railroad depots. As they followed the train tracks, they found a third larger Grand Central Station. A western street ran along the front. The name *ATLANTA* was painted over the front, faded and peeling now.

"I've seen this in movies or on TV shows before," Kyle said.

Off to the right of this, they stumbled onto a street they could not describe as anything other than the Chinese Street.

The writing or symbols were vertical in what they had to assume was Chinese. Within were pagodas, palaces, and strongholds, all surrounded by oriental metal work on gates and windows. A barricade stopped them.

"What the hell is this?" Cassady asked, looking up at the wall that ran a city block.

"It's the Great Wall of China," Kyle yelled out of pure excitement. That loudness caused them to duck down for a few minutes. "Do you think anyone is around?"

"I don't know if this place is well-guarded or not," Cassady offered. "That hippie guy kinda said no. At least not like the other Backlot."

They went through a tall palace-like building and walked out into a large square lined with medieval European buildings. At one end a castle loomed over the entire quadrangle.

"Now, I know I've seen this in movies like *The Three Musketeers* and probably others too," Kyle said.

They were slowly circling around, but before they completed the loop they stumbled onto a park, an orchard, a wooded area, and an Eden inside the Backlot. As they walked up they could tell it was different. They saw an ancient weather-beaten sign.

"It says *Eucalyptus Grove*," Cassady said

"This is like the forest in *Tarzan* or *Robin Hood*," Kyle said.

"Yeah, Sherwood," Cassady answered.

They stood transfixed, looking up at the huge eucalyptus trees. The wooded area was overgrown with several unusual kinds of vegetation, amazing plant life, shrubs, and towering dense bushes. Within the confines of the overgrowth they could make out a Polynesian-themed setting with thatched huts and water towers made out of stripped bark and reeds, faded and disintegrating.

One more turn brought them to a small, still intact, and seemingly used recently, beautiful cottage surrounded by more trees. Vines grew up the sides and outside walls. Cassady and Kyle started to walk across a small bridge, made of wooden planks and circular posts lashed together with timeworn rope, over a dry creek bed.

"Think it's safe?" Cassady asked.

"If we fall, it'll only be a few feet," Kyle answered as they were already halfway across. The cottage doors and windows were locked and they decided not to break in. They discovered it was actually made of stone and timber and not a false front with wooden panels. A real thatched roof hung over the walls. A feeling left unsaid and unshared was manifesting itself in their thoughts, not to hurt anything in the Backlot. They walked behind the cottage and found a wonderful stone staircase with a large Madonna and Child statue recessed into the wall, also overgrown with vines and several trees overhanging. There was a staircase leading nowhere, which didn't surprise them in the least.

"Movie sets don't have to go anywhere," Kyle said, smiling.

Walking around an extended corner of the building, they found themselves looking back at the big mansion. Kyle said, "I can't believe it's fake. It looks so real. You'd never know that it was a front with nothing behind it. It looks like an old Southern house."

Once again, the boys paused to listen and heard nothing but the rustling of the wind in the trees. Cassady had a peculiar feeling but couldn't put his finger on what it was about this day. He had never been there but had a memory either visually or embedded in his psyche that made it familiar and comfortable.

"I don't know what that guy at the beach was talking about yesterday," Cassady said. "This is soooooooooo cool. This makes me feel like a movie star. No, wait, like an adventurer deluxe!"

"I can't see anything bad about this at all. It's the most excellent place or thing I've ever seen," Kyle added.

As they continued walking beyond the railroad station, they crossed another open field and came to the edge of the small lake that ran back to the smaller mansion. A shabby bridge crossed over it at the far end, and a small rowboat was tied to a short pier. Again, bushes and trees were on the other side, hiding what lay beyond. They continued and saw the lake was part of a larger set.

"This looks like some kind of European Village," Kyle said.

"Yeah, but is that writing on the windows French, German, or Italian?" Cassady asked.

"My mom gets magazines and stuff and reads things like that. I think it's German," Kyle answered.

They walked onto winding streets leading up from the lake and bridge, and immediately got lost in the maze of stores, churches, bakeries, tailor shops, and what looked like ancient apartment cottages. The facades of the building had some French names and some German names; some the boys weren't sure of. Walking through a door would take them into a tight alleyway filled with weeds and bushes along with more scaffolding, platforms, and two-by-fours, reinforcing another wall that opened into another street within the labyrinth of cobblestone streets. They realized it was the set for a show they both had watched incessantly, *Combat!*

"We've seen Sergeant Saunders, Caje, Kirby, and Littlejohn, an infantry squad who battle their way across war-torn Europe," Kyle said in a simulated TV voice. "As we watch from the relative safety of our living rooms," he added. "It doesn't matter how real it looks, if we push the door open—it disappears."

"So, we don't go through all the doors. We leave them closed, and then it's real," said Cassady.

The entire village, except for two houses with staircases leading up to a second floor, were fronts with only the scaffolding in the rear. From the first upstairs window, they could see more fields and different movie sets in the distance.

They could clearly see a pool to the right of where they came in, with a diving board, and surrounded, again, by trees. An unkempt footpath led from the pool back to the eucalyptus garden. They hadn't noticed it before. They could see the pool wasn't filled with water, but with leaves and debris, empty and forlorn.

As he leaned out of a window and looked out over the Backlot, Kyle said, "This is unbelievable. This really feels like we're cut off from the outside world."

"Yeah, I don't feel like we're in the middle of Culver City. This is soooooo cool," Cassady said over and over again.

They explored for hours.

CHAPTER 3

The boys couldn't believe their good fortune in finding a place so completely strange and unique. It was a magical wonderland, but a little threatening at the same time. They felt at any moment they were going to get caught and, at the worst, taken to jail. That put their nerves on edge and heightened their anxiety, but it also increased their enjoyment.

"I don't care if we get caught. It would be worth it," Cassady said.

Kyle said, "I feel like my senses are on fire in here."

"Half the fun is how scared I am sometimes," Cassady admitted. "And it's not scared only of being caught. There's something else I can't explain."

The enchanting playground was a little less than a mile from their homes. They couldn't stay away. They never got enough and they never got caught either. Several weeks passed and it became their routine. A couple of times someone drove by in a Jeep and scared them almost to death, but they easily hid in the innumerable building facades, nooks, and crannies, and waited until the sound of the Jeep faded away. It was a charmed and wondrous place they had discovered in their backyard. Having explorations during the day was only the beginning.

When they decided to expand their search and when they explored the remaining parts of the Backlot, they found more than they ever imagined. On one end, a tall structure stood in front of them four or five stories high, but from the outside, it looked like two plank walls. The walls stood about a hundred feet apart, with thousands of two-by-fours and reinforcements, facing each other. On the inside, it was a New York street with a complete Brooklyn brownstone block with stoops, stairs, and railings going down to the street level, fully enclosed in a dead-end cul-de-sac.

The northeast part of the Backlot was a small sleepy town with cottage homes and tree-lined streets like something out of New England. It had a half-dozen twisting blocks with weathered houses. Alleyways ran behind several of the streets and bushes ran overgrown along the yards and the mailboxes sat on curbs of most homes, never having been used. Shutters covered the dirty windows and most of the paint was wearing off.

"I know what this is," Kyle said.

"What?" Cassady asked.

"It's the Andy Hardy set. I've seen it in old movies. They're the old stupid movies with Mickey Rooney and Judy Garland."

"You mean before *The Wizard of Oz*? It looks like the streets from *Father Knows Best* and *Leave It to Beaver*," Cassady said.

"Yeah, like the TV shows pretend our world to be. Nothing like it really is," Kyle added. "I hate watching those shows, they're so bogus."

The farther into this town they ventured, the closer they came to the sound stages and offices, so they rarely spent much time deep in its streets. To the south of this area of the Backlot were two warehouses. One warehouse was open with only a chain-link fence as a wall. They could see hundreds of military uniforms of all countries and wars. There was a pile of French Foreign Legion backpacks and fake rifles with hundreds of boots discarded like some forgotten war. Hats, helmets, and different wardrobe costumes were piled up almost two stories high in some places.

"If we climbed through the fence and took some of this stuff for souvenirs, we would be crossing a line. Cruising around inside the Backlot is a gift; stealing is something else," Kyle said.

"It would be, like, maybe disrespecting this place," Cassady said. "That's not what we want to do."

"We're not thieves, man," Kyle said.

"But we want to bring other kids into this place and share it. It's too good to keep a complete secret. Let's make a plan for playing army and other games with some serious hide-and-seek," Cassady said.

"Escalating this with other kids makes us obliged to develop a code," Kyle said.

"Very formal, but you're right," Cassady answered.

They used a strict system to decide who was and wasn't worthy. They had hours of discussion as to whether any school friend or neighborhood boy deserved the opportunity to be let in on what they felt was their own personal discovery and property. They felt like small gods during these discussions; it was a very powerful emotion.

"No one is welcome who would destroy something on the sets," Kyle said.

"That leaves Abilene out," Cassady stated with authority. "No one is welcome who would steal anything."

"That keeps Abilene out again, and Gram probably too," Kyle said, smiling.

"No one is welcome who would not follow directions and who wouldn't keep it a secret or..." Cassady started.

"And who couldn't keep up physically if we had to run..."

Kyle interjected.

"Or who we think would bring in others without our permission," Cassady finished.

"We're never getting stoned or dropping and coming in," Kyle said. "We can't allow anyone who would want to."

"It's cool enough already. I agree," Cassady said.

They almost always thought exactly alike on issues regarding the Backlot. Most times it was a needless worry. Few enjoyed the experience as they did. Almost everybody they brought in was extremely scared and nervous and could never let their anxiety go enough to enjoy it. Cassady and Kyle let the fantasy world they found themselves in overwhelm them and transport them out of the present and into their private imaginary world in the Backlot.

It became their secret place. They took care of it, they guarded it, and it seemed like it was taking care of them. They could hardly believe that they never got caught. Their games lasted hours. The vastness of the Backlot required rules about movement and courses of action, so they would eventually run into each other if they split up.

"We'll meet by the side of the smaller mansion across from the lane in about an hour if we don't see you before then," Cassady would command the other boys. "If there is a problem, go there and wait under the oak tree. There's a depression in the ground where you can't be seen from the field. Understand?"

The other boys sometimes would go straight there and hardly participate at all, waiting for the day to be over so they could go home. Cassady and Kyle were always ready to continue the games the next day, but most kids had had enough in one day and left the Backlot nervous wrecks.

As one boy put it, "This place creeps me out. Something's spooky here, and I can't put my finger on it, but it's a bummer so I'm outta here." Ironically echoing the hippie at the beach.

Cassady and Kyle were never deterred and never felt anything but completely comfortable after the first day or two. They sensed a connection immediately that transcended any worry about being caught and getting in trouble.

"It's like time slows down," Kyle said.

"Yeah, I feel we're experiencing things in a kind of slow motion, and then when we talk or something happens—or finding where someone is hiding—the distortion ends and things speed up to normal," Cassady answered.

It became a home away from home. It was their exclusive fantasyland. It was a wonderland, it was Europe, their personal Southern plantation, and Tarzan's jungle all rolled into one. It retained the enchantment and seductiveness from that first day of discovery every day.

Eventually, they decided to explore the Backlot at night. The second they climbed down the fence in the dark, the Backlot was transformed. As the sun always seemed to shine during the daytime, at night it was always very, very, dark and mysterious. Everything changed. The atmosphere was charged with electricity and their apprehension initially returned. The trees, most of all, seemed alive and swayed with a slight wind that didn't make its presence known at all before the moment they hit the ground inside. Every corner of every building and set and every blade of grass appeared responsive like a motion picture had started rolling the instant they walked by.

"It's dark, but I can tell where we are, no problem," Kyle said.

"Yeah, it's like, as dark as it is, it doesn't seem like night. I couldn't see my hand in front of my face walking here, so we must be getting used to where everything is," Cassady said.

They were city boys. They had grown up without ever really noticing the stars. Smog, haze, exhaust, and the lights reflecting off the city at night, however you explained it, they rarely noticed stars. Once they were in the Backlot though, they looked up and saw stars twinkling brightly, splashed all over the sky.

Like a painting of a dark sparkling rainbow washed against the heavens. It was bizarre and it was heavenly at the same time, but they loved the view too much and never questioned it.

"Cassady, look up, man," Kyle whispered that first night.

"Oh, wow, I've never seen stars like that, man, whoa."

The darkness hid the appearance of everything being a set on a movie studio backlot and allowed them to imagine, create, and transform it all into a living entity. They rarely, if ever, returned during the day after that.

Kyle and Cassady weren't completely sure if it was their imagination or not, but every once in a while as they walked along by some deserted façade of an old movie set, they would be jolted by a vision. It was a wonderful but scary feeling. It was the same sensation Cassady was having in his dreams, ones he hadn't confided in Kyle yet. Deep down he buried a slight feeling of fright. He could see people and things as they would have been if the Backlot was a real German village or the Atlanta train station filled with Confederate soldiers coming home from battle; always in gray, never Union Blue. It was as if a doorway opened and Cassady could see through it for a flash of a second. After all, it was a movie set and hundreds of movies had been made there. But at those times, he felt he had either been there before in another life or was returning to some place he'd visited. Then he'd be walking beside Kyle and the entryway would be closed as fast as it was opened.

"It must be the movies, man," Kyle said one night, but not clarifying what he meant. "I have weird vibes about this place." Cassady wondered if it was related to dreams also, but didn't ask.

"Yeah, that's probably what it is," Cassady replied.

Sometimes, though they both left it unsaid, they felt it was more than that. Cassady felt they didn't want to express any fear or worry about being in what they both believed to be a paradise.

CHAPTER 4

Close to midnight, Kyle and Cassady walked purposefully along the hot, dusty, alley. This alley ran parallel to Culver Boulevard and came out behind a large, vacant lot, overgrown with weeds at the intersection of Culver and Sepulveda Boulevards. They had scouted out the lot earlier in the day and decided the best course of action was to return late in the evening. They still felt inclined to skip the Backlot once in a while to do their usual escapades. Cassady carried a three-foot-long board. They had spent the earlier hours talking, listening to music, and waiting out the time in Cassady's garage room, the Shack, as they did most nights.

They walked into the field and immediately crouched down so as not to draw attention from the few cars driving along the boulevards. They were almost crawling when they moved up behind the shed. It was one of dozens of plank sheds, thirty feet long with wire mesh for windows in the front and large paper signs plastered over the front and sides advertising fireworks. The surrounding cities all had them, like so many fast-food eateries popping up in any open spaces left in the city. It was still empty, but any day now was soon to be filled with glorious streamers, waterfall volcanoes, sky rockets, roman candles, sparklers, and black snakes. They imagined boxes and boxes of the stuff sitting there in an unguarded shed.

They worked fast. In the rear of the shed, out of sight from both streets and prying eyes, the boys started digging. They had a hole dug underneath the frame in about ten minutes. It was deep enough to crawl under now. The shed had no floor, just the frame. The hole crossed underneath from the outside to the interior of the shed. The board, three feet long, was placed over the top of the hole. Dirt was filled in across the top. It was secure with notches dug along the edges. A person could accidentally step on the top of the board and not actually feel it. The inside ran under a counter in the shed, preventing that from occurring. It was perfect.

Two days before the Fourth of July they returned long after midnight. They advanced through the same alley, crawled through the high weeds, and approached the spot where the board bridged the outside and inside of the fireworks shed. They hunkered down in the dirt and began to dig out the board, but suddenly stopped.

"What's that?" Kyle said.

"What the...?"

They faintly heard a popular song from the summer's playlist.

"Hot fun in the summertime..."

"That's Sly Stone, man," Cassady said. He paid close attention to the current music scene and considered himself a burgeoning musicologist.

They crawled around to the front of the shed, slowly stood up, and standing side by side, peered through one of the wire lattice windows.

"What is that?" Cassady whispered, looking at several shadowy lumps lying on the dirt floor in the dark.

"It's sleeping bags, man. Shit!" Kyle murmured back. "Guys are sleeping in there. Guards. It's a radio playing. Let's go."

They slowly backed up.

"Oh well, let's go get our bikes and ride the hills of the Al Jolson cemetery. I only wanted a few free fireworks anyway. No big deal," Cassady said.

They walked off, next to each other, not at all unhappy. After all, they didn't actually aspire to steal anything. It was only an adventure, and adventures outside the Backlot seemed as important to them as sneaking into MGM. It was the gift of having the experience together. It seemed life would always be that way.

On the Fourth, at about seven o'clock, it was surprisingly cool as Cassady walked over to Kyle's house. The height of the wall next to the alley increased as he strolled up the walkway. The bushes surrounding the house camouflaged his arrival. Cassady looked through the screen door. Kyle was lying straight out on the couch with his long legs stretching into the middle of the living room and his head leaning against the screen of an open window. Kyle was completely focused on reading a book; completely unaware Cassady had walked up to the door. The only light came from a small lamp, which created more shadow than light in the room. Cassady backed up and crept around the side and eased through the bushes as quietly as possible. As he bent forward, the only thing that separated Cassady from Kyle was the thin dull screen. He leaned in and was less than an inch from the back of Kyle's head. Cassady inhaled deeply and then uttered a low guttural moan.

"Ahhhh..."

The reaction was immediate and intense. Kyle jumped up about ten feet off the couch, screaming.

Cassady ran back around to the front and looked in through the screen door as Kyle's mom came running into the living room hollering and asking what was wrong. Cassady stood there grinning.

Kyle glared at him and asked, "What the hell is wrong with you?"

Cassady shrugged. "I have no idea. What happened?"

The three of them stood there for a moment, looking at each other.

"You, you watch your language," Kyle's mom finally said. "And you!" she rounded on Cassady. "I'm sure you're not as innocent as you let on. Please refrain from making such a dramatic entrance upon your next arrival at our residence."

Kyle's mom always had something unique to say, no matter what the dilemma or situation. Cassady sometimes enjoyed getting in trouble with Kyle or his brother Lucas to hear what she would have to say next. She had lived in Europe as a child and retained a sense of decorum he loved to listen to. He was laughing out loud at this point.

Kyle looked over at him and said, "You're such a jerk. I can't believe it."

After the boys set off and watched the local fireworks with Cassady's family, and then watched a little TV with Kyle's stepfather, they went into Kyle and Lucas's bedroom pretending to go to sleep.

Tonight, the group would consist of Kyle, Cassady, Lucas, and the two other brothers, John and Davie. Lucas had befriended them and had asked to invite them. Cassady and Kyle had taken a chance on approving the two neighborhood newcomers, who had only moved in a couple of weeks before. They discussed it, knowing they might be nervous about trespassing late at night into the Backlot.

"What time did you tell John and Davie to meet us?" Kyle asked Lucas.

"About eleven o'clock. Their dad stays up a little later," he answered.

"Do you think they'll be cool?" Cassady asked.

"Yeah, I think so. They seem okay, but we'll see," Lucas said.

"Lucas really wants them to come. We can forgo the usual exhaustive screening process this time," Kyle said.

"We'll bring them, but it's always hit or miss with guys we don't know," Cassady said. Lucas rolled his eyes at that and smiled.

They left a few minutes after eleven o'clock, picked up John and Davie in the alley, and before eleven thirty the five boys approached the chain-link fence attached to the steel sharp-edged MGM one. To Kyle and Cassady, it was more than an obstacle to climb. It represented passing into the unknown and into the darkness of a quest. It was silent and shadowy once they hit the ground. The tall eucalyptus and oak trees surrounding them swayed in a soft breeze, unsettling the calm of the night. Within minutes the five boys were already moving past the Southern mansion down the deep dark lane formed from the overhanging trees in front of the other plantation houses. John and Davie hadn't uttered a sound. They stopped in front of a large hedgerow.

"Don't you guys dig this? Ain't the Backlot cool?" Lucas whispered.

Both brothers nodded their heads, and looked at each other while John choked out, "Yeah, ah, ah, I guess."

Kyle shook his head at Cassady. They knew what it was like when they brought dead weight into the Backlot. Some guys couldn't handle it. They'd freeze up and couldn't get into the game or let their imagination go for it. Cassady could tell John and Davie were miserable.

"The brothers are afraid," Kyle whispered to Cassady.

He could instantly sense and see it. Lucas was fine. He was an experienced trooper and infrequently came but always enjoyed the Backlot. They moved out from underneath the cover of trees and onto the football-field-sized open area.

Cassady looked back at John and Davie. They looked so scared they could hardly breathe, much less talk. They didn't look around, but kept insanely close to Lucas and their gazes firmly on the ground.

"I want to go home," Davie whispered to John. He looked away when he saw Cassady look back at him.

The five boys circled the European Village. They stopped again for a second or two.

"I don't think we can split up and play war tonight," Cassady said to Kyle.

"Yeah, no Sergeant Saunders and *Combat!* We'll skip the graveyard tonight also. That'll really freak them out. Whadya think?"

"No way, let's circle around for a little bit and head home. It isn't happening tonight," Kyle said. They glanced back at the brothers; they actually looked like they were shaking.

Cassady knew he and Kyle would be back. Their love for the Backlot never ceased. They felt at home there.

"I think John and Davie are nervous about being out in the middle of the night anyway, much less here in this bizarre place," Cassady said.

As they turned to walk back toward the Southern mansion and came around the *ATLANTA* railroad platform to the open field, they all froze. The boys gasped and all five hit the ground. John and Davie followed the example of the more experienced boys. It wasn't initially an identifiable sound they heard. It was a quiet din, but they really couldn't tell what it was. The sky lit up blue for a second, and then it was immediately dark again.

"What the..." Cassady said.

"I don't know," Kyle answered. Nobody else said anything. A couple of minutes passed with the boys sprawled on the ground in the tall grass.

"What the heck was that?" Davie urgently whispered.

"Well, that got a response from one of them," Kyle said. "I don't know, but we need to keep moving to get out of here."

"I didn't know he had it in him," Cassady said to Kyle,

almost sniggering.

Tentatively, Cassady, Lucas, and Kyle got up and started to move again. Kyle turned around and saw John and Davie still lying on the ground.

"Come on," he whispered hoarsely, waving his arm. He hissed to Lucas and Cassady, "Great, things are getting weird and the goon brothers are freezing up."

John and Davie got up slowly and reluctantly trailed Lucas with Cassady and Kyle leading across the field in front of the smaller Southern mansion. Once more they felt the noise more than they actually heard it. They stopped and the brothers and Lucas plopped down in the tall weeds once more. Kyle and Cassady were looking toward the big Southern mansion, as they always did for a point of reference at night, when they saw it. Cassady looked back over his shoulder and saw Lucas turn his head. Suddenly a flash lit all the windows closest to them in one of the smaller stately homes only a few feet away.

Lucas jumped and yelled, "Run, man, run!" John and Davie took off with him, running back the way they had come in.

Kyle yelled, "Wait!" But they were gone.

Cassady said, "Let them go. I want to check this out more. I don't think we should let this go without learning what's happening. Do you?"

Kyle took a few more steps and said, "Yeah, let's check it out."

Cassady and Kyle started walking across the south end of the open field. They had only walked about twenty feet when they heard the sound again and a pale blue light sparkled in a large cloud twenty feet high before rebounding off into the jet-black night.

Kyle and Cassady stopped dead in their tracks. They couldn't speak. They stood motionless, completely transfixed and stunned silent. They were standing frozen when something brushed by them. It was a luminous, glowing, sensuous presence in the shape of a girl. It was not simply a girl—it was an apparition of something strange, exquisite, and wonderful, but it was too much for them to handle.

Cassady and Kyle took off running across the small field toward the west through the graveyard and by the old haunted house and pool. They got to the fence in what seemed like seconds and found the best and quickest way out by crawling out on the limb of a huge oak tree that was overhanging Elenda Street. They were nowhere near their usual entrance and exit. The sheer sharp thin steel fence was below them. The drop to the sidewalk was about twenty feet. Elenda Street was deserted and dead this late at night. Both boys were drained, shaken, and out of breath.

CHAPTER 5

The next morning Kyle's mom woke all three of the boys up early getting ready before she left for work and to drop off their stepsister at the babysitter's. Lucas got up and went to the bathroom, but came back and lay right back down after talking to her for a minute. They all slept for another couple of hours. When they woke up, all three cooked a huge breakfast. Kyle's mom always had a huge amount of food for them on hand and always included Cassady in the shopping quantity calculation. There was always a vat of curry simmering on the stove, mountains of rice, and other food dishes perpetually available for snacks; the same with spaghetti sauce with pasta. This morning they made English eggs in a hole toast: eggs fried in the middle of huge slices of browned toast in an enormous pan. They went through almost a dozen eggs.

"She always asks if you're going to eat with us," Lucas said.

"Your mom is really cool. Did she ask you anything about last night?" Cassady asked.

"No, I don't think she even remembered me coming in like that."

Kyle and Cassady only passed occasional glances at each other. After eating Lucas jumped on his bike and headed out for a basketball game at Vet's Park. Kyle promised to join him in a few minutes. They started the dishes and Lucas wasn't gone for more than a couple of seconds when Cassady turned to Kyle.

"When we go back in tonight..." Cassady started.

"Wait a minute, who says?" Kyle asked roughly.

"What? Of course we're going back in. We have to."

"Why do we *have* to?"

"Don't you want to see it again, at least, see her again?" Cassady asked exasperated.

"I'm not sure. When I woke up it was like I couldn't believe it, but it couldn't have been real. It was either some kind of trick or something really bad!"

"We don't know that..." Cassady started. Before he could finish another sentence Kyle shouted at him.

"I'm scared shitless about that whole thing, man. Yeah, she was beautiful and all that, but it wasn't normal. I like things ordinary." Kyle launched a tirade. "There were so many things we should have seen as uncool; the ease of going in, the visions, or the feelings, whatever, the hardly ever having anyone else there. We ignored them. I don't like where this is heading. If this was a ghost or something... It wasn't right. I admit it scares me, but so what? It can't be good and I'm not going in," Kyle finished, letting out a deep breath. Cassady was quiet for a moment then something occurred to him.

"You know I used to be into magic tricks when I was young. For a while, I was really into it. I loved going to the magic shop when we went to Disneyland and sending away for tricks," Cassady said. "Then the more I got into it, I got bored because I always realized that no matter how cool I thought the magic trick was, when you got right down to it, it's still only pretend. There wasn't any real magic involved; maybe that's what's going on here. You can't see it from the other side. That led me to also read everything there was to read about Harry Houdini."

"Why?" Kyle asked.

"He was suspected of being something more than a magician. Do you know some people accused him of being a spiritualist, that he could magically transpose himself through walls and trunks, and that's how he was so good? You know that pissed him off. He always maintained he was simply a performer and that it was always tricks."

"You mean he didn't want it to be more than a trick?"

"Well, they were very good tricks—to the point of where it was an art. You know he spent the last part of his life dispelling the tricks of the people who said they could contact the dead."

"Why?" Kyle asked again.

"He loved his mom more than anything, but after she died he really freaked out and wanted to contact her. He realized these people were full of it, phonies. He went around the world exposing their tricks because he could see how it was all done—because he was so good at them himself. We have to go back in, so we know what it was. Maybe it isn't anything but a trick."

"I don't really think that could have been a trick, and why in there? Maybe we need Harry Houdini here," Kyle said. "And since it probably isn't a trick—I don't want to know."

"Let's think about it and talk some more. Go play basketball with Lucas and I'm going over to my grandmother's house," Cassady said as he walked out to go home for a while.

An hour later, Cassady left his house, climbed over the back fence into the alley that ran behind his street on Commonwealth Ave, crossed the deserted parking lot of Gates, Kingsley & Gates Mortuary, waited for the traffic on Sepulveda Boulevard to slow down, and then ran across. He was on his way to his grandmother's house, but was planning on stopping off at the diminutive library annex that was tucked between two small businesses on the busy street. He nodded to the librarian as he walked in and started to look around. As

Cassady was looking at the bookshelves, the uneasy feeling about last night still nagged him.

"Having trouble finding something to read again, Cassady?" the librarian asked. She was an elderly woman named Miss Rigby and was very helpful and very protective of the annex. Kids didn't last long who were loud or rude. Cassady always came here alone, and the librarian liked him and helped him look for books. He liked the librarian, even if she was very prim and proper. He thought her accent sounded English, somewhat like Kyle's mom. He treated her with respect and in turn, she turned him on to several books he loved. It was an easy trade-off. She had no idea that he always had two reasons for coming to the annex.

"Yeah, same old story. Looking," Cassady said.

"Are you looking for something in particular today?" she asked.

"I want to read something as good as *To Kill a Mockingbird* or *Huckleberry Finn*."

"That's a tall order to fill, as not many books are as good as those two," Miss Rigby said.

"How about *A Separate Peace* or *The Hobbit*?"

"Whoa, whoa, wait a minute. What got you to be such a reader anyway? Or who?"

"Well, I always read a little bit, but I met a friend, Kyle, and we talk all the time about books, ride our bikes to look for books, and we feel they have the answers to life. At least, our life. I had read *Tom Sawyer*, but he lent me *Huck Finn*."

Miss Rigby stood up and walked around the corner of the check-in desk, then motioned for Cassady to follow her and nodded for him to continue.

"Go on, Cassady," she said. They sat down around a desk in the open area.

"That can never be repaid. Even if I would have stumbled onto it through school or on my own, it is forever etched in my mind as being a gift from Kyle. We lie in the room I built in my garage and we spend many a late night, into the early hours of the morning, listening to music, talking, and thinking about what is coming in our lives... I've talked too much," Cassady said.

"No, but I have a question," she said. "Do your parents share much in your lives?"

This made Cassady stop for a second and think hard.

"I don't know. But nothing about what I'm talking about really. I guess not."

"It sounds like you two are helping each other grow up. That's nice."

"Yeah, well, earlier I had found *To Kill a Mockingbird* on my own. I've read it, and plan to read it at least every year from now on. I sent Harper Lee a letter with the help of my seventh grade English teacher."

"Really, that's beautiful. What happened?"

"I received a form letter stating, 'Unfortunately, Miss Harper doesn't respond to personal letters...' and blah, blah, blah. I loved that book more than any other I can think of."

"Have you read *The Catcher in the Rye*, Cassady?"

"Yeah, but I feel weird about it."

"Why, Cassady?" she asked. "I'd love to know about the issues. Speak freely."

"I thought I should love *The Catcher in the Rye* and did, in fact, enjoy it. It's one everyone I know has talked about. But I thought I should love it more than I actually did. I tried to love it," he said.

"It's not a long book," Miss Rigby interjected.

"It's not that. It's only a couple hundred pages," he said. "But during it I had this feeling that bugged me. I mean Holden was not quite as smart as he thought he was. Even with school, all my friends are too busy trying to make a few dollars and finding ways to scam a few bucks. We don't have time to whine and cry about the state of the phony world."

"Holden might have only been talking about the world as he saw it."

"Holden was a prep school teenager who, as I see it, didn't have really much to moan and drone on and on about. I couldn't get into it, but was told by friends and others endlessly, it's the classic novel about growing up."

"That's not a bad observation, Cassady. It's hard to wade against the tide. It's brave, but make sure you don't mistake his growing up, as he's trying to define himself, as the normal struggles against conformity. The people who do conform disappoint him, as you'll discover. I find the most feeling he expresses is fearing that his memories of his little brother Allie will leave him as he grows up and become a phony himself," she said. While talking, they had stood up, walked around the small library, and Miss Rigby stopped every few feet to look at a book, pulled it out, shook her head, and pushed it back into its place.

"Well, I'm more concerned with making a few dollars working at little jobs in the neighborhood or with my cousin once in a while. I don't have time to sit around complaining about how 'phony' everyone and everything is. I'd love a girlfriend. I don't have money to ride around in taxis all over New York City. Or go to a 'phony' wealthy prep school," he said. "It's not, all that *David Copperfield* crap, most times. I think I've had enough of all that JD Salinger crap."

"That's excellent, Cassady. I'll have to remember that and use it myself," she said chuckling.

"Sorry, it's well written and has many wonderful sections, but I..." Cassady trailed off and looked down at the floor.

"I think you're very insightful about the book, but young people have related to it for years now. I see what you're thinking though. Let's look around and see if I can find you something."

Cassady was always hoping she would show him certain books. Not only were they books he would enjoy reading, but they had a distinct signature on the checkout card in the back. It was the signature of a girl Cassady spent about twenty-three hours of each day thinking about. Nobody knew he thought about her or even knew, as he knew, that she was alive. Not even Kyle. They were in the same grade at Culver City Junior High. He figured she must live near his grandmother to use this annex as much as she seemed to. She had long blond hair and lovely brown eyes. Cassady thought she was beautiful. He'd only talked to her once, but he saw her at school all last year. One day he noticed that she checked out the same books he did, so when he dropped by the annex to pick up a book, he hoped he would run into her someday. The thought of that happening scared him to death. Last year when she'd started a conversation with him in social studies class, he was barely able to choke out a trite disappointing answer to the question she asked. The year ended without them ever talking again.

"I was thinking about something else I wanted to ask you," Cassady said as they were standing at the largest bookcase filled with fiction. "I was thinking about some of the movies made here in Culver City. On the Backlot, like on Culver Boulevard?"

"Oh, yes, there's been many movies made here, along with dozens of popular TV shows," Miss Rigby said.

"What were some of the ones that were filmed here?" Cassady asked. "How long have the Backlots been here?"

"One question at a time. Cassady. I think it's wonderful you're interested in the history of Culver City. Most young people aren't. If you really want to hear, let's sit down and I'll tell you. Do you have a few minutes?"

"Yeah, sure," Cassady answered.

"It started in the early 1900s. A man named Harry H. Culver convinced movie people to build their studios in this new city between Venice on the beach and the expanding city of Los Angeles," Miss Rigby said.

"Why here?"

"The weather and inexpensive land. Movie men bought and sold, wheeled and dealed different companies throughout the whole area. There have been dozens of different studios here at different times. Southern California must have been heaven on earth, a paradise with palm trees, the ocean close by, perfect weather, and plenty of jobs from this new picture industry," she said. Cassady looked at her and waited for her to continue talking. He realized he loved this history of Culver City.

"A man named Louis B. Meyer eventually bought Metro-Goldwyn Pictures and decided to build new backlots on a couple of large tracts of land in this new town called Culver City. The Metro-Goldwyn-Meyer studio was at its highest peak between the late twenties and the late forties."

"Do they still make movies here?" Cassady asked. They had never seen any activity while sneaking in; it always seemed dead in the Backlot.

"Wait, wait, I'll get to that. They made some of the most famous movies of all time here. Did you know all the Tarzan movies were filmed here?"

"Really?" He said this to pacify her and not give away that Kyle and he had talked about the jungle set on the Backlot.

"Yes, and *Ben-Hur*."

"Cool!"

"How about *The Wizard of Oz*?"

"All right," he said.

"How about *Romeo and Juliet*?"

"Here in Culver City? This or last year with Olivia Hussey?"

"Oh no, an earlier version. I know it well, right here on Backlot 2. But I realize a young boy like you would like the new one with her. The *Our Gang* series was also filmed here all over Culver City. Maybe not MGM, but here for sure."

"You mean Spanky and *Our Gang*? I've watched those shorts for years with friends."

"Yes, absolutely. If you watch those old shows closely, you can make out some of the old streets and landmarks like the Culver Hotel. All those kids lived and filmed their show right here."

"Wow! I'll watch them more closely next time I see the show."

"Did you know that Culver City had the world's shortest main street and the world's largest per capita payroll? Have you ever seen *Gone with the Wind*?"

"Yeah, maybe?"

"No, you'd know if you had seen *Gone with the Wind*," she said. She looked at him and he shook his head. "Oh, that's too bad. Yes, *Gone with the Wind* was filmed right here. Many other movies were too, and some still are, but most of them are on location now. Some are certainly still filmed on the big sound stages," Miss Rigby said.

"How about on the Backlots?" Cassady asked.

"There are three Backlots in Culver City and Backlot Number 1 is where the sound stages are located and where the famous entrance is on Washington Boulevard. I don't think Backlot 2 is used much anymore. Backlot 3 might have some filming going on, but not much. It's cheaper for the movie people to find the perfect locations in real places and go film it there. But much wonderful history is right here down the street from us. Why are you so interested?"

"I was wondering if you had any books that dealt with that time?" Cassady asked, deflecting the question.

"I don't know if I have anything that deals with the making of movies or that time period, but I do have a book you might like. I don't know if a boy your age would like it, but it does have action in it. It's the book that the movie *Gone with the Wind* was made from, by Margaret Mitchell. In fact, some people consider it a classic, and someone returned it yesterday. It's funny I was talking about it with her, a girl your age.

It's actually an easy read, and I'm sure you can handle it," Miss Rigby offered. Cassady was hoping beyond hope the girl who returned it was the one he was thinking about. He replayed the conversation he had with her again, for the millionth time, that Friday a couple of months ago when she actually asked him if he was going to hang out at the Teen Center in Vet's Park that evening. He stammered and didn't commit, not because he didn't want to, but couldn't bring himself to reply with a simple yes. He kicked himself almost daily since then for his shyness.

"Yes, I'd like that," Cassady said

"When you finish, and maybe if you ever have a chance to see the movie, come talk to me some more. I have a deep interest in the book and especially the movie," she said.

"Okay," Cassady agreed.

"Really, it might surprise you what I can tell you about that time and the movie. Cassady, I look forward to sharing it with you someday in the future."

When Cassady walked over to the counter to check it out, the thought continued. When he opened the book to sign his name on the checkout card, sure enough, the last person's signature on the card had the most beautiful sounding name in the world. The name he had said over and over again in his mind: Brie Ann Johnson.

CHAPTER 6

For the next two days, Kyle and Cassady spent time with other friends. It was the first time in what seemed like years they had spent that much time apart. Subconsciously they didn't even realize they didn't want to be with each other alone. What happened in the Backlot was unspoken with each boy thinking about it on his own. It was too weird to contemplate; did they see a ghost? Did they hallucinate the whole thing? They both knew they couldn't have actually, but couldn't wrap their minds around what it was that they saw. They needed time to process it before talking about it with each other.

Cassady knew he had to talk to Kyle one day soon, though. He was having shocking dreams—not because they were so scary, but unclear and hazy. He actually liked the feeling he had while the dreams were taking place. He saw a man dressed in flamboyant, colorful clothing and the beautiful girl. It was like the flashes they experienced in the Backlot that night, only in the dream he was walking and talking with these people. He couldn't make out what was being said, but it really didn't look like the Backlot, not like he knew it. It was bigger and more like a real place. But when he would wake up, he would only remember glimpses of what he experienced in the dreams and that was confusing.

They met up on the third morning. Kyle could tell Cassady was going to go right into talking about the Backlot.

"Let's not talk about it yet," Kyle said, preempting the conversation.

"Okay," Cassady agreed. "But then let's do something today."

"Yeah, let's see who's around."

Kyle and Cassady walked over to Gram's house. Usually, Gram and another neighborhood boy named George were either playing ping-pong or until recently working in their so-called garden. They were really good ping-pong players. Most days it was fun to sit back and watch them play. They stood about five feet from the table and slammed the ball back and forth to each other. Kyle and Cassady had forgotten how wild Gram was and how much fun it was hanging around his house. It had been several weeks, at least. Gram had four sisters, and it seemed like there was always something going on. Gram had a big goofy German shepherd named Strider that loved to play with anybody, anytime, all the time, and he never seemed to get tired. Gram's family also had a menagerie of several cats and a big white furry rabbit they named Bun Bun.

A couple of other neighborhood boys joined them and they played ping-pong in the hot sun late into the afternoon. Gram pulled out some excellent homegrown marijuana and they got righteously stoned. Earlier in the summer, Gram's dad, Mr. Miller, a lawyer and the YMCA Man of the Year, was talking to a fellow Y man and mentioned that he had been extremely worried about his son and his friends with their long hair and music, but was glad they were taking an interest in something, finally.

The other Y man asked curiously, "What might that be?"

Gram's dad replied, "Gardening. They have a garden with some beautiful four-foot-tall tomato plants." The man he was talking to happened to be a Culver City police officer.

"Have you actually *seen* any tomatoes on the plants?" he asked.

"Come to think of it, I was wondering when they would blossom out and we'd be able to enjoy some ripe huge tomatoes," he said.

"I hate to tell you, but they're probably growing marijuana in your backyard."

"That night my dad was so pissed," Gram told them the next day. "He tore up the five or six plants and threw them in the garbage that night. He didn't realize the trash went out the next day, and he didn't check before it got picked up. Early that morning I retrieved them, dried them out, and now I can supply the neighborhood with the best homegrown pot any one of us has ever smoked!"

After the ping-pong games ended, they all had the munchies bad, so they decided to walk down to Taylor's Liquor Store on Washington Boulevard to get snacks to drink and eat. Cassady was confused, but felt it was nice and relaxing to be with friends and not yet have to talk about the Backlot with Kyle. They stopped at George's house to listen to *Led Zeppelin II*. In the early evening, they were walking back down Center Street toward both Gram's and Kyle's houses.

Gram stopped and looking up the street asked oddly, "Is that my mom?"

Gram's mother was out in his front yard standing with her face in her hands, hunched over. As they got closer they could tell she was sobbing.

"Let's hang back a few," Kyle said as Gram walked over and asked why she was crying.

"Unngghhhhhhh unnnngggggggghhhhh deeeeiiiieeeedddd, ah!" she continued, almost coughing she was crying so hard.

"What?" Gram said as he put his arm around her.

"Aaaaaaauuuugggggghhhh unnnnnnnnnnnnnnggggggghhh dddeeeeeiiidddd," she wailed.

"What? Hot dogs again. Hot dogs for dinner? That's okay, Mom. We can have hot dogs for dinner," Gram said as understandingly as he could, nodding and patting her on the back, and looking over at the other boys, shrugged as if to say, "whatever."

"Uuunnn bunnnngh ddeeeaaaddd, aahh," she said again, choking a little.

"No, Mom, really. Hot dogs are fine for dinner again. It'll be okay," he said again, almost laughing.

She whimpered quietly a little longer without saying anything until she got her breath back. The boys stood there not knowing what to say or do. They were nervously looking at the ground and then at each other trying to formulate the words that could get them out of there without seeming rude to Gram or increasing his mom's embarrassment.

"Bun Bun's dead!" she finally screamed loud and clear. The shock on Gram's face was apparent. His mom resumed sobbing. He put his arms around her and looked at the group in shock over her shoulder.

They all immediately rushed into the backyard through the gate. They had forgotten to put Bun Bun back in his cage. Strider was there to greet them as usual, jumping up and down and running around in circles. There, in the grass, stretched out stiff as a board, his legs stuck straight out, was the fluffy white rabbit Bun Bun. Strider stood over him with his tongue hanging out as if to say, "Why won't my friend play with me anymore?"

"He ran the poor rabbit to death while we were gone," Cassady said.

George said, "Wow, this sure is a buzz kill."

George beat a hasty retreat and split. Kyle and Cassady stood around for a few more minutes, but feeling totally inadequate to help Gram in any way they could think of, walked over across the street to Kyle's house.

"We have to talk about this, right?" Cassady asked.

"I'm not going in again and that's final," Kyle said. "It's bullshit scary."

"I think we need to go in again, Kyle. Nothing's right with this and you know it," Cassady countered. "I think about it all the time. No matter what I do, it's there, all the time, right? Is it better to fill our time ignoring it and doing stupid things like helping kill pets?"

"Yes, it's always there, but eventually we'll forget about it. I don't know if it was real, and I don't know if I want to find out. Whatever it was, it isn't like it's out here. It's only a problem if we go over that fence at night. We should have never started to go in at night," Kyle said, raising his voice. "I don't think I can physically bring myself to go in again, Cassady."

"We'll do it together," Cassady said. "I know it's like a *Twilight Zone* episode, but... you know the truth is we have to find out what that was and if it was real. And that means going back in."

"Why?" Kyle asked. "I'm really scared of what happened, man. Can't you understand that?"

They looked at each other for a moment.

"And what about the dreams?" Cassady asked. He took a shot Kyle was having the same dreams he was.

Kyle looked at Cassady hard for a second before answering. "I don't know what you're talking about."

"You're lying, I know you're having the same dreams as I am, aren't you? We can't run from this!" Cassady yelled.

Kyle didn't answer. Cassady knew he had hit a home run.

"Okay. Listen, I actually thought I knew the people we saw. At least I recognized them. I've seen them in a movie my mom took me to years ago when I was little," Kyle said, irritated. "It was an old and long movie and I was too young to remember much about it now, but the uniforms, the dresses, and the hats were the same as the other night—but then, shimmering and glimmering in the dark. It couldn't be though, and that night wasn't part of some dream. It's too spooky."

"There's no way to prove we didn't see anything. But we can prove that what we saw was a hoax or has a sensible explanation. Do you think you can live with yourself if we never check it out again?" Cassady asked.

"I'm sure willing to try," Kyle answered, as he walked inside his house.

Kyle later told him he spent the rest of the day in the backyard tossing a football around. He felt bad about walking away from Cassady like that, but Cassady could push and push. The strangeness of this had them both acting weird. He knew what he saw and what he saw scared him.

CHAPTER 7

Two days later, Cassady was lying on the couch in the Shack reading *Gone with the Wind*. He hadn't seen Kyle since the argument. He was also listening to *Music from Big Pink* by The Band for perhaps the millionth time that summer. He was quickly fading and about to drift off when Kyle burst in.

"Let's go tonight," Kyle said.

"Why?" Cassady asked slightly taken aback, putting down *Gone with the Wind* behind a pillow. He was over halfway through it and was digging how he could place tons of scenes right in the Backlot where they probably filmed them for the movie.

"I don't know. You're right, I guess. We have no other choice. It's driving me crazy," Kyle said. "We have to see if it was our imagination or something else. Whatever happens, happens. Let's go tonight. If this turns out bad though, I'll kill you!"

"Yeah okay, let's do it. If getting busted at Abilene's, or helping Strider run a poor defenseless bunny rabbit to death is what our ordinary days are like—I'm up for finding out what happened that night in the Backlot."

They didn't talk as they made their way through the alleys. It was close to midnight since they had to wait several hours later than planned because, for some reason, Cassady's mom kept checking on them. It seemed like a bad omen. They cautiously waited an extra hour when they were sure his parents had gone to bed and were asleep. The night was spent talking and listening to music as usual, but the talk was about anything but the Backlot and ended as soon as they started on their journey through the alleys. They walked past Harter, Tilden, Huron, Milton, and Charles Avenues, crossed Elenda, and were on Arizona Street before they knew it.

A faint light was shining far off inside the big spooky house and Cassady attempted to gauge his feelings as they climbed the fence. He wanted to contrast them with feelings he had had on other nights. Nothing looked or seemed different, yet everything was transformed. Maybe it was nothing and yet the foreboding they were experiencing was metamorphosing the Backlot into something bizarre.

They hit the ground on the other side of the fence and waited.

Nothing.

The wind picked up again up as soon as they crept up to the backside of the big Southern mansion. No matter how calm it was before they entered, the branches on the large sycamores would begin swaying and the leaves on the eucalyptus would make a slight swishing sound. The oaks would bend in the late-night breeze and creak quietly. Cassady followed Kyle as they walked out on the porch of the Southern mansion and squatted down. In the pitch black, they could still make out the lane running up to the mansion and the trees bordering it.

"That's it," Cassady said with a nervous quiet giggle. "Let's get out of here while the getting's good."

"Yeah, I'm satisfied," Kyle jokingly answered back, feeling equally as nervous as Cassady.

Neither of the two boys wanted to continue, yet they felt powerless to stop.

"I don't want this place to be ruined for us," Kyle said. "We have to wait and see if it was our imaginations or what. I'm hoping it was. I don't know if I feel safe here anymore."

"Really?" Cassady asked. "I don't know what to think."

"Okay, let's go down by the lake and see if anything's up over there, and then circle around by the graveyard and then go home," Kyle said.

They stood up and walked down in front of the other mansion facades set back into the tree line. This was where they thought they were best hidden and had the advantage of ducking into several hideaways if necessary. It took them about five minutes to get to the lake. They walked out onto the bridge and looked back the way they had come.

"On one hand everything looks normal, but there's an undercurrent of weirdness in the air that I can't put my finger on," Kyle said.

They didn't do much talking as they walked through the darkness, mostly nodding to each other and grunting in response as one told the other to watch for a branch or to duck under low-hanging tree limbs, and not to step on something in the path.

"I don't know. Maybe it was a hallucination," Kyle said as they continued the circle to the graveyard walking past the entrance to the European Village.

"What? Both of us at the same time with the same thing?" Cassady answered back.

"Whatever it was, we can't depend on it being here all the time. Maybe it was a once-in-a-lifetime occurrence, and it's safe in here now. Maybe it's gone."

"Well, let's give it a few more minutes..."

They waited.

"I'm starting to think that the night is a bust, and I'm starting to feel like there's nothing here. I'm relieved, but at the same time slightly disappointed," Kyle said.

"Let's think about how we could come back with a fresh crew and begin the games anew," Cassady said. He wondered if the Backlot would ever be the same.

They were starting to walk into the graveyard, hoping they were feeling comfortable again, when they glanced back toward the open area that lay in front of the tree-lined lane leading up to the large Southern mansion. What they saw stopped them dead in their tracks.

"Oh, my God!" Cassady said.

"Oh, wow!" Kyle said at the same time.

They saw a mist rising from the ground like the fog at Toes Beach when it rolled into Playa del Rey from the Pacific Ocean. It was growing blurrily but without wavering. The mist had a bluish tint to it and moved slowly and faintly. It continued to ascend up into the air swirling and twisting into a funnel forty-feet high before gently flattening out and spreading over the ground. Cassady and Kyle immediately fell down in the grass behind two small bushes and watched as the mist languidly rose up again and gradually settled down to the ground.

"Wha... whaa... what do you want to do?" Cassady whispered. "Do you want to go? To run?"

"No, let's wait a minute and see what happens. This was your idea, asshole," Kyle choked back. "It's got to be some kind of special effect or someone's idea of a joke, right?"

Cassady's mind was screaming and he couldn't decide if they should stay or run and take off. "I'm too scared to run anyway," Cassady thought and then realized he had said it out loud.

"Okay, okay, we're here. Let's wait it out, whatever it is," Kyle said.

They were both mesmerized by the vapor as it darkened and swirled again and flattened and rose more slowly and then wafted around in a circle about fifteen feet off the ground. In the next minute, it began to settle more slowly. They watched, unable to say anything to each other.

"This is different," Kyle finally sarcastically whispered, not able to move a muscle.

Cassady barely made guttural sounds. At that point, smaller clouds started to form. The clouds in the mist were expanding, contracting within it, weaving, and circling. The clouds were about five feet by three feet. They were light brown-colored in the blue haze. They slowly started to change. Ever so slowly they were forming into shapes recognizable as human forms. They looked watery and liquid, but gradually hardened into silhouettes and then little by little, completely into human shapes.

"Oh, wow," was all Cassady could gasp.

"That's what I saw last week. Cassady, did you?" Kyle asked.

"Not this good of a look, no. Not like this," Cassady answered. "Is this like the movie people you saw? Are we going crazy or are we tripping?"

"Both," Kyle said. "And I was afraid of saying this out loud anyway. Now they're moving. Check it out."

The characters that formed out of the clouds were dressed in splendid clothes, the likes of which the two boys, growing up in Southern California, had never seen before. There were between twenty and thirty people in the mist. The women wore long dresses, shiny with sashes. Their hair was done up immaculately, soft curls surrounding their faces. They were frail, but statuesque, pale and thin, and carried themselves with an aristocratic air. Lace, ribbons, and beautiful trimmings draped off their dresses. They wore hats and carried umbrellas. The men all wore garish suits or uniforms. The military clothing was mostly gray with boots that came up to their mid-calf. They also wore hats with wide brims and had long sideburns and whiskers on their cheeks. Everyone was tall, elegant, and regal-looking.

The mist covered the front of the mansion now as it had last week. As it did, the paint looked fresh, and the mansion was apparently restored to its original grandeur. The pillars on the porch framed the building majestically. The grass was unexpectedly smooth and cleanly cut. The transformation was complete.

It was a flawless antebellum plantation manor. The people started talking and laughing among themselves. Some of the men leaned casually against the side of the pillars, and others walked from group to group joking and talking as they went. The boys couldn't make out what was being said, but as the conversations floated through the night air, they could make out mysterious Southern accents enveloping the words. Strange-sounding, otherworldly, one of so many things Cassady and Kyle were trying to make sense of, trying to comprehend, trying to believe what they saw with their own eyes. The mist rolled across the ground, circled and rotated on itself, and became fainter and fainter until the color was a pale light blue shrouding the people and mansion. It covered the open area but included the Southern mansion and the areas to the left and the right.

Cassady and Kyle stayed in the grass watching the scene unfold before them, petrified with fear. They were able to make out snippets of the conversations. The people in the mist were obviously comfortable with each other and friendly. They give the impression of a large extended family, although more formal in manner and talk. The boys remained with their mouths open. They could hear but not really process what was being said.

"What should we do? Maybe you were right. We shouldn't have come back. I don't want to get up and jam, but I might have to in a second. What do you think?" Cassady asked.

"Do you think they can see us? Do you think they'll do anything to us? I don't know how much more of this I can take," Kyle said. "They must be ghosts. Don't you think?"

The boys didn't realize they were answering each other's questions with another question. They were questions neither could answer anyway. Long lapses of time passed as they watched the figures stroll and talk in the mist.

"I have a feeling, uh, I don't think they're going to hurt us," Kyle finally said. "This is the second time we've seen them and maybe the second time they've seen us, don't ya think? They haven't even glanced in our direction."

"Maybe they don't recognize us from last week."

"I can't imagine they didn't know we saw them last week, or even now."

"Maybe they can't see us."

The gathering continued for five more minutes while they watched the couples and people stroll around the open area and in and out of the house. Cassady and Kyle smelled something roasting in a large open fire pit they hadn't noticed before at the side of the mansion. From where they were lying they could see the smoke rising and smell the delicious aroma.

"I remember this smell from the time my dad and uncles roasted a small one in our backyard," Cassady said. "It's a pig, but this is a big one roasting over that huge pit."

Slowly, subconsciously, without realizing they were even doing it, the boys crawled through the bushes they were hiding behind to get a better look, but at the same time, they didn't realize it made them more conspicuous. They lifted up their heads and arched their backs when one would point something out to the other. Suddenly, they saw a man and woman look directly at them.

"Let's run," Cassady whispered intently, getting up.

"No, wait a second," Kyle said while getting up and putting out his arm to stop Cassady. "It's her!"

The couple walked casually arm-in-arm over to Cassady and Kyle until they were about twenty feet from them. The man whispered something to the woman, smiled at her and then at the boys, and then proceeded to walk closer by himself. His smile broadened as he approached, and he held out his arms as if to show nothing more than curiosity to them. The man had curly dark blond hair and the woman's long dark hair was styled and contrasted with her deep green flowing dress. Kyle and Cassady were both up on their feet now, beginning to crouch a little, ready to dash away at the slightest warning. The man was dressed as ornately as the others and continued to smile at the boys as he walked slightly closer. They were glancing at each other, about to bolt; each knew the other was ready to go without a word.

"Kyle, Cassady, don't be so nervous, I won't hurt you," he called out to them in a friendly manner.

They didn't even take the time to look at each other in wonder, although they both freaked and blurted out at the same time, "How do you know our names?"

He threw his head back and laughed, put his hands on his hips, smiled again, and then spread his hands out again.

"He's obviously acting, man," Cassady whispered.

Cassady and Kyle both thought it was an exaggerated gesture. It smacked of pretension and it was clearly meant to throw them off, and make them think he meant absolutely no harm at all. Knowing what it was meant for didn't make it any less effective though, and they unintentionally relaxed a tiny bit and at least came off the balls of their feet.

"Why, we've learned quite a bit about you two since you've been visiting our home here."

Now Cassady glanced over at Kyle, while Kyle looked back at him. They both had their mouths gaping open with surprise, wonder, and fear. Neither of them wanted to run, but this statement caused them to brace a little and get back up on the balls of their feet.

"Home? What are you talking about exactly?" Cassady asked.

The man continued to smile, which actually was beginning to irritate the boys.

"Happy Jack," Kyle whispered.

"Well, I hope I can explain it. I don't mean to be patronizing, but this is simply, for lack of a better term, our home. All this. All that you imagine, all that you come for when you climb the fence. You feel it when you come close to the Sift though, don't you?" he asked.

"The what?" Cassady shot back. "We don't have any idea what you're talking about. What are you, some kind of hoodoo?"

"You've been listening to too much Creedence, man," Kyle said, chuckling.

Later it seemed funny, but at this point, something changed. They didn't doubt that they were talking to someone who had appeared out of a mist and might not have been real. Cassady and Kyle simply forgot to be so scared they couldn't talk or think, and took it for granted that they could converse with this man and ask him questions and he would answer them. Whatever he was, they were talking to him and trying to make sense out of what he was saying.

"Yes, the Sift. It's our place." He kept his arms spread and walked in a small circle. "Everyone must have a place, and this is ours. You discovered it and paid homage to it by being kind and most importantly, respectful and careful not to exploit it, even with the other boys you have brought here. We respect that. And so, we thought to share ourselves with you, and well..." He trailed off, smiling again.

"But what are you?" Cassady asked.

"Don't worry, we'll have plenty of occasion to talk about its significance another time."

Behind the man the party continued, but a few of the people in the mist stopped and looked in their direction. Cassady and Kyle continued to look at the man, the party, and now they noticed the pretty girl standing behind the man. She had slowly walked up, and now was only a couple of feet behind the man. Tonight, up closer, she looked perhaps a few years older than the boys. She continued to smile at them, and her smile was lovely and not irritating at all; it was pleasant and beautiful. Her hair was dark brown, straight, and long. She was a full head shorter than the man, but her presence was as formidable as his without even speaking. She had a few freckles spread over her nose and cheeks. Her bright green eyes sparkled in the blue mist and as long as she smiled at the two boys they found themselves smiling back.

Finally, Kyle woke up and asked, "But what are you? You never answered Cassady's question. Are you ghosts?"

"Well, you've posed an interesting question, and you deserve an answer, and you shall have an answer, but first let me introduce someone." He turned and said, "Scarlett, would you like to meet Cassady and Kyle, honey?"

The girl made an almost imperceptible bow while she spoke. "It's such a wonderful pleasure to meet you two finally, at last."

"At last?" Kyle murmured. That gave them both pause to think.

"Yes, how are you two this evening?" She laughed deliberately as she asked this, but in such a polite and delicate manner, and continued to smile so beautifully, that the boys were completely mesmerized. She was lovely and in the evening darkness with the mist surrounding her, she glowed. Cassady and Kyle thought back to the night they ran away from the Backlot and realized she was not frightening at all. It was obvious why she seemed to float by them in the dark.

They were spellbound and both barely able to mutter an answer, other than a grunt that was supposed to mean "fine." She was possibly the most beautiful girl Cassady or Kyle had ever talked to.

"We saw you the other night," Cassady said.

"You went by us in the dark," Kyle added.

"Sorry if I frightened you," she said.

Kyle and Cassady were suddenly conscious of a mild humming feeling almost imperceptible at first and nearly unnoticeable. As it continued it became pleasant and comforting, but not knowing the source of it made them uneasy.

"I feel like I'm a little high, but this different. I don't quite get it," Cassady said.

"Yeah, this is a different feeling altogether," Kyle said, glancing at Cassady before the man spoke again.

"Don't worry. It's being in close proximity to the Sift," he said, laughing.

"The what?" Kyle asked. "What are you talking about? This fog stuff?"

"Yes, it's the Sift that allows us to appear, but it won't hurt you. It changes your perception of what you know as reality. It allows us to become visible to you in the form we chose," he said. "When your perception is changed, it alters how you feel slightly. It won't cause you any harm, and it's quite pleasant while you are in it. In fact, you'll come to love it. Don't look shocked, and please, don't worry. We would never hurt you. Kyle and Cassady, we want to be friends with you."

"Why?" Kyle said.

"Again, what are you?" Cassady asked. "What's your name? You haven't told us even that yet," he asked, looking at the girl.

"I presumed you might know who we are by now," the man said. "You two are bright, resourceful, and thoughtful young men."

"Are you ghosts?" Cassady asked.

"That's entirely too simple of an explanation. What or who do we look like?"

"You look like ghosts to me, man. We don't know what's going on here," Kyle said loudly. "You look like characters from a movie, but I can't remember the name of it, and that mansion fits in with that."

"*Gone with the Wind*?" Cassady ventured.

"Very astute. Or was it a good guess?" the man said, shaking his head.

Kyle looked over at Cassady, and Cassady shrugged while he said, "I'm reading the book. I'm not sure if I believe it though."

"I'm not sure if I believe it either, but it looks like we're seeing it," Kyle said to Cassady and then turned to the man. "Tell us who you are or what you are, or we're out of here. Are you dead?"

"Would it matter to you at this point if I told you we were dead, and so by your understanding it would make us, by definition, ghosts?" he said.

"Do you think of yourself as something else?" Cassady said.

"Of course, we do. Our lives have ended in your time and we are what you might possibly become. If we have lived in a place we loved, or traveled to a place we enjoyed, we can relive it for eternity. If it is convenient and the possibility exists, we connect with the living, such as you, if everything works out. Many, many laws, you might say, or metaphysical rules, control it."

"What?" both Cassady and Kyle said.

"Oh, it has to do with the stuff of the universe, but don't worry about that. Simply know we're not here by chance. We have a purpose. Strictly speaking, we're not exactly ghosts, but we are also, somewhat," he said, laughing.

"Is this mansion called Tara, after the Southern plantation in the movie and book?" Cassady asked.

"Yes, we can create whatever reality we want to. MGM simply has called this building the 'Southern Mansion,' but this is one we wish to recreate for myriad reasons now. We have all felt fond of it from that time in 1939. Tomorrow it might be something entirely different. It works with the set on the Backlot already here. Don't you think we make it much nicer and prettier than it was before?"

"Why show us or reveal it or whatever?" Kyle asked.

"We chose to expose ourselves to you because of the questions you ask yourselves and the things you talk about. You have taken great pains to protect this place and your enjoyment is infectious," he said. "Now it's your decision to take the next step, to join us or not, simply by walking into the Sift and sharing our experience. You can always walk out, and when you do, you can decide to come again by as simple a thing as walking back in again. You have an open invitation to visit us here anytime you like."

"It sounds like a bunch of gobbledygook to me," Cassady said. "I don't understand half of what you've said. We could go in this thing and never come out again, probably."

"All I can give you is my word as a gentleman, and the fact that we've never hurt you and never will."

"How do we know when to come?" Kyle asked. Cassady looked over at him like he must be losing his mind. "I'm just asking," Kyle said shrugging.

"When you decide to come, we'll know, and we will be here," the man explained. "Don't worry about that. We'll be here. You'll want to come, and often. I'm rather sure of it."

"Why?" Cassady asked.

"Why would you not want to experience this?" he said, spreading his arms open wide and laughing again. "You'll want to meet and talk to Scarlett, I know." He leaned his head toward the beautiful girl beside him.

Looking around for a moment, they both realized while talking the night had exploded unexpectedly and spectacularly, flashing with wondrous color and dazzling beauty. The trees were alive and moving in a crisp breeze, the stars shining like diamonds. The grass was bright green; the mansion, the people, the clothes, the smells, and the very air they were breathing was exploding and bursting with an intensity and vibrancy the boys had never felt before. The woman, Scarlett, was looking at them, then turned and twirled in a small circle, her dress swirling out and slowly coming to a rest as the boys broke into smiles by the loveliness of such a small act of graceful charm.

"By the way, my name is Ashley," the man said, bowing slightly.

Kyle and Cassady looked at him and then shyly looked at Scarlett, who was looking back at both of them and smiling.

CHAPTER 8

They were back in the garage at about two o'clock in the morning. They hadn't said a word to each other returning from the Backlot. The night was especially dark as they walked through the alleys on the way home, and they only saw one or two cars on the way back. They hardly noticed, barely looking up from the ground, taking none of the normal precautions to duck and hide. They lay down on the bed and couch and then it all gushed out in a torrent of pent-up emotions.

"It's real. It really happened. We need to find out if we really talked to dead people though, and if they were, they talked back to *us*. I mean we were both there and saw it and we know we're not crazy. What could we do, go back with someone and they don't show themselves and then we'd end up looking stupid?" Cassady said in one long rush.

"I know, I know," Kyle said. "Maybe we're looking at this the wrong way. I don't know how anyone would react to this. Would they believe it anyway?"

"Wait a minute, you're right, I don't know if we should tell someone this story," Cassady said.

"Yeah, I don't know if we should even *think* about telling someone, Cassady. This is the coolest thing that could ever happen to us, or anyone for that matter. And I don't know if we should share it with anyone."

"I hate to think there was a reason to not tell Lucas," Cassady said. "And I feel bad about it."

"Yeah, I've never kept anything from him. He's my brother, man. But since he didn't see them the other night... maybe they didn't reveal themselves to him and the brothers for a reason and only did to us. But you're right, I'm sorry, but at the same time glad we didn't."

"Do you think they are what they say they are? What would happen if we actually went into the... what did he call it?" Cassady asked.

"The Sift, yeah, the Sift. Whatever, and I do think they are what they say. It seems they're only there for us. I don't believe they're going to hurt us," Kyle said. "He said we could leave anytime we wanted to, and I can't see any reason they'd go to all this trouble to reveal themselves and then hurt us. They're exposing something to us and we should take advantage of it. I want to go back as soon as we can. Think about how cool they looked. Scarlett was so unbelievably good-looking."

The talking continued and then slowed as both boys finally drifted off to sleep. In the morning Cassady's parents went to work, and he was slightly disturbed in his sleep for a few minutes when the cars started up, doors opened and closed, and the back gate closed. In the few minutes before Cassady fell back asleep, he realized he had been dreaming of the Sift and then he was in it. He was talking to Scarlett, and she was laughing at his jokes and touching him lightly on the arm as she was looking up at him. Cassady was smiling and thinking this wasn't such a bad idea. The Sift made him feel happy and giddy. The buzzing was nice and the people or whatever they were. They were pleasant and friendly.

Kyle didn't wake up with the morning noise, and both Cassady and Kyle had slept until early afternoon. When Kyle did sit up, he saw Cassady already looking out the back window of the Shack into the afternoon sky.

"Did you have crazy, but weird dreams?"

"Yeah, it was a crazy ride..." Cassady answered. "It was cool though."

They had awakened completely refreshed and full of energy, but ravenous. They made a huge breakfast of eggs, bacon, and pancakes in Cassady's kitchen, and cleaned it up listening to *Crosby, Stills & Nash*. They didn't talk about the Sift, but let it rest in their minds.

Kyle went home after the dishes were done, and Cassady read for a bit and then started to get ready to head over to his grandmother's apartment to check in with her. The last thing Kyle said before he left was that they should meet in the alley behind his house at midnight after watching the moon landing.

Cassady climbed the fence and headed across Sepulveda Boulevard. Without thinking about it before he did it, he stepped into the library annex. The librarian smiled at him.

"Good afternoon, Cassady," Miss Rigby said. "Are you already done with the book?"

"No, ah, well, almost," Cassady, said. "But I would like to ask you some questions if you have some time?"

"Yes, if I can. It's always a pleasure to help someone delve deeper into literature," Miss Rigby said, smiling. "Sit down, here at the big table."

"Uh, thanks. I want you to know I really like *Gone with the Wind*," Cassady said.

"Well, that's nice, Cassady. It's a wonderful book, and the characters are wonderfully drawn and developed. The historical aspect is obviously interesting, but there are aspects of the Civil War that are hard to reconcile with the movie, namely that slavery and the character portrayals are much too thoughtless."

"Yeah, the Civil War stuff is cool to learn about, but I was wondering if, well, do you know anything about the characters in the book?" Cassady asked.

"Yes, why I've read the book several times and I've seen the movie several times also..."

"No, I mean, yes. That's what I was wondering about, the characters in the movie. I'm sorry. I didn't mean to interrupt you, but I meant the actors that played the characters in the movie?"

"Oh, well most of them were famous before the movie, and then extremely famous after the movie came out."

"Do you remember their names?" Cassady asked as his heart raced.

"Why are you so interested in the movie? Have you seen it?" she asked.

"No, ah, I was thinking that they must have been pretty close to the characters in the book, in looks and everything. Maybe even personalities?"

"Well, I don't know about personalities. The movie was a big production, and movies always change things, but I think they probably came as close as they could to matching the physical descriptions with the actors that played them. At least after all these years, what we've come to believe they would have looked like."

"What were their names? In real life I mean, the main ones. Do you remember?"

The librarian suddenly got a strange look on her face, and Cassady thought for some reason he couldn't comprehend if he had pushed too much too soon. He thought he had better shut up and let her talk for a minute.

"Well, there was Clark Gable, of course, and Vivien Leigh. Let's see... the four main characters I guess would be those two, along with Olivia de Havilland as the neighbor who marries the extremely talented and handsome Ashley Wilkes played by Leslie Howard. The movie only touched on his wonderful talent. That's it for the four main characters. Is that all who you were thinking about?"

"So, Viviein played..."

"No, it's pronounced, Viv-ee-uhn. She was an English actress."

"Oh, okay, Vivien. What do you mean, was?"

"Well, she's dead now. She died a few years ago. She played one of the most famous characters in all of movies and literature. She was herself extraordinarily beautiful, and she played the gorgeous Scarlett O'Hara."

"Who else is dead? All of them?" Cassady asked, with obvious shock in his voice. He realized immediately he should have known that they were obviously dead, but it still was a startling confirmation of what he experienced. They were dead and they were ghosts.

"Yes, I'm afraid Leslie Howard is dead, Clark Gable also. I'm pretty sure from the main cast the only one alive is Olivia de Havilland."

"You said Leslie Howard played Ashley, right?"

"Yes, he played Ashley, of course." The librarian got the strange look on her face again for a passing second and inquired, "As I said, there is something I want to share with you, but now I'm most curious. Cassady, why do you ask who's dead and who's not from the cast of the movie?" Her eyes showed a hesitant but intense flicker as she looked at him.

"I don't know. I'm curious. I'd like to see the movie and see if the characters match the book," he said.

"Oh, very closely. I know they were all somewhat, what they call typecast, after that movie came out and were always looked upon and known as those characters. Leslie and Vivien both did many plays in the theater, but then World War II came along and that was the end. Unfortunately, Leslie Howard didn't make it through that terrible time," Miss Rigby said, her eyes cast down. She appeared visibly sad to Cassady, so he took the opportunity to say goodbye.

"Oh, please don't go yet. I'm all right. I'm a little bit curious as to why you're so interested."

CHAPTER 9

It took all he had to get out of the library without beginning to stammer and make a fool of himself. But she let him go without any more fuss.

Cassady only had one thought. They were really *dead*.

As he was walking away a car pulled up to the curb and sitting inside in the passenger seat was Brie Ann, the girl he was usually thinking about the whole time he was in the library annex. She waved at him and he waved back but kept walking, and then lambasted himself for his cowardly reaction, not stopping and talking for a minute. It wouldn't have been a hard thing to do. He could have asked her how her summer was going. He assumed it was her mom driving, but it could have been an older sister—he didn't get a good look. It could have been a natural, comfortable conversation. Anyway, the chance passed, and he was thinking about the dead people he had possibly met in the Sift. He would have to find out more about it somehow.

That night Cassady didn't wait to meet him but watched the first men land on the moon on TV with Kyle's parents, Lucas, and their little sister. The whole world seemed to radiate with possibilities.

"Before this, the world or here on Earth, we thought the moon was only an elusive powdery rock in the dark sky," Kyle's stepdad said. "Now, we know it's more than fluffy dust. They didn't sink in!"

"What is it made from, then?" asked Kyle.

"Well, it's obviously more than that. We'll have samples now, and since it's our only natural satellite, it's showing itself to be more like a planet. We know it doesn't have an atmosphere."

"How?" Kyle asked.

"If it did, stars would disappear when they came close. But now we'll know so much more about it. It's a new age of discovery."

"All the times I've looked up at the moon as the whole world has, and we can look at it differently now," Kyle said.

Anything was conceivable, and both Cassady and Kyle were having similar thoughts of themselves as astronauts or explorers of another type. They were experiencing magic, enchantment, myth, witchcraft, ghosts, spirits, and the dead coming to life and walking among them. Cassady realized, deep in his heart, that this wasn't a magic trick that would quickly disappoint him. It was the real thing. They were witnesses to the netherworld opening up here on earth. They might be able to enter it, stroll its streets, and be part of it. And that's what they planned to do.

Much later that night they were on their way. They didn't sleep at either of their houses. Cassady checked in at home, and then they met in Kyle's alley at midnight.

"Kyle, I found out they're really dead. I was at the library today and they've been dead for a while," Cassady blurted out.

"That makes sense..." Kyle started, but then stopped. "I mean, we saw men walk on the moon. It makes sense we can do this. I guess I assumed that without us talking about it. But how did you find out?"

"I talked to the librarian and asked her about movies made on the Backlot. She had no idea why I was asking though."

Kyle seemed satisfied with that answer. It wasn't spooky being out at that hour later than normal. It already felt natural and comfortable for both of them, and they didn't stop to question that feeling. They rushed through the streets and alleys in silence. They felt protected like the whole experience was a preordained destiny.

Soon they were climbing the fence and noticed a small light far off deep in the broken-down manor on the corner. As it happened only rarely, they didn't think much about it. The trees were again slightly wavering in the dark. Soon they were standing by the bushes across from the open field in front of the Southern mansion. It was gloomy and the air was heavy.

"What do we do if they don't come again?" Cassady asked. "I mean—can we rely on them appearing every night?"

"I think they'll come," Kyle whispered. He was looking intently at the area in front of them.

"Kyle, do you think we should be doing this? I mean, is it right?" Cassady suddenly asked. He didn't wait for an answer and asked another question. "Do you think this will change us?" He took his eyes off the field for a second and glanced at Kyle.

Kyle never had the chance to reply to Cassady's question, and Cassady thought back on it many times in the months ahead and wondered if his answer would have changed anything. Because as soon as Kyle's answer was forming on his lips and he started to speak, the mist arose from the ground, once more without warning. The mist had a bluish tint to it again, and moved slowly and swirled and twisted into a funnel high in the air and then flattened out and spread over the open ground, as it had the night before. The figures formed a little more quickly than last night, or maybe they knew what to expect this time. Abruptly, the figures were walking around, talking, dancing, drinking, and taking part in what seemed to be a wonderful party. It was the antebellum south during the Civil War coming alive before their eyes.

Kyle and Cassady watched for a while and when no one walked over to talk to them or invited them to join this time, they took several deep breaths, buried any reservations they might have had, smiled at each other, shrugged, and entered into the Sift.

Entering the Sift, the boys first felt a tingling sensation that was pleasant but wholly unfamiliar, and at the same time, different from any feeling they had ever experienced before. It was much more peaceful than any drug. Their breath was blown out of their lungs, and for an instant was replaced by the warmth of an oxygen that filled them with its indigo blaze, and most all conscious thought left them second by second as they walked forward. Cassady and Kyle were cognizant of the fact they were leaving their reality and entering into another sphere, another level, another world. They didn't care and crossed the threshold blissfully. They were nervous the first few steps and almost sick with anxiety, but now there was a simple ease and comfortableness they never imagined feeling.

"I'm on fire," Kyle remarked as the shimmering light enveloped them when they crossed over.

"I feel every molecule in my body," Cassady added.

They stopped walking and immediately Ashley and Scarlett walked toward them. The blue haze seemed to subside, and the boys realized that their attentiveness ability was increasing with an infinitely powerful feeling overpowering them and an overwhelming calm.

"This isn't like watching a movie..." Cassady began.

"I feel like I'm in one," Kyle finished.

"Welcome, my friends," Ashley said. "It's good of you to join us."

"Are we okay?" Kyle asked. "Can we leave if we need to?"

"Yes, yes, you are here to enjoy the Sift. Nothing else,"

Ashley said, smiling. "This is not death. You are not traveling through a tunnel, nor are you being pulled to a bright light or by force into the afterlife."

"I don't even feel like I'm on the ground. I could be flying," Cassady said.

The azure beauty pulsated around them. Looking up, they could see the outline of the Sift, and streaking across the contour and silhouette of the edifice were hues rotating in a beautiful blend.

"It's like a mixture of colors beyond the night. I can't believe this," Kyle said. "Can people on Elenda Street see this, or for that matter anywhere else in Culver City?"

"No. We are hidden from your world. We have allowed you, only, to see us in ours," Ashley said. "Guards, other kids, movie people, or anyone else who stumbles onto the Sift won't even know we're here. We will only show ourselves to you at night and when you desire to appear or I should say disappear within the Sift. We were here in toto the night you first saw Scarlett. You couldn't see us until we let you."

"In what?" Cassady asked.

"In toto. Totally, completely, as a whole... No one will ever see us here, even now. They can't. Do not worry. Let us enjoy the hospitality of Tara and your new friends. Come, come join the party."

Several people expressly walked up to them, surrounded them, laughing and smiling, and introduced themselves. Hattie McDaniel as Mammy, Thomas Mitchell as Mr. O'Hara, Oscar Polk as Pork, Everett Brown as Big Sam, Howard Hickman as John Wilkes, and a couple of dozen others as actors from the movie.

"I remember your characters from the book, *Gone with the Wind*," Cassady said, swept up into the introductions, and accepted their greetings with smiles and politeness.

"Come and let's partake in the gluttony of the feast." The Black man introduced as Big Sam shouted and waved them over under the beautiful oak trees casting a slight shadow across the wide lawn before the majestic plantation of Tara.

The food was barbeque—whole pigs were being roasted over open pits, along with roast rabbit, stewed mutton, fried catfish, corn pudding, cornbread, collard greens, coleslaw, black-eyed beans, peanut brittle, johnnycakes, and pound cake laid out on tabletops. Several long rectangle tables were wide enough for the Southern ladies and gentlemen to sit on both sides. Big Sam continued to host the festivities.

"While a meal serves the purpose of sustenance, we here in Tara have feasts. We enjoy—well, our meals are always obviously gluttonous excess and overindulgences!" he exclaimed happily.

Cassady and Kyle sat across from Ashley and Scarlett. Their nervousness peaked and then flowed away from them in the conversation. The people near them talked about the founding of Tara.

"Of course, my name is Gerald O'Hara, and I courted and married fifteen-year-old Ellen Robillard and bought one square mile of land and created Tara," a squat florid man said, sitting next to the boys. "I earned Pork there in a card game and as my wealth grew so did Tara. From a one-room shack to the beautiful mansion you gaze upon tonight."

"Eat, eat and enjoy," Big Sam interjected to the boys. They dug in.

"Of course, as the producer David O. Selznick said, nothing in Hollywood is permanent. Once photographed or the movie filmed, life here is ended. It is always symbolic of Hollywood. Our Tara has no rooms inside," Ashley expressed to them. "Neither was it here in this Backlot. It was a façade in what is called the 40 Acres Backlot, but that is no matter. So much of Hollywood is a façade."

The conversations continued around them while they ate. Other times they modestly glanced at Scarlett hoping that it wasn't noticed. Every time Cassady did he, in fact, got caught and she equally demurely smiled back at him, as she did with Kyle. He still couldn't believe how lovely she was.

"What does Tara mean, I mean, why the name?" Kyle finally asked. It was the first chance for one of them to say something.

"It was named after the Hill of Tara, once the capital of the High King of ancient Ireland," Ashley answered before Gerald could start another long story. "Or some such tittle-tattle."

"But it's a big, huge movie, right?" Cassady asked.

"Yes, but for us, it's what we live in for eternity. Since you are finished eating, let's have a tour of the Backlot within the Sift with more elucidation, along with what we offer here in the interior exquisiteness of the wonder you've entered."

The history of Tara and the Backlot was explained to Cassady and Kyle as they around walked with Ashley and Scarlett in the Sift. As they walked the azure expanded and contracted with their traveling—it seemed they walked for hours. Cassady thought about the contrast between the book and what the movie must be and these characters and the actors and actresses before him. It was confusing and amazing at the same time. They went from set to set within the Backlot and Ashley talked of what they were experiencing.

"This is Verona Square. One of my greatest achievements," Ashley said, leading the boys into the courtyard they had played and hidden in dozens of times.

"We've been here a bunch," Cassady said.

"Yes, but have you ever read Shakespeare—the Bard, the one and only, out loud, in front of cameras, with the beautiful Norma Shearer as Juliet?" Ashley asked dramatically, walking about waving his arms.

"Well no, but we loved it here," Kyle said, looking at the amazing authentic replica of the city in Italy named Verona. It was shimmering and an ethereal spectacular set with archways surrounded by flights of steps, colonnades, houses with entryways that were now obviously not facades, and one prominent well-known radiant balcony. "It didn't look like this when we came here. This is beautiful, is all I can say."

"They, and I mean Mr. Irving Thalberg, spared no expense on the set. As you see it now, a truly stunning array of fountains, churches, cobblestone streets, and stucco walls. For a temporary movie set, the construction was remarkable—and I present it to you as it was in the movie *Romeo and Juliet* in 1936, courtesy of the Sift. One day you can experience it with a beautiful woman and maybe fall in love on that marvelous balcony as they did in the true Verona in Italy, my friends," Ashley said.

Both Cassady and Kyle looked immediately over to Scarlett and she modestly smiled at them.

"This is Eucy Grove..." Ashley exclaimed on the journey to the next set.

"What?" Kyle said.

"I'm sorry. Eucalyptus Grove. It's famous for several movies. Clark Gable filmed a large part of *Mutiny on the Bounty* here. And I believe Scarlett became close to him several years later in another movie we all know extremely well, and have talked about and will talk about ad nauseam." With this statement, he looked back at Scarlett, who was frowning.

"He was a horrible man..." she said and paused.

"Scarlett has much to say about him, but we'll wait for another night for much of that obstinate conversation."

"How did they film *Mutiny on the Bounty* here?" Cassady asked. "Wasn't that on a South Pacific island?"

"Very good. They filmed most of the movie in that locale, but several scenes were filmed here supplementing with Catalina Island standing in for Tahiti. The beautiful trees here in the Backlot were used to a significant degree for that beautiful island."

"Wow," was all either of them could say. "We came by this dozens of times and played here hiding from each other and friends. But now, these trees are super cool," Kyle said, looking at the staggering palms and eucalyptus and other wonderful vegetation, shrubbery, and undergrowth that was now alive in the Sift, pulsating and effervescent with shadings of emerald. "It looks so incredible."

"And now another famous resident of the Sift is joining us to welcome you to the Sift tonight," Ashley said.

A relatively short stocky unattractive man, with curly blond hair, walked toward them from out of the bushy undergrowth dressed in a naval uniform of bygone times. He was holding a three-cornered blue hat to match his naval dress jacket protruding with, what they assumed, were officer epaulets. He stopped directly in front of Cassady and Kyle. Standing there for several moments, looking back and forth from Ashley to the boys with a malicious scowl, he suddenly stepped close to Kyle, waving his arms, and shouted, "I'll cut your water rations in half to nourish my beloved breadfruit plants! I'll shackle you in iron chains. I'll flog you within an inch of your miserable lives. I'll keelhaul you under my ship, the HMS *Bounty*, even after you're dead and your carcass is rotting. I will not stand for mutiny on board my ship. I am Captain William Bligh and you'll rue the day you were drinking in that tavern to be kidnapped into service of the Royal Navy in Portsmouth, England, in 1787!"

The boys stood there in shock. They looked back at Ashley and Scarlett for help. They were both frozen in place. Unexpectedly, Scarlett stepped forward, laughed, and said, "Really William, you'll scare the poor boys to death."

"Gentlemen, allow me to introduce one of the greatest actors of all time. Mr. Charles Laughton—Academy Award winner for *The Private Life of Henry VIII* in 1933, and of course, the New York Film Critics Circle Award winner for his defining role of Captain William Bligh in *Mutiny on the Bounty* in 1935, from which he has designed to live out eternity with us in the Sift," Ashley proclaimed.

"It is wonderful to meet you both," Charles said. "I also have a star on Hollywood Boulevard, which I understand has fallen on, shall we say, rough times lately. And I was *not* nominated for my greatest role as Quasimodo in *The Hunchback of Notre Dame*, if you please."

They could barely understand him. Scarlett stepped forward again and said, "Please, Charles, keep that North Yorkshire dialect under control for our colloquial American friends."

He laughed and took a stance and said, "Aw wonder how yah can faishion to stand thear i' idleness un war, when all on 'ems goan out! Bud yah're a nowt, and it's no use talking— yah'll niver mend o'yer ill ways, but goa raight to t' divil, like yer mother afore ye!"

"Very good, Charles. Boys, he has quoted from Emily Brontë's *Wuthering Heights*. He was also a famous and remarkable theater actor of quite renown," she said. "He spoke Yorkie or Tyke dialogue and I will only partially interpret and quote, 'I wonder how you can stand there in idleness and worse, when all of them have gone out!'"

"He also has a history with the infamous Clark Gable, don't you, Charles?" Ashley asked. He glanced over to Scarlett and smiled while he said this. She shook her head mischievously.

"That bastard," Charles shouted. "I was the reason that narcissistic pea brain had to shave his pretentious mustache off. He hated me for that. The Royal Navy, at the time, was clean-shaven, and he fought like the devil to keep it on during the filming. In fact, right where you are standing we had our biggest argument about that ugly caterpillar on his upper lip."

"Why did you care?" Cassady ventured to ask.

"Look at me! If you had to stand next to that handsome, slick, masculine horse's ass, you'd be self-conscious too. I did... Well, I guess neither of you two brawny young California beach bum juveniles would have to worry about that..."

Right at that moment, they heard a sound they had heard several times before in their night sojourns in the Backlot. A Jeep was driving through the area. They looked around wildly at Ashley.

"This is excellent. Cassady and Kyle, you will now witness the power and grandeur of the Sift. We are under the dome, cupola if you will, of the Sift and it is by what means we have watched you and others unhindered for many years. Do not move—actually, it doesn't matter. Stay with us, though." The group stood still and observed.

The Jeep pulled up to the entrance of Eucy Grove and stopped. The tall, bushy-haired security guard got out, leaving the engine running, and walked toward them without hesitation. By doing so he entered into the province of the Sift. He looked around and acted as if they weren't there. The boys noticed a light hazy beige glow accompanied him. His actions belied absolutely no indication that he could see, hear, or place them, or was aware of either the existence of the Sift or the present unearthly beauty of his surroundings. He walked close by them and shined a flashlight into the brush for a moment. Cassady and Kyle had seen this very action several times and were usually well hidden and knew in their past explorations to simply stay quiet and the guard would move on. This time, however, they were flabbergasted while standing openly within the Sift. It seemed terrifying and eerily shocking.

Ashley unexpectedly shouted, "Hey, you dodgy git, please turn off that torch, you're disturbing our revelry tonight! Please don't come back here again and bother us."

Cassady and Kyle jumped and started to move...

"Relax, you two novices... Once again, understand he can't see us much less hear us. This is how we watched you two for the longest time. While we are within the Sift, others are not conscious of us or the Sift."

"What the heck is a torch?" Kyle ventured, asking quietly.

"A flashlight in American," Charles said laughing.

The guard turned around, walked purposefully back to his Jeep, jumped in, gunned the engine, and drove off kicking up dirt on the path, disappearing into the night out of the proximity of the Sift.

"How is this happening?" Cassady asked. "Did we walk through this without knowing it before?"

"Oh, absolutely. We allow you in when we stipulate or desire to. Many times we followed you within the Sift and more than relished your presence and your appreciation of the Backlot," Ashley exclaimed.

"Those times when we felt something strange and at the same time those amazing flashes of weirdness," Kyle said. "We should have known during those times when it was unnerving and the Backlot felt haunted, we felt it, huh?"

"The Sift is, you could say, multifaceted and inexplicable," Ashley said. "Let's continue the tour, shall we?"

CHAPTER 10

Cassady was in the large Culver City library on Overland Avenue late the next morning, researching some of the strange things that were affecting him from the previous night. He looked in several books but wasn't sure exactly what he was looking for in any of them. He was searching through thick books as hefty and as big as dictionaries, listing articles from newspapers and periodicals. After finding what he considered interesting, he had to fill out small forms on paper and give them to the librarian standing at the large counter and she would go back into another room and bring out the microfilm. Cassady would then have to take the rolls to a microfilm reader, set it up, scroll through it until he found the correct date, and then look for the particular article. After several hours, he found things about the characters or the people or the ghosts or whatever they were. They had troubled lives, but nothing stuck out to make him think this was expected or predictable.

He was leaving the library and walking out the entrance when he glanced back over the checkout desk, through into the offices that were enclosed by glass windows and he saw, looking back at him, Miss Rigby. Why was she here, instead of the small branch annex miles away? Cassady quickly walked through the front door, jumped on his bike, and didn't look back again until he was cutting through the large field down the block on Overland Avenue, half expecting to see her following him. It left him more puzzled than anything else.

Cassady made it to Kyle's house and plopped down on Lucas's bed. Kyle was lying across his bed reading and hardly glanced up when Cassady came in.

"Hey," Kyle said.

"Hey," Cassady answered.

They both lay there for a few minutes and both seemed to be waiting, maybe each waiting for the other to talk first. Cassady was thinking this was one of the first times in his life he didn't feel that talking to Kyle would change anything, improve it, or be necessary. They warily caught each other sneaking a look and grinned.

"Was that the craziest thing you could have ever imagined or what?" Kyle roared at Cassady.

"I can't deal with it. What we did last night is too much to think about. I don't know what to say about it," Cassady yelled back.

"Have you been freaking out all day or what?"

"Yeah, I can't believe what it was like, and I looked at some things in the library on Overland this morning..." Cassady started to say when the door burst open and Kyle's mom came into the room excited and shouting.

"Do you and Lucas still use Right Guard or any spray deodorant?" she yelled.

Cassady wondered why she was shrieking. Kyle had to think, he didn't really use that much deodorant at all, but Lucas did and he thought it was Right Guard. He shrugged.

"Yeah, I think so. Why?"

"I need it all right now. I have to have it, and we have to get rid of it. The aerosol cans are ruining the earth's atmosphere."

"What?" Kyle asked.

"The chemicals in aerosol cans, the chlorofluorocarbons, are having adverse effects on the earth's stratosphere. It's doing bad stuff, and we have to get rid of all the cans," she said while walking toward their bathroom.

"*Our* cans are ruining the atmosphere?" Kyle said and looked over at Cassady.

"No, the stratosphere," she yelled back at them. "It's part of the atmosphere, or something. We'll all be killed by ultraviolet radiation!"

He often complained to Cassady about how his mom could get excited about things she would read in newspapers and magazines. Kyle's mom was in their bathroom throwing things around and came out with her arms full of various cans of deodorant and air freshener and anything else they assumed she thought must be dangerous to the earth.

"What are we supposed to use for deodorant now?" Kyle yelled at her back as she walked purposefully from the room.

The boys sat on the bed and looked at each other. Cassady had wanted to broach the subject of what they saw and did last night with what he read this morning, but he could see Kyle was upset at his mom.

"Forget it, man, she's out to lunch sometimes," Kyle said to Cassady. "Lucas is going to be pissed off when he gets back and all his deodorant is gone." They both started laughing at the same time.

"What's ultraviolet radiation?" Cassady asked, still laughing.

"I don't know. All I do know is that I guess to avoid it we all have to smell bad now."

They sat there for a few more minutes thinking about everything. It seemed overwhelming. Cassady wanted to talk about some of the things he'd looked up in the library microfilm.

"What about the library?" Kyle asked, almost reading his mind.

"It's like, they're like Marley's ghost in *A Christmas Carol*. 'Old Marley was as dead as a doornail.'"

"So they're really dead. I mean, I guessed that, at least, it had to be true..."

"Kyle, do you believe it really happened?"

"Yeah, I'm wondering if it did myself. It doesn't seem real now. I don't feel tired like we should be. Did the time seem weird to you? It's as if no time passed at all. Is that possible?"

"Well, I checked the time when I got back and you know the only big amount of time that passed was the time it took us to walk back and forth. It was only about one thirty, so we didn't lose much time. I guess it's possible because... I guess, is any of it possible? I mean, if the *what* we did was possible, maybe time, like, stands still, or at least slows down while we're in the Sift."

"Yeah, okay. That makes sense, if any of it does," Kyle said. "Are you okay with sneaking out every night?"

"Yeah. My parents work too hard and get up too early to notice and they've been okay with me sleeping in the Shack most nights so I can listen to music and read. They'll never notice."

"Yeah, me too. Lucas sleeps way too hard and one night he got up and saw I wasn't there and the next morning he asked me where I was. I told him I couldn't sleep, so I went for a walk and he thought for a moment and said, 'That sounds about right. You're getting crazier as you get older.' So I should be okay also."

"I woke up feeling rested, but it was more than that. When I rode over to the library and was looking some stuff up and started thinking about how tired we should be, I realized I was more energized than worn out," Cassady said.

"What else were you looking up?" Kyle asked.

Cassady took a deep breath. "I was looking up..." he started to say.

Lucas burst into the bedroom and angrily tossed his gym bag and basketball around. "Mom's crazy, man. What's with all this taking our deodorant and stuff?"

"I know, relax. We'll get some more later. You know how she gets, man. She thinks she's saving the world, and we usually have to suffer for it. We'll get roll-on or something."

Cassady and Kyle looked at each other and Kyle said, "Let's do it."

"Do what?"

"Papa Bach's Bookstore! Man, we really need to do something normal."

"Another mindless bike ride seems like the perfect thing."

Kyle on his older, but iconic reliable Raleigh, Cassady on a newer Schwinn 10-speed derailleur bought from Lonnie Johnson for $25 *with* a receipt. He didn't even want to actually contemplate where Lonnie got it. Out to Culver Boulevard, two blocks later, a right immediately onto Sepulveda. Riding crazily off and on the sidewalks and crossing streets, up and down curbs, obeying some laws, most, at least, not strictly enforced. Danger at every corner, every light, and every ride mingled with close encounters with automobiles. Didn't matter, wasn't a thought, simply the journey for the day, one more adventure. A hypothetical quest to a place that possibly had all the answers they were looking for in life. They were headed toward a place that contained books. Books they couldn't find in a library. They were learning to share them and talk about them and treasure them. They had turned to reading as a way for the world to explain itself. Cassady found with Kyle that one of the most reassuring objects in the universe, the greatest and most promising of things, is a book. They simply carried the possibility of uplifting their spirit. They couldn't remember who discovered Papa Bach's Bookstore, but likely, once again, Cassady thought it was Kyle's discovery.

Once on Sepulveda, it was a straight shot of a few miles. From their home base in Culver City to crossing some of the main arteries in west Los Angeles: Washington, Venice, Palms, National under the Santa Monica Freeway (about a halfway landmark), Pico, Olympic, and finally Santa Monica Boulevard. On the northwest corner sat Papa Bach's Bookstore. They parked their bikes, partially hidden in the small parking lot in the tall weeds that were never cut.

Kyle and Cassady separated and sat between two aisles reading ravenously for several hours. Kyle walked over to Cassady and showed him a big book.

"Check it out," he said opening a huge book with the title *MGM Movie History*. A double-page picture showed a still from *Gone with the Wind*. It was Scarlett standing in front of Tara.

"That's it, man. How cool!" Kyle said. "We wouldn't have found this anywhere else. Thank you, Papa Bach."

"I looked in the library and didn't find any picture books, only some biographies," Cassady said. "That's one of the things I was looking for there."

"It's too much to buy. We'll look through it," Kyle said as they scrunched down together behind an aisle. "So, what did you find in the library this morning anyway?"

"I read about their lives and newspaper articles and looked up some stuff about a guy that believes people can come back from the dead."

"Who?" Kyle asked.

"I found out some more stuff about Harry Houdini and another guy who wrote a book in 1693 called *The Wonders of the Invisible World*. His name was Cotton Mather, but he was more interested in how witches and stuff come back with evil magical power to overtake places and are tools of the devil. Weird other stuff and people too. It doesn't mean much to us in the Sift, I guess."

They spent another hour reading and looking at the pictures of the movies and stars but were more interested in the Backlot images appearing in the background. They rode home, and as they split up Cassady looked over at Kyle and thought he'd talk about it later.

"I'll see you tonight, man." He waved goodbye and rode on.

CHAPTER 11

Cassady, standing with Kyle, watched the Sift rise up out of the ground and finally level out to what the boys had been waiting for. In the dark from Tara's steps, Kyle and Cassady walked toward it, mesmerized by its presence, nearly hypnotized, waiting for the rush of entering into the warmth of the mist. Entering the Sift, the boys first felt a tingling sensation that was pleasant and familiar, but at the same time, different from any feeling they had ever experienced before. As their breath was blown out of their lungs, and for an instant was replaced by the warmth of air that filled them with its indigo blaze, almost all conscious thought left them second by second as they walked forward. Cassady and Kyle were cognizant of the fact they were leaving their reality and entering into another sphere, another level, another world. They didn't care and crossed the threshold blissfully. They were nervous the first time and almost sick with anxiety, but now it was with a simple ease and comfortableness they never imagined feeling.

"How do you feel now that you've been in the Sift a dozen times?" Ashley asked.

"It still feels like we're, like, kinda submerged for a while, but then it goes away. It's a feeling that wears off and then we have that tingling sensation and bigger-than-life feeling. It's like echoes of things or thoughts of the same things happening over and over," Kyle said.

"I don't know, but I guess I think the same thing," Cassady started. "It's actually better than any high I've ever felt. But I wonder at times if, it's as if... have we always been here? And since we're here now..."

"Yes, in a way since, you're here now, you can be here this day, every day, and you may, if you like, always be here," Ashley finished.

"How's that?" Cassady asked.

"It's like most things in life and even in death. It's a choice. We have been the same as you are and one day you will be as we are," Ashley said. "If you're lucky."

"I need to think about what that means," Kyle said.

"Do you celebrate your birthdays in the Sift?" Cassady asked. "Do you go to the bathroom? I see you wear different clothes every night. If you're spirits or ghosts, do you get hungry? I mean we noticed you guys didn't really eat much at the feast."

"I thought you might be the one to question simple things like that, my friend," Ashley said. "You're caught up in the minutia of natural life. Let me ask you a question since you are compelling us to talk about the mundane. Do you, or have *you* needed to go to the bathroom while here with us for the last few weeks?"

Both Cassady and Kyle thought.

"I haven't realized we haven't had to go to the bathroom or eat anything at any time since we entered and stayed in the Sift," Kyle said. "We did at the feast, but I didn't really feel like I had eaten later; at least, the next morning we both realized we were hungry again."

"Yeah, we haven't gotten hungry, even when there was a

barbeque or dinner prepared by what seemed to be the servants," Cassady added. "We've been like, we're part of a scene or production. I mean the food is always great and appreciated, but what we call the tingling sensation seems to suppress those natural needs while we're in the Sift and for several hours after we leave."

"The cosmos is made up of countless diverse dimensions, and they are as unlike and dissimilar as the possibilities. It can't be explained yet, and you're not ready yet to comprehend or appreciate the capabilities," Ashley said. "And now that you've entered into another realm, let's have you enjoy a setting within that realm I know you will like."

When they left the Tara region in the Backlot and went into, as Scarlett called it, "another locale" to do something different, they continued to have the same sensations and extremely pleasant vibrations. It was like being on the best high they could imagine without taking a drug.

"Being here *is* the drug," Cassady said to Kyle one night. "Let's accept it without thinking about it too much."

"Basically I don't know exactly what to think about it. But, yeah, hey, let's simply enjoy it," Kyle said.

The Tarzan set was small on the Backlot, but as with the other locales, it expanded exponentially with whatever Sift activity was being presented. On most of these sojourns, Scarlett abstained from participating. She didn't join if there was any difficult physical activity involved. This night a man they didn't recognize was walking behind them as they left Tara and walked toward the Tarzan set. The Sift enlarged and moved along with them.

"You mean we can actually swing through the vines here like Tarzan did?" Kyle asked.

"Yeah, like Johnny Weissmuller from the movies?" Cassady said. "Is he dead? Is he here?"

"No, Cassady, he isn't here or deceased yet. We're working

on it, but you know the best-laid plans..." Ashley trailed off, amused.

"What do you mean—you're working on it?" Cassady asked. "Can you contact people like you did us?"

"Sometimes, but it's always indistinguishable. Do either of you know what an apparition is?" Ashley asked.

"Are you a ghost?" Cassady asked in return.

"You *are* going to continue to ask these questions, so I'll help. The source of our energy is a spot of light through a portal, a veil. We are the creation of a vacancy of light and fill it like a black hole in space. I know that doesn't make sense, but we marginally pull open the curtain or veil and bridge the realm of your physical world and our spiritual one."

"Are you Ashley or are you really Leslie Howard?" Cassady asked.

"Both! As Scarlett is Vivien and everyone else you'll meet in the Sift. I am his doppelgänger. That explanation is why we are apparitions and not ghosts per se. As Mr. Weissmuller will be... as you can be..."

"But is Tarzan going to be in the Sift?" Kyle asked, seemingly to move the conversation away from things that didn't make sense.

"You're right about that," Ashley exclaimed with the same seeming relief. "There are times when a person would be a good selection for our domain and the Sift. Mr. Weissmuller is now residing in Florida, where he owns and runs Tarzan's Jungleland or Tropical Wonderland, or something equally clichéd. He's been hosted and is biding his time until he will join us."

"You've approached other people to join here, or what?" Kyle asked.

"Yes, we can contact others and invite them. Everyone we talk to about the Sift is special and so are you," Ashley said. "Now, please try to enjoy yourself." He walked forward into the wilds, laughing.

Cassady and Kyle followed Ashley through the growing density of the jungle within the Sift as it was enlarging and filling out. The world they were walking into was suddenly humid, warm with a light mist filling the air, thick with vegetation, tangles of vines, shrubbery, and impenetrable greenery.

"Tonight Denys Finch Hatton will accompany you." Ashley continued as he turned and nodded to the man who had been following them. "He was a world-famous English aristocratic and big-game hunter. I might add he was the companion and friend to Baroness Karen Christenze von Blixen-Finecke, a Danish noblewoman, who wrote the wonderful memoir called *Out of Africa*. Though she used the pen name Isak Dinesen. I always promise to bring you many wonderful phenomena and people."

"What'd we do to deserve this?" Cassady asked. "Why us?"

"When your time is right, if it is your destiny..."

"You mean when we die?"

"Tonight, I want you to simply have a good time," Ashley said, ignoring the question.

The man stepped out of the shadows and introduced himself while shaking their hands. He was dressed in the clothes they expected from a hunter. He wore a large floppy hat, a cambric shirt, and work pants tucked into knee-high boots. He didn't carry a gun. Kyle asked him why, and he gave a long, pleasant answer.

"This is the finest way to experience the African jungle. All the pleasure and beauty with none of the danger," he said. "I look at it differently now than I did when I was hunting. In the last hundred years or so, there are things to take into account now that we didn't have to then: colonialism, imperialism, horrible triumphalist white males, ethical behavior toward animals, ecological concerns, and so on."

"What's triumphalist?" Kyle asked.

"I'm glad you asked that question. It's a disproportionate or unreasonable celebration of successes and virtues of a given group or ideology over those of another, namely in Africa, what we did with the Africans."

Both Cassady and Kyle looked at each other and shrugged. "You sound more like a college professor than a big-game hunter," Kyle said.

"Ha! You're right, that was a little bit haughty. I won't do that again. I love to pontificate on many subjects. I favored photography later in life anyway. There are many things we could discuss, but let's get on with enjoying the jungle. Remember, if you see a native—just raise your hand and grunt *Ungawa!*"

"Hey, that's the stupid shit Tarzan says to communicate with everyone in the movies," Kyle said, laughing.

The lake now looked immense. A stone bridge spanned the lake on one end and eucalyptus trees along with jungle foliage seemed to go on forever. The trees got taller, and the leaves had fully grown over each other, with vines reaching up their trunks creating an umbrella of darkness and a green canopy. The shores of the lake were beautiful with tropical lushness, and off in the distance the boys could see rising hills, evenly covered with primeval jungle.

Animal noises rapidly filled the night and spooked them on and off for hours. From the dark shadows came the wild calls of beasts they couldn't see. Lions roared deeply and cheetahs screeched, running silently by in the darkness.

"Do lions or cheetahs live in a dense jungle?" Kyle asked. "I thought they were on a savanna in Africa?"

"You're right, the savanna in Africa covers roughly five million square miles, and many animals you might see there don't belong here. They do in our jungle, though, and try to remember the Tarzan movies. It didn't make any difference there either," Denys said, laughing heartily. "Remember, as Thomas Friedman said, every morning a gazelle wakes up and knows it must run faster than the fastest lion or it will be killed and eaten. And every morning a lion wakes up, it knows it must outrun the slowest gazelle, or it will starve to death. No matter who you are, when the sun crests the hilltop you best be running."

"Who's Thomas Friedman?" Cassady asked.

"He's a writer who's probably never been in a jungle, or hunted either," Denys said, laughing again.

Cassady and Kyle never saw natives or any people. Denys pointed out birds like the African gray parrot that yakked at them, and other small animals that were in constant movement and clamor.

Walking along a path made by some kind of large animal, they were astonished to see a deer leap in front of them and tear through the night.

"That's a striped antelope called a bongo," Denys said. He kept up a patter of explanations of everything they saw. They came across something that took their breath away and stunned them into stillness.

"Whoa!" Kyle said catching his breath. "Check it out."

"Quiet," Denys ordered, and they all kneeled down waiting and watching.

Kyle and Cassady were amazed and couldn't believe where they found themselves. Cassady thought he couldn't have imagined or hallucinated anything this outrageous.

"Although they are the largest living primate, they're also peaceful and usually attempt to frighten off intruders without physical violence. But if needed, the male there can tear us apart without even trying," Denys whispered to them.

"I thought everything in here was safe," Cassady murmured back. Denys smiled. "It is, but why take the chance? You aren't completely legitimately of the Sift yet, are you, boys?"

They watched the mountain gorillas move around slowly

eating leaves, stems, and buds and chewing thoughtfully, for an hour. All Cassady could think was how this was beyond tremendous. The large male was magnificent with a streak of silver coloring on its back. Its head was huge, with a thick trunk and broad chest, and its stomach stuck out like several basketballs. Later they saw an animal rushing across an open area a few feet in front of them, scaring them into jumping back and falling on each other.

"What the hell was that?" Kyle yelled.

"What do you think, zebra or deer?" Denys asked pointedly.

"How can we tell, it looked like it could have been either of them," Cassady said.

"You city boys have much to learn. That was an okapi," Denys said, laughing. "It's a cross between a zebra and a deer but is actually more closely related to the giraffe. It's a very solitary animal that lives in the dense jungle like what we're in now. And since we're in a dense jungle, have you noticed the vines hanging down?"

Cassady and Kyle did, in fact, swing through the trees on vines. Denys took them to another part of the jungle where he gave them some instruction. They swung sometimes thirty feet across at extreme heights from vines connected to the forest top and were always able to grasp the other vine with unerring precision and never failing or falling to the floor of the jungle.

"It makes me feel indescribable, strong, intense, and crazy!" Cassady yelled. "I could do this all night!" He landed on the ground flush with a physical intensity and emotion of being beyond power. "It's almost supernatural."

"You can do anything here," Denys said. "In the Sift, that is. But in actuality, if you swing from one vine to another that is hanging dead still and vertical, you wouldn't swing anywhere beyond that. Unlike the movies, you'd be left dangling there looking ridiculous. Not here though. Have fun."

They learned quickly to virtually fly through the air from vine to vine and descend dozens of feet rapidly and catch the next vine before alighting on the ground. Denys watched and laughed quietly after every pinnacle achievement. The Sift allowed them to soar like trapeze artists as easily as any circus specialists. After one breathtaking flip, Kyle landed on the thick floor of the matted jungle and bowed to Denys.

"Really? Is the Sift allowing us to do this?"

"Absolutely. Don't you feel it? I told you the truth. That is truly the magic of the Sift."

"You said we weren't legitimately of the Sift. Will we be?" Cassady asked.

"That's a question for Ashley. I'm here to show you a satisfactory and enjoyable time. You can explore things you've never imagined..."

"Whatever we want to do, we can do?" Kyle asked.

"Yes, you've mostly been talking and enjoying the texture of the Sift in a quiet casual mode with Ashley and Scarlett. That's Tara and the *Gone with the Wind* set. There's not much to do but feel and talk..."

"Which isn't bad," Kyle said. "We've been enjoying the time getting to know them."

"I can imagine," Denys said grinning.

"Yeah, it's called Scarlett," Cassady said laughing, but without the normal sarcasm that recently had begun to seep into the conversations regarding her.

"There is an indefinite realm of possibilities within the Sift. How do you feel tonight?" he asked.

"It's like we could go for days like this. Do you think we could explore the other sets like this? I mean, the World War II European sets and everything?" Cassady asked. "And always have this feeling of invincibility and electricity flowing through us night after night?"

"Yes," Denys simply said. "Whatever your mind's eye can

envision."

As the night closed and they returned to the Tara mansion, they exclaimed what the night was like to Scarlett and Ashley.

"I'm glad you've enjoyed the night. I understand you're quite the Tarzan," Ashley said to Kyle.

"Yeah, it was great," Kyle said.

"I missed you," Scarlett said, looking down.

"You can come next time," Cassady said wondering what exactly or how she meant the comment.

"I wish you'd stay around Tara for the next couple of nights," she said, primarily looking at Kyle.

Walking home, Cassady questioned Kyle if he knew what that was all about.

"Nothing, man. She likes us there, we'll explore this whole place, the French Courtyard, the Chinese Street, the New York Street, the Three Musketeers court, and all of it!" he said shouting. "It's never-ending."

Cassady could never quite peruse Scarlett's and Ashley's minds or thoughts or how they really felt about things. They couldn't realistically become friends like their friends in school or family, and he said so as they walked.

"I mean, obviously, they're ghosts, man," Kyle said. "We can't figure what they're all about. We can try with Scarlett. I'm sure going to try."

"Ashley talks in circles. I don't understand half of what he's saying and as far as Scarlett goes..." Cassady trailed off. "Do you feel you can really get close to her like you could a girlfriend? I don't feel like I could, not like the girls we have talked about."

"Those were our fantasy girlfriends. This is a real girl," Kyle said.

"Really," Cassady asked. "That's what you think? She's real?"

Kyle didn't answer that question.

CHAPTER 12

One late afternoon, Gram and Abilene, righteously practically burst into Kyle's house and sat down with Cassady and Kyle in his bedroom.

"We haven't seen you guys for, it seems like, weeks, man. What's up?" Abilene asked.

"Nothing," Cassady said. Kyle nodded.

"Bullshit!" he answered. "We're here to fix that. You're spending some time with us. Right now and tonight. Period."

"Well, okay," Kyle answered a little reluctantly. "Doing what?"

Gram went into his pocket and pulled out a piece of tinfoil, opened it, shook the contents out into his hand, and held it out to both of them. Inside were a couple of orange sugar cubes. Abilene looked intensely at them both.

"Psychedelics?" Kyle asked. "Orange Sunshine?"

"Si, senor. We've already indulged. Do it."

They'd skipped taking it with other friends a couple of times because of going into the Sift night after night. They had the time, but not the inclination. It was always hard to say no to Abilene though; especially when he was in this kind of mood. Cassady looked at Kyle, shrugged and reached out to choose a hit, picked it up, and popped the acid in his mouth. Kyle did the same. They sat around for a good hour and talked about school coming up, especially high school for Cassady, music, girls none of them really knew, or maybe Gram's sister's friends at his house. Cassady thought it would freak them out if he and Kyle could tell them about Scarlett.

"We're going to a movie. It should be good on acid," Gram said.

"What is it?" Kyle asked.

"It's some crazy old stupid movie playing at the Culver Theater. Let's go," Abilene said. "What does it matter?"

Kyle and Cassady had seen so many movies there, some good, some not so good. It sometimes didn't matter—going together was the purpose. Thinking back on those experiences he realized they had to continue to do *normal* things—it possibly made the Sift even more special; the spending time with friends was one aspect of that feeling. Cassady had a feeling this night was going to be decidedly different. Maybe they could still go in later. But upon reflection, he realized they might not make it. But maybe that was okay too. These were lifelong friends.

"Gram, what's the movie playing?" Cassady asked.

"It's something called *Gone with the Wind*, or something like that," Gram said as they got on their bikes. "I have no idea what it's about, but it should be really good in about an hour or so."

Cassady stopped stunned and looked over at Kyle. Kyle was looking back at him as keenly.

"Yeah, who doesn't love old movies on acid," Kyle said hesitantly.

"Can I double up with you?" Cassady asked Gram. He didn't have his bike at Kyle's house. Gram's eyes were dilated and spinning around in his sockets.

"Sure, man, no problemo. Hop on the handlebars."

It was several hours after they dropped when they finally sauntered into the Culver Theater and went straight into the huge men's lavatory room foyer. It was vast and lengthy from a long-ago forgotten era of Los Angeles and Hollywood, and the movie connections in Culver City. Cassady and Kyle floated down the ramp, but couldn't stop flowing with the tidal wave that was carrying them without acquiescence. This night the foyer seemed as lengthy as a football field, and it was packed.

"I'm completely tripping," Cassady said.

"Where are Gram and Abilene?" asked Kyle. They looked around and they were both long gone.

"Weren't they right behind us?" Cassady asked. Kyle shrugged.

Packed in the foyer appeared to be at least two or three groups of outlaw bikers, crammed in the lobby, milling around. They were tatted, dressed in Levi's and leathers, long greasy hair, patches on their vests with their colors, chains dangling from pockets and belt loops, and bandanas. Every one of them was smoking. They grew taller and taller until some stood seven feet tall or more. They towered over both of them and Kyle and Cassady had to look up to bring them into focus. Cassady could see them in great detail before they passed by or walked behind them and shrank back down to nothing. They smelled so horrible that Cassady and Kyle literally gagged. They tried to make their way out, but could only look at each other stupidly for what seemed like eons before they were walking again and stared around at the bikers and at each other.

"We need to get out of here or possibly get killed," Cassady said.

"Follow me," Kyle answered. "I don't even know if that was real," Kyle said as they walked through the deep green velvet curtains instead of doors into the theater.

Again, something simple seemed to take them an indefinite period of time, but they finally found seats in the mostly deserted theater. They never discussed what happened to the bikers, or for that matter what had happened to Gram and

Abilene, but they felt safe in the front row now.

As the opening credits of *Gone with the Wind* rolled, the music cascaded down on them. They were transfixed watching it come alive. Suddenly there she was sitting with the Tarleton boys discussing the possibility of war.

"They're sitting on the front porch steps of Tara," Cassady exclaimed.

"We've been there," Kyle said. "God, she's beautiful."

"Yeah, Scarlett looks the same as she looks in the Sift."

Cassady looked behind him. Two rows behind them and slightly to the left, a man was sitting with his arm around a pretty girl. When the next scene in the fields started and the slaves stopped working as the bell lightly sounded, the man stopped talking to his girl, looked straight at Cassady, stretched out an arm, and loudly, theatrically, and along with Big Sam and another slave, voiced the exact words they spoke: "Quitting time!"

"Who sez it's quitting time?"

"I sez it's quitting time."

"I'm the foreman. I'm the one that says when it's quitting time at Tara! Quitting time!"

Shocked, Cassady looked at Kyle for validation. Nothing. He was staring straight ahead, as if nothing unusual was transpiring behind them.

As the movie progressed, Cassady couldn't make out anything about the plot of the movie even though he had read the book and knew it. He turned once again to Kyle and said, "I'm confused. This is incomprehensible nonsense."

Kyle had the same quizzical look on his face. Cassady couldn't remember who said it first but one of them practically shouted; "We'll figure it out in the morning."

The movie continued with the plot still unfathomable. "We'll figure it out tomorrow," they'd alternately murmur, holler, shriek, bellow, and whisper, depending on their frame of mind. During the movie, waves of bliss broke over Cassady. The ecstasy seemed like it would never end. The bigger-than-life feeling that came with the ingesting of LSD washed over him like a twenty-foot wave. Concentrating on the movie, Cassady watched the gears turning inside of Rhett Butler's head.

"Now, look, his face has red and blue neon stripes on it. So does Melanie. Are their eyes whiter than the white of anything you've ever seen?" he asked Kyle. "It's like big snowy glass marbles staring at you. The walls in the background are like looking at a merry-go-round."

The next thing Cassady knew the movie was over and they were riding home on Kyle's old but usually dependable Peugeot. Kyle was giving Cassady a ride on his turned-up handlebars—like Gram had done.

"We're floating along the Mississippi like Jim and Huck," Kyle yelled. "We're not on a bike, we're floating along on the raft," Cassady answered.

Rudely and suddenly they melted into Culver Boulevard. They sunk several feet into the street. They were going downward; Cassady felt like he was pushed off, and then they stopped. He looked back at Kyle and couldn't fathom what had transpired. Kyle was bending over his bike, muttering, looked up at Cassady, and raised his bike up into the air. The front tire, rim and all, was bent in half, completely and thoroughly. One half was bent at ninety degrees.

"What happened?" Cassady screamed.

"I don't know." They looked at each other and giggled and hooted and howled and might have laughed forever except for having to trade off carrying the bike the rest of the way home.

Back at the Shack in the garage, they both sat down and then stretched out across from each other and fell into an intense euphoric state. After a period of silence, without forethought or premeditation, they began to recite the entire dialogue from

Gone with the Wind. Line by line. They didn't act the scenes out physically, but verbally they were able to remember and perform the entire movie. They exchanged lines—taking turns initially and then simultaneously, first as the Tarleton twin brothers with Scarlett on the steps of Tara that they knew so well.

Brent: What do we care if we were expelled from college? Scarlett. The war is going to start any day now so we would have left college anyhow.

Stew: Oh, isn't it exciting, Scarlett? You know those poor Yankees actually want a war?

Brent: We'll show 'em.

Scarlett: Fiddle-dee. War, war, war. This war talk is spoiling all the fun at every party this spring. I get so bored I could scream. Besides, there isn't going to be any war.

Several hours later they finished.

Scarlett: Rhett! If you go, where shall I go? What shall I do?

Rhett: Frankly, my dear, I don't give a damn...

Scarlett: Tara! I'll go home. And I'll think of some way to get him back. After all, tomorrow is another day!

After they finished, they chuckled for a moment.

"Did we memorize the entire movie without realizing it?" Kyle asked.

"That is or was impossible. But we did it, didn't we?" Cassady asked rhetorically.

"I guess so. It's like we're embedded with weird super-natural powers, or something," Kyle answered anyway.

The morning light was streaming into the small window in the Shack.

"Are you okay?" Cassady asked.

"Yeah, that was incredible. I always knew there was more going on than they were telling us," he said, smiling. They slept into the late afternoon.

CHAPTER 13

The next night, when the Sift whirled around them, they didn't feel like they would ever need acid again, especially as they took those first steps into the cobalt blue light.

"I swear I'm never dropping again," Kyle said. "Smoking some weed is one thing, but I'm done with tripping. It seemed cool at the time, but that was crazy."

"I don't think I want to go through that ever again," Cassady said. "I promise also. I can't imagine that we'll ever need it."

Kyle and Cassady always paused for a minute when they entered to look at each other, gasp for breath, and feel themselves be pulled further and further into the Sift. The intensity of their happiness was overwhelming, and the humming of the Sift drew them deeper and deeper. Cassady and Kyle were pulled through the blue and center of the Sift. A melody of radiance played around them, and they felt light and airy as the blue fell away. Scarlett and Ashley walked toward them, welcoming them once again into the phenomenon that was the Sift. They had something to share with Scarlett and Ashley this night.

"We saw the movie last night!" Kyle exclaimed. "I saw it before, but didn't remember it that well. And well, I didn't really understand it any more than I did until later. And then it all became crystal clear."

"I wanted it to make more sense," Cassady said. "And it did after we got home. Do you know what we do outside of this?"

"No, we don't really need to, but surmise much of what your generation of teenage boys do during their days and nights outside of the Sift," Ashley said shrewdly.

"We saw it at the Culver Theater," Kyle said quickly changing the subject. They had talked about whether sharing their day-to-day activities with Ashley and Scarlett was what they should do or not. They really didn't find it necessary.

"You could probably see many of our old movies there, yes?" Ashley asked. "I remember that theater. It was beautiful."

This, Cassady counted, was well over a month after the first time they entered the Sift. It had now become a rush they lived for, a rush they waited for all day, a rush they anticipated with a delight they hadn't considered possible, and one from which they thought they might never want to return. Kyle and Cassady spent hours of the night in the Sift and only missed an hour or two of the actual night going and coming. They had limitless energy and a wealth of strength for playing pickup games of basketball, baseball, or riding their bikes during the day. As the summer melted away, they never stopped to consider why they had vitality and intensity, only how much fun they were having night after night. Their new life was pleasing to them, as were their new friends. A secret life that took on a reality of its own during the long nights that rushed in front of them like a never-ending train. Cassady realized he and Kyle were weird and wonderful travelers but also exclusive invited guests on this continuous procession from one province to another, from the plantation to the jungle set to the Chinese Street, to the European Village to the New York brownstone, to the small sleepy Andy Hardy town set and back again.

"Welcome my friends, welcome," Ashley said, always with open arms.

Cassady and Kyle always took a minute to adjust to actually being in the Sift. No night was the same as the night before. As the Sift welcomed them, their bodies relaxed, the evening seemed brighter, colors more vivid, and they always began to giggle as the feeling grew. They felt tranquil and lightness invade their bodies as the euphoric peace entered them.

They talked and walked with Ashley and Scarlett and the other members of the Sift and never felt a moment's hesitation in the conversation. The connection with these people was instantaneous and deep. All their thoughts seemed enhanced. The sky above the Sift was ablaze with colored patterns and geometric configurations, blue, red, green, and yellow. Time was meaningless.

"What would you like to see or do tonight?" Ashley would ask them.

"What's left?" Cassady asked back.

"You've been to our wondrous Southern plantation barbeques, our beautiful German fests, also traveled its vast and deep forests, the nineteenth-century European towns, the dazzling French Alps, the emerald green Amazon jungles, the Foreign Legion Sahara desert forts and bazaars. How about an evening walking along the striking European Village?" Ashley asked. "That makes up the set for the wonderful TV show *Combat!* You mentioned watching that show for several years."

"Cool, let's go," they answered.

They hadn't realized the Backlot had so many sets they could explore. Every time they thought they had traveled around a set, Ashley would come up with something they hadn't even thought possible. The smallest corner of an old set that had been discarded and left to rot turned into a night full of adventure and amazement.

One night they were almost overcome with the ethereal overpowering colors, buoyancy, and the sensations of the night.

"Wow," Cassady said as he stumbled into Kyle walking along the cobblestone street of France.

"I'm lightheaded also," Kyle said looking around and up and down the street. "Is it something I'm seeing or experiencing for the first time or is it being in Europe that's making me feel this way?"

"Take a minute, you'll feel better than fine," Ashley would say.

"Why is this happening?" Cassady asked. "Is it doing anything to us?"

"No, of course not. I'd never let anything happen to you. Just give it time, you'll be back to existing the way you should."

And Ashley was right.

"I'm feeling great again," Kyle said after another minute.

"It's like I'm looking through a kaleidoscope and sensing that larger-than-life thing," Cassady said. "How can anything that feels so good actually be good? It goes against everything I've been told about stuff like this."

"You ask too many questions, man, go with it," Kyle said, a smile plastered on his face. This made Cassady start laughing, and he let the giddiness slide back into his being.

"This isn't stuff, Cassady, it's the Sift. It's something that few in the history of the world have ever experienced," Ashley said. "Billions of people have lived and died, but few are chosen to feel what it is to be in the Sift."

"But we aren't dead," Cassady said. "How are others chosen? Have they all died?"

"Kyle's right, Cassady, you do ask too many questions. Relax and enjoy."

"I'm trying to keep my thoughts straight. It's hard with

this, almost overwhelming."

"Relax, my friend. I'm going to convey to you some things," Ashley said. "The Sift is an astral setting. Many kinds of people or spirits reside here and in other planes. There are many types of Sifts or realms, with different layers to each one. It is a physical dominion or province. Many names can be used. It does not have the same physics that the planet does. Do you study physics in school?"

"I don't even know what the word means," Cassady said, smiling.

"Of course you don't," Ashley said laughing. "Anyway, the actual geography doesn't matter. We're here to visit and see what we can accomplish in our time. Our invitation may or may not be extended to people in the etheric plane."

"The what?" Cassady asked. "Why us?"

"I'm joking with you. The etheric plane is the lowest level of the human energy field or aura. But remember this: the Sift is yours alone. Do not share it with anyone else. That is a truth you must obey," Ashley said as a final pronouncement. "It is an honor we bestowed on you two alone. Now, let's enjoy the next adventure."

"I know my questions are going somewhere, but I can't keep my concentration for long enough. The heavy air is on us in here," Cassady said as he started giggling again, walking down the cobblestone streets of the European Village. He realized, once again, that Ashley didn't answer his questions.

As he and Kyle looked up a soldier dressed in the World War II Infantry uniform was walking straight toward them. He was dressed in a dark olive, drab-colored field jacket that came down to his upper thighs. It looked made of cotton, but maybe windproof, with several large pockets filled with ammo magazines. The trousers of the same color and material were also stuffed with army gear. His uniform was dirty and well-worn from use. His helmet was lopsided and he hadn't shaved in several days. He had sergeant stripes on his sleeves. He looked hard at them both for a moment and forcibly spit out, "The coward dies a thousand deaths, a hero dies but one."

"This, my friends, is Sergeant Saunders," Ashley said with a flourish.

"Nah, we know who Sergeant Saunders is," Kyle said. "And this ain't him."

"We're too close in time to the actual TV show, so these are actors who have played on the show one way or another," Ashley said. "But *Combat!* has only been off the air a couple of years, and for us in the Sift that is comparable to a nanosecond."

"So they're not dead?" Kyle asked.

"Checkmate King Two, this is White Rook, over," Cassady said, laughing.

"I see you're an aficionado of the show," Sergeant Saunders said. "I need you two to fall in and follow me to the action!" Several other soldiers appeared and as they walked by identified themselves: Lieutenant Hanley, Private Kirby, Private Caje, and Private Littlejohn. All were characters from the show, but not physically the actual persons as on the show. A nondescript soldier and two others handed Kyle and Cassady a weapon each and small light green backpacks filled with ammo.

"Training will take place for the next couple of nights, and you'll learn to handle the M1 Garand rifle," he said in a clipped Southern accent. "This is a semi-automatic, fed by a clip, of which you'll find a dozen in your pack. It is a gas-operated, self-loading, and shoulder-fired weapon. Its weight is 8.94 pounds, it's 43 inches long, and has a maximum range of 5,500 yards. Any questions?"

"What?" Kyle said. "We don't know what you're talking about really."

"I've fired a shotgun with my dad, but that's about it," Cassady said, remembering the intense hatred he had for hunting. He wondered about the contradiction and reconciling of those two feelings with playing army and now almost a real, lifelike game.

But learn they did. They remembered the show and missed the regular actors that played the parts on TV, but soon enjoyed the actors that filled in for them.

"I'm a little nervous about this first night's battle, aren't you?" Kyle asked Cassady.

"Yeah, but we have to trust this whole crazy thing. I'm hoping it's fun," he answered.

"This is all for you two to enjoy and do as you have done for months in the Backlot; play army," Ashley said, as they marched away from him and the Village to a hillside and ridgeline above it.

"Saddle up, and bring up the rear!" Sergeant Saunders ordered Kyle and Cassady.

They smiled at each other as they tried to keep up. Later, neither one of them told the other how scared he felt, but the thought of getting killed never crossed their minds. They knew that they couldn't be killed, but they forgot while they played. They were having too much fun.

"Of course, this is a typical scenario for us tonight," Sergeant Saunders said, falling back beside Kyle and Cassady. "We've been given the arduous task of taking a nearly unattainable hill with two German bunkers, guarded with MG34 and MG40 machine guns. What makes matters worse: we have to take it without armor support or even without platoon mortars. I will spend most of the night trying to convince our command that the hill cannot be taken and they, no surprise, will answer in the negative and keep pushing us *to take the damn hill, no matter the cost.*"

Within minutes they were pinned down on a ridgeline with the Germans' automatic weapons firing and mortars dropping on them.

"On my order—we're going to double-time down to that

low ground and set up an attack line and set up fields of fire while advancing!" Sergeant Saunders yelled over the crescendo battle noise.

They ran down the steep decline and set up as Cage tried to raise the company on the walkie-talkie.

"Checkmate King Two, this is White Rook, over. All I hear is static," he yelled to the sergeant. "Typical," was the answer.

"We're moving out and up the hill," Sergeant Saunders shouted. "Watch for the Krauts. They might counterattack; be ready when we move."

The Germans did, in fact, come down as the squad led by the Sergeant surged up the hill. Cassady and Kyle moved with the squad as they drove forward. They fired continuously and crossed the draw and moved up to meet the German soldiers. Explosions went off all around them with bright flashes of light—almost like an inferno erupting within feet of them. They fell down several times—again amazed they didn't get hurt or even banged up.

"Get up and continue the attack!" Private Kirby screamed at them. They followed him without thinking. Blasts peppered the hill in front of them and without understanding how it was possible they were unexpectedly cresting the hill and firing into the bunkers with the air around them streaked with fire, smoke, and detonations going off again and again. Rifle and machine-gun fire surrounded them for several minutes. The Germans suddenly laid down their arms and surrendered. Kyle and Cassady took a minute to process what they went through and catch their breath.

"I feel exhausted but great at the same time," Kyle said. "That was so cool that the Germans who we shot fell down, but later got up without a scratch. I swore several of those guys looked like they were shot to pieces. I thought for a second, *Wow, I really killed somebody.*"

"That was a gas," Cassady replied.

"We need to gather up these guys and call for relief and POW transport," Sergeant Saunders said. Cassady looked over and saw Private Cage now easily talking on the walkie-talkie, making arrangements. They played out two more combat scenarios much alike throughout the night.

"That was the time of my life," Cassady said to Kyle later that night, walking home. "But you know, I don't think war, I mean actual war, should be a game."

"I thought the same thing." Kyle agreed. "But we've had fun playing army in here for months and months, but that was obviously the most fun I've ever had. And just think, this was all happening in the Backlot!"

"I never ran out of ammo. I never even had to reload," Kyle continued. "It's really like the movies or TV. The good guys never run out of ammo. That's crazy. And the Germans kept running right in the open to be shot..."

"Yeah, it's like, hey, I've got cover and concealment behind this dirt hill, like they taught us over the last few nights, but then the German guys get up and run right over to a stupid bush to hide behind!" Cassady exclaimed.

"We'll do it again tomorrow night, huh?"

"Heck yeah."

They felt they could stay as long as they desired and left when they felt their time was up for the night. Sometimes Ashley had to remind them they couldn't stay indefinitely.

"The Sift only exists at night during certain hours. Because we are above ground and, like your vampire lore, cannot exist with exposure to sunlight. A realm is a vacuum in which energies or charges flow through and carry electrical rushes that are both positive and negative. It cannot produce light. Understand?"

"Not in the least," Kyle said, smiling.

CHAPTER 14

When Cassady walked into the library annex Miss Rigby immediately got up, walked past him, and flipped the sign on the door over to *Closed*. Cassady was spooked and started to think twice about staying. He knew he could push her out of the way and force his way out, but instead, for some reason, he didn't.

She looked at him and said, "Cassady, please don't be afraid. I won't try to hurt you. I have to talk to you about some of the things that are going on."

"What do you mean?"

"Let's go in the back room and talk, so we won't get interrupted."

They walked into the storage room, which was only slightly larger than a closet, and sat down at a small table. Miss Rigby paused while looking at Cassady before speaking.

"Basically, Cassady, I would like to know what you were doing looking up information on my father a few weeks ago at the main library."

"Wait, what? Who?"

"I checked after you left and saw what microfilm magazines and articles you were looking at, and it had to do with my father, Leslie Howard. He died in a plane crash more than twenty years ago. I also know you looked up articles on Vivien

Leigh, and a couple of spiritualists, mainly having to do with ghosts or specters. Why?"

"I didn't know that he was your father. I didn't do anything wrong," Cassady said. He was stunned and didn't know what to say.

"I'm not saying you did anything wrong. I would very much like to know why?"

He knew he couldn't answer her and tell her the whole story, but he couldn't believe she already knew what she did and that she was Ashley's daughter—or the actor who Ashley played... wait, he had to think clearly. He knew Leslie Howard was the actor who played Ashley in the movie *Gone with the Wind* but not that this was his daughter.

She sat there gazing at him. He could still run out and never come back. No one would believe her about this whole thing. Only Kyle and he *knew* Scarlett was actually Vivien Leigh, the actress who played Scarlett O'Hara in the same movie. They sometimes talked and acted like the movie stars, and sometimes they didn't, although they only wanted their movie identities in the Sift. None of it made any sense. Cassady's mind was racing a million miles an hour.

"Can I say something and maybe it will help you relax and let you know I really only want to be your friend?" Miss Rigby asked.

He didn't know if he wanted to be her friend, but said, "Yeah, sure."

"I have put a few things together over the last couple of months. Cassady, I know you're sneaking into Backlot 2 at night, right?"

His mind blurred with the fact that someone had stumbled upon Kyle and his secret, seemingly so easily. He had to deny it. "What? Why would we—I mean, why would I do that?"

"Cassady, I remember when you first asked questions about MGM and Backlot 2 in particular. It wasn't idle curiosity, now was it?" She was looking at him more intently and spookily than anyone ever had, except maybe Ashley, and he saw it in her eyes. Cassady was certain this was getting strange now.

"Okay, yeah, sure." Cassady couldn't think of why he should deny that. He and Kyle always knew they could only get in a little trouble for simply trespassing, so it wouldn't be the end of the world for them.

"I also obviously know you read about *Gone with the Wind* and now know who my father was and who Scarlett was. Am I right?"

"What does that have to do with anything? I was interested, that's all."

"Cassady, I'm not trying to trick you into anything. I'll tell you a story and hope you have the patience to indulge an old lady. All right?"

"I guess," he answered, lying. He was more than interested.

"I grew up here in the United States. I loved my father more than anything in the world. He was a ladies' man and once said that he didn't chase women, but couldn't always be bothered to run away either. Leslie had an affair with my mother while he was acting in a play here in America before he later became quite famous as an actor in *Gone with the Wind*. He had much success in many motion pictures, and he sent my mother money over the years and visited me as much as possible. We never lived with him, but we had our lovely home here in Culver City and many wonderful friends. Life was actually brilliant even though he didn't recognize me in public. He chose to be in my life if only marginally, but then sent me to school in England so he could also see me often. I remember very wonderful times with him. I knew we would have continued to be close with each other more in time."

"I'm sorry," was all Cassady could think to say.

"Thank you. Well, when World War II broke out he did his duty as a civilian by traveling to England and helping in the war effort. He was flying back home from southern Europe in a plane that was a commercial airliner with no military personnel aboard. A whole squadron of German Luftwaffe fighters shot down his plane. It was rumored that the Germans thought Winston Churchill was on board, and even more terrible are the rumors that Leslie was a spy, with other spies on board, and the Germans knew it.

"My father wasn't a spy. The *Ibis* was his plane and it was only one of a few commercial airliners downed during the war. It took off from Portugal, which was a neutral country. They had been flying planes back and forth from England and Portugal since the war started. Why would they shoot it down then? I have to know. I'm not sure but I think you can help me somehow."

Cassady couldn't imagine what she was talking about. "I don't know how I could."

"What do you do in the Backlot most nights?"

"I don't know what you mean."

"I know you *do* go into the Backlot almost every night."

"No, I don't." He thought it was the best thing to deny it. He and Kyle never had any idea anyone knew about their nightly sojourns.

"Cassady, I know you and your friend go in almost every night so there's no use in denying that to me. I know it to be true."

"How could you possibly know that?"

"You know the house on the corner on Arizona and Elenda, where you climb the fence every night?"

"What?" He thought hard about all the times they scaled the fence and what they obviously never saw was someone actually in the old decrepit house.

"Did you think it was deserted?"

Cassady's mind was reeling and he couldn't sit still. He

knew he was fidgeting, but he couldn't stop. The house always looked abandoned, and they never gave any thought to anyone living there. They went by it night after night without worrying about anyone seeing them or caring. They used the chain-link fence to climb over the tall steel one. Several times when they first started going into the Backlot at night, they noticed a small light deep within the decrepit old mansion, but they never gave it any more thought.

"Cassady, I live there. Leslie bought it for us and it's been our family home for decades. I'm alone now and keep to myself, but I've seen you and your friend."

Cassady didn't have an answer to that, so looked down at his feet.

"I know something is going on and I must impress upon you, I'm not trying to get you and your friend in trouble. I actually want to help—if I can be of any help that is. And if not, there is something I would like to ask of you, if you would be so kind as to be of service to me?" she asked pleadingly. Cassady had only one thought—he wanted to talk to Kyle more than anything in the world and ask his advice.

"What does your living there have to do with us?" Cassady asked.

"I think you know the answer to that question. Let me tell you another story first. Or at least ask you a simple question."

"Okay."

"Cassady, do you believe in magic?" She leaned forward with a slight, almost imperceptible smile showing.

"No, not really. I mean, do you mean as in magic tricks?" he asked.

"Not really, because that's a trick, as the name defines it. I mean real magic, or the supernatural," she said. "Maybe the spiritualism you seemed so interested in looking up in the main library? You also looked up Charles Webster Lead-beater?"

"Maybe. Why?" he asked curiously.

"He was a Theosophist and founded the existence of the etheric plane..."

Cassady vaguely remembered reading about that in the library and also remembered Ashley talking about it the other night, but didn't connect the two.

"What does that have to do with anything?"

"I have to contact my father, Leslie. I have been trying to contact my father for several years through many mediums, psychics, and spiritualists. I have conducted many séances with many spiritualists and..."

"Did they work?" Cassady interrupted. She was giving him too much information to think about. He needed her to slow down and cutting her short seemed like the only way. His heart was racing, and he felt an eerie tingle from the way this conversation was going.

"I'm sorry, I know I've been rambling on, and it's more than you probably found in your research, isn't it?"

"Yes, I only found a short biography on both Ashley and Scarlett. I only found a little information on the real people, I'm sorry, I mean your father, ma'am."

"Please call me Eleanor."

"Well, I don't know much more than when and how they died," Cassady said, suddenly feeling like he had said too much. "I didn't make much sense out of the other stuff or people." He got caught up in the conversation and realized he still didn't know if he could trust Eleanor and whether he should even be talking to her. He had to stop and talk to Kyle about this before he went any further.

"I've learned to distrust most people in my hunt for the truth, but in your innocence, I feel I can trust you," Miss Rigby said. "I have refuted many fake mediums that used cheap stage magic and tried to pass off tricks as the work of spirits, while mainly trying to actually make contact with Leslie. I have ways of knowing within minutes if we are actually talking to him. In our own way, we were extremely close and I can ask a question or two that only he would answer correctly."

His mind was whirling. He wanted time to think. "I'm sorry, but I have to go now," Cassady said.

"Oh, Cassady, please don't go and cut me off."

"I know, I'm sorry about your father, but..."

"Please don't stop talking to me. I know you know something. I know it and I know it's in the Backlot. I want you to help me contact my father. Can you?"

"Maybe," he accidentally blurted out. He couldn't believe he said something like that. But he had to admit it felt like a relief and made him reflect he wasn't crazy.

"Oh, God! I knew it. What have you seen in the Backlot?"

"I don't know, but what is it you want to know?"

"I have to know that he loved me and, maybe what happened to his plane and... I'm planning another séance and want you to help... Oh, I don't know exactly but I'm obsessed with him dying like that..."

"I'll ask or see what I can do for you, okay? I'm not sure it's him..."

"Can I see him also?"

"No! I'll explain it to you..."

"Please."

"It's some crazy thing called the Sift, and it's ghostly and it's bizarre and it's spooky, but it's great at the same time. I've met several dead people. I can't even believe it myself most days. He says he's Ashley and I've looked up the others also..."

"Oh, God! I believe you. Somehow I know you are telling the truth. I saw the things you looked up in the microfilm. And I also saw you looked up Cotton Mather, Allen Kardec, and Charles Webster Leadbeater, and a few other spiritualists and occult writers. Did you find out anything? Are you interested in that? Some of them deal with spirits and actually devil worship, don't they?"

"Whoa, whoa, yeah, but if he's your father I'm going to have to ask some more questions. I don't know if he'll answer or not, but I'll try. It could take some time and I can't let my friend know. I *have* to take my time... I can't talk about this anymore now. I'm sorry, I have to go."

Cassady got up and started backing out of the small office and into the library. He didn't want a scene to take place and felt it was about to. Eleanor was following him at an arm's distance and looking at him pleadingly with her hands open in front of her.

"Please help me, Cassady. Please say you'll think about it." She was almost crying. "Please say you'll come back again sometime and talk to me."

"I'll think about it."

"Promise me and I promise I won't tell anyone what I know."

"I promise I will. Give me time."

A sob broke out from her throat. "Yes, I promise I will. Please ask Leslie what he was carrying back from Lisbon for me as a present on the plane when he died."

Cassady shook his head and didn't answer. He knew that he had admitted to someone that the Sift was real and even if he wanted to, he knew he shouldn't have done that.

As he was going through the door, he heard Eleanor say one more time, "Ask him what present he was bringing me home, please..."

CHAPTER 15

Cassady walked over to Kyle's house late the next morning and found Lucas and Kyle lying around their bedroom reading.

"What's up?" Cassady said.

"The ceiling," Lucas answered.

They had dozens of comic books strewn all over the floor. Cassady found an empty spot and picked up a Zap Comix and started reading. It was the famous *Keep on Truckin'* issue. They had passed many hours doing this very activity, and it still seemed normal and comfortable. Cassady and Kyle preferred reading books but were never opposed to reading silly things either. They loved the hippie-inspired comic books, funny and graphic, that dealt with sex, drugs, music, and the Vietnam War. It seemed a whole new world was opening up. No more Batman and Superman.

"You guys want to go to a movie tonight?" Lucas asked.

"I don't know. I guess not," Kyle said.

"You guys don't want to do anything anymore, man! Just forget it," Lucas said as he got up, walked out, and slammed the door.

Kyle and Cassady exchanged a look.

"He'll get over it," Kyle said.

"I think he might be right though. How many times have we turned him down to do things lately?" This was reminiscent of the feeling he had been having lately and thought doing the possible crazy *normal* activities with the neighborhood kids was a good thing, and at least they would be together.

"I'll see if he wants to play ball, you want to come?" Kyle asked, biting his lip.

"No, you go ahead, but let's go to a movie with him before we go back in tonight. There's always plenty of time, and it's not like we need the rest. I've been feeling great. We've been turning down things a lot lately. Talk to Lucas and I'll stop by later," Cassady said, getting up to go home.

As Cassady walked home he thought about what happened. They had never cut Lucas out of anything. But this was different; this was something no one else could know about. He remembered some of the things Ashley told him concerning the Sift. He had broken one of the cardinal rules by talking to Miss Rigby and compounded it by not confessing the transgression with Kyle.

"The Sift is yours alone. We have shared it with you, and you are not privileged to share it with anyone else. I'm sorry, but that is the way it is and must be. It is an honor we bestowed on you two alone," Ashley had plainly said.

Kyle and Cassady agreed not to argue with his logic or rules. They enjoyed the Sift too much to ruin it. Cassady now wondered if keeping it from Lucas was a good thing or not. Was the Sift real? It seemed real enough. What was happening that he couldn't share it with other friends? It seemed to draw them in further and further every night. He couldn't or wouldn't tell even Kyle about Miss Rigby.

"This feels like it's a good thing," Cassady had said one night.

"We've been chosen to experience this incredible adventure—no, more like a metaphysical quest. We can't turn our backs on it," Kyle said.

And yet, if Cassady admitted it, there was a small nagging fear growing deep within his heart. Maybe this wasn't something, as great as it was, they should be pulled into.

Later that evening when Cassady was walking back up to Kyle and Lucas's house, he thought of how beautiful the night was and how strange it all seemed. They were in the middle of something really bizarre and it was still okay to go to a movie with Lucas. He realized he had little desire to see any of his other friends, and he sensed they had noticed and wondered if that was good. Abilene had. Cassady realized he wouldn't miss some of the pitfalls having a wide range of friends brought along with it. Several of his friends were a couple of years older than he was and maybe not the best influences. He didn't miss some of the undertakings.

Two years earlier, Gram, George, Abilene, and Cassady were considering ditching school for the afternoon and driving up to Topanga Canyon to go swimming. The ponds and creek were full, and it sounded like a great idea. The car they were planning on going in, though, was a Ford Mustang that Abilene had stolen and stashed in his garage for a week or so. They had stood on the old railroad tracks running down the middle of Culver Boulevard arguing about the merits of using a stolen car, Gram and Cassady literally standing on one side of the tracks, and Abilene and George on the other side.

"You're such a pussy, Cassady. I can't believe it!" Abilene yelled.

"This is uncool, man. Don't do it. It's crossing a line we haven't crossed yet!" Cassady pleaded to Gram.

"Fuck you, pussy. They don't even look for stolen cars after a day or two," Abilene spat. Cassady couldn't believe Abilene's improbable reasoning.

"That can't be true. That doesn't make sense. Gram, this is something bigger than we really want to do."

"You're a fucking punk, Cassady, and you are too, Gram. Don't go then. But we'll be swimming in the tide pools in an hour."

In the end, Gram went back to school with Cassady. George and Abilene pulled out of Abilene's alley, drove two blocks, heard the wail of a siren, and were busted for grand theft auto. That night at the police station George spilled his guts to his dad, also a YMCA man, about how Cassady talked Gram out of going along with him and Abilene. George's dad called Gram's dad and told *him* the story. After that, Cassady could do no wrong with Gram's dad. Cassady had saved his son from having a felony record, and he loved Cassady for it.

Cassady and Kyle hadn't seen Abilene for the last couple of weeks since dropping acid with them, and honestly, Cassady was glad for it. But when Cassady walked into Kyle's house that night, there sat Abilene and Gram.

"We're crashing a party in Beverly Hills instead of going to a movie with Lucas," Kyle said, shrugging.

"Where's Lucas?" Cassady asked shocked.

"Lucas split."

Cassady was immediately jealous, he always knew Lucas as a smart guy. Abilene had another car—his mom's it turned out—and they drove up to Beverly Hills and had to park down the crowded street from a beautiful castle-like home. They walked into the huge foyer and gasped at the stairway circling up to two or three stories. They made their way out to the massive backyard with a massive pool and beneath a ramada, two gargantuan fish tanks filled with large colorful fish.

"What the fuck do they have these big ugly goldfish for?" Abilene asked Gram.

"They're obviously koi," smirked a guy with glasses and a corduroy jacket standing next to them.

"And obviously, I could shove your head in there to see

how long you could hold your breath," Abilene countered.

Gram steered Abilene away and Kyle and Cassady went in another direction, laughing.

"This could be trouble," Kyle said. At the party, they circulated around for a while and eventually Cassady had a couple of uncomfortable conversations with kids who didn't know him.

"Do you go to Beverly High?" a pretty girl asked him.

"No, I go to Uni High," he answered. He had learned that University High was the other super upper-class school in Bel Air or somewhere near. He awkwardly turned away from her and immediately overheard a conversation between two guys that didn't bode well.

"I heard Kathleen found two guys going through drawers in her parents' bedroom," one of the guys nearby said. "They took off and we can't find them."

At that point, the party was thinning out and Kyle and Cassady couldn't find Abilene or Gram either.

"I'm sure they were the guys rifling through the rooms, so let's get them out of here," Cassady said.

"Yeah, it won't be pretty if anyone braces Abilene."

They wandered up from the pool into the huge mansion. They found them both with a couple of other guys running down a long hallway into a huge bedroom on the second floor flipping onto a king-size waterbed. They'd sprint down the hallway and as they flipped over and landed, the waterbed would swoosh up into the headboard looking like the next flip would break it wide open. A crowd of boys was standing around laughing their asses off.

Suddenly, a girl walked up from downstairs and began screaming, "Who are you guys? I want you out of here or I'm going to call the police."

Kyle and Cassady managed to talk Abilene and Gram into leaving at that point, as Abilene was about to get in a fight with the girl's boyfriend.

"We could go to my dad's office in the Culver Building downtown," Gram offered.

His dad had given him a key to his law office for emergencies. Cassady smiled and thought that was a major mistake. He couldn't imagine what the emergency could be. They went through the underground parking garage, which opened into an alley, and the front of the building was on Washington Boulevard. His dad's plush office was on the fourth floor. The only music he had was 8-track tapes of people like Neil Diamond or Simon & Garfunkel, and that was okay for a few minutes. They got high and sat around in his office relaxing for a while. Gram and Abilene were a couple of guys who would destroy some stranger's waterbed for a laugh, so sitting around listening to Peter, Paul, and Mary and being mellow was not going to last long.

They began to run up and down the hallways chasing each other and playing hide-and-seek, Kyle and Cassady against Abilene and Gram. They were having a gas. At one point, Kyle and Cassady hid in someone else's unlocked office on the third floor and waited. They couldn't hear Gram or Abilene and several minutes passed. They had filled up some cups with water and were going to bomb them when they came by. Nothing. They slinked out and went into the stairwell. They walked down toward the first floor and stopped.

"Do you hear that?" Cassady asked. "Wait a second."

"What is it?"

It was the faint crackle of a police radio transmission. "One Adam 12, see the man…"

Cassady looked over at Kyle and his eyes were as large round and opaque as Cassady's were. They slowly walked down to the bottom, opened the stairwell door, and cautiously peeked around. Parked in the garage toward the back entrance were two Culver City police cars; fortunately, no cops though.

"Let's get outta here, man," Kyle said.

Kyle and Cassady walked out between the police cars, climbed a fence, and continued east down the alley. As they walked around the corner past Culver Center Flowers, they looked out on Washington Boulevard, saw nothing, and turned toward home.

Without thinking they walked down the sidewalk, sauntering as if it were noon as opposed to after midnight, passing back in front of the Culver Building. Later they realized that stupid, ignorant, unthinking move saved their asses. As they walked by the front foyer, there, with all the lights now blazing, sitting on the floor handcuffed with a huge cop standing over them, were Abilene and Gram. Later Abilene said the cop nodded his head at Cassady and Kyle and sarcastically said, "I bet those are your dumbass friends, right there, huh?"

Abilene shook his head and didn't give them up although they were both busted for possession of cannabis. It was lucky Gram's dad was a lawyer. Cassady didn't save him that time. Cassady and Kyle's names weren't mentioned.

"I don't want to do anything with those guys again," Kyle said later.

"Yeah. Something like that, being stupid with Abilene, could screw up the Sift, couldn't it?" Cassady asked.

"Yeah, more than the Sift. Our parents would be watching us really close and then we wouldn't be able to get out. Let's break free from this crazy shit. The Sift is a thousand times better."

CHAPTER 16

Kyle and Cassady were listening to Scarlett talk. Scarlett loved to talk. She was telling them stories about *Gone with the Wind* and Clark Gable. She had them laughing so hard Cassady thought he was going to pee. It never occurred to either of them that actors and actresses could be so mean to each other. It took all this time for Scarlett to open up about her movie life.

"Clark had false teeth and it was hell kissing him," she said. "I wanted to gag. He was lazy, indolent, and slothful. He wasn't the sharpest pencil in the cup, nor the sharpest tool in the shed, nor the sharpest knife in the drawer, nor finally, the yellow of the egg."

"No way!" Kyle said.

"Really?" Cassady asked.

"Yes, but I do have to say, he was kind to me, and he enjoyed my potty mouth," she said. "He did make a clumsy effort at seducing me, but I was so incredibly enthralled with Larry that I naturally rebuffed his unwelcome lame attempts."

The boys didn't say anything to this, as it was simply too much to comprehend. "How did you get the part in the movie?" Kyle asked.

"I was made for the role. As soon as I did a screen test, they knew there was no other person in the world who could play Scarlett better than me." Cassady and Kyle glanced at each other and both thought they couldn't have agreed more.

"What was it like making that movie?" Cassady asked.

"All I remember is being exhausted. I had to do dual roles at times."

"Dual roles? What does that mean?" Kyle asked.

"I was in almost every scene in that damn movie. In the morning, I had to play myself as a sixteen-year-old and then come back in the afternoon and play myself as a widow in my twenties. On one day off, which was few and far between, I went to my friend's house—George Cukor, the director, who had these incredible ladies' pool parties. As Baroness d'Erlanger said, 'Then in the evening naughty men would come around and try to eat the crumbs.' Anyway, I fell asleep next to his pool, wet, still in my bathing suit, and all he could do was throw a blanket over me until the next morning. I probably averaged over fifteen-hour days, most days." Scarlett tossed her hair and grimaced. Cassady immediately thought of what she must look like in a bathing suit.

"It must have been hard work. I never thought movies were such hard work," Kyle said.

"The worst was during and immediately after my divorce and getting married to Larry," she said.

"Oh," Kyle said.

"Yes, poor Larry had to put up with all my problems and..."

"Who was he exactly?" Cassady asked. He detected that Kyle was feeling a tinge of jealousy even though he thought it was crazy.

"Laurence Olivier, my husband and the love of my life. Larry filled my life with desire, romance, and passion, but unfortunately also much heartbreak, infidelity, and sorrow," she said. "My God, I sound so melodramatic."

Cassady could tell Kyle, unexpectedly, was falling in love with Scarlett. Cassady enjoyed the attention she paid to them both, and Cassady felt a tinge of what he thought was love, but couldn't really put his finger on what he was feeling. Talking with a woman so incredibly beautiful was wonderful, but also made him nervous. They were spending much of the time with Scarlett, as she preferred to be called, never Vivien. She had accompanied them, at times, but now rarely, to other facets of the Backlot. One night she stopped. Scarlett seemed to prefer to stay in either the *Gone with the Wind* set or the European Village, but without the war scenes playing out. Mostly sitting around talking.

"The Southern mystique and the lifestyle had always fascinated me, especially during the filming of the movie. I miss those days and often wished I had actually lived during those times," she often said.

"What about slavery?" Cassady asked out of the blue.

"The slaves we had in *Gone with the Wind* were well taken care of and more or less happy," Scarlett said. "We clothed them and fed them. Their time was..."

"You're kidding?" Cassady said, interrupting her.

"Listen to me, Cassady... We cannot expect fairness and justice in this world or life. The best we can hope for, including slaves, was and is a paradise after the misery of it is all over," she said in a final tone to end that night's conversation.

Cassady felt sickened. He couldn't believe what he heard. His feelings for her changed in an instant. He was confused, but also unwillingly entranced by her beauty. He would sit back and listen from now on.

The next couple of nights Cassady noticed Kyle was becoming obsessed with her marriage to Laurence Olivier and constantly asked her about him and their relationship. Scarlett answered happily some nights, but Cassady noticed other times she answered rather coolly. One night it was both.

"What made you fall in love with Larry?" Kyle asked.

Scarlett smiled. "I was drawn to his incredible charm and

magnetism, and of course, he was the most famous actor in the theater world at the time. We had met, but I cemented our relationship one night with our first conversation when I went backstage to talk after his performance in *Theatre Royal* in 1934. He wasn't going to let me go after what I said to him that night. And I know he was drawn to me in a way he never had been before with another woman, including his wife," she answered with a sneer. That sneer threw them both off. From there it got worse. She appeared to be another person, an ugly person, as she ranted through her mistakes in life.

"I ruined my love for him and his for me. I smoked incessantly and drank far too much. It didn't help my lung condition, and it certainly didn't help with my accelerated hysteria and what they called my manic-depressive periods," she wailed. Cassady looked at her and saw a face that was losing its beauty and was quickly turning into a horrid mask of pain.

"Drugs, shock treatments, and so-called psychotherapy didn't help either," Scarlett added. "Well, I longed for Ashley through that entire dreadful movie and I finally have him now, at least, in one way or another. Don't I?"

Cassady felt like getting up and running away. Kyle sat there and finally held her hand while Cassady walked over to the Southern mansion and talked to some of the people there. Ashley came up.

"Are you having a good time tonight?" Ashley asked.

"Well, I was until Scarlett had a meltdown. I didn't know what to say," he confessed.

"In the Sift, we bring shadows of our former lives with us. But what we have now is this wonder we have been gifted. Vivien had a wonderful life, but with many challenges, and as Scarlett she can continue for eternity. She has chosen to live here in this existence now and forever."

"Will this stay here forever?" Cassady asked quietly. "I

mean the Sift."

"How long is subject to interpretations and those answers are not for me to answer yet. Give it time. Don't let Scarlett's being upset disturb your time here tonight. She has had things that even now in this afterlife trouble her. She's taken with one of you, and since you're here and not comforting her, that person seems to be Kyle," Ashley said, smiling.

They walked to the barbecue together and Cassady forgot about all of it for several hours while talking to the actor who was Big Sam from *Gone with the Wind*. He was so nice and kind. He was the foreman on Tara and Cassady was amazed he was happy here in the Sift.

"Can I ask you why you are a slave here in the Sift?" Cassady asked before thinking what that question represented. "I mean, I know you're not a slave here, but you represent one."

"That's quite the question, young man," Big Sam said. "We're in a place that was simply characterized in a movie, right?"

Cassady only nodded.

"But it's a place we have all vanished into that exhibits a piece of history. But the history is not reflected in authentic historic times. It's a version of history that didn't actually happen; it's what people *want* to believe. This..." he said lifting and opening his arms, "is not the truth, but an imaginative shadow of the reality that the Sift falsely epitomizes—especially to novices such as yourself and your friend."

Cassady didn't know what to say to that. He was somewhat shocked by that information so he simply asked, "Were you in other movies?"

"Yes. Did you ever see the original *King Kong*?"

"Yeah, did you play one of the guys on the island?"

"Yes, I played the savage who danced around like an idiot, and did so in tons of movies. I was in over forty in my career.

Many of them were unaccredited. My reality here... it's not real. It is a supernatural falsehood. When you enter that sparkling blue light it's an indescribable feeling, right?"

"Yes, for sure," Cassady answered.

"You'll never experience anything like it again. All the years that follow, none can compare with that glorious blissful first moment of entering the Sift. But you'll then participate here through an unnatural occurrence by falling into the trap of this realm that supports torture and enslavement because I ignored the fallacy. It would do you well to think about that."

"I'm not sure I can understand, are you really Mr. Brown or Big Sam? Ashley won't clarify that for us, or me really."

"I'm both, but the mystical experience... It's a choice young man. The stakes are obviously higher than you can imagine..." He stopped and looked around.

Cassady didn't have a chance to ask Mr. Brown more. At that point, Ashley came sauntering back up with Kyle and looked on as Mr. Brown turned and walked away, and they called it a night.

Walking home that night was tense between them. Kyle was exclaiming how much Scarlett told him about her life. "She wanted children, and had a daughter with her first husband, but couldn't have any with Laurence Olivier and that was the misery of her life. Larry thought she was the most beautiful woman in the world and I have to agree. I've thought that from the first night we saw her, right?" he asked.

"Yeah, I guess, but she's not real. So I don't know," Cassady said.

"What? She's mesmerized everyone who's ever been around her. She went to school in India. Isn't that cool?" Kyle said wildly. "You said so yourself, I remember—what did you say right before we fell asleep?"

"You're right, there's no denying her beauty, but what is she to us now?"

"She's a girl who's spending time with us, man. That's enough," Kyle said.

Cassady thought he shouldn't push things, so he let it go. "What else did you learn about her life?" Cassady asked, changing the subject for Kyle.

"They interviewed 1,400 women for the part of Scarlett and she's still pissed that she only got second billing behind Clark Gable," Kyle went on. "She met the director—I think his name is Selznick or something? Right on this Backlot on, I remember, December 10, 1938, when they built fake Southern plantation houses and other fake plywood and paper-mâché buildings along with old abandoned sets to make the burning of Atlanta scene so real."

"That's pretty cool. They filmed that here?"

"Yeah, can you imagine? She said the flames shot up and could be seen all over Culver City. People thought the town was burning down."

"I would have loved to have seen that," Cassady said. "Did she ever say why she came here to Tara and *Gone with the Wind*?"

"It's where she likes to be here and always has, even before she had the chance to join them. The Sift is here on the place they like to call home now."

"And what kind of home is that exactly?" Cassady asked.

"I don't know." Kyle said and then suddenly blurted out, "She let me kiss her."

"Wow. What was it like?" Cassady asked, genuinely entranced, but still troubled by her thoughts and beliefs on slavery. Could someone so beautiful be either crazy or stupid?

"Heaven," Kyle said, smiling.

CHAPTER 17

The next afternoon Cassady was back in the Sepulveda library annex reading a week-old copy of *Rolling Stone* at the farthest table away from the door. Cassady didn't know exactly why he couldn't avoid the annex, but felt too much had happened in the last couple of weeks and felt overwhelmed at times. Miss Rigby hadn't had a chance to ask him any more questions, and he didn't have any new information for her, so was waiting for the right opportunity to tell her. She was busy with another lady who asked for some help. There were only two weeks left until school started after Labor Day. It would be his first week of high school. It didn't seem like a very big deal to him as Kyle had started last year and most of Cassady's friends were a grade or two ahead of him, and he was looking forward to joining them. He was reading about a concert that had taken place in upstate New York a week ago. They called it Woodstock, and it seemed as if every band in the world had played there.

As Cassady was reading, the unthinkable happened; suddenly the door opened and in walked Brie Ann. She glanced at Cassady, and he quickly looked down at his magazine. She returned a book and was talking to Miss Rigby. His heart jumped up into his throat, and he couldn't breathe. He tried concentrating on the magazine article, something about Creedence Clearwater Revival playing after the Grateful Dead, but it all swam together before his eyes.

"Hi, Cassady." Brie Ann had walked right up beside him.

"Oh, hi," Cassady choked out, his voice sounding like a frog.

"What are you reading?" she asked, sitting down across from him.

"I'm reading about Woodstock," he answered. He waited but couldn't think of anything else to say, and thought, oh no, here I go again. He also thought, *Oh, by the way, I sneak into MGM Studios at night and converse with ghosts on a regular basis, never sleep, and I'm never tired either. It's not that weird, but I'm beginning to think I'm getting pulled into something waaaaay beyond supernatural, and my best friend's freaking out falling in love with a ghost. But other than that everything's cool.*

Cassady wondered if he could talk to this girl that he had a crush on for almost two years. Unexpectedly, he found himself wondering if she was as beautiful as Scarlett. Immediately he regretted the thought of trying to compare them.

"My sister told me about that. It would have been great to have gone," Brie Ann said sitting down next to Cassady. "I heard Crosby, Stills & Nash were great. I love them. I play their album about a thousand times a day." She saved the moment from being uncomfortable and continued talking.

"I would have loved to see Jimi Hendrix play the 'Star-Spangled Banner.'"

"I saw him, I don't know, maybe a year ago," Cassady said.

"Really, cool, where?" Brie Ann asked.

"At the Forum in Inglewood with a friend named Donovan," Cassady said. "He got tickets and we went. It was a gas. But Hendrix came out and only played about forty-five minutes. He never said a word to the audience, finished, and walked off the stage. We had to walk down to a gas station to call his mom to come and pick us up. She had just gotten home from dropping us off. She was a little pissed." Cassady couldn't believe he was talking so much and thought he better slow down.

"That's weird, but still cool. How'd your summer go? I can't believe it's almost over."

"Good, it's gone by so fast. Are you looking forward to high school?" he asked almost dizzy with apprehension.

"Yeah, but I'm nervous. My best friend Gloria moved away this summer and it would be nice to have someone to hang out with and talk to..."

"You can talk to me," he almost shouted. "I mean, we read some of the same books, you know. And I always have time. I mean I spend time with Kyle, but I always would have time for you."

Everything froze in time and Cassady swallowed. Brie Ann stared at him with a penetrating look and then smiled. "I noticed the books a long time ago too, Cassady. Talking to you would be nice." She slid her chair an inch closer to the table and started talking about how different things in high school were going to be and what teachers she had heard about.

Cassady only heard about half of what she was saying. He nodded and was smiling like crazy. He looked at the long blond hair that framed her face, her eyes, her smile, and decided she was at least as pretty as Scarlett. Maybe more so, because she was real and, more importantly, talking to *him*. As he listened, he saw Miss Rigby looking back at him with a smile.

"Cassady, doesn't your grandmother live around here?"

"What? Oh yeah, I'm sorry. Right behind here." Cassady looked back at Brie Ann. "That's where I'm usually going when I stop in here. How did you know that?"

"Oh, I know a bunch of things about you, and I hope to find

out more. Is that okay?" Brie Ann smiled.

All he could do was smile back. It was a dream come true.

"If you didn't already know, I only live a couple of blocks around the corner at Washington. I also know your name is the modern English version of the Gaelic or Celtic," she said. "That's why it's spelled with an 'A' right?"

"Wow, how do you know that? My grandmother is the only other person other than my mom to know that."

"I looked it up. Now if you answer a question I've had for, I don't know, maybe a couple of years. You can walk me home..."

"What question?" he asked.

"Tell me what's the Shammy Whammy?" she asked.

"Oh wow! I don't know if I should. That's a crazy kinda nasty story?"

"Please, I've heard that said for years and whenever it's said, guys start laughing but will never tell me why. I figure since you're the guy who told the health teacher 'I would gladly take a case of gonorrhea and a shot in the ass if it meant having sex,' you'd be the one who could tell me."

"You remember that?" Cassady asked, flabbergasted, suddenly remembering Brie Ann was in that class also.

"Yes, it made you famous for a while, didn't it?"

"Yeah, but not with the right people," he answered, smiling. "Well, she shouldn't have told us that gonorrhea and syphilis were in epidemic proportions in Los Angeles and the surrounding cities."

"And you shouldn't have said 'that's bullshit,'" Brie Ann said, laughing. "Now, I figure the boy who said that would be the one to tell me about the Shammy Whammy."

"That got me a suspension. No way. I can't tell you that story. We don't know each other well enough," Cassady pleaded. "It's beyond gross."

"How about we make a deal?" she asked.

"What would the deal be?"

"If you tell me and walk home with me, I might give you a kiss," she said, smiling. Cassady thought this might be the luckiest day of his life. The story was incredibly disgusting, but she asked for it. He also realized there wasn't much he *wouldn't* do to get a kiss from her.

"You're tougher than I thought," Cassady said, laughing, and he realized he liked it.

"Yeah, yeah, tell me the story."

"Okay, so we also used to play with a boy who lived on the corner of Center Street and the alley that ran parallel to Washington Boulevard. His house sat on three lots with a backyard that ran almost a hundred feet. In the middle of this huge lot grew two enormous apricot trees spaced about thirty feet from each other. Remy was his name. They've moved now, but one day in early summer about, I think about five years ago, our goal was to sneak into Remy's backyard and climb the trees and gorge on the ripe apricots until we were sick. The catch was Shammy. He was this huge mammoth monster of a Great Dane that roamed the backyard and patio."

"I remember people talking about that dog," Brie Ann said, nodding.

"We usually were not allowed to even be around him—only when Remy's mom was home and could control him. She usually locked him in the garage when Remy had friends over. He would howl like in that movie the *Hound of the Baskervilles* until they let him out to run around, circling the trees, cutting sharp corners, free from his imprisonment, furious, frothing at the mouth for several minutes."

"Shut up, that's not true," Brie Ann said, giggling.

"I know, I'm being dramatic," Cassady said.

"You see too many movies." She smiled. "Or read too many books, but that's good."

"Anyway, late one spring, as the apricots were ripening, Gram, Donovan, and a new kid in the neighborhood named

Wyatt, and I were walking down the alley and had earlier seen Remy's mom out with his brother in his wheelchair, heading the opposite direction on Center Street."

"Does Wyatt still go to Culver?"

"No. Luckily for him, he coincidentally moved not long after this day," Cassady said. "Not exactly because of that day, but it wouldn't have been a bad idea."

"Okay, go on," Brie Ann said, reaching out and touching his arm. Cassady felt faint.

"We stopped and hung on the fence and looked longingly at the ripe luscious apricots literally falling off the trees," he continued. "'Let's climb the fence and get some apricots,' Wyatt said. 'I don't know where Shammy is right now, but we have to wait until we know he's in the garage,' Donovan said. 'You guys are such chickens,' Wyatt answered back."

"So, I assume you all went right over after that challenge," she said.

"Yeah. We all immediately climbed the fence and ran for the first tree," Cassady continued. "Donovan and I were the last ones over the fence, and as we ran for the trunk of the biggest tree, out of the corner of our eyes we saw the shadow. Shammy was coming around the corner of the garage and heading for the same tree. We veered to the second tree and made it right as Shammy, distracted for a second, swerved toward us. His split-second hesitation gave us enough time to get up to the first branch and pull ourselves to safety."

"Whoa," Brie Ann said.

"Shammy wailed and barked like crazy and was really pissed. He stood up on the trunk of the tree Donovan and I sat in, reaching up, shook his head, flinging saliva in showers over the tree and into the air. We climbed up to the highest branch that could hold our weight and put our hands over our ears. He ran over to the other tree and commenced the same act. He continued for like five minutes, running between the two trees howling horribly and scaring the shit out of us, and like, caused us short-term madness. We howled along with him and then laughed like crazy.

"Shammy eventually calmed down and lay down in the grass between the two trees, seemingly dozing off but obviously still keeping a watch on us. We waited for another ten or so minutes and every time we even shifted in the trees, we could see Shammy's eyes follow us."

"'We're going to have to wait until Remy's mom comes home or someone finds us and gets him in the garage,' I said to Donovan. 'Yeah, I'm not getting down until he's long gone!' We yelled this plan to the others. 'I'm going to run for it!' Wyatt yelled back to Donovan and me. 'No, don't!' Donovan answered back. 'You guys are so chickenshit, I can't believe it. I'm getting out of here!' Wyatt yelled.

"What worked the first time had no takers this time. I yelled for Gram to stay put. Gram looked over and nodded.

"Shammy looked for all intents and purposes like he was sleeping. Wyatt hung from the lowest branch, still a few feet from the ground and looked over at us, dropped and started running. He made it about twenty feet. Shammy was up in a flash, bore down on him like a freight train, and ran right over him. Wyatt went down hard and rolled into a ball. Shammy turned, reared up, and pounced on him. He didn't bite Wyatt. He didn't gnaw on Wyatt. He didn't lick Wyatt. He held him down and moved him around like a rubber ball, showing his incredible strength for a few seconds. Then, Shammy pulled him in tighter with his long front legs and paws, jerking Wyatt closer, and suddenly moved up on top of him.

"'What's he doing?' Donovan asked me, shaking his head. 'I don't know,' I said.

"Shammy was slowly and deliberately humping Wyatt. Wyatt began to scream like a banshee. He screamed like I had never heard anyone scream before. Thinking about it now, it sounded as if he was being gutted. We couldn't see how Shammy was hurting him but didn't understand what he was doing. In our, at the time young, minds, none of this made sense. We were always afraid of being bitten, even eaten, but not wrestling with Shammy. We started to giggle and laugh. Wyatt had stopped screaming and was moaning now."

"Oh, my God!" Brie Ann said, putting her hand over her mouth.

"Yeah, exactly. Don't forget you asked for this."

"I know, I know. It's okay, go on."

"Suddenly Shammy stiffened and pulled Wyatt in even tighter. Wyatt let out a howl that matched anything he had let loose before. We looked over and saw Wyatt covered in white goop. Shammy was tottering a few steps off of Wyatt weirdly. We, not having any conception of what took place, laughed again. At that exact moment Remy's mom came running around the corner with a broom held over her head and smacked Shammy on the side of his face and then on his back as he turned and ran around the side of the garage. I saw Gram, a blur, heading for the fence and Donovan and I were seconds behind him. Remy's mom screamed something muddled at us, and I remember looking back for a flash, as she put her arms around Wyatt, still covered with white slime dripping off him, walking toward the corner of the garage."

Brie Ann was laughing and crying at the same time. She kept her hands over her eyes, wiping them. "I've never heard anything so gross in my life."

"I bet you're sorry you asked, huh?" Cassady asked. "Sorry, but you insisted."

"Yes and no," she said. "At least now, I know to never ask what the Shammy Whammy is. Can you walk me home now? I have to get going."

As they were walking out, Brie Ann turned and waved to Miss Rigby, who motioned for both Cassady and Brie Ann to come over.

"I'm certainly glad my two best readers have finally met and are going to be friends," Miss Rigby said, smiling. Cassady smiled and looked down at the floor.

"Cassady, I would like you to come back sometime. There are a couple of questions I'd like to ask you. It's nothing bad, just something I've been wondering about."

Cassady and Brie Ann walked out and started up Sepulveda. Cassady pointed out where the back of his grandmother's house was and how he jumped the fence to get there. They were almost to the Big Doughnut, with the outlandish doughnut replica looming almost forty feet in the air when Brie Ann stopped and turned toward him.

"What do you think Miss Rigby wants to talk to you about?" she asked.

"I have no idea. I don't have any books out. The last thing I read I put back into the overnight slot several weeks ago."

"You don't have any idea?"

"No, I swear," Cassady said.

"You won't start out having secrets from me, will you?"

"No, after I talk to her, I promise I'll tell you what she said."

Cassady's mind whirled and he truly was at a loss.

"Even if she asks you not to tell anybody?"

"Why would she have something to ask me she would want a secret?" As soon as Cassady said this he realized how crazy it was to promise to not have secrets when he and Kyle had one of the biggest secrets he could ever imagine, maybe in the history of the world. Cassady was keeping an earthshaking secret with Kyle *and* Miss Rigby. He walked Brie Ann home, got a swift kiss, nearly skipped back to his grandmother's house for dinner, and didn't think about Miss Rigby's request the rest of the night.

CHAPTER 18

"Welcome, my friends. I am King Louis XIII and unfortunately the only true actor from *The Three Musketeers*, the movie you will be experiencing tonight on the beautiful Backlot in the beautiful Sift. I'm afraid D'Artagnan, played by Gene Kelly, is yet to join us in the Sift. Lana Turner, who was the beautiful Milady de Winter, June Allyson the irredeemable Constance, Van Heflin as Athos, Gig Young as Porthos, and lastly Robert Coote as Aramis, are not yet among us."

"He means dead, right?" Kyle whispered to Cassady.

"Yeah," Cassady answered. "They must not be dead yet. It was the same with the guys from *Combat!*"

Cassady looked at the portly man dressed in a blue coat made from what looked like silk. A colorful enormous hat spiked with feathers sat crookedly on his head. A red robe draped off his shoulder. He stood in a dominating stance with his feet far apart, which displayed red socks up to his mid-thigh and bright, red-heeled shoes. Something about the man seemed incredibly familiar. The flamboyant manner in which he presented himself was somewhat out of character, even dressed so outlandishly, with what they sensed they remembered. He, in reality, looked somewhat like a befuddled man with a deeply lined face that appeared suspiciously recognizable to Cassady.

Ashley had brought them to the *Three Musketeers* court and castle set for the next several late evenings, for, as he put it, "an adventurous romp of chivalry, honor, and escapades set in France in the 1620s. A night filled with heroes, heroines, kings, queens, cavaliers, and criminals, along, of course, with conspiracies, vengeance, scandal, and larger-than-life characters. One, whom you'll recognize and be amazed to meet."

As they looked around, they were astonished the formally decaying vacant movie set and flaccid crumbling walls of the old European fortress had become alive. The stone courtyard was vibrant with color, the ladies dressed beguilingly as seductresses, the men of repute dressed as swashbuckling cavaliers, all wearing fashionable clothes, walking about transformed into the residents of seventeenth-century France. But suddenly something appeared a little off to Cassady and Kyle.

"Wait, forget the king stuff, I know you, you're the Wizard of Oz, aren't you?" Cassady mockingly asked the man standing before them dressed as a French monarch. "I see it now. I've seen that movie a bunch of times and you're Oz."

"No!" the man exclaimed. "I am the king of France and you will be my musketeers who swear allegiance to my family and me in a time when we must besiege the Huguenots in the port city of La Rochelle. The Musketeers of the Guard fight in that conflict..."

"No, you're the man behind the curtain," Kyle said interrupting him. "I recognize you also."

"No, wait; pay no attention to the man behind the curtain. I want a heart, a brain, and..." Cassady started to say, laughing.

"And courage," Kyle shouted, finishing, laughing along with Cassady.

They both looked at the man expectantly and waited. After a flash they saw a change in his stance and realized the king was defeated and relented.

"I *am* Frank Morgan. You're right, I was Professor Marvel and the Wizard of Oz in the movie with that title. I will forever be known for that role, although I was in over a hundred movies and actually had five roles in that movie..."

"I remember, weren't you also the guard at the door?" Kyle asked.

"Yes, along with Professor Marvel, I was the doorman, the cabby with the 'horse of different color,' the guard to the Wizard, and, of course, the Wizard. I am a tad proud of that role, but have chosen to become part of *The Three Musketeers* here in the Sift for eternity. As I did not live to see *The Wizard of Oz* become one of the most beloved movies of all time—I chose to make this my home and wait for many of my fellow actors and actresses to join me in the wonders of the Sift and this wonderful movie from 1948, the year before I died."

"Is this where they filmed the movie?" Kyle asked. "Only people who were in the movie and are dead can participate here, right?"

"Hasn't that been made obvious to you?" he said. "I'm sure Ashley has attempted to explain much about the Sift, but it is something that defies enlightenment and understanding. Let it be that for you and enjoy the experience of seventeenth-century France and the world of *The Three Musketeers*. This is the famous Copperfield Street with its own Musketeers Court added in 1948, the last set built here on the Backlot. It is not meant to be realistic, in the movie or the novel. It is a world of romance and battle, not a world of uncertainty, but one of absolutes—especially for you two."

"If the actors who played the roles aren't dead, who will we interact with?" Kyle asked.

"Oh, there's an abundance of fellow actors and actresses for whom this is the chance of a, well, not a lifetime, but a time without end we shall say, and who want to partake," the king said. "They might be workers from the movie, gifted stunt-men, or had other small parts, and were given the chance to join the Sift and interpret different roles as we all do in life. As it was on the *Combat!* set. Let's get started, shall we?"

"I'm Athos," a man said stepping out of the darkness next to Kyle.

"I'm Aramis," a man behind him said to Cassady.

"And I'm Porthos," another said, walking into the light. "I will be overseeing your training and education. Not unlike your time in the other European Village and the *Combat!* stage set, you will take time and learn the fundamentals of sword fighting."

"We had fun on the *Combat!* set," Kyle said. "Even the training."

"We learned a bunch on the job, so to say," Cassady said. "I guess we had some practice playing in here for months, though."

"Understood, but you will learn the basics of swords-manship which will be timing, distance, and reaction, along with the slash, thrust, and slice. You will learn to only spend seconds grasping your opponent's style and abilities before you endeavor the attack!"

The actors who played Athos, Porthos, and Aramis in the Sift spent the next few nights teaching Kyle and Cassady. The Musketeers wore elaborate uniforms, all trimmed with silver and gold lace, blue tunics embroidered with more gold, the color of the guard, with elaborate hats with feathers and mid-arm gloves and mid-calf black boots. Cassady thought with humor that he and Kyle, of course, wore Levi's and t-shirts with tennis shoes, as they did in life and all the other aspects of the Sift.

After several nights of training, Kyle and Cassady were actually fighting, each taking turns playing the role of D'Artagnan.

"If I offended you, I do not contest the truth of the umbrage, but will meet you where and when you chose," Cassady said remembering the scene correctly or close enough to suit Frank Morgan as the king.

"I demand satisfaction," Aramis shouted as he advanced on Cassady.

Cassady walked forward to touch swords with Aramis, who ignored the rules of proper protocol and lunged at Cassady. It caught him unaware and luckily he quickly sidestepped the thrust and immediately fell into the magic of the evening's sport. They fought, slashed, and moved quickly around each other. It did not last that way for long. Several times Cassady lost balance and barely regained his footing as Aramis moved in closer and closer. Cassady found himself simply defending and unable to make any of the moves he had practiced so diligently to learn night after night. He had no choice but to let Aramis advance him up two or three stairs on the castle's courtyard's flight of steps to the tower. A crowd of onlookers in the courtyard murmured, shouted, and cajoled him in support of his match with Aramis.

"Stop him from moving you away from the open court," Kyle shouted at Cassady.

"He must get back down to the open area," the king said worriedly.

Cassady was directly grazed on the arm by Aramis' sword. He didn't feel any pain and thought it would come to him later and didn't have time to consider it as he took one more step retreating from the flashing of the sword blade. Cassady couldn't remember the next moves he had planned or what he was taught and his mind went blank. In his fright, he wrenched his body sideways and thrust his sword at Aramis's head at the same time. It presented an oblique indirect target to Aramis, and he fatally hesitated. Cassady, again in his panic, slashed, terrified, like a windmill at Aramis and unbelievably connected. Aramis fell to the ground as Cassady's sword sliced his neck with enough power, Cassady thought, to cut his head off. Cassady stood frozen and looked around.

"Magnificent, excellent, Cassady," the king bellowed.

Cassady looked down, but Aramis was already up and striding toward him to shake hands.

"Congratulations, Sir Cassady, or should I say Sir D'Artagnan. It was a marvelous contest. You performed better than expected and bested me fair and square," Aramis said. "Ah, but maybe luck played a small part in the parlay, yes?"

"Absolutely," Cassady said. "Of course, you can't die?"

Aramis merely smiled.

He looked at his arm and saw not a drop of blood or the slightest scratch, where there should have been a wound. Cassady's attention was diverted immediately by a noise at the gates.

"There is an assault and a Huguenot on the castle grounds," shouted Porthos. "I need the next knight to step forward and defend the king. That means you, D'Artagnan," he said, looking at Kyle. "Attack!"

The Huguenot came through the gate and rushed forward toward the group standing, as the others closed ranks around the king. Without thinking, Kyle did, in fact, step forward and rushed to meet the large man dressed in the uniform of a formidable warrior, but different from the Musketeers of the Guard, shabbily and modestly outfitted compared to Aramis, Athos, and Porthos. They engaged instantly in a tremendous battle.

"C'mon!" Cassady yelled at Kyle. "You're doing great. Watch his thrusts." Kyle was also moving up the staircase in the courtyard defending himself against the advancing Huguenot swordsman.

"He's repelling and defending every thrust magnificently," the king said. "I could never ask more of my guard."

"But defending he is," shouted Porthos. "He must attack!"

"You know, the Huguenots were nothing more than Protestants, or actually French Calvinists, persecuted by Catholic France," the king said, giggling. "Oops, I guess that's me, uh?" he said.

"Are you the king now, or Frank Morgan?" Cassady asked.

"Well..." He answered by shrugging and laughing.

A burst of lunges, thrusts blocked, and slices thwarted had Kyle moving the Huguenot back down the stairs. As they got to open ground the momentum slowed and they both slackened the attack, even going so far as to wait moments before answering each other's lunges and slashes.

"Yes, yes, go on the attack now, don't stop," Porthos loudly commanded Kyle.

At that point, it seemed exhaustion kept them both standing in one place, but still battling it out. Cassady watched as Kyle held his own, but then slowly was being moved up stair by stair again every few moments.

Suddenly Kyle was struck by the Huguenot's sword. He fell.

"Can that happen?" Cassady cried. "It looked too real. Is he really hurt or killed? We were never shot in the war scenes. It was all, like, play!"

"Oh, my, my," the king calmly said. Cassady rushed across the courtyard and up the stairs. As soon as he got there, he saw Kyle sitting up.

"Are you okay?" he yelled. Kyle stood up in front of him and looked around.

"Yeah, it was weird. I felt it go in, but it didn't hurt. I must have blacked out for a second from the shock of it, but look, nothing."

They both looked at Kyle's shirt and Cassady even lifted it up and they looked at his belly.

"No mark, nothing. Not even a scratch," Cassady said,

walking behind Kyle and thinking it out and remembering. "Like my arm."

"Oh, my, my," said the king, again walking up to them. "You've learned a little lesson here in the Sift, haven't you?"

"We can't die?" Kyle asked, still a little bit shaken.

"In good time," the king answered. "But not here, tonight, or *ever* in the Sift."

"You have obtained *another* important lesson tonight," Porthos said. "The untrained novice who picks up a sword, at times, can do better than someone who has spent their entire life working on sword skills. After a while, we teach you rules to fight by. You held your own against the Huguenot swordsman longer than you ever should have, precisely because you didn't fight by the rules. Kyle, you were more dangerous, as you were also, Cassady, to Aramis." Porthos said this while looking at both boys. "Why do you think this was?"

"I was only flailing at him, scared and not paying attention to what I was doing and barely remembering the rules about slashing and thrusting," Cassady said.

"Exactly," Porthos exclaimed. "You both were unpredictable and as apprentices much more dangerous. Kyle was eventually worn down and made rookie mistakes that would have ultimately cost him his life. But as the Sift shows, it is a merciful and magical place for us who spend perpetuity here."

Nights later, at one of the magnificent feasts given in their honor with a dozen Musketeers in attendance, King Louis XIII sat next to them. They hadn't had much interaction with him the last few nights. He kept his distance, as was expected from a king and his guard.

"I'm still not as hungry as I wished I was," Kyle said. "This meal is unbelievable."

Large turkey legs, beef ribs, pork ribs, corn on the cob, roasted chicken, duck, quail, baked potatoes, crepes, soup in bread bowls, black tea, and mead made fresh hourly. Topped off with fresh fruit were dozens of pies of all types.

"Yeah, it's what Ashley told us, we can eat but we're never really hungry in the Sift," Cassady remembered.

"Have you thought of what could bring you here permanently?" the king asked, suddenly turning to them both with an intense stare.

"You mean after we die?" Kyle asked.

"Well, yes, but that's another issue. This is our life for eternity, what do you think about that? And you can call me Frank now."

"Why did you come to this part of the Sift, Frank?" Kyle said. "I really want to call you the Wizard or the Great and Powerful Oz. Sorry, but it's hard not to see you like that."

"It's okay. That was only one role, as I mentioned, out of many films. It didn't become a special movie to the public until long after I passed. For the ten years after it was released—it may be hard for you to believe, it wasn't very popular. Your generation and probably many to come now see it as a special movie, as many do with *Gone with the Wind*."

"Yeah, they play both on TV every year. The monkeys used to scare the crap out of me," Cassady said, smiling.

"As they do most children on first viewing," Ashley said as he walked up and sat down across from them. "Margaret Hamilton, whom you may or may not know played the Wicked Witch, has recently said, whenever she watches the scene in *The Wizard of Oz* where Frank is handing out the diploma to the Scarecrow, ticking heart for the Tin Man, and medal for the Cowardly Lion, she cried because she knew Frank Morgan was actually that exact kind of person," he said.

"She'll be joining in the Sift?" Kyle asked.

"I think not," was the only answer Ashley gave.

"I don't think she will either," the king said.

"Why not?" Cassady asked.

"She doesn't think the Wicked Witch of the West was a

true representation of who she was, or is, and who she will be," the king said. "She always felt bad about scaring children, and after being badly burned in Munchkin Land, she doesn't have fond memories of that role. Margaret wouldn't fit in here..."

"Why not?" Cassady asked again.

"She's not the type of person who actually is invited or would want to join. And come to think of it, I don't know if you are either, Cassady," the king said, looking sullen and down at the table.

"What do you mean?" Cassady asked. "I thought you guys didn't watch or follow or even know what goes on in our world?"

"We have many realms or venues to follow our fellow actors or friends once we pass. Margaret has an innate goodness within her that would preclude her from..." He stopped and looked pensively around at Ashley. "Never mind... Well, I know for a fact that another person from the Oz movie has made a debut recently in the Sift?" He looked carefully at Ashley again.

"It's permissible to let them know, especially Cassady," Ashley said, looking at him. "The Sift attracts many people from all walks of life, but particularly from the movies here at MGM."

"Who?" Cassady asked. "And why especially me?"

"Tomorrow night will be your night, Cassady. They're extremely interested in meeting you. But you'll have to wait and see, my friend."

"Can't you give me a hint?"

"The king did. They are from *The Wizard of Oz*. That's enough for tonight," Ashley said. "It's time to head back to Tara and Scarlett, don't you think?"

"Yeah, sure," Kyle said. "We always end the night where we started."

"Yes, you must leave where you entered."

Cassady didn't say anything but looked at Frank Morgan

as he was getting up. All the king did was shake his head sadly. The boys didn't return to *The Three Musketeers* set again.

CHAPTER 19

The next morning late, Cassady found himself with Gram and Abilene down on the Venice Beach boardwalk. It was the same stretch of boardwalk where he and Kyle had first talked to the freaky guy that turned them on to Backlot 2. Smelling the salt water, the feel of walking along the sand, the sunshine hot and warm, and they could detect marijuana in the air from the Dogtown locals. Hippies were everywhere, although the three of them never considered themselves hippies. They felt that was newspaper and TV garbage. The boardwalk promenade was still filled with flaky guys playing their guitars, fortune-tellers, bad artists, and, not really vendors, but guys selling food they wouldn't think about eating—even when high.

"Do you remember when we used to ride our bikes by Gold's Gym and stop and yell in the door, 'Hey muscle head!' and ride away?" Gram asked.

"Yeah, that was crazy," Cassady said.

"I remember a time or two when they'd run out the door yelling that they were going to kill us and we flipped them off," Gram said, laughing.

Cassady had been on his way over to Kyle's house, but saw

him riding away with Lucas on his newly repaired bike, probably going to a pickup basketball game at Vet's Park. They had been doing that the last couple of days. That was okay with Cassady, though. He and Kyle surely spent enough time together. He had one of those feelings about doing ordinary things with friends that kept intruding on his thoughts. Abilene and Gram were walking down the street and he, spontaneously, joined up with them and hopped on the bus to Venice. Doing something different, maybe even considered commonplace, felt good. Even with his prior reservations about hanging with Abilene, Cassady wanted to not think about the Sift, and who he was going to meet that night, at least for a day in the sun.

The three of them walked along looking in the bistros, boutiques, and tourist traps and stopped—a young guy was playing "Blackbird," by the Beatles, and not badly.

"He's the kid from that TV show about being lost in space," Gram said.

"I hated that show," Abilene said and kept walking.

Cassady stopped for a minute to watch and listen.

As he walked to catch up with Gram and Abilene he smelled the same odor he'd had several times in the last few minutes.

"What is that?" he asked as they walked by a couple of older girls and boys.

"It's patchouli," Gram said. "My sisters have been wearing that crap for months now. It's like some kind of musk stink. I hate it. I push them away from me when they come near."

Venice was always a swirl of colors, commotion, and crowded humanity. It was continuously bursting with over-powering smells, he thought to himself. He smelled crazy stuff all mixed up: food being fried, suntan lotion, incense mixed with pot wafting up from the waterline, some guy selling sickeningly sweet cotton candy. It was like a carnival. Always the girls, though, made the trip worthwhile. They wore tie-dye, beads, headbands, dashikis, bikini tops, macramé, and crochet that hid nothing with low-cut bell-bottoms fully exposing belly buttons. He loved it. They stopped to watch the muscle guys work out at the Muscle Beach site. Cassady dug the whole atmosphere, especially down a ways on the exercise bars and rings with guys doing acrobatics swinging around. They were incredibly strong and coordinated to do what they were doing. He thought of Kyle and himself in Tarzan Land swinging on the vines without having to work as hard, and smiled.

"Check it out, check it out..." Abilene said and pointed down the promenade about half a block.

Cassady looked and saw a crowd following four guys casually sauntering towards them. The guy in front was wearing striped pants with a white shirt, long dark hair and sideburns, with dark sunglasses. The others following a step behind him had on Levi's, but with long hair and strange shirts. One had a scarf around his neck and they all wore various boots or moccasins. They strolled along without being bothered by the small group of kids shadowing them at a polite distance. A photographer was taking pictures as they sauntered.

"Shit, it's the Doors," Gram said. "Cool," Cassady whispered at the same time. They watched them walk by—all four smiling and enjoying the sun, beach scene, and the day.

As they were winding up the day and started to turn back, Abilene said, "Hey, let's cruise up through the canals."

"Yeah, okay," Gram replied. "I haven't been into the 'slum by the sea' for a long time."

"We can walk up Twenty-Fourth Avenue and then cut up to Venice Boulevard afterwards to catch the bus back to Culver City," Cassady agreed.

"The waterways are nasty and gross, but let's check it out;

see if we can score some weed," Abilene said.

The houses were old and dilapidated. It reminded Cassady of some of the buildings in the Backlot, aged and decrepit; nothing like the small, neat California bungalows in Culver City. As they were walking up Howland Canal crossing Grand Canal, Cassady looked over and saw something he didn't expect. Cassady saw the guy with the long grimy hair in a ponytail from a few months ago who had first told them about the Backlots. He was standing in front of a really run-down house that looked like it was abandoned. Cassady caught his eye and the guy smiled. Abilene and Gram kept walking and didn't look back.

"Hey man, how's it going?" the guy said.

"It's good. How about you?" Cassady said.

"It's always cool. Have you been inside yet?"

"Yeah, a couple of times," Cassady said, nodding

"Okay, are we talking about Backlot 3 or 2, now?" he asked.

"2," Cassady answered, and didn't offer anything more.

"You didn't find it a bummer?"

"No, not really. Why?" Cassady asked. He immediately comprehended, for some reason, that hiding the truth from this guy was not going to be easy, because he sensed this guy knew something about it. He fervently wished Kyle were with him now.

"You sure, man? I mean, I'm wondering if you know what I'm talking about. Maybe it's nothing, but I detect you might really know what I'm talking about," he said, suddenly dropping the hippie persona, taking a step closer, and staring intently into Cassady's eyes. "I don't think you're telling me the truth. I think you didn't listen to me when I told you not to go in there, and you saw the something I told you was a bummer, but it was actually much more than a letdown. Right? It was beyond weird and it's not real, but maybe even nefarious."

Cassady wondered what that meant, but actually had an idea. He wanted to turn away and run. He thought whatever this guy looked like he was perceptive enough to know that Cassady was, in fact, not telling the truth. Who the hell was this guy?

"No, it's nothing like that. We're done with it and it's over," Cassady said.

"Now don't get the wrong idea," the guy said walking even closer to Cassady. "I'm cool, my name's Rick. I don't want you to get involved in something that you can't handle. The world has many inexplicable phenomena we can't make clear and sometimes these strange things are centered in places we would never expect them to be," he said as he put out his hand to shake. "What's your name?"

Cassady hesitated to put out his hand but did as he said, "My name's Cassady." When he gripped Cassady's hand, Rick pulled him in tighter and whispered in his ear.

"Don't go back in there! Stay out, no matter how far you're in. Be sober, be vigilant; because your adversary the devil, as a roaring lion, walketh about, seeking whom he may devour..."

Suddenly, Abilene was there and stepped up in between them. Rick broke contact and stepped back.

"What the fuck's your problem, man?" Abilene said.

"Nothing, nothing, we're just talking. It's good. No harm, no foul," Rick said, turning away and walking onto the porch of the house.

"It's all right. Thanks, Abilene," Cassady said. They started walking away with Cassady hoping Abilene probably supposed it was another freak on the streets of Venice. Cassady looked back one more time and saw Rick nodding at him before he ducked into the old derelict house.

"What was that about?" Gram asked.

"I don't know. Kyle and I talked to that guy a long time

ago, and I was saying hi and the next thing I know he's pulling me in and..." Cassady shrugged.

"What was that guy's name?" Abilene asked as they walked back to the bus stop.

"Rick. It's nothing, forget about it," Cassady said.

"Okay, yeah, but what I think that Rick needs... is nothing less than a Shammy Whammy!"

CHAPTER 20

Cassady was going to the library annex several times a week after school to meet Brie Ann. They didn't have any classes with each other this year but spent lunch together instead. Kyle went his own way in school, ate with an assortment of guys they knew—Gram, Abilene, and George—and never asked him about Brie Ann. Cassady thought this was only one of the weird things that were changing. He ultimately kept eating lunch with Brie Ann and waiting for Kyle to ask. Along with reading books and doing homework together, they read the newspaper. One day, Cassady had gotten into an argument with a long-term substitute math teacher about Vietnam. Cassady really didn't know what he was talking about, but since everybody he respected was against it, he thought he should be against it too.

"You need to know who General Westmoreland, Robert McNamara, Henry Kissinger, Ho Chi Minh, and Lieutenant Calley are and what they represent before you argue about what's going on," Miss Alexander said. She was right. He couldn't believe all he didn't know. The Sift was still there, and he was never tired and had all the energy he needed, but the combination of the Sift and meeting Brie Ann was almost overwhelming at times. The extreme changes in the country were getting thought-provoking. It was hard to reconcile the Sift with real life.

"I can't believe the Hells Angels killed that guy at the Stones concert," Brie Ann said.

"I can't believe Paul is dead," Cassady said.

"I know. There's like a million clues," Brie Ann said.

"Yeah, they say you can hear John say, 'I buried Paul,' at the end of 'Strawberry Fields.' And Paul's the only one barefoot on the cover of *Abbey Road*," Cassady said.

"What about the VW license plate that says 28IF; he would have been twenty-eight if he hadn't been killed," Brie Ann said.

"I don't have that album yet, but Paul was supposed to have died in a car crash in 1966 and was replaced, in secret, with a lookalike. All I know is this new guy wrote some of the best songs ever. Maybe that's a good thing. That means we wouldn't have had any of this new guy's songs on *Sgt. Pepper's* or the *White Album*, not to mention 'Hey Jude.' So I say, good, this new Paul is better than the old Paul," Cassady said. "He's a better bass player too."

"You're crazy," Brie Ann said, laughing.

The librarian stayed out of their way most of the time and let them be together without any interruptions. Miss Rigby was kind to them both and hadn't bothered Cassady with questions about where, or why, and had he talked to her father yet. He was able to separate the two parts of his life fairly well. They didn't bleed over into each other except while he was in the Sift and felt pulled away thinking about Brie Ann. She was quickly becoming someone he wanted to spend more and more time with and talk with and do everything with. He was dying to tell her about the Sift, but couldn't even begin to think of a way to broach the subject. They were so much alike and enjoyed the same type of books. They had both recently finished *Slaughterhouse-Five* by Kurt Vonnegut.

"I had a hard time with the time thing and jumping around, and the Tralfamadore thing didn't work at first, but it made sense after what he experienced in Dresden," Brie Ann said.

"I wonder how many civilians were really killed in that bombing?" Cassady asked.

"Let's ask Miss Rigby," Brie Ann said.

Miss Rigby had a book on World War II, and as unbelievable as it seemed, there was very little in the book about the firebombing of the German town Dresden.

"You'd be better off checking in the main library. You'd probably find a big history reference volume with it mentioned, or possibly a book concerning the whole mission," Miss Rigby said. "Cassady, I know you know where that is. And since you're reading Vonnegut now, and I saw you returned *Gone with the Wind* over a month ago, right? That makes it another book you both have read, so do you both have an interest in the characters and the filming here?" Brie Ann looked at him.

"I read it a long time ago and I never cared for it that much. I couldn't really get past the whitewashing of slavery," Brie Ann said. "It made it hard for me to enjoy the movie also."

"Oh really, Cassady has asked me, it seems, dozens of questions about the book. And maybe as many questions about the people in the movie and the Backlot story here in Culver City," she said. Cassady was immediately regretful about asking her any questions about anything.

"What's that about? Was the movie filmed here?" Brie Ann asked.

"I should let Cassady tell you about that. He probably knows as much about it as I do," Miss Rigby said. "But what else did you take away from the book?"

"I thought it was more about Scarlett and Rhett Butler and not so much about the actual war," Cassady said. "Like, it was a fantasy about the Southern or Confederate loss of a glorified style of life and a horrible invasion of the South. Not really much about the horrors that must have been life for the Black slaves." Cassady was thinking about that very subject nightly lately.

"They called it the Lost Cause," Miss Rigby said. "And since it was written from the perspective of a slaveholder, it makes sense you would feel that way."

"I don't think they meant to portray the Black people as... I don't know, as being mistreated. I mean Big Sam leaves Tara and is forced into the Confederate Army. At least working for them, and then he *still* remains loyal to Scarlett," Cassady said.

"That's ignorant," Brie Ann said. "Nothing about slavery gave slaves any choice. You can't think it's okay to own slaves and the people who did were good people." Cassady felt of touch of pleasure that Brie Ann didn't let him get away with anything. All his months in the Sift, he realized he hadn't really confronted what slavery must have been like, or why the people he interacted with would ignore the reality of doing that to millions of people. He never reconciled his feelings about Scarlett.

"No, no, of course not. I'm thinking that the owners of the plantations... I don't know what I'm trying to say. I guess I thought the story was about other things rather than the war and that the slavery was a backdrop to the main story," Cassady said.

"I bet if you were a slave, you'd feel differently about it," Brie Ann said. "It's an ugly stain on our country, and I don't know if we can ever erase it. I think Atticus had it right in *To Kill a Mockingbird* when he said, 'It's all adding up, and one of these days we're going to pay the bill for it.'"

"No, you're right. It's like what goes around comes around. Not only is hatred and prejudice wrong, but also it will come back to visit us," Cassady said, understanding and agreeing. "And not only for those who did it directly. The longer it goes on, the worse the return will be. At least we have laws now, but it's not over. I mean the laws only happened in our lifetime."

"Hmm," Miss Rigby said.

"I agree," Brie Ann said. "But the part of *To Kill a Mockingbird* that led to my only problem with the whole story is after that Atticus told Scout that women can't serve on juries Scout says that 'Perhaps our forefathers were wise.' I hated that she said that, and I'm glad that's changed now."

"I think Harper Lee might have been mixing her point of view in that section. It was meant to be said and shown through Scout's young eyes," Miss Rigby said.

"Maybe, but I still didn't like it. I wanted her to be smarter than that," Brie Ann said. "She had too much insight for a little girl. A little too precocious but not about that."

"That's a complaint many people have about the book, but it's still a great one. Harper Lee messed up telling the story, for many people, by using a six-year-old talking like an adult and staying in the voice of the child," Miss Rigby said. "But I'm guessing you have more than that one problem with the book."

"Yeah, you're right, but you agree she's a little too smart. Anyways, now, what's the interest in the people in the *Gone with the Wind* movie, Cassady?" Brie Ann asked.

"Yes, Cassady. I'm still interested in your interest in that myself," Miss Rigby said deliberately.

"Nothing really, since I found out it was filmed here. That's all."

"Really, there's nothing more to it than that?" Miss Rigby asked, smiling knowingly.

"No, really, I swear," Cassady said. He didn't want to share this with Brie Ann. Cassady couldn't understand himself yet, why he couldn't. He wanted to, but thought it best to still keep these two parts of his life separate.

Later that day, they walked across Sepulveda, scooted around the mortuary, climbed both the mortuary fence to the alley and Cassady's back fence, and were in the Shack. Cassady was amazed at what a trooper Brie Ann turned out to be.

"I never thought being friends with a boy could happen so fast," Brie Ann said.

"What?" Cassady asked.

"Well, I've always thought that boys my age would never be like the boys I read about in books and movies. But you're close to what I had hoped for, at least."

"Close?" he asked. He felt a lump in his throat and thought his heart might stop. He reasoned he'd take close.

"Yeah, I always hoped to be the best person I could be, and then something would happen. I didn't think you were ever going to have the nerve to talk to me, so I had to walk into your life. I mean, Miss Rigby told me you were checking out the same books I did for a while."

"She told you that?" Cassady asked.

"Don't be mad. It's what made me want to start talking to you in the first place, remember?" Cassady thought of all those days hoping he could finally talk to the girl who read those books, and he smiled.

"Are you liking school this year?" Cassady asked, trying to change the subject. He felt weird talking about his feelings, especially since he didn't know what they were and felt they changed all the time.

"Yes, but I've always been a loner, and now that Gloria is gone and I have you, it makes everything easier. I've always been that, maybe, I was too brainy for some of the girls and too harsh for others. I hung around the edges, and everyone thought I was sullen and moody."

"You're anything but that. I don't see any of that in you. You're beautiful and smarter than I'll ever be. I never thought I'd be able to spend time with anyone like you," Cassady said as the words rushed out. He was talking to the girl he had fantasized about for what felt like forever.

Brie Ann thought for a minute. "I thought that teenagers couldn't really fall in love, but I don't know," she said. "I'd rather feel what I'm feeling right now, than not, and weeks ago I wanted nothing more than to be invisible and be like everyone else in our school and not think about anything important or deal with what someone else is feeling."

"Love might be rare, but what I feel doesn't feel like it should take years or whatever. I feel it right now," Cassady whispered.

They spent the next hour kissing while listening to Brie Ann's copy of Joni Mitchell's new album *Clouds*.

Later, Cassady started once again discerning what his deepest feelings were and how his fear of never being good enough should have already disappeared, because he had a girlfriend and she was real.

Brie Ann was wonderful. He thought he loved her but didn't know how to go beyond the kissing. She pushed his hand away several times, so he stopped. Then she moved a little to make it happen again. After the third, fourth, or millionth time he was so confused he didn't know what to do. He didn't necessarily want any pleasure himself. He wanted to make her feel good. But at the same time felt an overwhelming desire. Cassady couldn't understand why she didn't want, that but he accepted it, and it was still nice.

After they stopped Brie Ann said the nicest thing anyone had ever said to him in his life. "I know now exactly where I should be and what life should be like and that's being with you here and now. I don't want this to ever change. Ever."

After all this the pressure and confusion about sex, being in love, the Sift, and having absolutely no idea about what to do next, the only thing Cassady was certain of and felt the most incredible sadness about was the simple fact that he was losing his best friend to talk about it with anymore. The Sift was interfering with his real life or maybe what he and Brie Ann had was private between only them.

CHAPTER 21

The next night Cassady still felt that going into the Sift was like walking through a field of light with a mild electric shock that made him feel slightly unstable. It was a little traumatic to his equilibrium, and he had actually stumbled once or twice. It always took a few minutes to start talking again. Tonight, Ashley nudged him away from Tara and walked Cassady by himself to the *Andy Hardy* set. Cassady saw people, dressed nicely, walking around, and even some children riding bikes and playing along the street.

"Why did you want me to come here alone, tonight?" Cassady asked. "Kyle and I haven't spent much time here. We couldn't see the adventure in it."

"Have patience, my friend," Ashley said. "Enjoy the loveliness of the town, see the chapel with a steeple at the end of the beautiful street, the towering elms, the gorgeous houses, and see the people enjoying their wonderful neighborhood. The people are all perfect American families, in their perfect American town..."

Cassady could see that the bucolic elegant New England town was transformed into something special. Two-story gable houses with columns supported porch roofs, Grecian doorway moldings, and window frames, almost all painted white. It was pleasant, but he knew from all the families in his world that life was far from perfect.

"You mean the way movies try to pretend life is, rather than the way it really is. That's what movies and TV shows are about. It's like you and the Tara of *Gone with the Wind*. You don't show us the bullshit that was slavery..." Cassady started.

"Enough, Cassady! I'm here with you to introduce someone... and luckily she is coming out from her house right now. She can introduce herself to you, my friend. Enjoy!"

A lithe pretty girl, petite, with brunette hair tied back, but falling down in front and framing the contours of her beautiful, fresh, striking face, seemingly walking on air, strode up to them. She was the quintessential perfect girl next door. She was about his age but much shorter than Cassady, and he recognized her instantly.

"Dorothy!" he shouted. He looked over to Ashley, but he was already walking away.

She stuck out her hand by way of introduction and said, "It's delightful to meet you, Cassady. But I'm afraid I'm Betsy, Betsy Booth, and this is the *Andy Hardy* movie set, of which I only made three appearances, but they were the most innocent, sweet times of my life. It's actually set in Idaho, not New England, although the houses look like that."

"But you're Dorothy from *The Wizard of Oz*, aren't you?" he exclaimed with passion. She was beautiful in a different way, and it was wonderful to see her even in this unexpected site in the Sift. "Your name is Judy Garland, right?"

"Yes, that was my name, and I was also Dorothy Gale from Kansas, but that was for a very short time and I chose another for eternity, one more to my fulfillment," she said, smiling. "And for time without end, I felt I couldn't have anything more comforting than the time without end here in the perfect world of *Andy Hardy*."

"I'm sorry, but I didn't really ever watch those movies. I

look at you and see Dorothy and think of you singing 'Somewhere Over the Rainbow.' The Wizard didn't want to be in *The Wizard of Oz* in the Sift or movie either. He's the king of France."

"Oh, Mr. Frank Morgan you mean. He wasn't initially a success as Oz with that role either, but we chose what we're best suited for and my eternity is as Betsy. My memories of that movie are skewed rather sharply. They only let me sing that one song by myself in *Oz*, and they almost cut it from the movie, those idiots. They let the Munchkins sing more than me."

"But that must have been so cooool, being with Oz and in Munchkin Land," Cassady said, gushing. He couldn't help it.

"It wasn't all you think it's cracked up to be. Let's sit down on this bench and talk for a while."

"Okay. Why didn't you like it? We heard about *Gone with the Wind* from Scarlett..." Cassady started.

"Yes, I'm sure she had many things to say about that movie. As for me, first thing was I hated those too-tight stupid ruby-red shoes, but I had it easy. Those costumes were pure hell for those guys."

"You mean, the Scarecrow, Lion, and the Tin Man?"

"Yes, they sweat and were miserable. They couldn't eat and we worked way too hard at times. We went through four producers, and Victor Fleming, the director, slapped me one time because I couldn't stop giggling," she said, looking down. "He also left to work on *Gone with the Wind*. I know Vivien, or Scarlett, also had troubles working on that movie."

"Yeah, she didn't seem very happy at times being an actress either," Cassady said. "But what was it like working with the Munchkins?"

She stood up and motioned for Cassady to follow her. "I know we need to get past some of these questions. Everyone wants to know about the Munchkins, don't they? Well, they could be a pain in the ass sometimes. Remember, those little rascals were real people and not simply stereotypes. They didn't always keep their hands to themselves. They had a way of putting their hands up my dress. I had to kick a couple."

"Get outta here," Cassady said. He was now walking with her down the street with the beautiful perfect houses. People smiled at them and waved from their porches.

"Yes, they were maybe only having fun, but I had to do what I had to do. You know the Culver Hotel near the MGM Studios in downtown Culver City?"

"Yeah, of course. We're only about a mile away from there."

"That's where they were housed during the filming. The late-night parties were so rambunctious, and they got so drunk and disorderly, the police were called and a few were arrested. Payoffs were made to keep it quiet," Betsy said, smiling. "But you can't blame them. For many it was the first time they had been around people like themselves and away from home."

"Is that true? They seemed to go crazy?"

"Not really. Most of it was exaggerated over the years," she said, laughing. "The worst was the monkeys."

"I bet. You must have had an interesting life, though?" Cassady said, changing the topic again.

"It may have been interesting, and I love my two daughters and son, but here is where I want to be now. I wanted to meet you, Cassady."

"Why did you want to meet me?" Cassady asked.

"I'm told you're at a crossroads and I want to show you the possibilities that the Sift offers. Ashley has talked about you and told me so much," Betsy replied.

"What crossroads?"

"I know you love the Sift—we all do. I've been waiting a long time to belong here. I, well... we thought you might enjoy being with me here. Would you like that?" she asked Cassady with unbelievable intensity in her eyes.

"I feel like I'm asking a lot of questions. But my life is right now only starting. I'm not ready to be with anyone that's not, I guess, I mean, alive in my world."

"But you can be here."

"How?" Cassady asked.

"You can join us. Ashley can set it up. At least when the time is right..."

"I feel uncomfortable with this conversation," Cassady interrupted. "Let's talk more about your life. What was singing all those years to people like?"

"Oh, all right, we'll talk of my life. But I will come back to the possibilities the Sift can bring to you. At my funeral, the famous actor James Mason said, 'Judy's great gift was that she could, by singing, ring tears out of the hearts of rock.'"

"You really could sing," Cassady said.

"I could sing, dance, and act—a triple threat. I truly had a great love for an audience, but I wanted to prove it to them by giving them blood. But now I want to live here quietly and I think the best would be if I could with you, Cassady."

"I can't think of that right now, sorry. That doesn't make sense to me, really."

"Oh hell! I thought this might happen..." She stopped and looked intently at him, unsmiling and harsh.

Cassady saw an abrupt change. From Betsy Booth in a small town in Idaho to a brash, unpleasant, drug- and alcohol-ridden, aged has-been—and then she smiled and that person disappeared and was immediately replaced with the beautiful vibrant teenager. It was much like what had happened to Scarlett.

"It's okay. I understand. I'll tell you the rest of the story about my life. I left the world you belong to only weeks ago and especially the horror that the success *The Wizard of Oz* brought to my life, although it did open up many possibilities for me. I'm afraid much of my life was made unbearable by different pressures. All through those early years, the movie people made my life a terror. They monitored every aspect of my life. From the time I was thirteen, there was a constant struggle between MGM and me. They were controlling how much I ate, what to eat, and when to eat," she said. "They had several people watching what I ate. It was terrible, but I wanted to be a success so badly I was prepared to do anything. Even sacrifice my young years. I remember this more vividly than anything else about my childhood."

"But you were Dorothy," Cassady said. "You're beautiful..."

"Thank you," Betsy said. "They actually wanted Shirley Temple for the part, that spoiled little brat! But remember, I was around women like Ava Garner, Lana Turner, and even the magnificent, stunning Elizabeth Taylor. Try to compete with that. I was making big money but face it, compared with those women, I was the ugly duckling. I was prescribed diet pills for my weight and barbiturates to help me sleep; it was a habit that stayed with me for the rest of my life until my accidental overdose. Mind you, it wasn't suicide. If I had committed that I wouldn't have been allowed to be here."

"What's that all about?" Cassady asked. "Who made that rule?"

"I guess it's something we don't talk about. It's a little depressing, so it doesn't come up. They have been talking about it after I died and I wish I could make it known. I was chosen as you have been."

"Why have we been chosen? I don't get this anymore. We aren't planning on dying any time soon..." Cassady faltered. "How is this home? Why couldn't you make a home in the world?"

"The couple of movies I made with Andy Hardy, who you know as Mickey Rooney, especially the first one, *Love Finds*

Andy Hardy, were the most beloved of all the movies I made. I saw how it could be, even a fantasy world, with everyone loving everyone and accepting them for who they are. It was that way for that short period of time and I wanted it forever, and the Sift offered me that," she said. "I can be sixteen years old for eternity and don't have to ever worry again about my weight or looks... Don't you want that? We could have it together."

"I'm happy in my life. I'm getting happier day by day. I want to grow up. I'm sorry for the troubles you've had in your life, but I have to have mine too. Can't you have the Sift in the *Wizard of Oz* set or Land?"

"Yeah, that's one of the problems. We need a semblance of appropriateness to visit in your realm. It was filmed entirely on a sound stage. It wasn't really that pleasant of a time in my life," she said. "It was a make-believe world for *real*. But making the movie wasn't a joy."

"Yeah, I guess. Oz is really a weird story when you think about it," Cassady said, warming to talking and being with her again. "You're carried away by a twister to a bizarre fantasy world where you kill the first person you meet. Then, you meet three really weird dudes dressed up as strange... I don't know what, and they help you go on to kill that first person's sister, huh?"

"Yes, that's a great way of putting it," she said, laughing. "You know even though it wasn't an enjoyable time, I've always taken the message of *The Wizard of Oz* very seriously. You know, I believe in the idea of the rainbow. And I spent my entire life trying to get over it. The Sift is a fantasy world that is existing forever and a day and it *is* over the rainbow!"

"Is it?" Cassady asked.

"Well, yes, but there are things you should know about it."

"Can you tell me?"

"I shouldn't, but you seem really nice and you should know

what it's all about."

"Please tell me. I have so many questions that Ashley won't answer and even Frank Morgan wouldn't," Cassady said.

"You mean Professor Marvel wouldn't answer," she said, chuckling. "Of course he wouldn't. Ashley would never allow it. There would be a price to pay."

"Like what?"

"That you don't need to know yet. What are some of your other questions?"

"Why are you all in certain characters and why do you stay in them, I guess, for eternity?" Cassady asked. "Like Ashley or Scarlett, or even more so, Everett Brown as a slave?"

"When and if you decide to join us, you are given an opportunity to choose whom you want to inhabit, and that is your character, but maybe better understood as a specter, for eternity. I chose Betsy because I was the happiest in my life during the filming of those movies. I was innocent. I can only be that innocent again here, now. Do you understand?"

Cassady said, "I have no idea if I understand."

"I chose this life when I had to. While it was bizarre and crazy, it was also more familiar. It was my truthful condition and what to you is seemingly real, for me was becoming clumsy and ordinary. That world was the one I was leaving behind. It will be for you also."

"So we'll be given an identity?"

"Yes, it's beautiful and wonderful," she said with a dreamy look in her eyes. "Or one will be chosen for you. Talk to Ashley about that."

"Why is Kyle flirting with this—when he's never even been in a movie, or had a character to choose from other than himself?"

"It's very rare that happens, but sometimes the choice is given to outsiders. It's usually people that have those special moments in their life that they truly don't want to let go of. Those moments when everything is perfection and they've stumbled upon the Sift by accident, like you two have. Other kids have snuck into the Backlot, but never connected to it like you and Kyle," Betsy said. "It's a decision that can never be taken back, so be careful, but think hard about spending time with me, Cassady. But please *do* consider it."

"I have someone I'm getting close to. You're nice, more than nice, but it doesn't seem right," Cassady answered. "I haven't lived my life that I'm now starting. Haven't you *ever* been happy?" Again, he wanted to change the subject from himself.

"I had unwanted advances from movie people since I was a young girl, five unhappy marriages, drug use, alcohol abuse, starvation diets, and the only time I felt wanted was when I was a kid on a stage either singing or acting. As much as I loved singing, every time I sang, I died a little. And here, I was happy in this beautiful Carvel, Idaho town with Andy Hardy. I could have, and wanted to be again, maybe with you, Cassady."

"Who are you all? And especially, who is Ashley? He seems like a leader or someone who controls this..."

"Ashley doesn't come in horrid regalia or an ugly face, he comes as he is and offers what most of us hope for..."

She stopped talking and when Cassady turned around, Ashley was standing there scowling at them.

"I thought it might be too soon, Betsy. I was right. Leave us now!" Ashley said sternly.

As she was walking away, she looked back lovingly at Cassady and said, "I'm sorry it didn't work out, be careful and follow your heart..." Betsy, Dorothy, and Judy were gone.

CHAPTER 22

Walking back with Ashley, Cassady was still trying to process the whole meeting with Judy Garland. "Can I see Judy, or I mean Betsy, again?" he asked Ashley. He immediately felt guilty about asking while thinking about Brie Ann. He was torn between the pull of the Sift and a beautiful girl wanting him, but luckily Ashley resolved the dilemma for him.

"No, I'm sorry it didn't work out. It wasn't meant to. Betsy wasn't ready. She hasn't been with us long enough to help you in the long run."

"What is it that you want from us in the long run here?" he asked. Although he was still curious, he felt a huge relief he didn't see coming about not being asked to spend any more time with Judy Garland.

"I don't want anything from you, Cassady," Ashley answered a little sharply. "I thought you'd like Betsy. Most boys your age would."

"I have someone in my life that is giving me what I want, or maybe need, right now. I'm sorry, I didn't mean to mess anything up. I was wondering, that's all," Cassady said. "Forget it. It's okay."

He was still walking with Ashley alone for a few minutes and while they were walking, Cassady stopped and again forced the conversation with Ashley.

"Did you ever meet a guy named Rick?" Cassady suddenly asked.

"Maybe, yes, now that I think about it. I'm sorry you and that disappointment met. He was on the periphery of our world but we saw right away he wasn't going to embrace the Sift like you and Kyle have. So we sent him and his friends on their way. That was a fun night," Ashley said, smiling.

"Why? What did you do?" Cassady asked.

"You remember you and Kyle's first glimpse of us. At least, Scarlett?"

"Yeah," Cassady said.

"Our introduction to Rick and a couple of his friends was, let's say, a little more complicated, and wasn't as welcoming as yours was... Let's leave it at that," Ashley said, amused, and added, "They ran for their lives."

Cassady tried to process this and couldn't help but wonder what had happened. "I need to ask you something else," Cassady said. "How long can this last? I mean, do you eventually move on, or is the Backlot here at MGM the only place this happens?"

"Good question, Cassady. As I realized before, once again, I knew you'd be the first to ask some questions and you've proved me right," Ashley started. His face grew darker and his manner seemed anxious. "Kyle is much too in love with Scarlett to want to change or have reservations about it. There is no time limit. The Backlot is an enchanted place to be trite about it. Don't get wrapped up in the why. Simply enjoy what we have given you here. We can still make it work with Betsy, or Dorothy if you prefer. The Backlot was special to you before you found us and... Let's say it has been part of your life, and it will always retain that innocence and wonder you've loved."

"Is it right, though? For us to be doing this—is it okay?"

"When you live your life knowing there are possibilities beyond what you see and understand, you can count yourself as one of the luckiest people in the world," Ashley said. "The ordinary person doesn't have the proof of life beyond what they know, so they must deal with life on simpler terms. You have proof that the cosmos is much more greatly expanded than you thought."

"But maybe that's the way it's supposed to be. Maybe the fact that the majority of people don't meet ghosts or apparitions is the way it's supposed to be and we should live our lives like that," Cassady said. "Maybe we're supposed to embrace the mystery of life."

"Maybe, for that matter, death also. We chose you because you are who you are, and you were here at the time of choosing and reckoning. Kyle has already made a choice."

"Why us? Why Kyle and me? What reckoning? What choosing? What's so important about us?" Cassady asked.

Without warning, Ashley's demeanor changed, and his face grew large and frightening. He looked different and wholly grotesque for a flash of an instant, especially his eyes that became enormous with striking pupils radiating fire within them...

"Because you're here," he shouted, "and we crave you!"

Because your adversary the devil, as a roaring lion, walketh about, seeking whom he may devour... These words somehow ran through Cassady's mind like a shout. Rick had seen it.

The change back was instantaneous. Ashley regained his composure a second later. Cassady wasn't sure what he had seen, but his gut told him whatever it was it was, was nasty and frightening. He felt sick.

"I'm sorry, Cassady. You upset me. I don't really want to talk about where and what I've come from. Isn't it enough for you to know I'm here for you and Kyle and will always be here for you?"

"But where's *here*? That's what I need to know. And why can't you talk about who you were?"

"Because *that* doesn't matter. My life, as you probably have researched, quite admirably I might add, is over and this is what is real for me now. I'll show you something. Look at my bracelet," Ashley said, as he stuck out his arm and jiggled his wrist, turning the chain over for Cassady to read.

"That's nice, but what's the significance of that?" Cassady asked.

"It was for my daughter," Ashley answered, but immediately said, "It's really of no concern to you."

"Okay. That makes sense—why show me then? But what I'm really wondering is who and what you really are?" Cassady barely glanced at the writing but was able to read it.

"I've said it once, and I'll say it again: I don't want to talk about that right now. Now come along and let's not discuss that again," Ashley said.

"I've got to know," Cassady said loudly, stopping and facing Ashley.

Ashley turned and looked at Cassady. He glared hard at Cassady while he continued to stare for several moments and merely said, "No."

Cassady ran back to Tara to find Kyle.

Ashley stood there for a minute and slowly followed.

CHAPTER 23

Cassady could tell Kyle knew something had gone wrong. When saying goodbye to Scarlett and Everett Brown and leaving with Kyle, it took everything Cassady had to not scream and tell him what he saw. Mr. Brown stood there watching both of them intently as they left the Sift and it slowly dissolved from view. While walking home Cassady tried to bring it up several times and failed.

"I need to tell..."

"I don't want to hear it, man," Kyle said, interrupting him. "I had a great night and you've become bad news. I don't *want* to hear it..."

"You've got to hear it, man," Cassady started to say as Kyle walked on.

They parted without speaking another word.

The next morning Cassady found himself on the bus alone heading west to Venice looking for answers to the questions roaring through his mind. He got off at the Pacific Avenue stop and walked up the couple of blocks again to the small intersection avenues of Howland Canal and Grand Canal. He cautiously strolled up to the trashy house he had seen Rick go into and knocked softly on the door. He waited for over a minute and knocked again. The door opened slightly and Rick, disheveled, his hair hanging down around his face, glassy-eyed, clothes wrinkled and unkempt, looked at Cassady as if not even faintly recognizing him, but abruptly said, "Oh wow, it's you. I thought I might see you again." He looked beyond Cassady. "Are you alone?"

"Yeah. Hey, I have some questions for you." Cassady said quickly to reassure him he didn't mean anything else. "Is that all right? I really don't know what I'm looking for..."

The door opened all the way as Rick said, smiling, "No, it's early for me, man, that's all, and I don't sleep well anyway, so come on in and let's have a heart-to-heart."

They walked into a living room filled with obviously discarded beat-up furniture, beanbag chairs, and clothes lying in piles all over the place. Old pizza boxes, empty soda cans, beer bottles strewn around the floor, and ashtrays overflowing. It took Cassady by surprise that Rick lived like this since he was so well-spoken and seemed intensely knowledgeable when they were talking on the beach.

"Don't judge what's going on here," he said, waving his arm around. "I share this place with two other dudes. Remember, one person's untidiness and chaos is another one's competence and familiarity. Ha! But I do want to talk to you about what I know you saw and how far you're into it."

"Okay," Cassady said. Rick dropped down on a beanbag chair and motioned Cassady to do the same. Plopping down, he thought it was actually pretty comfortable and he should get one for the Shack. He looked up at a huge Doors poster and said, "We saw those guys the other day. That was cool."

"Yeah, that was big news, but they used to be around here all the time and nobody cared and now it's a big deal when they come back and slum for an hour or so." Without warning he said, "Listen, I know you've met or seen some strange shit. Tell me what the fuck is going on with you in this. I have my own story, but you need to tell somebody what's going on.

Don't you?"

Cassady told him a sort of peripheral sketch of the story and left out many of the details and nothing about how long, or the adventures, or the falling in love with Scarlett, or the other characters they met, or his worry about Kyle making some kind of crazy decision. It was simply a basic terror story. During the telling, he stuck to the lie that they only saw the Sift (without naming it) a couple of times.

"You were lucky—you didn't see the complete horror show then?" Rick asked. "What did you think it was? Did they come after you?"

"No, they didn't. We didn't know what they were. What do you think it was you saw?" Cassady asked him back.

"Personally, I think it's a glimpse into hell," Rick said. "What else could it be? The characters formed in that blue shit the first time and we ran. It seemed magical though, so I went back, of course. The first time I was only with one other friend, but the second time they materialized I was with two other different friends. Of course, they didn't believe me until they saw—whatever it was, man. We didn't really understand what was going on at all. Then they started to come after us. We didn't know what they were or what they wanted, but we got the hell out of there, literally. They turned from those cool characters from the Old South, or whatever, into some kind of hellish monsters and chased us back across the field, and it only stopped once we made it and were over the fence."

"It didn't get that bad for us, but again, what do you think it was?" Cassady asked.

"I'm not sure. But it was like I said to you before, the gates of the netherworld opened up and showed us... I mean *really* showed us Hades. Only what I could imagine. Well, more than I could have imagined. I read this stuff now and I'm still not religious in the normal sense," Rick said pointing to a Bible laying on one of the scratched and beaten-up crooked tables.

Cassady noticed it for the first time and saw it wasn't worn or shabby up like most of the things in the house. There were several other new books next to it. He couldn't read what they were, but had the feeling they dealt with what they were talking about and what Cassady had researched in the library.

"I've gone to church a couple of times, but I don't really feel a connection to what I experienced. I'm not sure there's a battle between Heaven and Hell. It might exist in between. My friends simply wanted to forget about it. I couldn't and still can't. But I sure don't want to experience it again. Where's your friend, by the way?" he asked Cassady. "He wasn't with you that second time. Were those guys you were with in on this?"

"No, they don't know anything about it. The friend I was with isn't interested in finding out either..." Cassady trailed off. He couldn't bring himself to open up completely. He realized, obviously, that Kyle and his experience was much more profound and intense than Rick's, so thought it best to keep the conversation where it was now.

"I don't see the friends that were with me either," Rick said. "We definitely didn't really talk about it again and we drifted apart. They're dealing with it however they can, I guess."

"Why did you go into Backlot 3 then?" Cassady asked.

"I had to see if it was there also. It wasn't. I checked out Backlot 3 with a couple of different guys and then let it go. It's only movie shit and that's cool, but not like Backlot 2. I talked to you that first day at the beach after doing Backlot 3 a couple of times to make sure."

"Why would they do this? I mean appear for us, and why here in the Backlot?"

"Like I said, I've read about it and the nearest to it is what the Tibetan cults have a name for. They call it the tulpa. It's a concept from their thing called Theosophy, mysticism, some bullshit, but what you do is—through willed spiritualism or imagined beings, they appear, and that's what we tapped into."

"Why us and are there rules or anything like that?" Cassady asked, wanting more than anything answers to some of the questions he had and answers that weren't forthcoming from Ashley, Scarlett, or Everett Brown.

"Yeah, a ton of them. You can join only if asked. You can hook up with another tulpa or ghost. And I mean sexually, or at least romantically also. You are persuaded by the overwhelming desire, or a conclusive emotion—a certainty that you belong there and always have..."

"What do they get out of it? They have already lived their lives, why do they want to do, whatever it is to someone else? Have you read Charles Webster—"

"Leadbeater. Right? Yeah, his book is there." Rick said, interrupting, pointing to the table. "He's not in the same ballpark. His shit is weak compared to what this is. They've asked you to join, haven't they?" Rick asked, looking intently at him.

"I don't know, but I'm more than curious, I guess."

"Okay, I'll leave it at that. According to the Tibetan shit, you can't commit suicide to merge with them. It's kinda like the Catholic thing. But to answer your question; they need new people to continue as legitimate deities or whatever and they feed off of new lifeblood, if you will, like vampires. Not often, maybe every decade or so. I don't know, but bringing in new people, especially a young unfocused being strengthens their existence. Oh, yeah, they only have their power in the dark."

"Why as movie characters, or are they the real people they were?"

"Again, according to the books," Rick said, waving his hand again over the table with the piles of books and manuscripts, "they inhabit whatever form is desired or, remember the imagined beings, by the intended, say, victim. They can inhabit any form or person they want. Whatever is convenient to taking control, or possessing whatever? You thought they were cool, didn't you? And how cool was the Backlot when you first found it?"

"Pretty cool," Cassady admitted.

"Understand then, you could be inviting them into *your* world without even knowing it. The tulpa will talk gobble-dygook to obscure their real intentions. Shit about the universe and other crap to confuse the targets. These entities are comprised of energy... they draw the strength required to sustain their existence from the psychic or even physical strength of live people. They steal souls, man."

"Who do you think they really are?" Cassady asked. He thought about all the times Ashley said things that were incomprehensible.

"Even though it was on a Backlot—it sure wasn't a Hollywood movie," Rick said, sniggering. "It scared the shit out of me. With all the reading, what I've come to believe, whether it's biblical or not... demons don't show themselves in a cloud of smoke or fire necessarily. They can have a physical manifestation, it's rare and unusual, but they aren't colored red and don't have horns and tails. We can forecast our feelings or expectations and they can assume any form to meet those passions. When demons claim or disguise themselves to be either angels or dead human souls, these infestations eventually have to be busted out as false. There is still no conclusive proof of dead people coming back as ghosts. The evolution or process is very subtle and you're communicating with a demon, but you don't even realize it."

They sat quietly for a few moments. Cassady was shocked at how close Rick had come to their situation. What he could do with this information he didn't know yet. He knew he had to tell Kyle about what he saw last night. He got up.

"Thanks for talking to me. I think I'll let it go also. Maybe

I'll see you around sometime."

"Yes, stay out and learn whatever you can from this. We've experienced something most people don't even realize exists. Do what you may with that information. I'm trying. Maybe I'll see you on the boardwalk again someday." He walked Cassady to the door and shut it firmly behind him. Cassady felt humbled and confused. But realized he'd have to take it slowly with Kyle. He was hooked.

CHAPTER 24

That night, as unbelievable as it seemed in contrast, turned out to be one of the most relaxing nights in the Sift Cassady could remember. He didn't start the conversation with Kyle on the way as he felt deeply it wouldn't work yet. Mainly, through the whole night, he also only asked a few questions and didn't make any waves with Ashley. He pretended the whole conversation didn't happen, and he didn't see what he saw the night before. He wanted to take it all in and talk to Kyle when he had the chance to confront him, or at least get the conversation started without fighting. Cassady and Kyle spent the night in the Esther Williams pool. Cassady let it all go and for a few minutes, it felt like old times. Instead of the run-down scruffy dirty pool they had walked by during the many months' sojourns into the Backlot, the Sift had transformed it into a beautiful, wondrous, miraculous, blue water oasis. They spent the night swimming and diving with some of the *Gone with the Wind* people who were adventurous also. The boys swam in their underwear and no one cared or even mentioned it.

"Do you remember when we got caught skinny-dipping in the outdoor YMCA pool on Culver and Elenda over a year ago?" Kyle asked Cassady with a huge smile on his face.

"Yeah, it was past midnight that night too. Who would have thought that weird guy would have been working late that night?"

"At least—he let us go. He didn't even let Mr. Miller know. One more time with a clean getaway!"

Scarlett lounged by the poolside and enjoyed the fun they were having. She didn't join in the water games, although Kyle also spent several hours talking closely with her.

"Why do you call this the Esther Williams pool?" Cassady asked Ashley.

"She made several movies here, until she was such a box office success that the studio built her the larger cavernous tank on one of the sound stages to use in many more movies," Ashley said.

"Is she in the Sift?" Cassady asked.

"No, no, she's still very much alive and well. But, like Johnny Weissmuller, we're working on it. In the meantime, we can enjoy the pool dedicated to her movie history. Many famous actors and actresses have filmed and played here. Clark Gable swam here and had to do several takes to dive instead of belly flop. Elvis also swam here in *Jailhouse Rock*, but it was cut from the movie. John Wayne landed a plane in here during the filming of *The Wings of Eagles*. Luckily, because he was and still is a dreadful swimmer. Paul Newman spent a whole day here swimming here while filming the movie *Sweet Bird of Youth*."

That was the only conversation Cassady had with Ashley. He didn't talk to Scarlett at all.

Cassady waited until they were completely out of the Backlot walking home and with an effort, he finally brought up Ashley.

"He's the devil, Kyle. Really! He showed me a glimpse of it, something I can't explain. It was monstrous, horrible, ugly, and he had fire in his eyes! He all but admitted it to me."

"Really, you think he's the devil. Don't be stupid. He was

messing with you. I knew he'd do that if you blew off Judy
Garland." Cassady realized Kyle again knew something had
gone really wrong but was still reluctant to talk about it, or he
truly didn't want to believe it.

"Why don't you want to hear about what happened?"
Cassady asked. "You *have* to know this, what I saw, what
Ashley is..."

"I know, I know. So it didn't work out with Judy."

"No, don't you want me to tell you what I saw, man?"
Cassady yelled. "I can't believe you're being so flippant."

"I set up the rendezvous with her, *man*," Kyle yelled back.

"I'm talking about Ashley..."

"Maybe he got a little pissed. We're trying to let you in on
this. This is the greatest thing that could happen to anybody
and we have the chance to do it," Kyle said calmly. "I can't
believe you don't want to be with Betsy or Judy or whatever.
She's beautiful, smart, sixteen, not to mention she can sing,
you idiot," Kyle said.

"Not to mention dead," Cassady replied. "She seemed a
different kind of pretty, yes, but I can't even contemplate
spending time with her, Sift or not. Please! Stop! Listen to me!"

He pushed Kyle and Kyle immediately pushed back. They
backed a step off and raised their fists. Cassady suddenly felt
completely shattered. The friend with whom he had so many
adventures, and who was closer to him than anybody in his
life, was about to come to blows over something he couldn't
even explain. He dropped his fists and cried out one soft sigh.
He thought of coming at this from another angle to try and get
through to Kyle.

"You know, we both thought she was beautiful and wanted
Scarlett's attention, so I backed off and let you spend more and
more time with her alone," Cassady said.

"She chose me, asshole," Kyle replied.

"Fine, I know that. That's not what I meant, but anyway it

meant at times I had to spend more time with Ashley. I've been asking him dozens of questions about his past. Not always about Ashley, but about being Leslie Howard, his family and friends and movies. Ashley was not always forthcoming with that information. I'm not even sure that's who they are. Judy Garland was neat to meet and talk to, but I could tell I'm being placated. Was it a coincidence, or maybe an accident or maybe not—she died, and then chose to come into the Sift while they wanted to offer me something?"

"Neat? You blew it," Kyle said. "She was a gift."

"I don't want the gift of a ghost. I want what I have—a real girlfriend."

Kyle shrugged his shoulders at that, once again seemingly ignoring his relationship with Brie Ann. Cassady realized he didn't want to push it, at least not yet. He didn't want to even think about Ashley's face again or see what he had shown him. He realized Kyle didn't want to hear it or see it.

Almost to their homes, Kyle asked Cassady, "Why aren't you into this anymore? This has turned out to be more than anything we could have imagined or dreamed of. You were with Judy Garland night before last night. Can't you dig that? And I haven't begun to get tired of Tara yet."

"I was hoping for Glinda the Good Witch of the North."

"Do you have to be such a smartass, all the time?" Kyle said, smiling. Cassady thought they were back together again for a minute.

"So, tell me about your girlfriend." Kyle suddenly said.

"Why have you waited all this time before saying anything?" Cassady said. "Why not before while we've talked about all this?"

"I thought it would end on its own. You know, she would fade away..."

"Her name's Brie Ann, and she's not a someone who will fade away. I haven't had an opportunity to talk, I mean, you could see us together, and you never asked about her."

"It's really not a big deal. The Sift is the main thing here. We shouldn't give it up. I can't."

"I know now it's wrong. It was cool and everything, but I know I can't do it much anymore," Cassady said. "Man, I'm sorry."

"It's still Scarlett, isn't it?" Kyle asked. "It isn't that you didn't like Judy that much. Is it?"

"No, I swear it's not really her. I want to do other things."

"Other things like what?" Kyle yelled. "You're jealous of me and Scarlett."

"No, I'm not. That's your problem now. I don't care, you win, and you can have her. She wants you—I get that. What does it mean anyway? What would you win? She's dead and we're not."

Kyle ignored most of that and said, "You know she's not truly dead. You've felt what it is. I've done more than kiss her, man!"

"How? I never asked but she only looks real. She's only a spirit. Can she even feel?" Cassady was astounded by this realization.

"Ashley told me how it works. We all exist in an energetic and physical form. It's like a duality. The spiritual body senses what's unseen and the physical body senses what's present— they both sense what's tangible. So I feel her and she can feel me until it changes presently."

"Man, you're whacked out," Cassady said. It was all he could think of.

"This is the best my life has ever been. We have more energy than anybody I know and we hardly sleep. I can't imagine what else you could want to do. I played basketball with Lucas yesterday for three hours and feel great. I had hoped you'd be with Betsy and I'd be with Scarlett. All I can think about is that we have it made. We shouldn't do anything to mess this up."

"Like what?" Cassady couldn't imagine what he was doing to mess this up.

"Anything! Don't mess this up, that's all. Ashley said you could mess this up somehow if you freak out on us."

"When did he say that?"

"Oh, one night when you were distracted and weren't paying attention. We weren't talking about you behind your back. We're concerned you've become sidetracked or something. He didn't say freak out, that's me, but he said destroy an opportunity of a lifetime, or something, and then laughed. That's all."

"You're scaring me now Kyle, it's not us—or me—against them. I'm part of this too."

Cassady decided not to bring up the horror he had seen with Ashley during the night before again. He didn't think it would do any good and Kyle probably still wouldn't believe him anyway. His mind was in a fog.

As they were almost home, and Kyle was talking about how they should appreciate what they had here, Cassady finally tuned into the conversation when he heard him say something about living it instead of visiting. Cassady couldn't concentrate and so didn't respond to what Kyle was saying.

"I don't want you being distracted from the Sift and that is exactly what's happening." Kyle was starting to raise his voice.

"I don't see Brie Ann in the middle of the night and..."

"We feel she's taking too much of your energy, and you may not want to participate in the next phase of completion in the Sift," he yelled. "We have big stakes here and you might be blowing it. I knew that's what happened with Judy!"

Cassady stood there looking at Kyle amazed with wide eyes.

"What phase of what? What are you talking about? Do you hear yourself? Who're we? Do you have a mouse in your pocket, or are you letting someone else think and talk for you now? My losing interest in the Sift has more to do with what and who these things are, Kyle. They're not people. We have to be careful about what's going on here."

"That's not true! Are you thinking about telling her about the Sift?" Kyle asked.

"Why not? If it's such a cool thing, why should it remain a secret? I have a girlfriend for the first time in my life, and we talk about the same things you and I used to talk about. I want to do everything with her. Why should I not be able to tell her about the Sift and the Backlot?"

"For the same reason we don't tell anyone. We were given this as a gift. We were favored. Don't ruin this, Cassady," Kyle said. "And don't even think about bringing her into the Sift. It won't be allowed."

"Favored? Allowed? Now you sound like Ashley again."

"Is that such a bad thing?" Kyle asked. "Wait, it's going to get better."

"Yes, and I've had about enough. Something isn't right here anymore."

"This is bigger than us! We—I have to know if you want to go further within the Sift, Cassady."

Cassady stood there without having anything to say for a moment.

"Of course I don't. Haven't you listened to me? How can you... are you thinking about staying in the Sift?"

"Who told you that's even possible?" Kyle asked.

"Betsy or Judy... whoever. She said sometimes outsiders could be invited. Are you thinking about that?"

"I wouldn't be an outsider, but an invitation was offered to me and an identity was debated."

"By who, who would make that decision? Ashley? He's evil. Don't do this, Kyle, or even contemplate it. Please don't do this..."

But Kyle, once again, walked off.

CHAPTER 25

Cassady walked into the library annex after school, by himself, sat down behind a table, and waited for Miss Rigby to finish with a customer checking out a book. It was a lady he'd seen before in the annex, though. It was never busy, and usually the customers were regulars. As soon as she left, Miss Rigby turned toward him and faced him with scrutiny of obvious questioning. He nodded. She walked over and turned the sign on the front door to *Closed*, then walked back to the counter and motioned for Cassady to follow her. They went into the small storage room.

"Finally. Please tell me what you can and don't leave anything out," she gushed out.

"I really don't have much more to tell you. Who I'm talking to might very well be your father, or not. It's not a good situation."

"Why not?"

"I don't know who they are. They're either actually Ashley and Scarlett or they're pretending to be Leslie Howard and Vivien Leigh. It depends on which night it is and I can't promise you the truth. It's eternal confusion. All I can do is tell you what I've been going through and what we both can think or not."

"I want to believe he's my father to such a degree that I can't be sure I'll be rational about this," Miss Rigby said.

"All I can do is tell you what's happened so far," Cassady said. "I'll start from the beginning..."

An hour later Cassady finished. They both sat there and looked at each other for a long time.

"I'll have patience for you and we'll get through this together. I might continue to try other methods to contact him, though," Miss Rigby said as she hugged him. He nodded his acceptance.

Cassady walked out the door and made a turn between two buildings and was walking down the alley, when out of the shadows behind the next building walked Brie Ann.

"How did you know I was here?" Cassady asked, trying to steer the conversation away from the obvious, and knowing with Brie Ann, that was going to be impossible.

"She asked you to come in and talk to her a while ago, and I was coming down the street when I saw you go in. I thought I'd surprise you, but when I got here, I saw the *Closed* sign on the door and decided to wait. That's all. Well, you promised to tell and now you can. What could you have been talking to Miss Rigby about all that time?"

"I don't know. Nothing. Books, about books."

"Why are you lying to me? Miss Rigby wanted to talk to you. We've been hanging out now for weeks and the one thing I counted on was you not lying to me."

"I know, but I don't know how to tell you, that's all."

"How about telling me the truth?"

Cassady let out a deep breath. "Okay, but we can't do it here. Let's go back to my house."

"All right, but you have to promise to tell me the truth," Brie Ann said.

Cassady could only think about how many promises he had made in the last hour. They walked the rest of the way in silence. Cassady spent the time trying to sort things out. He felt like he had to share this with someone besides Miss Rigby. He couldn't all the way with Rick. Kyle was about to make a decision about something; Cassady knew it in his heart. What could happen if he told Brie Ann about the Sift?

Then he realized it would have to be something beyond telling her. He might have to show it to her. That could be dangerous, but he didn't know what else to do. She would have to see it. No one would believe it unless they saw the beautiful azure color of the mist, wonderful swirls, and the inconceivable creation of the Sift people. Cassady would have never believed it unless he had lived it with Kyle, and now the same thing that he loved about it somehow seemed to be threatening to take his best friend away. He'd have to give Brie Ann a chance.

Back in the Shack Brie Ann sat down and graciously she didn't say anything, waiting for him to start talking. Cassady sat quietly, let out another deep breath, and started his story.

"I want you to know something. I think you're beautiful, and I feel I'm lucky to have this time with you, and I don't think we've even begun to get to know each other. I never thought someone like you would ever like someone like me, and I feel like it's more than liking you. It's better than that. And I'm going to tell you something today I can hardly believe myself most of the time, but I'm going to take a chance and tell you. Then whatever happens will happen. But I want you to know that keeping this secret has nothing to do with you. I felt I couldn't tell you when we first started talking because of how strange this thing is." It all came out in a rush. He was nervous to the point of being sick, out of breath, and lightly shaking.

"I'm sure it'll be all right, and I promise to not judge you and try to understand." Brie Ann smiled and touched his arm, nodding, and said, "Go ahead, Cassady."

He looked at Brie Ann intensely, quietly, let out a deep

breath, and for the second time Cassady started his story.

"So, you know the MGM Backlots we were talking about, or really Backlot 2 down a little bit on Culver Boulevard?"

CHAPTER 26

Cassady was waiting for Kyle where they had been meeting at about eleven o'clock every night. Cassady hadn't been there for several nights running and was wondering if he had missed him. A few minutes had passed when Kyle walked up. They didn't talk for a moment but stood there looking away from each other.

"Are you going in with me tonight and getting back to normal?" Kyle finally asked.

"There's nothing *normal* about this at all. Don't you know that, Kyle?" Cassady yelled. "Ashley is not what you think he is. He's wicked."

"That's not what I see. He can be numerous things. I know Ashley can be cruel, unfair, unapproachable, emotionless, self-pitying; all these things," Kyle said, laughing. "But I also know he can be the most precise consistent soul, kind, thoughtful, and a caring head of these people..."

"You mean ghosts or phantoms?" Cassady said sarcastically.

"Yes," Kyle said, ignoring the sarcasm. "But, like I was saying, sympathetic at times, maybe arrogant, but also likable, delightful, passionate, and a remarkable friend."

"That's quite the rap. Did he tell you all these things or do you really, really see this in him? You see him as a friend? Not me?" Cassady asked.

"He can be a friend to both of us. I don't want to leave you out of this. I know it's hard because I'm with Scarlett now, and we're closer than ever. You should have joined me these last few nights," Kyle said.

"How can you be with Scarlett?" Cassady asked. "She's not real."

"I told you, she's as real as your girlfriend is to you."

"I don't have to sneak into the Backlot in the middle of the night to see her. We are in the real world together. I was hoping we'd both have a real girlfriend someday and I do, and you won't as long as you keep coming here."

"There's nothing you have that I don't have here. There'll eventually be a girl here for you. Ashley told me to tell you that. Also, are you trying to tell me you don't want the adventures, excitement, and cool things we can have in the Sift, anymore?" Kyle asked.

"Of course I'll miss that and it was beyond fun, but it can't be good. We've had so many real crazy times and all those close calls. Don't they mean anything to you anymore? I think about all those times and... I don't want to have times like that with anyone but you. It can't be better, and nothing can be as nice as it is with Brie Ann."

"Believe me. What I have with Scarlett is fun, much more than fun. You could have it too."

"I've never really had an interest in her, not because of jealousy, but precisely because she's not real. I'm only interested in Brie Ann. We've talked too much about this."

"That's not what I meant and you know it. We can have whatever we want in the Sift. Whatever you or I dream of—it can become genuine, real. And anyway, what was it you saw in Ashley that made you think he's so evil? It was a game he played with you."

"These are people who have *slaves*, man. They want to exist, maybe for eternity, with the thing we fought a Civil War to stop!"

"Everyone who is in the Sift is there by choice, it's the movie set that works for it, for them, I mean," Kyle said slowly.

"That doesn't even make sense. I talked to Big Sam..."

"Forget it," Kyle said. "Why don't you see the good in Ashley?"

"His eyes. They were one moment clear and calm. He stares at you with a self-confidence, but his gaze then came from somewhere else, somewhere deeper, from eternity. I saw a blaze in his eyes and what they spoke wasn't obviously *of* this world or goodness. All I know is this is genuine evil come to life for us and I don't want anything else to do with it."

"I'll miss my friend," Kyle said, walking away.

Cassady walked down the alley on the way home. At Commonwealth he suddenly stopped and turned around and ran back to the alleys and streets they normally walked to Elenda and Arizona Streets. Luckily in the quarter moonlight he could barely see Kyle in the distance and waited a minute to keep enough of a gap that Kyle wouldn't see him easily if he turned around. It looked like Kyle was walking quickly and with purpose so as not to be bothered. Kyle climbed the fence alone and so did Cassady several minutes or so later. The Sift had already risen forty feet high and swept down, swirling while it flattened out in the dark. Cassady hid in the other old Southern mansion on the edge of the Sift. He was close enough to hear—he thought—without being seen. He wasn't sure if that was possible but didn't care if he was caught. Out of the gleaming azure fog, the figures slowly developed in the cobalt blue mist. As they evolved into the soldiers and Southern ladies and gentlemen, Kyle joined them at the party. The antebellum south had never looked so color-washed, rich, and wonderful. Kyle calmly walked over to Scarlett and Ashley.

"Welcome, Kyle, how are you tonight?" Ashley asked. He asked him, as he had asked them together, the same question every night. Cassady could hear clearly and amazingly felt he was concealed and undetected.

"We had another big blowout tonight," Kyle said.

"Kyle, I know you miss Cassady and know he has made a personal choice, but if Cassady doesn't want to take part in these nights then that is up to him. It's another glorious evening, Kyle, and I'm glad you have chosen to continue to attend our gatherings. We'll have to give up on Cassady, I'm afraid, unless you want to give it one last try?" Ashley said.

"I'll see, but I also don't want to waste any more time. He'll do what he feels like. It won't change my decision one way or another," Kyle said.

"I'm especially glad of that," Scarlett said, stepping up. "Are you sure you don't have something else to tell us about Cassady?"

"Well, we had that blowup. It wasn't pretty, and I'm sure he isn't coming back," Kyle said. "Actually what he said was he thought this was—I want to remember this the best I can: 'This is genuine evil come to life for us and I don't want anything else to do with it.'"

"How do you feel about that, Kyle?" Ashley asked.

"I'm confused and disappointed," he said dejectedly. "One time he asked me if we'd be friends when we were thirty-five and I said sure, why not? Now, I guess not. I thought we'd be friends forever, and forever is now."

"We'll talk about your decision later tonight, with or without Cassady," Ashley said. "What Cassady is discovering is who we were before we were part of the Sift, and it doesn't have anything to do with what *you* are going to do. Cassady has some things to work out, and I wish him all success with his endeavor."

"You know those things? How?"

"It's completely reasonable. We have very little information actually on life outside of the Sift, but enough to ruminate on some things, though. His meddling is a sad attempt to give someone who was close to my doppelgänger help, but I'm not actually who she thinks I am. If he can give her a little peace of mind and happiness, I am more than glad to give them my best. If the information I provided Cassady helps in that undertaking, then so much the better for all of us. Cassady might even help end the charlatans and spiritualists performing tricks like foolish séances from taking advantage of her, but nevertheless, he must soon make his own choice. Let us enjoy this beautiful nightfall."

As they walked away into the depths of the Sift Cassady knew it would be unwise to follow. He suddenly grasped he shouldn't have been able to view the whole thing without Ashley wanting him to. But as he started to move to stand up he saw Ashley unexpectantly turn toward him, nod his head with a small wave of his gloved hand, and give him a horrifying smile.

CHAPTER 27

Several nights later, Cassady and Brie Ann walked along the well-traveled route he and Kyle had walked along for months. Brie Ann had told her mom she was staying the night at a new friend's house she had met recently at the library annex, and snuck into the Shack after dark and stayed there until Cassady came out to get her.

They came to the corner of Elenda and Arizona Avenues and instead of walking all the way down to where the steel fence started, they walked to the entrance of the tall chain-link fence gate, opened it, and stepped onto the grounds of the old, dark, forbidden mansion. They stood still for a minute and listened to the tall trees sway in the familiar way of the Backlot and now this house. Both Cassady and Brie Ann looked for the small light deep within the menacing house.

"She said to lock the gate behind us, didn't she?" Brie Ann said.

"Yeah, I got it. Are you sure you want to do this?" Cassady asked Brie Ann.

"Yes, I've always felt she was nice. Now, I only think she's kind of strange, but still I know she's okay."

"Okay, I was checking, I'm not sure I want to do this, but I have to do something."

"No, *we* have to do something," Brie Ann said with a slight smile.

"Thanks," was all Cassady said.

They walked up to the tall door and Eleanor was standing there on the porch in the dark. They both jumped back.

"What the..." Cassady started.

"I'm sorry. I didn't mean to scare you. I only wanted to make sure the gate was locked," Miss Rigby said sheepishly. "I'm glad you came."

"It's locked like you asked me to," Cassady said.

"I'm glad you've agreed to help me. My guests don't know anything about what you've told me. I arranged this several weeks ago and now know it may or may not do any good, but thank you both for coming. I want to keep an open mind. What you've experienced with Leslie might mean this is hogwash, but maybe, just maybe, he might want to contact me this way. We'll try at least. Come into my house, please," she said as she turned, opened the door, entered, and walked down the hallway. Over her shoulder, she said, "Please close the door behind you; it will lock automatically."

The hallway was lit with a couple of candles, and so Cassady knew now why the lights didn't project outside at night. There was a light farther down the hallway. Both he and Brie Ann were looking at the walls and into the couple of rooms as they walked down the extremely long hallway. Everything was old but colorful. It didn't quite look like either of their parents' houses. It wasn't too scary; a little dark. Eleanor had many little knick-knacks on bookshelves and doilies on comfortable leather chairs and other old but beautiful furniture. At the end of the hallway, she turned to them.

"Are you surprised by my home? It doesn't look like much on the outside, but I like it to be pretty on the inside. I like my privacy, and the external tackiness keeps people away."

"It's beautiful, ma'am," Brie Ann said.

"Oh, we've been through that enough. Please call me Eleanor. Cassady has finally learned, haven't you?"

"Yes, I have," Cassady quickly answered.

"Come into the study," Eleanor said. "Go ahead and look around."

This room was immediately different from the rest of the house.

"Look at all the posters," Brie Ann said, drifting around the room.

Enclosed in glass were almost a dozen of Leslie Howard's movie posters. "Look at this one. *The Petrified Forest* with Humphrey Bogart," Brie Ann said, sounding awestruck and impressed.

"*Romeo and Juliet*, from or at the Verona set. He showed me the balcony." He smiled at Brie Ann.

"This poster declared his nomination for an Oscar for his portrayal of Henry Higgins in the 1938 movie *Pygmalion*," Eleanor said proudly, pointing one out.

The rest of the room had prizes, scripts, and pictures of Leslie Howard with other movie stars, at dinners and maybe award ceremonies.

"This stuff is amazing," Brie Ann said.

"You could not have known or realized Leslie was so successful," Eleanor said, smiling.

In the center of the next room they entered was a large wooden table with big, cozy, and welcoming leather chairs surrounding it. Brie Ann and Cassady had been told there were others invited, but still were somewhat shocked. In two of the high-backed chairs sat an elderly man and a woman. The two people would glance up and then look down and close their eyes and sigh heavily and then barely glance up again. They didn't speak and Brie Ann and Cassady didn't say anything.

"Oh, I'm sorry. I haven't introduced you to my other guests tonight. I'm being rude. This is Arthur Ford and this is Sarah Harper. They are going to help us tonight. Arthur and Sarah are my friends. I was hoping you would help in our quest, too. We very much would like your participation in tonight's séance," Eleanor said.

"Okay?" Cassady said. He thought, *We already agreed,* so he would. He had never thought about what that would entail, much less who the other people would be.

"Do you think we can help?" Brie Ann asked.

"Eleanor seems to think that you have some sort of special connection to her father, and I would very much like to see what you can do," the very old man said. He spoke laboriously and very slowly. Every word was enunciated as if it was its own sentence.

"Why would you think I would know anything?" Cassady answered.

"Eleanor seems to think, that, in fact, you *do* know something, and I'm here to check that claim out."

"Please, Cassady, I don't want to beg, but I will," Eleanor said with a knowing nod. "Sit down and observe and contribute if you can. I won't bother you again and will only ask this one favor from you." Cassady didn't know if this was for the couple's benefit or not, but he checked his temper for her sake.

Brie Ann reached out and touched Cassady on the arm and faintly pulled on his shirt sleeve. She whispered, "Please play along—you never know."

The many things about the Sift Cassady had discovered over the months mostly scared him and worried him, and he didn't know what to do about it. He thought back on several of his last conversations with Kyle and Ashley, and none of them had turned out well. Since he had stopped going to the Sift he didn't know what else could be done. Ashley had only briefly mentioned his daughter and Cassady thought perhaps he had accidentally found out what she wanted to know. He felt it was his duty to relay that information to her, but wasn't sure with these other people here, so he would stay and play along and see if the opportunity presented itself to give her something of what she wanted.

Brie Ann somehow, against all odds, believed him and they had talked about her going to visit the Backlot. But she saw what he was going through and naturally had some serious reservations about seeing it firsthand. She also understood that it might not be a good thing,

"Sit down at the table and let me tell you a story, young man," the man said. "My name is Arthur Ford..."

Cassady and Brie Ann sat down across from the couple, and Eleanor sat at the head of the table. It was warm in the room and they all immediately focused on him.

"I have been a clairaudient all my life," Arthur continued. "I have been in touch with the spirit world as long as I can remember, well over fifty years. I founded the Spiritual Frontiers Fellowship of New York during World War I. I witnessed deaths from the influenza epidemic in army camps and in the trenches. I realized my psychic abilities by having visions of knowing the names of those who would die several days before their deaths. In 1929, I interposed and broke the secret code that Harry Houdini and his wife devised to test the afterlife and for him to communicate with her after he died. He relayed the code to my partner Francis Fast, and I have been involved in this and know what is real and what is not. Now I am a very very old man and Sarah here is a spirit guide who has spent time with Eleanor and so will make the first contact."

"How?" was all Cassady could think to say. He had promised Brie Ann he'd have an open mind no matter what happened here, so he kept his reservations and knowledge of

Harry Houdini to himself.

"We would like to conduct a séance tonight, and I will be the spirit guide to whom Leslie Howard will contact his daughter Eleanor and let her know he is within the spirit world and can tell her things that they alone can validate," Sarah offered.

"How?" Cassady asked again.

"It's Cassady, isn't it?" Arthur asked, not really desiring an answer. "You're asking about the afterlife or spirit world, aren't you?"

"If that will tell me how you expect to communicate with Ashley, then yes."

"Neither of those places are a static existence; spirits live in a place where their life forces evolve. Spirits advance to a higher plane and are more developed than humans. Contact with them is conceivable and probable if one is as advanced as I am."

"How so?" Brie Ann now said.

"Some spiritualists are open to receiving knowledge about matters such as moral and ethical issues and the nature about our existence. I have been able to become one of those spirit guides," Arthur said. "Let's begin this night, but to have success we must have trust, faith, and belief."

"You think you can contact Ashley through a séance?" Cassady said.

"I find it interesting that you continue to refer to Eleanor's father by the name he played in a ridiculous movie," Arthur said.

"Well, that's the way I thought of him when I learned about the history of the Backlot," Cassady said defensively.

"I understand, but why would you still refer to him as his character?"

"It's what we've been doing for a long time, sneaking into the MGM Studios Backlot. We run around the old set. I was interested in what was filmed there and learned his name from the movie and book, that's all."

"I'm aware of that. Eleanor has told me of this connection, but I still don't really see your interest in Leslie. We're the ones interested in Leslie. Your only link to him is through Eleanor."

"I confess, I didn't correct Cassady initially and wasn't entirely truthful about who I was when we met, Arthur," Eleanor interjected.

"That's the way I remember his name, that's all," Cassady said.

"If you have any information about Leslie Howard, please let us have those specifics now. Holding back information or essentials from a medium is detrimental to the success of contacting the spirit world."

"You mean, give you stuff you can use during it, so we think it's real?" Cassady asked.

"Do you want to participate in this séance with an open mind, Cassady and Brie Ann? Or will your presence be a problem?" Arthur said, more slowly than his normal speaking rhythm.

"Yes," Brie Ann said, looking at Cassady. "We'll do it."

"Okay, I'll stay, no problems, and we'll participate, I guess," Cassady said.

"Fine, I'll explain what we are going to do and how we are going to do it," Arthur said, in his agonizingly slow method of talking. "Please sit down now, and we will begin." They sat down around the big table and waited. Cassady felt sweat form along his brow and wiped it quickly.

"No one must speak but me and, when the time comes, Sarah. Be respectful, the dead cannot laugh with happiness, so do not provoke them with merriment or cynicism."

That, Cassady knew was categorically wrong. He had witnessed Ashley, or Leslie, laughing dozens of times. He kept his mouth shut for Eleanor. Brie Ann touched his arm, as if to tell him, once again, it was all right.

"We will place a picture of Leslie in the middle of the table, and we must all concentrate on his image," Arthur continued. "Our hands have to be placed palms down on the table. Two candles will be lit on either side of Leslie's picture and will be the only lights in the room. In a bowl of quartz, I will place a drop of my blood to draw his spirit, and a lily, the flower of death. Do not break the circle until I instruct you. I will read from the Bible to begin to draw the spirit world into our world. Do you have any questions?"

Brie Ann glanced at Cassady as they both shook their heads. Cassady thought how easy it would be to simply walk into the Sift and ask Leslie or Ashley himself, realizing, though, he might get the usual roundabout ambiguous answer.

Arthur picked up a large Bible from underneath the table and opened it, as Eleanor placed the picture and two candles on the table. She also brought a small crystal bowl filled with liquid. Arthur reached for the bowl and put it in front of him and took a small pin out of his inside coat pocket and pricked his finger, letting a tiny drop of blood fall into the bowl. He wrapped his finger with a handkerchief. Eleanor moved the bowl to the side of the photo, dropped a lily into the middle of the bowl, lit both candles, and turned off the overhead light. She smiled at Cassady when she saw him looking her way, and then she looked down at the table.

"Place your hands palms down on the table and clear your minds of daily clutter and any negative thoughts concerning the possibility of linking with the spirit world," Arthur slowly said.

He looked around the room at each person at the table and then moved the Bible in front of him and began to deliberately read, "Samuel 28:1. 'In those days the Philistines gathered their forces for war to fight against Israel.'" As he continued, Cassady glanced up and thought of what Arthur would do first to make them think that a spirit was in the room. "'And his servants said to him; Behold, there is a medium at Endor... And Saul said, Divine for me a spirit and bring up for me whomever I shall name to you...'"

Suddenly one of the candles flickered. Arthur barely slowed his measured reading. The candle then shot a bluish flame two inches above the wick.

Everyone jumped, including Cassady. His sweat broke out again, and he glanced over to Brie Ann and saw the shining glow of sweat on the tip of her nose. Arthur hardly hesitated before he continued to read, "'And the old woman said to Saul, I see a god coming up out of the earth. He said to her, What is his appearance? And she said, An old man is coming up; and he is wrapped in a robe. And Saul knew that it was Samuel, and he bowed with his face to the ground, and he did obeisance.'"

A loud knocking came from somewhere behind Arthur. It started slowly and then grew louder, so that he had to stop reading. As he looked around the room the knocking slowed and then faded away.

"Please move your hands so that the little finger of each hand is touching the little finger of the person sitting next to you," Arthur said. Everyone moved slightly to do that and relaxed to some extent after making physical contact with another human.

"Tonight we have opened every avenue to aid in the access to the spirit world. Here in Eleanor's home, all that is left of Leslie's physical remnants are available to make you comfortable and to help bring you to her again," Arthur now spoke stronger and louder. "Leslie Howard, you who were born on the third of April in the year of our Lord 1893 in the city of London, England, and who perished over the ocean in the Bay of Biscay, on the first of June in the year of our Lord in 1943. Are you here? Are you with us? If you can show us a sign, show us evidence that you are willing to communicate with your daughter, so that she can know you are fine and being a faithful servant in the spirit world. Can you answer her questions about your—"

"Iiiiiiiiiiiiiii aaaaaammmmm heeeeerrrrrrrreeeeeeeeeeeee," Sarah started to wail and moan over and over. Cassady sat on the edge of his chair.

"Iiiiiiiiiiiiii am hhheeeerrrrreeeeee, I am here, I am here, I am here," her wail turned into a chant, with her face contorted and anguished, as the loud knocking started up again.

Cassady looked at Brie Ann and saw dread on her lovely face. He then looked at Eleanor and saw such longing on her face; he felt torn and ashamed. He wanted to believe for her sake, he wanted it to be real for her. But he knew it couldn't be real; real was Ashley in the Sift, not here in this room; but he waited.

"Leslie, please continue to talk through Sarah and use her to make your connection to our world. Let us know what you would like to communicate to your daughter. Tell us now," Arthur said.

"Iiiiiiiii wwaaaannnnttttt heeeeerrrrr to know oooooofffff my looooooovvveeeee. My love, my love, my love," Sarah cried.

"Yes, I love you too, Leslie," Eleanor cried.

"Do you have any further message for us, or for your daughter, Leslie?" Arthur asked.

"Iiiiiiiiiii, plaaaaaaane, morning, home, plane, plane, home, morning," Sarah moaned and cried.

"What are you trying to say to us?" Arthur asked.

Cassady looked over at Brie Ann realized what was happening and mouthed the word, "Bullshit!"

She shook her head at him and he then looked over at Eleanor, who seemed like she was about to pass out from the whole thing.

"Ask him about the present," Cassady said to Eleanor. "Ask him what he was bringing you?"

"Yes, oh god, yes. Leslie, what were you bringing me from Lisbon? What was the present you were bringing me on your trip, darling?"

"Iiiiiiiiiiii, plaaaannneeee, home, plane," continued Sarah.

"The spirit world can only give answers to questions they feel the need to respond to," Arthur jumped in. Cassady thought this was much like the gibberish that Ashley in the Sift ran by them at times.

"But we can try to receive the answer to that question," Arthur continued. "What were you bringing to your home to your daughter on your return trip before you crossed into the land of death? Leslie, can you answer the question, yes, please give your daughter the answer to her question?" The knocking was thunderous.

"Iiiiiiiiiii have changed the present now, home, plane, present, now, changed, not what she thought, changed present, now, home, plane," Sarah was almost chanting the answers.

"Yes, Leslie, what did you change the gift to?" Eleanor shouted. "Yes, tell me."

"Iiiiiiiiiiii have new present, plane, on plane, new, rug, rug, rug, present, brought from plane, brought from Portugal, rug," Sarah sang now.

"Yes, Leslie, you were going to bring me a rug from Portugal. I know we talked about it, but you said something else, but I wanted a rug. Yes, love, yes, I wanted a rug."

"Alllll, done, gone, done, alllll gone, finished," Sarah said as she slumped forward on the table and put her head down.

Nobody said a word for several minutes. Eleanor cried softly throughout the time everyone sat and looked down at the table. Arthur leaned over and patted Sarah on the back and cooed quietly to her. The knocking was gone, but in its place was a silence almost as deafening. In the dark the knocking could have been anything, even, he had read, the cracking of fingers or other joints. He knew it was fake.

Cassady let everything that had happened to him in the last half a year run through his mind and tried to sort out what the right thing to do was. What should he do here? He thought the right thing to do was bust Arthur and let Eleanor know what Ashley had told him.

It was simple—he couldn't entirely understand what the Sift was or how he fit into it, but he knew Leslie had become Ashley. He wasn't Leslie Howard the movie star anymore. He was a ghost and spirit that had revealed himself to Kyle and Cassady, and they had been spending time with him in the Sift. Even knowing he had exposed it to Eleanor, he sorted through how he should go about presenting the facts without exposing the Sift to strangers, and whether they believed him or not wasn't his problem. Arthur brought the problem to a climax.

"Now that the spirit of Leslie has departed, we should not linger over what was said or done. We first must thank the spirit of Leslie Howard for appearing, and I will now dampen the candles and have Eleanor turn on the artificial light and close the Bible to signify the end of contact with the world of spirits," Arthur said.

"Why can't we talk about what happened?" Cassady asked.

"It is detrimental to the experience of communicating with entities of the other world," Arthur replied.

"Do you want to talk about it, Eleanor?" Cassady asked.

"I, ah, I don't know," Eleanor said. "I feel confused."

"It is not permissible to converse and linger over the encounter," Arthur interjected. "I will not permit it. Sarah is exhausted and we must now depart."

Cassady was about to let it all go and talk to Eleanor later and clarify what he knew to be the truth, but Arthur was really being an idiot about the power trip thing, so he couldn't help himself.

"You're a fake, you were probably always a fake, and fifty years later you're still trying to fake people out of money,"

Cassady said, looking at Eleanor.

"Young man, you are presumptuous. You're out of line and have absolutely no idea what you're talking about. I have more experience than you'll ever understand," Arthur shouted.

"You seem to be able to talk a little faster now than during that hoax you pulled off," Cassady shouted back. "Eleanor, he's taking advantage of you. Don't believe him!"

"Cassady, please, the proof was in the rug. I had talked to Leslie about bringing one to me, and now I have proof that he was going to do that for me," Eleanor said in between the yelling.

"Eleanor, think about all the things you told Sarah and Arthur when you talked to them while you prepared for this. Did you say anything about a rug? Because I know you thought Leslie was bringing you something else," Cassady said. "You might have mentioned a rug from Lisbon would have been nice, but he couldn't have transported a rug on the plane during the war. But there was something else you knew he was bringing you, wasn't there?"

"Oh, Cassady, no one could have known that, only I have kept that secret and..."

"This is preposterous. We have finished the séance, and there is nothing left to discuss. It is detrimental to further communications," Arthur yelled.

"What it's detrimental to is you getting paid. I don't know how you pulled off the flickering light or the knocking. I read where Houdini said it's usually done with your knees. Houdini spent years of his life dedicated to exposing what he called 'vultures who prey on the bereaved.' I know she's a fake and all I ask is why you would take part in something like this? Huh? Why would you, Sarah? It's so uncool."

Sarah continued to sit quietly and refused to look up at Cassady or Eleanor.

"I'll ask you not to address the medium further, and we

must now leave."

"What was it, Cassady? What was he bringing me? I'm tired of all this and wanted to believe so badly," Eleanor said as if Arthur wasn't even there.

Cassady looked down and took a deep breath. He looked intently at Eleanor. Brie Ann reached out and touched him on the arm.

"He was bringing you a bracelet," he now spoke slowly.

"Oh, God, yes, I've never told anyone. I did mention the rug to several people over the years, and I probably did to one of these two also, I don't remember..."

"He's guessing, the little twit. He's more of a sham artist than anyone, Eleanor, don't believe him," Arthur started to say.

"Don't sound so heavy now, do you?" Cassady laughed.

"Shut up, Arthur. There is something else you can tell me, isn't there, Cassady?" Eleanor said as she looked deep into Cassady's eyes.

"Yes, he had something engraved on the inside of the bracelet," Cassady said.

"All these years I've waited..."

Cassady pushed away from the table.

Eleanor reached out to him and said, "Tell me, what did he have engraved? No one has ever known what the words were he told me he would have put on a bracelet for me in Portugal. I know it has to do with the Backlot, but how, I don't know. Please tell me. I know you know and are telling me the truth, Cassady."

"Walk with me," Cassady said in a low voice.

Cassady, Eleanor, and Brie Ann walked into the hallway. Cassady waited until he was sure they were out of hearing of the room where Arthur and Sarah still sat.

"I know you *have* seen Leslie. Please tell me what he said," Eleanor pleaded. "I didn't really doubt it, but couldn't be sure.

I know a young man like you wouldn't have had any reason to play a trick on me like this."

"He's all right, but where he is—it's like I said, the Sift is someplace bizarre, but he is part of something with my friend that I want to stop if I can and I now realize I have to try."

"What? Tell me now," Eleanor said forcefully.

"The words Leslie had inscribed on your bracelet were: *Ashley Lives!*"

"Yes, yes, yes, you are right! You couldn't know unless Leslie told you," she sobbed. "It was our little joke. It's what Scarlett said in *Gone with the Wind* when she found out Ashley was alive after the Civil War was over. For the next few years whenever Leslie would travel, he made it a point to get that message to me—that he was safe and coming back to California—but only we knew what it meant. I know it's real." Eleanor moved forward but stumbled as if she was collapsing, and Brie Ann took her arm.

"I can't tell you anything more yet, and I have to go, I have to do something myself tonight." Cassady said. "I'll tell you more another time, I'm sorry."

"You've helped me enough. But I do have one thing more to ask of you. I almost forgot, but please come back tomorrow afternoon. Since it's Saturday, can you both get away? I saw something in the paper and thought, *Well, I think it could answer some more questions for us...* I'm sorry."

"What, Eleanor? What is it?" Cassady asked.

"Can you ask some questions that have to do with communicating with Scarlett?"

"I don't think I can guarantee that yet," Cassady said slowly.

"It's all right, I understand, but please come back tomorrow. There is someone we can talk to. He might meet us and talk to us. He was extremely close to Scarlett. We can try."

"I don't know." Cassady hesitated. He felt he was losing

control of the whole thing. Eleanor knew too much, and it was scaring him. "It may not happen right away. I'll see you after we do what we can."

Brie Ann touched Cassady on the shoulder and nodded at Eleanor. "We'll be here as soon as we can, okay?"

"Yes, please, please. This is, I mean, he might have the more answers we've all looked for. If anyone had some answers, this man would."

Eleanor walked with Cassady and Brie Ann out of the door and down the path to the gate. She unlocked the gate and gave them both a hug. She immediately turned away and walked back up the house.

CHAPTER 28

Cassady and Brie Ann walked the few feet to the place where the chain-link fence met the tall MGM steel fence. He hadn't seen Kyle since the argument. Cassady had been somewhat physically ill after he stopped going in and was now feeling a little better, but they both were incredibly tired from the emotional roller coaster the night had already put Brie Ann and him through. Cassady and Brie Ann climbed up the fence to the top of the steel railing and he guided her over and down the other side. They crouched in the tall weeds and listened. They heard nothing. Almost imperceptibly the wind blew through the tall eucalyptus trees, making them sway in the dark night. The sky looked whitewashed with stars spread out over the heavens giving them enough incandescent light to see the backing shapes of the buildings and fictitious scaffolds before them.

Without a word, Brie Ann followed Cassady across the dirt path and through the grass grown up around the wooden beams and then up on the floorboard in the back of the Southern mansion. He walked with her through the front door out on the porch of Tara. After giving Brie Ann time to take in what lay in front of them and what an old dilapidated but glorious building they stood in front of, Cassady led her down the porch and down the tree-draped lane to the open area in front of Tara and the lesser mansions.

"You're right. This place is incredible, strange, spooky, but darkly beautiful."

"I knew you'd think that. I wish we were only enjoying the night in here, instead of..."

"It's okay. I get it. Where would they be? Cassady, is this where it takes place?" she asked quietly.

"It has been, but I don't know, and I also don't know if we'll see it," he answered. "They have a choice to either let us or not."

They continued walking down to the edge of the European Village and then back around to the lake. Brie Ann was now silent as they walked. The magnificence of the Backlot was almost overwhelming. It seemed like such a bizarre atmosphere even without the weirdness of the story that Cassady had told her. The Backlot's pull and magnetism were apparent to her, and she immediately understood what the boys saw in the Backlot at night. Cassady knew their mission tonight frightened her, but for him she went to great pains to not let it show as they walked through the different sets. He knew she believed him; he knew she felt she had to trust him.

"Let's head back. Maybe I can't do this, at least not this way," Cassady whispered. "I'll talk to Kyle tomorrow."

"Okay, if that's what you want to do," Brie Ann said.

"Let's walk to the far edge of the large field and stop. I want you to at least have one night and feel the experience of taking in the mansions and the full atmosphere of the Backlot at night," Cassady said.

After a minute, Cassady touched Brie Ann on the shoulder to continue, and as she took one step with him, the sky lit up, exploding with the blue azure light.

They both froze. This was a familiar sight for Cassady, but

he was nervous along with feeling the same wonderment and fear as the first time, because Brie Ann was here. The cobalt swirl began to turn into a tunnel in the sky as the light faded from blue to a light sapphire and flattened out against the ground. Cassady looked over at Brie Ann who gripped his arm tightly. He smiled and she looked at him for a second, then looked back at the sight in the field before her. She wasn't smiling, but wasn't as scared as she thought she should be, maybe because Cassady had told her what to expect. In a minute, the figures began to form out of the blue haze and Cassady then realized the seriousness of having to acknowledge to them he was breaking the Sift's cardinal rule of bringing an outsider into their world. At the same time, he comprehended that they were allowing her to see it and that had to mean something.

Out of the clouds the shapes turned and slowly formed into the people that were well known to Cassady. They dressed in the familiar splendid clothes of the deep plantation south for Brie Ann like they did months ago. The members present tonight numbered the same as most nights, several dozen, and Cassady felt they were dressed even more flamboyantly and colorfully than normal. Could they have known he was bringing someone in to see them this late evening? Cassady saw Ashley glance their way for a flash as he turned back to the group of people he was conversing with.

Cassady and Brie Ann stood there for several minutes as the gentlemen and ladies walked among themselves in the Sift, not acknowledging their presence. Cassady felt a strong pull to walk into the mist and begin a night of revelry and festivities like all the other times he had come into the Sift. He couldn't believe how strong the draw and yearning to step into the pleasures of the shadows were to him.

"Do they know we're here?" Brie Ann asked in a trancelike voice. "That man looking at us is... Leslie, I mean, Ashley, I can tell from his pictures, and that beautiful girl next to him is Scarlett, isn't she? You were right, she's unbelievable, I can tell," Brie Ann gushed.

The women wore their long dresses made of silk with sashes. Their hair shone with soft curls surrounding their lovely faces. They were frail, pale, and thin, as Cassady said. Brie Ann told Cassady she could see how they still carried themselves with an aristocratic air. Lace and ribbons draped off their dresses as they did every night, and the men all wore dazzling suits or Confederate uniforms.

"I've never seen any men with long sideburns and whiskers on their cheeks like that. The hippies at Venice Beach don't count. These men carry themselves much differently," Brie Ann said quietly. "I realize you're right, Cassady. Everyone is tall, elegant, and regal-looking. This is beyond anything you could've explained in words."

"It is, isn't it?" Cassady was glad she could see it and believe him.

"What should we do?" Brie Ann timidly asked, still intent on watching every aspect of what was transforming in front of her. "I'm scared, but I'll stay, okay?"

"Ashley will eventually come over, I hope. It's probably a test to see if we have respect for the Sift or something. But he will see who you are and will want to know what we want, if he doesn't know already."

The men and women began to glance their way more and more often. Cassady looked within the groups without trying to show his impulse to take Brie Ann by the hand and walk straight into the haze and feel the wonderful electricity and hum that the Sift provided. He was looking for Kyle and couldn't see him in tonight's party, although this was still early for him. Although he knew Kyle could be in other parts of the Sift, he also knew that didn't make sense with Scarlett here. Suddenly, Ashley and Scarlett turned and walked straight across the picturesque green lawn and stood inside the edge of the blue hue, as they had that first night long ago.

"Are we okay?" Brie Ann whispered. "I feel funny."

"Yes, it's the Sift. It's being in the same proximity as its magic," Cassady said as he reached down and took hold of her hand. He realized he was using the same language as Ashley. "As long as we don't actually go into it close is good enough."

"Excellent clarification, Cassady," Ashley said. "You've learned well. I see you will take much more away from this experience than you now know or can envision, but I must ask why are you here tonight and might I also ask, why is someone who hasn't been invited here with you? Haven't we made the rules clear for fulfilling our promise of the wonderment of the Sift to you after all this time?" Ashley asked.

"I've done what I think is right, Ashley, or should I say, Leslie?" Cassady said.

Ashley shook his head sadly and sighed. "I hope you know what you're doing Cassady, but actually I forgive you for how you've transgressed tonight. I understand that coming here was not going to be easy for you. At least not as easy for you as it became for Kyle."

"Where is Kyle?" Cassady blurted out.

The rest of the party was not quite crowding around Ashley and Scarlett, but they were looking and moving almost imperceptibly closer to the edge of the Sift and forming a loose half-circle and listening intently.

"Cassady, this is an unusual occurrence for us. We don't usually handle protocol in this manner, and I don't think, in its history, the Sift conducted business in this unorthodox way. You should be honored to have this discourse with us."

"I said, where's Kyle? Damn you!" Cassady shouted. "I don't want to hear your bullshit anymore."

"Cassady, you might say we're already dammed, but that is another matter. You can always step into the pleasure of the

Sift, and we can discuss it further,"

"I want to. I feel it with every cell in my body, but this isn't right and it never has been; I know it now," Cassady said as he squeezed Brie Ann's hand again. "I'm afraid that we might not be strong enough to resist what it brings to us."

"Very astute. You've always been very perceptive. Now, Cassady, I will answer your every question tonight, but first, we've all been terribly impolite to our new—invited or not—guest," Ashley said.

Cassady knew something was happening and was powerless to fight the force Ashley and the Sift had. He knew he had to play along with the rules Ashley laid down. He also knew Ashley, in a strange way, *had* been straight with him as far as the experience of the Sift.

"Ashley, Scarlett, this is Brie Ann, she's a friend of mine," Cassady tentatively said.

"Oh, Cassady, she is much more than a friend. Without her presence, short of you meeting her, we might not be having this conversation at all. Why, without her, you might have had the urge to join us here in the Sift and continue to enjoy the enchantment of the night, possibly every night forever," Ashley said.

"It's not my fault," Brie Ann couldn't help but say.

"Oh no, dear, we are aware of that. It's your luck to meet Cassady at this juncture of his life, and he couldn't help but bring you to the peripherals of our world. Nobody is at fault, but nevertheless, some decision must be made, and aspects of life and, I'm afraid, death, must be accepted. I have to thank you both though, for being so extraordinarily kind to my aforementioned sweet daughter. It was good of you to let her know that I think of her and love her and did love her during my time on earth," Ashley said wistfully. "Cassady, I would like to thank you also for your help in continuing to debunk the con artists and fraudulent spiritualists. Mr. Arthur Ford is one of the worst and he tried incredibly hard to take advantage of my daughter."

"Is or was she your daughter?" Cassady asked. "And how do you know what or where we were tonight?"

"In a manner of speaking. Again, as always, it's complicated. The Sift, and I must say we who live within its boundaries, have access to other realms, and when you've been aboard an aircraft that's been shot down over the Bay of Biscay, with flashing spears of light threading through your airplane killing many and causing your aircraft to plunge into the sea sinking like a stone..."

"What does this have to do with anything?" Cassady interrupted.

"Before that nightmare took place I was offered the Sift and took advantage of its pleasures. Now that I'm here I have the possibilities of eidetic visions. Not only of memory, but denoting vivid mental images of life presently outside the Sift. At times I've been able to follow your lives with visible detail."

A man stepped forward who was dressed somewhat differently than the rest of the Sift Confederate gentlemen and officers. He was a tall Black man, powerful-looking, extremely muscular under a suit that didn't fit with the Confederate regalia worn by the other participants. He looked at them with intense piercing eyes. He stood a few feet behind Scarlett, seemingly waiting for an introduction.

"Big Sam," Cassady whispered, but loudly enough for everyone to hear.

The man nodded and stepped forward.

"I would like to introduce Mr. Everett G. Brown to you. I'm assuming he has something he would like to say," Ashley said. "Although, I remember you've met."

"Yeah, I remember talking to him," Cassady said and then looking at him said, "You're a nice man. What are you doing here?"

"I enjoyed talking to you also. I wanted to say... after my initial sojourn I wasn't given a choice in the matter, young man," Mr. Brown said.

"Wait, can I ask you a question?" Cassady interrupted.

"Yes," he answered, but he glanced at Ashley and then stepped back.

"I want to know... uh, I want to... I guess... how can you take part in all this? All you did was act in a movie, but in that movie, you were a slave." Cassady threw his hands in the air as if to accentuate his point. Mr. Brown looked at them, his face becoming downcast and sad.

Stepping forward and jumping in to help Cassady, Brie Ann said, "I think he means he can't believe you'd participate for eternity as a slave. It seems so wrong. We want to know why all this is happening and why did Cassady and Kyle become involved in this and why are we seeing it? Why did they get let into the Sift?"

"Once the decision is ultimately made none of us have a choice, in a manner of speaking. What seems wonderful and beautiful can quickly become something out of control. Ashley has told you all you need to know, and some of it is inexplicable. The rest is incomprehensible, so even Ashley and Scarlett can't explain it to you. You have to simply accept it as true. And we simply converse with a few, but in the manner we choose and are allowed to. You should leave and never come back. With or without your friend," Mr. Brown said as if in a final manner.

"You were so nice the night we talked. You're not below these people," Cassady said.

"Yes, I was in over forty movies, most of them unaccredited and usually treated like garbage by the very people I was working for..."

"There are many other dimensions to the Sift that you can learn to appreciate and come to know if you wish," Ashley said, interrupting and spreading his arms.

"But Mr. Brown, help me, can you? I want to know where Kyle is and what is going on tonight. Why isn't he here?"

Cassady asked.

"Your friend has made a choice that he might very well regret, but if you can help him," Mr. Brown said. "Maybe..." Ashley moved up in front of Mr. Brown with an ugly expression on his face.

"That's enough, Big Sam. You aren't helping here. Why don't you go back to the party?" Ashley said.

Looking from Ashley to Cassady and Brie Ann, Mr. Brown said, "I'm not Big Sam and I'm not even Everett Brown. It's bad enough I'm participating in this horror, but I'm not going to rope this boy and girl into your repulsion. And there's not a damn thing you can do to me that hasn't already been done."

"Wait, Mr. Brown, what do you mean?" Cassady asked. "Can you help me?"

"Don't think that slavery is the worst that can happen. It was the worst for millions of good people. This doesn't show what a true slaveholder plantation was like. You don't have to be a historian to know that. What's happening here... The decisions we make, the choices that you make here and now in your life, can last an eternity," Mr. Brown said, shaking his head.

"That's enough," Ashley shouted, turning to look at Mr. Brown.

"I'll have my say. *This*," he said looking back over his shoulder at the party. "Doesn't show the horrible cruelties of slavery, or a family separated, or bloody whippings. And this was numbers in the millions. Body parts hacked off for attempting to escape, women raped to produce more children for the plantation. Even beautiful Tara would have had involuntary breeding! Every character in this damn movie was a shallow silly depiction of *real* people and we all made the same mistake your friend has made."

Mr. Brown started to walk away and then stopped. He turned and said in a powerful voice, "The cruelty of Satan, who seeks by all means to devour us, is overcome by watchfulness and faith."

The change in Ashley was immediate and powerful. As he had appeared before to Cassady, he reddened horribly in anger and bellowed at Mr. Brown's back as he turned again and walked away. "Never quote that book, and never speak to this boy and girl again. Leave now and don't return!"

"Who are you?" Brie Ann cried.

"You're not really Ashley, are you!" Cassady said, but not as a question. "And you're definitely not really Leslie Howard, are you? Eleanor is not your daughter. What you are is either devils or phantoms but maybe more than that." Cassady said. It made him sick to his stomach to say this, for himself, for Eleanor, but mostly for Kyle. "I was right when I told Kyle that this is genuine evil come to life."

Yet again, the change in Ashley was immediate and powerful. He grew several inches, darkened exceedingly in fury, and roared at them. Out beyond the hues, colors, and wonders of the Sift raised another realm—one that Cassady and Brie Ann could view clearly. Smoke billowed up from what looked like lava and magma. Plumes of smoke, not the beauty of the Sift, but ugly, blurred, murky dark fire raging, and the barely heard but distinguished screams of millions of damned souls crying out filled their ears. Shadows without bodies were floating in the ominous inferno. The smell wafted up and over them, making Brie Ann gag and choke and then vomit. In another instant, it was gone and the tranquility of the Sift was back.

"Who are you?" Cassady cried. He wanted to run and take Brie Ann with him, but he couldn't.

"I am who you think I am. You thought this was all for fun and games. But you're learning, and as the Bard says, "Tis now the very witching time of night, when churchyards yawn and hell itself breathes out Contagion to this world,'" Ashley said, laughing like the demon he obviously was.

"You're not really Ashley, are you!" Cassady said again. He knew in his heart it was much, much worse than that. "And you're definitely not really Leslie Howard, are you? What you are is either a devil or phantom but maybe worse than that." It made him sick to his stomach to say this and realize what they had done and gotten themselves into.

Suddenly, Ashley shrank done to his normal size and pale color. As if knowing what Cassady was thinking, he bowed and swept his arm to his side. "Kyle will be here when it is time for him to arrive, and I'm afraid we must also take our leave. Cassady, it has been a pleasure, but with you not joining us and deciding to stay out of the Sift's magnificence and glory, I must bid you goodnight and good luck in all your future endeavors,"

"Were you a spy in World War II?" Cassady blurted out. "Were you shot down? How did you know your daughter wanted to know about the bracelet? And needed to know about it?" He wanted to keep the conversation going and tried anything to not have it end until he knew what was happening here.

Ashley simply shrugged and said, "I can be whoever I need to be..."

"And you're not really Vivien Leigh, are you?" Cassady asked, instantly knowing they wouldn't answer these questions. "Wait, please answer me. Where is Kyle and are you saying he's going to stay in the Sift?"

"Yes, he has decided to join, chosen to remain with us, and we know you will handle the grief of his family and friends like the gentleman you are, Cassady. These events were determined long ago, and there is no culpability involved. But I know you two will handle it like the gentleman and lady you are." Ashley drifted off.

The pain in Cassady's stomach suddenly got worse. His fear grew large and foreboding and grew immense inside him.

"Wait, what are you saying?"

"No remorse. Kyle is where he wants to be. We possess his nephesh."

"Cassady, I'm sorry it didn't work out like we wanted, but I've enjoyed our time together. I'm glad you have Brie Ann with you," Scarlett said condescendingly, nodding at both Brie Ann and Cassady.

"Wait, please," Cassady said.

"Good night and good luck," Scarlett continued, but as she did she smiled wickedly and said, "Don't you know, 'Hell is empty and all the devils are here.'"

The Sift flashed brightly and then the swirl reversed itself, and the figures clouded up and faded. The mist turned to its familiar cobalt blue and whirled around into the soaring tunnel and flattened out and weakened. The clear blue light flashed in an indistinguishable illumination, fading gradually, as it disappeared. Soon nothing was left in the field in front of the old decrepit mansion but a weak vapor and haze, already fading into the darkness. The grass was yellow, brown, dry, and dying. Nothing was left but a slight breeze murmuring through the eucalyptus trees in the nighttime.

CHAPTER 29

They walked through the alleys and streets without the ability to speak a word. Cassady didn't know what to say. Brie Ann was dizzy with all she had experienced and felt worried and didn't know what to say either, so they both walked muted. They went the back way down the alleys, skirting Kyle's house without discussing it. As they walked up Cassady's driveway, he had the idea to leave Brie Ann in the Shack and then go back to Kyle's house and find out what was happening. But as he looked up he could see his dad standing in the dark by the gate. Brie Ann slowed down behind him.

They looked at each other and his dad shook his head, seeming to think he knew where Cassady had been and immediately forgiving him for being out with Brie Ann so late, and said, "Cassady, I'm sorry."

"What?" Cassady said. "Sorry, for what?"

"Where have you been? Don't you know what happened?" His dad was obviously in some sort of shock. His shoulders dropped and sank as if his whole body shrunk several inches. His hands covered his eyes.

"What? Tell me what?" Cassady felt like he had been slammed in the stomach without even hearing whatever it was that his dad was going to say.

"I hoped I'd never have to be the one to tell you something like this. I thought you knew. I'm so sorry, Cassady..."

"What?"

"I'm sorry, Cassady, but Kyle was killed in a bike accident while crossing Sepulveda Boulevard with Lucas late this afternoon."

Cassady fell into his dad's arms and sobbed, "No, no, no!"

"It'll be all right, son, it'll be all right."

But Cassady broke away and ran down the driveway. His dad yelled at him, but he didn't stop. He ran down his street, down the alley and across Center Street, and up the walkway to Kyle's house. He stopped running when he came to the screen door, the door he had snuck up to and looked in without being seen millions of times before. He looked into the living room and saw Kyle's mom and Lucas sitting on the couch. A light was on in the kitchen, and there were people sitting around the kitchen table talking in low whispered voices. Kyle's mom looked up as if she knew he was going to be there.

"I've been waiting for you, Cassady," she said in a soft voice.

Cassady opened the screen door and walked in and sat down next to her. She put her arm around him and held him as he cried.

"I don't understand..." Lucas was repeating over and over. Cassady didn't have the faintest idea as to what to say. He had never lost anyone before and could never have imagined losing someone under these absurd horrible unworldly circumstances. He felt as if his world was ending and he was being gutted from the inside out. Cassady sat and let the tears drip down his cheek and couldn't say anything other than, "I'm sorry, I'm sorry."

"I've probably repeated the details of what happened to Kyle to everyone who's come to the house tonight. They've brought food and made snacks and drinks. I have a dozen frozen casseroles already, but I don't remember to whom I've talked about it and to whom I haven't. I start to talk to someone and they tell me back details that they couldn't have known unless I'd already told them. Does that make sense, Cassady?" Kyle's mom said.

"You haven't told me," he answered. He immediately wished he hadn't said that and really didn't know if he wanted to know.

Kyle's mom swallowed hard. "I know. Kyle and Lucas were riding their bikes over to Tito's Tacos at Washington Place and Sepulveda. I don't know why I think that's important, probably because I know it's one of your favorite places to eat. As they went out into the intersection, Kyle, of course, jumped the light as soon as it turned green. Lucas saw a car coming fast. He thought it looked like the car was going to run the red light and yelled for him to stop, but he said Kyle kept going and never wavered. Lucas said it was almost like he couldn't hear him or didn't care the car would hit him. He flew about ten or more feet off his bike when the car hit him. When I went to the hospital to identify him..." She stopped and cried for a minute. Cassady sat without moving and waited.

"There were a couple of teeth missing and bruises, but he still looked like Kyle." She stopped again and blew her nose. "I thought he would be completely torn up, but the impact didn't tear him up at all like I'd thought." Cassady couldn't bring the picture to his mind. He agreed with her and assumed Kyle would always look like Kyle. "It doesn't matter now. I know you are going to miss him as much as we are, Cassady."

He still didn't say anything. She patted him on the back and left to make another couple of phone calls. Cassady couldn't understand how this was happening. It didn't feel real. Nothing had felt tangible since the day they entered the Sift, and he had this overpowering need to scream at them about the Sift and tell all their secrets. He wondered if it would make a difference. Should they know? Would they believe it? Cassady was running the accident through his head and had the worst, most unrelenting fear that Kyle had wanted to die, that he had to die because he had been invited. He had accepted the invitation. Maybe he was powerless to stop the accident. There was only one way to permanently remain in the Sift.

He stayed the night with Lucas. They sat in the bedroom they so often had shared without saying much. He assumed Kyle's mom talked to his dad sometime during the night.

That next night, long after his parents went to sleep, he walked the familiar walk down the back alleys and streets until he found himself at Arizona and Elenda and climbed the fence. Cassady didn't even glance at Eleanor's house. He walked through the back of Tara and out into the open field and waited for hours.

"They could be here and not allow me to see or feel their presence. Kyle could be right next to me. Ashley isn't going to allow me to see him again," Cassady said to himself, but out loud, hoping Kyle would maybe respond to his fervent wish.

The night was eerily familiar but distorted. Not like the transformation that occurred when they first encountered the Sift, but in a way that made the manifestation of normality ugly and sad. The trees swayed and the breeze wafted, but without the comfort of familiarity. He continued to wait until he was certain the Sift wasn't going to return. They weren't going to let him in again. He felt forsaken. He walked back home without the assurance that time had paused—it was almost morning. The next few days he kept away from everyone, including Brie Ann, and didn't go to school.

The day of the funeral Cassady walked over to Kyle's house an hour early because his family asked Cassady to drive to the funeral home and sit with them during the service. They drove together silently and sadly out on Culver Boulevard from Center Street and then a right two blocks down on Sepulveda and then only another block to the mortuary. As they pulled into the entrance, Cassady realized he could have easily jumped his backyard fence as he had a hundred times to go to his grandmother's apartment across Sepulveda on Tuller Avenue. When they pulled into the Gates, Kingsley & Gates parking lot, he glanced back and saw the library annex where he had met Brie Ann. It seemed like years ago.

After everyone arrived at the service the atmosphere was depressing and dark. He took his place next to Lucas in the front row. They glanced at each other and Cassady reached out and lightly patted his knee. Tears sprung from Lucas's eyes, and he nodded and looked away. Every person Cassady could think of was there. Every member of Kyle's family, some from out of California, Gram and his sisters, their parents, his own parents, Regis, Abilene, George, Donovan, several of Kyle's teachers, and dozens of people he didn't recognize. Brie Ann was with a classmate Cassady didn't know—he assumed for support—she was quickly introduced as Desiree. The name didn't register with him.

Suddenly, he noticed the casket was open. He would be able to see Kyle one last time. On each side of the casket, two tall candles were burning. Brie Ann walked up beside him and handed him a piece of paper. Cassady put it in his pocket and looked up. She smiled and went back to her seat with her friend. He didn't know the family even had a minister or were religious at all until a man in a black suit walked up to the podium. Religion had never come up in conversation with Kyle's mom or dad, or Cassady's family either.

After that, he didn't hear a thing that was said. The words washed over him but he couldn't concentrate on what was spoken. One thought crashed through his brain. He had to get up and shake Kyle awake, or at least shout the minister down and tell everyone it was a mistake. Cassady could knock this old man down and take over the service and tell everyone what had happened. He'd confess everything and they could see that it wasn't his fault.

But deep inside, Cassady thought it might very well have been his responsibility. He should have tried harder to keep Kyle from making the choice he did. It was guilt that was dominating his thoughts, and Cassady hadn't yet realized you don't have to *be* guilty to feel guilty. He thought of Kyle being in the Sift while the preacher droned on about a boy he had probably never met. Cassady longed to believe the Sift was something that had happened to another mysterious person and not Kyle, but some part of Cassady would eternally be close with Kyle. Now its buildings became Kyle's refuge, its landscape Kyle's haven, and only its memories were Cassady's reality. He understood his life would never be the same. This was his certainty, to never forget. To survive this, he'd have to stop everything—believing, feeling, existing, loving, and being—and become nothing. After the service was over, he stood up with Kyle's family, followed them up to the casket, and walked by without looking down at Kyle.

When he got home that afternoon, he opened the note Brie Ann had given him. It said, 'I found this poem and thought of us and, no matter what, I think you should think of Kyle when you read it:'

> *I give you this one thought to keep. I am with you still—I do not weep. I am a thousand winds that blow. I am the diamond glints on snow. I am the sunlight on ripened grain. I am the gentle rain. When you awaken in the morning's hush, I am the swift uplifting rush of quiet birds in circled flight. I am the soft stars that shine at night. Do not think of me as gone—I am with you still—in each new dawn.*

After Kyle's funeral, Cassady stopped talking. Completely. He slept eighteen hours a day and when he was awake, he lay on his back looking up at the ceiling in the Shack in the garage and stared at nothing. He felt as if the Shack could separate itself from the garage and he could float away, realizing not a person in the world, even Brie Ann, could find him, talk to him, or ask him how he felt.

Cassady had an outwardly complete breakdown. After several days, he occasionally nodded for answers. He'd eat a few bites or sip some water and then look away. Brie Ann visited twice, but wasn't comfortable, not knowing what to say, and vacillated between telling what had happened, and not knowing what they would think of her either.

"I don't know what to say. Please talk to me," Brie Ann said on the last day she was allowed to see Cassady. She reached over and touched his arm.

"Don't tell," he whispered and closed his eyes.

Before his father led her out, she leaned over quickly and whispered, "I won't, I promise. I love you." Brie Ann continued to try to visit him, but her parents forbade her to go to his house, telling her it wasn't healthy.

Over a week later, a doctor came in to see him. Cassady initially didn't talk. The doctor continued to ask questions and it seemed to wear him down. He comprehended this was not the time to talk about the Sift, but he couldn't very well not talk at this point. He thought he'd play it off as his mourning for Kyle and being really tired. All he could think about was that the doctor's overgrown eyebrows covered his whole forehead.

"Cassady, do you know why you don't want to get up and join the rest of your family?" the doctor asked.

Nothing.

"Do you think this had to do with your friend being killed?" Asking obvious questions trying to get him to talk. "Do you feel guilty about his accident? Did you have an argument with him before he was killed and feel badly about that?"

"He wasn't killed. He was taken," Cassady suddenly whispered in a hoarse voice.

"Excuse me, I was told he was killed on his bicycle. No?"

The floodgates opened. He didn't think about what he was saying. Cassady couldn't control what he was saying, and he purposely wouldn't stop what he was saying. He didn't consider the ramifications of what he was saying. It was a stream of consciousness outburst that included everything that had happened to them. He confessed in detail about every day since Kyle and he went into the Sift and how the people in the Sift revealed themselves to be evil spirits and then took Kyle into the Sift. His confession had been well rehearsed by telling both Miss Rigby and Brie Ann. It went on for twenty minutes. The doctor was not able to stop him and was having trouble understanding anything of what he was saying.

Finally, he was able to discern a few things from the outburst and ask a question as Cassady took a pause for breath. "Certainly, Cassady, you don't believe you met Vivien Leigh and Leslie Howard and others from *Gone with the Wind*, do you?"

"Not only did I meet them. I've spent hundreds of hours of my life with them and have gone for hours and hours during the night for months and have all the energy I want every day. It was no problem until I stopped going." He never mentioned Brie Ann, and later he was glad he didn't. He hoped he saved her from the indignity of trying to explain what had happened. Cassady continued for another long period, more or less talking to himself while the doctor stood up and outside the door to the Shack talked to Cassady's parents. They didn't try to hide their own hysteria and talked without realizing that Cassady could hear every word they said.

"What's wrong with him, what's he doing and talking about?" his mom asked frantically.

"He's definitely had a psychotic break or episode," the doctor said. "I suggest he go to a hospital immediately."

"What does that mean?" his mom asked. "What's a psychotic break?"

"Hearing, seeing, or believing things that others either don't see or know to be real. It seems to be persistent. These are extremely unusual thoughts and visions far beyond a hallucination. Cassady's fantasy world is quite detailed, realistic, and almost convincing, if still preposterous. His brain is basically in an overload gear right now. I think it could be coupled with the grief and death of his friend. It seems Cassady doesn't want to accept that reality. It can be common with loved ones or close friends. Were they close?"

"They were inseparable," his dad said.

"That kind of loss and trauma could account for this manifestation. He's obviously exhausted. Do you know if he and his friend actually ever went into, or as he stated, *snuck* into the MGM Backlot here in Culver City?" Cassady took a quick look at his parents while they both shrugged and looked at the doctor and waited.

"It doesn't actually matter, at this point," he said. "There is a place I think it might be advantageous for Cassady to go for a while to get the help he needs."

Cassady was taken to Camarillo State Mental Hospital north of Los Angeles, near Oxnard.

CHAPTER 30

Cassady was led into his new residence without his parents. They had left him at the small reception building, and he followed along the walkways that traversed the spacious green lawns, grounds, and surroundings of the massive hospital buildings.

"This is what they call the House of Style. It was built in 1934," the hospital aide said, talking incessantly like Cassady was on a tour instead of being committed. "That's the Bell Tower. It was built in 1936. The kitchen and dining area are attached to the South Quad and the rest of the South and North Quads were built in the next decade. We will now proceed to the Receiving and Treatment Buildings. Last year, the Adolescent Division was separated from the Children's Division and now we have four different treatment units and an exclusive school for all grades. I assume that's what you will also start attending after admittance."

All Cassady saw were the bars and layers of grates on every door and window up through several stories on each building. After being escorted through several wings and then admitted to the hospital in Receiving, they left him sitting for an hour or more while people came and went.

While waiting, Cassady was given a bag lunch consisting

of a tuna sandwich, Fritos, chocolate pudding, an apple, and a carton of milk. More time passed, and he was finally taken to another part of the hospital by a nurse who didn't say anything except, "follow me." In the next building, all his belongings were taken and bagged. He asked for the book he brought with him, *To Kill a Mockingbird*. He was told it would be given to him once it was scrutinized and he was assigned a room. He was stripped, examined, and a blood sample along with vitals taken. He was allowed to shower with an escort supervising, who was actually very polite, and finally taken to the psychiatric ward in the Boys Adolescent Division. Cassady was introduced to the daytime staff, whose names were a blur, and shown his room down a long hallway. It had two single beds, two desks, chairs, and a closet on each side of the room. A standup lamp was next to each bed and desk. It was one of a dozen rooms overseen by four nurses, two female and two male. Cassady was told his door would remain open, and he would be observed regularly throughout the night. Even though it was only early evening he was given a sedative and out of sheer exhaustion and misery he fell immediately asleep.

In the morning, awakened at six o'clock, Cassady met an aide who told him his name was Julian.

"Here are your toiletries," he said, showing Cassady a plastic bag. "Put them in your top drawer and use them every morning. It contains a bar of soap, shampoo, toothpaste, a toothbrush, and deodorant. Try not to lose them or misplace them; if your roommate steals yours let one of us know. If there are problems with them, you'll have to ask for them at the station every morning. Don't let that happen. It's a big hassle." Cassady started to smile thinking of Kyle's mom panicking and taking away all their spray deodorant, but looked over at Julian staring, and stopped.

"Are you into hassles?"

"No," Cassady said. Julian looked hard at him for a moment.

"I don't think so, no I don't think so at all," Julian said. "After hygiene, we'll line up for breakfast. You guys all line up and we go down together. A straight line all the way. Don't get out of line. It's a hassle. When we get in the dining hall, get your food and sit down and eat. You can eat with friends, if you have any. No hassles at breakfast or any of the meals. There're four or five of us watching. We don't like anyone hassling anyone. Understand?"

"Yes, I understand. I don't want to hassle anyone."

"Good, go ahead, use the bathroom, we're late. I'll take you down to breakfast myself after you're done."

During breakfast, Cassady ate by himself, alone at a table, and didn't look around. It wasn't anything like the breakfasts he and Kyle and Lucas made. He could tell the other kids were looking at him and talking about him. Nobody came over to talk to him and he was grateful for that. After he was settled in, within an hour, he was seen by a shrink who made a big deal out of identifying himself as a doctor but didn't even give Cassady his name. They met in another room down at the end of the long hallway in what was called the Reflection Room. He quickly went over Cassady's essentials, like name, address, his parent's names and phone number, his age, sex, height, weight, hair and eye color, grade in school, and last but not least, his admitting diagnosis: emotionally unstable personality disorder (EUPD) with an overall diagnosis of depression.

"The majority of the day here will be utilized learning coping and survival skills and speaking about your life with the professionals on staff, including myself. We will make a list of medications for you to take and you will be watched to make sure you take them. Don't make the staff force you to take it." Cassady couldn't conceive of making his life any harder than it already was. He was thinking about how to get out as soon as he had arrived.

"I won't be a hassle to anybody," Cassady said.

"Good. I'm glad you've met Julian," he said, but without the slightest sign of a smile. "He's one of the straightest shooters here. Listen to him. If you've seen the general-purpose lobby—you can earn time by watching an hour or two of television. You can also read, the lobby has books. Do your homework in your room with the door open. We'll check on you. If you don't read you can sit quietly and meditate on yourself. You *cannot* sleep. I repeat—you cannot sleep during the day. After a week, you will start school. You earn that also. Believe me, it's better than sitting around here all day. Please don't create distractions."

"Hassles."

"Exactly. Your roommate is not here right now because of that. He should be here later today though, I haven't checked yet. Now let me ask you a question, Cassady. Why do you think you're here?"

Cassady thought. He remembered when a school counselor called Kyle incorrigible one time, and Kyle jumped up and started to hit the dirtbag, but stopped realizing that's exactly what he wanted him to do. So Cassady immediately comprehended it would be healthier to stop talking about the Sift and meeting Scarlett, Ashley, and the others. He continued to have dreams about the Sift every night. It felt so real, but it also instantly felt to be in his best interest to not repeat what he had said to the asshole doctor who had him committed. He already couldn't remember what he was feeling then. It already seemed like weeks ago.

"I said some crazy things to a doctor. I think I was, or maybe I *went* crazy when my best friend died. That's all I think happened," Cassady said.

"Well, we'll talk about this some more in group and individually. I'm just checking you in. Do you have any questions for me?"

"I think it would be nice or polite to know your name?"

"My name isn't important, but it's Dr. Jones." He got up

and walked out the door. *What an asshole*, Cassady thought. He hoped every doctor in here wasn't an asshole. With the one at home, he'd met two already. He might have to learn to watch what he said around here.

When his roommate showed up later on that first day, it continued to reinforce the feelings he was having. Ezra was super skinny, had bad acne, and talked wildly, at times incoherently, but talk he did. Cassady laughed a great deal listening to Ezra.

"Man, this is crazy, I'm from Culver City too." Ezra started to tell Cassady Culver City stories the first minute they met. "You know my brothers Joe or Harold? It doesn't matter..." He barely took a breath. "I got nailed for stealing a car and then I fought the cops. They had me in juvie, but I got out and escaped, then I broke into the Surprise Store on Washington and stole a bunch of clothes and stuff and took them to the hippie store on the boardwalk in Venice and got busted again. Back in juvie I started to act crazy..."

"How?" Cassady asked. "Why?"

"This is better than juvie. It's easy, do things like say everything is groovy—I mean all the time, to every question you're asked or even when you're not asked. And get upset at things that don't really make sense or bother you, and then calm down fast and sit quietly for long periods of time doing nothing. Why, I mean, are you really crazy? I mean, why are you here?"

"No, I mean... I had a hard time for a while," Cassady said. Julian stuck his head in the door and said, "Ezra, it's time to see the doc."

As he was leaving, Ezra turned to Cassady and said, "Remember, when you see Dr. Howard, be sure to tell him about the new doctor who found one of his patients lying on the ground beaten, bloody, booted, and out cold."

"What?" Cassady asked.

"Yeah, he found him knocked out bleeding in one of the rooms down the hall, and the first thing he said was, 'My God, whoever did this must get psychological help immediately.'"

Cassady glided into a familiar and yet similar reality. He constantly wondered if Kyle was still in the Sift, and if so, what was happening to him now. Cassady also wondered if coming out of the Sift after all that time was collective and sent him over the edge. Or was it Kyle being dead? Where he was now was similar in some ways. It felt real and looked real, but the people around him were either a little bit crazy, pathologically insane, or for lack of a better term lazily identified as delinquents.

After several days, another doctor came to see Cassady. They sat down in the private counseling room.

"How are you this morning, Cassady? My name is Dr. Howard."

"Good," he answered. A doctor who told him his name was a positive start. He went through a series of questions: did Cassady feel suicidal? Did he have thoughts or urges of violence toward himself or others? He replied in the negative to all the questions. He didn't ask about hallucinations though.

"Now, let's talk about why you're here, shall we?"

Cassady nodded.

"I think you should tell me exactly what you can about going into the..." He looked at his notes, "The Backlots in Culver City, and why that is important or how it relates to your friend's death."

"Well, I don't think it really does. It was a fantasy we cooked up while we snuck in."

"How's that?" He asked.

"We snuck in at night and started to talk about who made movies there and I researched it and found many of the actors and actresses that were dead—we could fantasize about meeting them. It became part of the game."

"So, you don't believe it really happened?" Dr. Howard asked.

"No, of course not. I went crazy about Kyle dying and don't remember or know *why* I said the things I did. But I guess I made it up to freak everyone out and... I don't know."

"What got you in here, I feel, was that you gave the appearance of someone who has gone through a severe trauma of some sort. We used to call it a moral invalid crisis or an incident that overwhelms the mind and causes a period of oblivion. That would fit, but grief can explain many of the episodes that look like trauma. What do you think, Cassady?"

"I don't know, but I don't quite see it that way."

"Would you say you were emotionally attached to your friend?"

"Yes, we were close and I miss him."

"Do you think you're going to be okay? What do you think or how do you feel about your friend now?"

"Yeah, I'll be okay. I miss Kyle and I think life will be harder without him in it," Cassady said sadly. "But I want to move on. And that has to be without him."

"We'll try and help you make that transition. We'll talk every week or so, maybe more if I think you need to. Right now you seem in control of yourself. Be careful of some of your peers here," Dr. Howard said as he was going out the door. "You should know that Ezra, along with other issues, is a pathological liar."

Cassady quickly realized Ezra, like many of his hospital companions, was actually fairly smart, but off a little. Many of his friends back in Culver City were essentially like these guys. They learned to cope better. He also learned this world he now existed in had many of the same attributes as the Sift, but he learned he'd have to differentiate between this physical world, the outside world, and the illusory world of the Sift. He sat through the support group therapy classes along with the supposed academic classes without saying much and trying to simply get along, which he felt was the best policy for managing not being crazy. Studying turned out to be a safe haven, so Cassady developed habits he had never had before and it looked good.

During the next weeks, Julian also often talked to Cassady during the down times. Looking through the small library one day, Cassady spotted a book he had heard about many times but had never had the chance to read. It was *One Flew Over the Cuckoo's Nest* by Ken Kesey. George's sister Martha had read it and he remembered her talking about it at Gram's house one night. He read it straight through in the next two days.

"You like that story?" Julian asked him when he was almost done with it.

"Yeah, I can't believe they let us read it," Cassady answered.

"You're probably one of the few that reads anyway, and *they* don't have any idea what's donated to this place."

"Yeah, I guess so. But it seems weird reading this in here."

"How's it going with Dr. Howard?" Julian asked. Dr. Howard did become the main doctor Cassady saw weekly now.

"Good," he said. "He's not an asshole."

"That's good. It's important to get along with him. I mean, he has power in here, and if he likes you, that's good. And remember, young man, don't lose your laugh, 'cause like he says in the book, 'Man, when you lose you laugh, you lose your footing,'" Julian said, chuckling and walking away.

Right after Julian said that and Cassady was scanning *Cuckoo's Nest* for that quote Ezra came over with a boy named Brook and plopped down across from him.

"Hey check it out. Brook has a joke he heard. Go ahead, tell him, Brook," Ezra said.

Brook was a really huge overweight guy with rolls around his stomach that bowled over his belt. He had to sit with his legs apart. He was essentially, in fact, a nice guy, but never talked normal and only communicated with jokes. He seemed to know a million of them. Everyone gave him some space. Once in a while he'd go off though and couldn't be controlled by anyone, so nobody really messed with him. Cassady assumed Ezra befriended him for protection.

Brook took a couple of deep breaths and started. "So, this doctor was taking a newbie, a possible admittee, around the hospital. Dig it, he wasn't yet determined to be a patient. They wanted to see how he reacted to the place. It was a test, see? The doctor asked him a question. 'We fill up a bathtub with water and then we give you a teaspoon, a cup, and a medium-sized pail. What would you use to empty the bathtub in the quickest way possible?' So the boy answers, 'I'd use the pail of course.' The doctor immediately has the boy restrained and taken to a room. As the boy is carried away he's screaming, 'What did I say was wrong?' The doctor said, 'Oh, you didn't say anything wrong, but you wouldn't use the pail, you'd obviously simply pull the plug in the drain, you crazy fucking bastard. Welcome to Camarillo!'" Brook tried to sit up, but had to rock his large body to make it. He never laughed out loud, but a small smile showed through his fat cheeks and brown teeth. Cassady laughed along with Ezra.

CHAPTER 31

The weeks rolled by. Cassady initially got a letter every week from Brie Ann. He never answered them. His parents were on his ass constantly to answer her. They visited every Sunday afternoon. He couldn't explain it to them or himself.

"Please, send her a note. She's a very nice girl, and she's concerned about you. Why won't you put her on your visiting list?" his mom asked him for several weeks.

"I can't. I don't deserve her and don't want to have her involved in this mess," was all he would say until his non-answers finally won the argument and they stopped asking and the letters stopped coming. He did well in the academic classes and contributed as well as he could in the group sessions. Cassady didn't genuinely have to contribute much to make the appearance of participating. So many times, the sessions collapsed into anarchy, and sitting quietly while someone else went off looked good on his record. In the individual sessions, Cassady kept the same refrain of his depression about Kyle's death and said he didn't remember why he brought up the Backlot fantasy with the doctor his parents had committed him with. It seemed to work in the long run. He thought he had convinced them that he couldn't even remember the incident.

Every other day Julian and two other aides took the boys on Cassady's wing out for physical education. A doctor was supposed to oversee the class but rarely accompanied them. They could play basketball, do calisthenics, play catch with a softball, or sit around the court and do nothing. Julian tried every session to get a few of them to jog around the playing field. He was rarely successful. Julian had played football on a scholarship at UCLA, but tore his shoulder up and now ran diligently for fitness. After the third time of being asked, Cassady agreed to run with him. He was tired from not doing anything but listening to the other boys bitch, moan, and complain. He thought of the long bike rides he and Kyle used to take and the unknown veiled energy that must have taken, and what good shape they must have been in without realizing it.

"C'mon you're thin and can do it. I remember you bragged about riding your bike with your friend all over the place. We'll go easy for a couple of loops," Julian prodded.

"All right, all right," Cassady said.

They decided to run a little over three miles. Julian had measured it out over the years of running every day. The distance was agreed upon because of Cassady's biking background. They started off at a slow jog. As the distance increased nothing prepared Cassady for the excruciating pain and lactic acid distress of that last mile. He and Julian had forgotten about his numerous weeks of sedentary life in the hospital. As Cassady's wheezing continued to grow worse, not a word was spoken other than Julian asking a soft question if he was all right and wanted to continue. Cassady nodded vigorously, although he didn't truly think he would be able to finish. After it was over, Cassady collapsed on the grass and almost passed out. He had played pickup games and one sport or another since elementary school. Even when getting high with friends they always made time to ride bikes, go swimming, or play pickup games at Vet's Park. But nothing compared to the larger-than-life feeling of having actually run three miles without stopping.

"You should never have to run less than that now," Julian said.

Unbelievable, Cassady thought. His parents sent him a pair of new shoes for running. They were called Adidas blue Jaguars. He loved them, and he never missed a run with Julian, now almost every day. Others attempted to join them, but no one stayed with it like Cassady did. He even ran on Julian's days off and felt free from the pressures of the hospital while he ran.

"You people represent the oppressive force in modern society and I think you're no better than Dr. Mengele," Brook yelled one day in group. A young doctor was running the day's therapy session. He was new. He forgot to tell them his name.

"I don't think that's accurate in the least, but why do you think that, Brook?" the young doctor said. Dr. Howard was watching him, probably evaluating him.

"You can't answer a statement like that with, 'I don't think that's accurate' and a question," Fred said. Fred was really crazy. He had told Cassady he was sent to Camarillo because he studied too hard. He tried to study twenty hours a day before being committed. Fred *was* smart, but angry and often outraged.

"Why do you say that, Fred?" the doctor asked him.

"Who do you want to answer? Brook, for calling you a Nazi or me, for questioning you for asking him a stupid question?" Fred said.

"How about you answer first and we can get back to Brook?"

"I think that if everyone who's been disillusioned in love were sent to Camarillo, all the rooms would be filled up within an hour or so," Fred said.

"I'm not following you, Fred. Could you clarify that?" the doctor asked. Cassady saw Dr. Howard writing something down.

"When I was growing up, all I heard was study, study, study. Get good grades, get good grades, push, push, push!" Fred started.

"I thought we were talking about being, what did you say, 'disappointed in love'?" the doctor said.

"No, no, no. I said *disillusioned* in love! Shithead!"

"Could you clarify that for me?"

"No!" Fred screamed.

"Okay, we'll come back to that another time." He was completely flustered.

"Cassady, do you have anything to add to the discussion?" Dr. Howard asked him, jumping in and helping an obviously relieved young doctor. Cassady sincerely liked Dr. Howard of all the ones that had come through the days and nights.

"The only thing I can contribute, I think, is we're all chronics or acutes. Maybe we're machines with flaws and maybe we can't be repaired. The faults are born in, or maybe they're theoretically beaten into us."

"I see someone's done some reading," Dr. Howard said. "Do you think that's true, Cassady? Was Ken Kesey correct? Or maybe Chief Bromden? Is it irredeemable?"

"No, not really. We can learn to adapt and change," Cassady said sheepishly. "And we can improve with time and help." Dr. Howard nodded.

"Sorry to interrupt the love fest, but I have something to say to Fred," Brook said loudly. Cassady was, once again, glad the focus was taken off him and thanked his cohorts in the group for saving him by acting out.

"Not about Nazi doctors, Brook. Please spare us that again."

"Okay, but how 'bout this? I've heard that we should dance like there's nobody watching, sing like there's nobody listening, love like you've never been hurt, and live like it's heaven on earth."

"That's very nice Brook. Thank you for that," Dr. Howard started to say.

"But... but... none of those people I parroted are here to vouch for us when we end up in Camarillo Insane Asylum!"

At these times, the noise and yelling rose to a crescendo and the screaming and several times fights broke out. Not every group session, but many descended into bedlam. Cassady was reminded of the craziness of Gram's house, stoned or not. He knew from experience to sit out the aggression and madness and display how to remain calm.

Later Ezra told him a story about Brook.

"Do you still not remember who he is?"

"No, why, should I?"

"Yeah, man. He's the Bozo the Clown kid from years ago."

"What?"

"The Bozo the Clown guy. He's fat and scary now, but he really wasn't a nice guy even then. Remember that show... almost ten years or so ago."

"Yeah, vaguely."

"Yeah, yeah. TV was live then, and they didn't have any delay or whatever they can use. We were little then, but sometimes they let kids in the area be on the show. Brook was on and he was as mean then as he is now. Most of the kids were happy as shit to be there, but not him. During the show Brook was sitting there crossed-legged and his head in his hands looking down, and the stupid Bozo is trying to get him involved in some kind of game or something and starts bugging him. 'Don't you want to play the game, kid? You can throw the balls into the bowls and win a prize like the other kids. C'mon, kid, lighten up and have some fun.' So Brook finally looks up at Bozo and loudly says, 'Cram it, Clown!' That was the end of Brook's TV career."

"What did Bozo say?"

"It was great... He goes, 'That's a Bozo no-no.' Don't ever say that to Brook though."

Dr. Howard continued to come to talk to Cassady several times a week. They talked around the Sift and didn't bring it up and it seemed a dead subject. He didn't tell the doctor he still had the dreams, but they were fading. They did talk about Kyle. Many sessions were about his friend.

One day after talking about the mundane, Dr. Howard asked, "Why did you cut off communication with your girlfriend, Cassady?"

"Did my parents tell you that? It doesn't have anything to do with why or how I got in here."

"I was simply wondering. There's no right or wrong answer. She was a part of your life and it could be of interest for us to discuss why you cut her off."

"I don't know. I guess I was ashamed and after so much time went by, I didn't think I could again. Maybe, I thought it was best for her that she move on."

"Well, I think that's reasonable, but the only question I have is if you plan on talking to her when you're home?" Dr. Howard asked.

"When's that going to be? Years?"

"No, actually very much sooner than that. You see, we've been dealing with people who were thought to be 'insane' this way for decades. But, that's changing. Quickly. It's treatable and I don't think exhaustion and grief qualify as insanity anyway. There are many ways to describe your delusional episode at home. It surely isn't a psychopathic personality disorder, and I see absolutely no evidence or symptoms of schizophrenia. The hallucinations haven't continued, have they?"

"No," Cassady said, thinking—they can't because I'm not

in the Sift.

"Something has happened in California that precludes you from staying here any longer."

"Really?" Cassady blurted out. He felt a growing fear of distress in his stomach.

"Yes, they passed the Lanterman-Petris-Short Act, and it eliminates the indefinite commitment of people and requires an annual reconsideration of involuntary treatment. And your hospitalization was really, sort of, voluntary. I don't see any complications about what you went through continuing. We've had many good talks and your attitude and behavior have been exemplary in the last few months. You're doing extremely well in your academic classes also. I see no reason for you to be unable to integrate back into your life. I'll give you my phone number and I want you to call me if there is ever an issue with which you're uncomfortable. We're discharging you within the next week. We've informed your parents, and they'll be here when the formalities are completed to pick you up."

Cassady couldn't believe it could happen so incredibly fast. In five days the doctor walked him to Julian, who was ready to take him through the discharge procedure.

"They don't waste any time getting people out when they need the room, and you are far from a problem, my man," Julian said, laughing. Cassady went through the almost exact same procedure in reverse as when he was admitted. Ezra was in lockdown for getting in a fight at lunch the day before, so he didn't get a chance to say goodbye.

"He got in a hassle," was all Julian said when asked. He said goodbye. "Keep running and reading and do well in school, man." He handed Cassady a pile of magazines called *Track & Field News*.

When he got home, his parents had fixed up the Shack in the garage for him to live in full-time. It had a new full bathroom, real door, bed, and new couch. His uncle had helped his dad fix it up. He even offered Cassady a part-time job learning to do construction the next summer. It was really good money.

The thing about coming home that affected him the most was on the desk in the Shack. He found four albums. In a pile, which he found astonishing, were *John Barleycorn Must Die* by Traffic, *Tea for the Tillerman* by Cat Stevens, *The Band* by The Band, and *Abbey Road* by the Beatles. And a book, a new hard copy of *To Kill a Mockingbird* by Harper Lee, to replace the one that was taken away from him his first day in Camarillo and never returned. With the albums and book there was a note from Brie Ann:

I'm sorry you don't want to see me or talk to me. I hope you change your mind some day. All you have to do is call.

Love, Brie Ann

CHAPTER 32

"I didn't have anywhere else to go," Cassady simply said to Gram one day a week later.

Cassady and Kyle along with the neighborhood boys and girls had always casually strolled into Gram's house, and even if no family members were home, they could sit down and watch TV by themselves, or with friends, girlfriends, neighbors, or friends of friends of the family. It was the house Kyle and he visited regularly during their friendship. The family never locked their doors that anyone could remember. Gram had four sisters, three older and one a year younger. Cassady and Kyle, like several of the neighborhood boys, spent many fruitless hours vainly attempting to lose their virginity in that unhinged house on Center Street.

There were days in Camarillo Cassady thought everyone who hung out in Gram's house could seriously use some of those social-behavior classes he received.

"People look at you weird, huh? Everyone wants to know what Camarillo was like, man," Gram said. "I do too, but I'm not going to ask. You'll tell us when you feel like it."

"Yeah, eventually. Everywhere I go this weird sensation follows me. Like, people constantly give me these creepy glares and then turn away when I look back. They expect me to freak out or act like a scared puppy dog."

"So what. You're comfortable here at my house, aren't you, man?" Gram asked.

"Yeah, it's crazy and I dig it. I was a friend with you before Kyle and during all this time. I want to thank you for letting me fall back into this scene so easily."

"Yeah man, don't think about it. Don't forget we sure as shit took those bricks off his wall together, first and foremost," Gram said, laughing. Suddenly Cassady comprehended somewhere deep inside that even if you knew someone, maybe your entire life, you might never be devoted, profound friends. But you could still be friends.

"Shit, man. We were in first grade together..." Gram started to say.

"Other than my family—no one's known me longer. So many strange things have happened here—it would impossible to remember them all."

"Just chill. All the time you were gone, George and me have still been playing ping-pong in the backyard in tribute of you."

"Yeah, and the whole time I was in Camarillo I often thought about you and George playing stoned in the sun. You are a chill guy, man. It's great to see that you're still a couple of the best ping-pong players anyone's ever seen."

"We've been taking on a couple of my sister's new boyfriends. They have no idea how good we are, so it's always fun to humiliate them slowly. They think they're going to impress their new girlfriend. But really end up going down in flames while these young longhaired kids lie around laughing at them."

It was a comfortable return. Cassady didn't know exactly why he felt he couldn't return to Brie Ann, but he wasn't going to start school until January, so the rest of this fall was his. He returned to Gram's house and started the old routine. He stayed away from the library annex also, but he saw Kyle's face everywhere. At times his grief overwhelmed him and he would spend an afternoon alone in the Shack in the garage rereading books they had shared.

One afternoon a couple of weeks after he was back, when Gram's parents were out of town for the weekend, Cassady thought he'd stop by.

"Let's go down to Taylor's Liquor and get some beer," Gram said as soon as he saw him.

They went down to the store on Washington and stood outside asking men to buy them beer.

"Hey mister, would you buy us some beer?" Gram asked three men before one stopped and looked at them. They either said "no" or looked disgusted and kept walking.

"Yeah, okay," said a younger guy, probably in his early twenties, with long hair. "What do you want?"

"Colt 45 Malt," Cassady answered. "Two tall ones, the twenty-four ounces."

"More bang for our buck," Gram explained. The guy laughed.

They chugged the beers and were in the process of lying around his backyard enjoying the buzz when in walked George's sister Martha and her friend Kathy. Both were older than Gram and Cassady by two years, and were part of the group of friends that all the boys consistently lusted after. They were usually out of their league both socially and clearly sexually.

It happened right when they were at the peak of a strong powerful overwhelming malt liquor beer buzz. Martha and Kathy began acting a little strange. All Cassady could remember was Gram and Kathy were suddenly gone, probably in his garage room, much like Cassady's.

"Hi," Martha said, sitting down practically on top of him. "I think it's so cool you were in Camarillo."

"Well, it's not really that cool of a place, really..." he tried to answer.

"I bet it was like *One Flew Over the Cuckoo's Nest*, wasn't it?" Martha asked, gushing. Cassady remembered she was the one who had read it a year or two ago.

Cassady thought for a moment, *What in the world is wrong with this girl?* Then said, "Yeah, exactly."

And the next thing he knew Martha was kissing him. She had to initiate it, he would have wanted to, but had been rebuffed several times before for even stupidly and clumsily suggesting it. They lurched, hanging on each other, around to the back of the garage. It was a beautiful early fall evening and the longer uncut soft willow grass was the only pillow they needed. Martha initiated him to things that up until then had only been reading material and fantasy. Unfortunately, he found out, at certain times and with certain people, fantasies are better left that.

They were still vigorously engaged, when Cassady suddenly stopped. He was still on his hands and knees, looking over her, into the grass thinking this ought to feel better, and he should be having a great time, thinking this girl was willing to do anything; thinking he shouldn't feel awful having sex with an older, more experienced, attractive girl; and thinking, gosh, they really ought to cut this grass, when the malt liquor and other stomach contents for possibly the last week all rushed out into that same willowy grass, making quite the mess and smell.

"You pig!" Martha yelled.

"Ugggggggggh!"

A minute or two later, Cassady was still staring intently into the grass dry heaving when he faintly heard Martha squeal. She was whispering something intently, and he didn't have the energy to look over.

"What?"

"I said, I sat on a nail, asshole."

She thrust her hand under his face and in the late twilight Cassady could faintly make out the dark wet discoloration on her palm.

"Is that blood?" he asked stupidly.

"Yes, you moron, when I went to put on my pants, I sat on a nail."

"Have you had a tetanus shot lately?"

"Fuck you, asshole."

"Shit, I thought you loved me," Cassady said, laughing, still inebriated, thinking, so this is how I lose my virginity, and unexpectedly not wanting to with her. He thought, maybe this doesn't count, but also why was he being such an asshole. They didn't finish, at least, he didn't. He reasoned he'd have to check with his best friend and consultant, Kyle, for a determination. He suddenly realized gloomily he'd never be able to do that, but now that it was all off his stomach, he did feel a little better. Unknown to Cassady, in the interim of playing in the backyard, a number of kids had shown up when Martha and Kathy did, and a party had been raging for a while. Then, not wanting to miss the excitement, Gram's parents had unexpectedly shown up early, and his mom finally made her way into the backyard, probably going to knock on Gram's outside door to the Shack, when she heard Martha and Cassady exchanging murmurs of love.

"Hey, get a flashlight, some of them are out here in the dark."

Cassady remembered his bike was back there too somewhere, so he got dressed while Gram's mom continued to yell, found his bike, hopped on, and rode right by her out the gate down the driveway to find Kyle, once again, not remembering he couldn't get a ruling on virginity loss and consummation of the act. More than anything he wanted to be able to talk to Kyle, but more he still wanted, hoped, at least theoretically, to retain his virginity. He believed with his whole heart Kyle would agree with him that this night shouldn't count. The next day he was summoned to Gram's house and found out his dad had called everyone's parents in attendance but his. With Cassady, he even joked around about "getting some" from an older girl and snickered. Of course, Cassady promised to never do it again. He was *still* the golden boy who had saved his son from grand theft auto with Abilene.

Cassady realized the whole time he was thinking about Brie Ann. He felt a profound sadness not sharing his life with her and he didn't enjoy this new lifestyle, but felt powerless to stop it.

A week before Thanksgiving, Gram's dad made them an offer they couldn't refuse.

"Do you guys want to accompany me to Yosemite National Park, as part of the Culver City YMCA contingent, for a conference and retreat seminar?" he asked one day. "You'll only miss a couple days of school."

"What kind of conference, Mr. Miller?" George and Cassady asked.

"Well, it's something I have to go to, but you guys would go for the fun of it and not have to participate in the planned events," he assured them. "I'll give you a cut-rate price. I'll call your parents. No problem."

They were caught, hook, line, and sinker. George, Cassady, and Gram rode up early Friday morning with the driver, a young annoying guy named Ralph from the Y in town, and a young girl they didn't know. The girl was pretty and was quiet the whole ride. Her name was Desiree. Ralph wanted to repeatedly tell the story of how he met Cassady.

"Remember that night two summers ago, when I caught you and Kyle skinny-dipping in the outdoor Y pool about midnight," he said.

"Yeah," Cassady answered softly the first time and then, "yes," more forcefully the second.

"I think I was a very amiable guy not to turn you in to the

police or even call your parents."

It got really annoying for Cassady. He didn't want to talk about anything that included Kyle and it was a long drive with this guy continually trying to impress Desiree with his bigheartedness. He vaguely remembered Desiree from the depressive haze and confusion surrounding Kyle's funeral, but couldn't remember why.

Immediately upon their arrival at Yosemite, Gram's dad disappeared and Ralph informed them they were to be separated and sent to different cabin groupings for the "Sensitivity Training Retreat." They balked but didn't know exactly what to do, who to talk to, or how to find Gram's dad—who they didn't see until Monday evening on their way back. Cassady looked back at George and Gram with Ralph, who had a stupid smile on his face, and had to walk away with a group of strangers to a set of three cabins. Each group had about twelve people with the boys and girls split fifty/fifty. Each cabin was a duplex, divided with one side for boys, and one side for girls.

Cassady gathered with the others in his group into the leader's cabin to tell their stories. Desiree was there, but since he couldn't remember how he knew her, it didn't help. Most were active members in their respective YMCAs and were legitimately attempting to get something out of this experience. Cassady cringed and refused to participate and was being lambasted, mostly by the leader, for not "opening up to the experience."

"I choose to not talk," Cassady stated flatly. "I think you should move on without me. I was brought here under false pretenses. Find Mr. Miller from Culver City, and he'll tell you." He was flashing back on the intense talks with the counselors at Camarillo and he had learned it wasn't an effective counselor who forces people to contribute.

"I'm afraid we can't do that," the group leader named Ethan said. "We all have to share in the experience, or the group dynamic won't jell, Cassady. We want you to join in, really, we do."

It was really uncomfortable for a few minutes. Cassady looked down at his shoes and didn't answer any more questions. Ethan didn't realize Cassady could do this for months.

"If he doesn't want to participate, I don't think he should be forced to," a young guy, maybe middle twenties, said. Cassady wanted to hug him. "I mean, we're wasting time riding him and if he didn't know what the long weekend involved, I don't think it's productive for us to try to force it. I would rather hear from people who want to participate."

"Yeah, I second that," the pretty girl named Desiree with long brown frizzy hair, on Cassady's left, said. Cassady looked over and wanted to kiss her.

Right at that split second, they could hear a barely recognizable wail coming from directly outside the cabin.

"Caaaaaassssaaaadddyyyy, come out, coooooommmeeeee out, leave them!"

"That sounds like a friend of mine. I better go see what's wrong," Cassady said getting up.

"We're not supposed to leave the cabin until introductions and convictions have been completed," Ethan said emphatically.

"Sorry, gotta go. Can't leave a friend in need out in the cold."

He walked out and there was George standing there with his arms open looking as shell-shocked as Cassady felt.

"Is this unfucking believable or what?" he yelled. "Are those people in there as crazy as the nuts in my group?"

"Yeah, I want to kill Mr. Miller," Cassady said.

"He's long gone. I tried to find him and he's not even staying here."

The door to the cabin opened and Ethan was standing there looking at them.

"What's that chump want?" George said. "He's geeking

hard."

"Let's get out of here, anyway," Cassady said as they immediately started walking quickly away. "Let's go rescue Gram and get stoned."

Earlier in the week, George and Cassady had scored some dynamite hash from a friend of George's from school. They rode their bikes over to Aiden's house one afternoon and he took them into his bedroom. Cassady had never met Aiden before, much less been to his house. In the background, he could faintly hear a vacuum cleaner running as Aiden took them into his bedroom, sat at his desk right next to the door, and started cutting off a large chunk of hash. Suddenly, the door opened and Aiden's mom was standing there holding the doorknob in one hand and the vacuum cleaner tube in the other. Aiden and his mom had a ten-second staring contest while she looked up from him with the hash spread out on his desk and then at them. George and Cassady stood there struck silent—two tall longhaired strange kids standing in her son's bedroom, obviously making a drug transaction. She glared at them all one last time and backed out, slamming the door.

Aiden calmly turned toward them and said, "Did you guys enjoy meeting my mom?"

They walked along, checking in with various groups, and were constantly questioned as to what they were doing and why they weren't in their group, but answered they had an emergency message for Gram Miller. They finally found Gram in the assembly hall. When they walked up, Gram was standing on a chair with his back to his group with the members standing around him chanting for him to open his trusting senses and fall into their welcoming trustworthy waiting arms. After he did, Cassady and George shouted for him, and he looked at them, sauntered over, and asked oddly what was going on.

"Come on, let's get out of here," Cassady said.

"Why would I want to leave?" Gram said with a strange curious look in his eyes. George and Cassady looked at each other, shrugged, backed up, and George said, "I guess we'll see you later."

As they walked out of the hall, George said, "That figures, in less than two hours they've turned him into a pod person."

They were still laughing about that when later in the evening, after indulging, they found themselves in the foyer of the main lodge of Yosemite Village where several of the group members were also sitting around listening to a couple of guitar players.

The older guy that had defended him was there. They listened and enjoyed themselves talking and laughing. Cassady ended up sharing sleeping quarters with the older guy, Martin, and another guy his own age. Only a thin wall in the second part of their cabin separated Desiree and Cassady's cabin mates from each of their rooms. He later learned one could hear everything said in either room. They spent most of their time laughing.

"I'm not sure many of the campers are that enamored with Mr. Ethan and the program, but I came for personal reasons," Martin said. "I'm getting married soon and have been involved in my YMCA, so I'm taking one last solo journey."

Cassady couldn't remember what all was said, probably driven by a hash haze and loss of inhibitions, but they did have fun before they crashed, and he passed a test he didn't even know he was taking.

At breakfast the next morning Desiree approached Cassady.

"Would you like to go hiking?" she asked. "I've dropped out of the sensitivity schedule also. I remember you from your friend's funeral. There's a friend of mine in another cabin. We'll go meet her also."

"What?" Cassady asked, confused. "Wait." She took off walking quickly and he had no choice but to follow.

"Go with me. It'll be someone you like. I guarantee it. Relax," she said, continuing the walk down the row of cabins. "They've joined our mutiny also."

"But who? Why don't we go on the hike with the others?" he asked. "Who did you know at Kyle's..."

"Did you know I also know your name is the modern English version of the Gaelic or Celtic name C a s s i d y?" Desiree said, interrupting as she walked ahead, looking back over her shoulder.

"Wait a second," Cassady whispered, as they continued down the row of cabins. "Only two people cared enough to find that out and knew it. My parents didn't even bother to look that up."

"Yeah, it was also the last name of the Beat Generation guy Jack Kerouac used for *On The Road*."

Cassady glanced down to the last cabin. "You were at Kyle's funeral with... You're friends with... I remember!"

"Too late," Desiree said, smiling and pointing down to the last cabin. There, sitting on the steps partially hidden from the overhanging tree branches, was Brie Ann.

CHAPTER 33

Before meeting up with the others, Brie Ann and Cassady went for a walk alone along the Yosemite Falls trail to the first waterfall. It was a cold but wonderfully crisp morning.

"I'm sorry for setting this up without your permission. I couldn't wait for you and didn't care what happened. If you didn't want to see me—I was prepared for that," Brie Ann said.

"No, no... you're right. This was good. I needed a push and didn't know it. It's truly what I want."

"We need to talk about Kyle and what happened. Don't you think?"

"Yes, but I don't have any more answers than I did when I left. We can't know what happens when people die. Maybe we all go to a Sift, or heaven, or maybe they were really in hell. At least, a type of hell. It's unknowable, that's all I know," Cassady said.

"I think that's a good start, but is anything like that meltdown going to happen again?" Brie Ann asked. "I don't want you to ignore me again. I can stand anything but that."

"I don't think so, but don't take me into the Sift again and have me lose my best friend," Cassady answered. He thought it a good sign he could say that without tearing up, and instead be really happy he was back with Brie Ann.

"Wow, I didn't expect that for an answer," she said. "Are you really as good as you seem to be?"

"I think so. This secret is bigger than both of us, but we can get through it. I think. As long as we're together." He really did think so. "Now, fill me in on what you've been doing. And how did you get to know Desiree?"

"She started school a little before you left, and was dropping by the library annex, and we started talking," Brie Ann said. "When she heard about Kyle, she offered to go to the funeral with me, and since then she's been a good friend. I joined the swim team with her. It's been something to do at least. I know I told you on the sly at home, but I really want you to know I've never whispered a word about the Sift to her."

"Was it hard keeping it in?"

"Yeah, but having Eleanor to talk to helped, and I spent time with her and talked," Brie Ann said. "She said it looked like we both suffered a shock from the experience and she knew it was real after the séance. She thinks we both will still have issues for a while and that we can talk to each other and her if we need to."

"I thought of that, but I pushed so much away in my mind that I couldn't really let myself think about this being real or you being real. I don't know why this happened and now I'm glad you're here and I'm with you again. At least, I want it to be that way."

"We have to be together on this to make sense of it," Brie Ann said.

"Maybe I... or maybe we can now. I'm glad you had her to talk to."

"She did. She's open to stuff like that. We should have known with the séance. I told her what I could and what happened, and she was open to it. I also didn't tell her about the horror we saw at the end with them. I let that be my own hell and besides, it helped me when you wouldn't communicate. She told me to give it some time. That you would come around, and you did," Brie Ann said, smiling. "You simply needed a little push and Desiree helped plan that."

"To tell you the truth, I was never so glad to see someone in my life. Keeping you away was stupid."

"Cassady, remember what Eleanor told you the night of Kyle's death, about meeting someone who could help. She said it might come up again and she'd let us know."

"Who was it?"

"I don't know. Some actor I think. Until then we'll keep it a secret, at least I promise I will."

"Who'd believe you anyway? You'd end up in Camarillo too."

"We can talk about it. How bad was it?"

"It wasn't good, but it really wasn't that bad. I was able to spend time thinking and acting normal. Which I realized I wasn't acting like, even with you some of the time, because of the secret about going in. But so you know this feels really good."

"Maybe if you act normal long enough, you'll be able to be normal, whatever that means. Eleanor said that. But I don't think we'll ever be completely normal again, 'for what it's worth.'"

"Great song. What else have you been listening to? Thanks for the albums by the way, and I needed to have *Mockingbird* again. That was the coolest present and the best thing I've been given in a long time."

The walk lasted several hours and they forgot about the other campers. They talked records, movies, TV shows, books, and more books. Brie Ann filled Cassady in on her life without him. They talked about everything they could think of and then more. When they felt they didn't have anything else to talk about they talked about the sky, water, flowers, the universe, their friends, relatives, school, stupid philosophical things, and even their future goals and dreams. Hours passed and they never thought a conversation could encompass and take them around the world covering places they wanted to see together.

"What's with the running?" Brie Ann asked. "A couple of people told me they'd see you early in the morning. It's funny every time they saw you it was either on Culver along the Backlot or on Elenda."

"I don't know, but it feels like a release. I'm dealing with things better and starting to look at it with a sense of accomplishment," he said. "It's like Julian gave me another gift. Other than yesterday, hanging with George, I've had no real desire to get high again, so I hope that's a good thing."

"That can't be a bad thing. I feel the same way about swimming."

Cassady decided to refrain from telling her about the Martha fiasco at Gram's house. He was almost certain Kyle would have agreed that it didn't count, so he let it pass. He felt guilty about not communicating with her and still couldn't explain why it happened, not even to himself.

"I'm sorry this whole thing came to pass, but I wasn't really over everything and still don't know *how* the whole thing came to pass. I really don't have an excuse for cutting you out of my life. I didn't want it to happen. I used to think about you for hours. I wondered what you were doing and wished I were with you. Every time I didn't walk into the annex, I hoped I would see you somewhere else. I couldn't think about what exactly we were going to talk about, that I wanted you to be the one I was talking and being with. I really, hardly ever got around to thinking about kissing you or maybe more, but being with you was enough. Whew! Sorry," he said.

"Never more than kissing, really?" Brie Ann raised an eyebrow at him.

"No, I guess that's a little lie," he said, laughing.

"I was resentful and a little angry, but I mostly felt sorry for you and wished I could have helped. I can get over my feelings though. Let's make sure our time counts now." She leaned into him and kissed him. The next two days they had a great time tripping around the park.

CHAPTER 34

It was a couple of weeks after the Yosemite weekend and they'd been easing into being together, and even gentler about talking about what had happened.

Cassady and Brie Ann showed up at Eleanor's late one Saturday morning and walked up the path to the front. When Eleanor opened the door, Cassady knew she knew everything that had happened and didn't say anything, but hugged them both. The house still had a darkened pallor to it, but it never occurred to Cassady or Brie Ann to be frightened or even nervous. The worst had already taken place and nothing, it seemed, could scare them again.

Brie Ann had set this meeting up. Eleanor called Brie Ann and said the same opportunity had arisen about meeting someone who might either have information or actually know something about what happened to Kyle. Cassady reluctantly agreed.

"We'll obviously take my car," Eleanor said as she closed the door behind her and walked them around the side to an old, dilapidated garage that housed an old Chevy that she had been driving for years.

"Where are we going?" Cassady asked.

"To the Beverly Wilshire Hotel. Have you ever been

there?"

"No," both Cassady and Brie Ann answered.

"It's nice and maybe today, nice is what we need right now. I'm so sorry about Kyle."

Cassady sat in the back, and Brie Ann in the front passenger seat. They drove up to Overland Avenue and east on Pico while Cassady looked out the window thinking about going through all that had happened in the last year or more. He wanted Kyle back and wanted to be friends with Brie Ann and more than that. But at least he felt that he now might have a clue how. One dream had come true, and another had turned into a nightmare.

They made a left onto Beverly Drive and wound through the big houses that kept getting bigger as they went north. Eleanor turned off before Wilshire Boulevard and went up and down a couple of residential streets.

"We can find a parking place here, so we don't have to use the valet parking," she said.

"What's that?" Brie Ann asked.

"It's where you pay someone to park your car."

"Pay someone, really?" Cassady asked.

"Yes, it's crazy, but some people pay other people to park their car for them," she said and laughed.

"I can't see paying someone to park a car, even if I had one," Cassady said, and a small grin turned up at the corners of his mouth. He saw Eleanor looking at him in the rearview mirror.

She smiled and said, "When we get there, I know you have many, many questions to ask, but let me talk first, so we can get started and not get thrown out. I talked to him on the phone and had to tell a couple of white lies to get him to see us. He didn't really remember me, but because of Leslie, he agreed to meet us. I told him you were my niece and nephew, so we have to take it slowly."

"Why do you think he'll know anything?" Brie Ann asked. "What's his name?"

"His name is Laurence Olivier and some people think he is one of the greatest actors in the world. It's a coincidental chance that he's here again this week. He's here for some sort of movie meeting, looking into a couple of film possibilities. He was married to Vivien, or Scarlett to you, but please try not to call her that, even if it comes up. They weren't married when she died, but I think they were still friends. I don't really know if this will work, but I was hoping he might have some insight or something. I really don't know, but think we should try."

"Why are we doing this then?" Cassady asked. He remembered Scarlett talking about him and being married to him. He was getting nervous and felt bad and was tired.

"I don't know if it will, but don't you want to try and get some answers as to what happened and if there is anything we can do? Don't you want to know what happened to Kyle?"

"Kyle's dead, and so is Leslie, so what's the point?"

Eleanor had parked the car and slumped forward and started sobbing.

"Stop," shouted Brie Ann throwing a furious look at Cassady. "He didn't mean that, he's still upset at times and doesn't know what he's saying, do you?"

"I didn't mean to upset you," Cassady answered. "I mean I thought I might have been able to stop it, but now I don't know. You're right, Eleanor, I guess we should learn what we can, so let's do it. I'm sorry, really I am."

Eleanor sat still and collected herself for a minute or two. "Okay, let's go. We're supposed to meet him in the restaurant and let the concierge know when we've gotten there."

"Okay, but what's a conseeage—" Cassady asked.

"Concierge. It's French for somebody who runs things in an exclusive hotel like the Beverly Wilshire," Eleanor said, laughing quietly, wiping the tears from her eyes, and taking a deep breath.

They walked a couple of streets up toward Wilshire Boulevard on Rodeo Drive and marveled at the size of the hotel. It seemed to take up a whole block, and there were people walking in and out, along with cars pulling in and out, so nobody really noticed them. Eleanor was dressed nicely, so Cassady thought maybe they didn't look as out of place as he felt. They walked into the huge lobby and Brie Ann and Cassady felt overwhelmed. It looked as big as a football field with a gigantic chandelier hanging in the foyer, and the floors were polished to a mirror.

"It's going to be fine," Eleanor whispered and motioned for them to wait.

Eleanor walked right up to the long ornate desk where several people in blue suits with embroidered badges were working and talking on phones. She talked to a man, and he pointed back behind them and gestured, and another man standing outside a large office walked toward Eleanor. They conferred for a minute and then she walked back to Brie Ann and Cassady.

"We can go on up to his room. He's running late and can't come down to the restaurant right now. Maybe we'll have more privacy," Eleanor said, but her voice had a slight quiver to it.

Brie Ann and Cassady looked at each other, but didn't say anything.

"He's in a luxury suite on the top floor. We can take the elevator right over there," she said, pointing to a hallway off the main foyer. They took the elevator up to the penthouse floor and walked down the private hallway. The walls were strikingly white and the carpet a deep golden beige. Eleanor knocked on the door, ignoring the button that they thought was a doorbell. The door was immediately opened and a man an inch or two shorter than Cassady stood there looking at them. He appeared full of, Cassady could only think, of passion. His eyes were dark, clear, and sharp. He was thick in the waist and had a pronounced chin and a mass of dark neatly combed hair. He stared at them and waited.

"Mr. Olivier, I—I—I'm Eleanor, and this is my niece and nephew, Brie Ann and Cassady."

"Of course you are, dear. Come in, come in." He turned and walked into the large room that didn't look like any hotel room Cassady could think of. This was not the bedroom; obviously there was another room or two. The room was actually a living room of sorts with gold sofas and love seats. The man walked with an ease that suggested everything he did was rehearsed and performed flawlessly.

"I insist you call me Larry. I allow my friends to, and I do believe you mean to be at least friendly, do you not?" He smiled as he talked. "Now please, sit, and make yourself comfortable and delight me with why you've come."

They all three sat down on two corner love seats, Cassady and Brie Ann on one and Eleanor on another, Laurence Olivier directly across from them. He crossed his legs and put his hands over his knees.

"Well Mr. Olivier, I mean, Larry. We've come to talk about Vivien and my father, Leslie..." Eleanor hesitated.

"What could I possibly have to discuss with you concerning Vivien, or for god's sake, your father, whom I only met on the set and at a couple of screenings and the like? I do remember him being somewhat of a pensive fellow, sucking on a pipe incessantly."

"I was hoping we could ask you some things that you could possibly give us answers to. If not, we'll be on our way."

"I wonder what they have in common after all these years other than both being gone now? Have we met socially, you and I, if at all? I've been racking my memory to think of when we've met and can't for the life of me when exactly that was, my dear?"

"Please let her explain," Cassady interrupted.

"My dear boy, politeness is the missing ingredient here, I do believe."

It poured out, not unlike it had with the doctor who had him committed.

"I'm not your *dear boy*, and she's trying to tell you that I've recently met and talked to Vivien; she was dressed as Scarlett O'Hara. I've spent hours, nights, and months with her in something called the Sift on the Backlot here in Culver City and she and Leslie have taken my best friend and I want him back. So shut the hell up about being polite and listen." Cassady howled this out and Brie Ann put her arm around him. The room was silent. Everyone looked down and waited. Only Eleanor looked not up, but also attentively at Cassady.

"I've come to believe him and as incredible as it seems, well, it's worth your time to listen," Eleanor said.

"He's telling the truth, I know he is," Brie Ann said. "I was there also."

The room was silent. Nobody spoke for almost a minute.

Finally, Laurence Olivier dropped his head into his hands, looked up pensively at all three of them, and cleared his throat. "I realize this may sound as crazy to you as what you'd expect it to sound like to me. As difficult as it is to believe, which I certainly think you will, but I not only believe you, I've been waiting several years thinking this very thing might happen, but fearful it might also. But I do have a question or two,"

"What?" Eleanor said.

"We never made public what our first conversation was when Vivien came backstage to talk to me after my performance in *Theatre Royal* in 1934. Did it ever come up in all these astonishing nights, weeks, or months?" he asked demurely with a slight smile on his face.

"Yes," Cassady said. "She went backstage, and you were

sitting on the stool at the mirror still sweating, and she leaned over and kissed your shoulder and said, 'We'll be together soon forever, my love.'"

Olivier slumped on his couch and held his hands up to his head again. After maybe two minutes he got up and went over to the bar set inside one wall and made a drink. He walked into a little foyer off the room and picked up the phone and made a call. He talked in hushed tones for a minute and the only thing they heard was his voice as it raised telling someone that someone else would have to wait.

Cassady whispered to Brie Ann, "If he tells us to get out we'll leave and pretend it was all a joke. I don't want him to laugh or yell at us. We know this is real and maybe he can't handle it." He stopped and looked up.

Olivier walked back slowly and sat back down. He paused for a breath and...

"Oh my God, you have seen her, haven't you? A young boy from Culver City, California, couldn't have possibly known that unless you met her somehow."

"Yes, I'm telling the truth."

"I don't know what I can tell you other than what I know," he said to them, sloshing his ice around in the glass and taking a large gulp of his drink.

"We want to know what this is, if you know and what can we do about it?" Eleanor said. "Can we reverse anything about this or make contact again. Have you?"

"No, I'm eternally sorry, there's nothing I can do to help you. But yes, I was aware of it. After we divorced, but actually long before that, Vivien was visited by these visions, and we— meaning friends, family, and her doctors—were completely convinced she was mentally unstable and was having periodic nervous breakdowns."

"I know the feeling..." Cassady whispered to Brie Ann. "Sorry," he said to Olivier.

"There were times when we would have friends staying with us at our home, Notley Abbey, and we would stay up incredibly late watching movies on the old projectors, until almost four a.m. And after we slept in, Vivien would have already been up for hours or not slept at all. She'd have the whole day planned. This intense erratic behavior began soon after she was in *A Streetcar Named Desire* with Marlon Brando. She was never the same," he sighed. "I begged her not to play that part."

"Is that when she had shock treatments, or whatever?" Cassady asked.

"Yes, we didn't know what else to do. Vivien always wanted more than I could give her. We divorced in 1961, and she had already been having the visions about being back in *Gone with the Wind*. It was quite detailed. Leslie always had a part of the dream, but I knew he had been dead for years by then so I assumed it was, in fact, vis-à-vis *Gone with the Wind*. Everyone thought it was the stress of the divorce. I sold our home at Notley Abbey and she purchased her country home she called Tickerage Mill and spent gobs of money refurbishing it. It had a lake and gardens where she could walk, and where I hoped she would find peace."

"Did she?" Eleanor asked.

"No, but we remained friends—or at least we tried. She would call me and tell me these outlandish stories of a Sift, a blue cloud that would envelop her and take her back to Tara, where she could live happily there forever. She asked me to join her. I naturally placated her and told her that would be marvelous. Her new husband, Jack Merivale, became more or less her caretaker, a dear man. They had a simple but caring relationship. But he had no idea about what she was going through. She would have one breakdown after another, and years later I put it together in my diary entries and they fell in place after a hysterical phone call concerning this thing she called the Sift. When she died, they put it down to a recurring bout of her tuberculosis, but of course, she hadn't had TB in years and was completely in remission. She passed too quickly for that to be the cause. At the time I had a sinking feeling it was somehow a choice on her part. That she didn't want to live with it any longer."

"My friend got sucked into it because of falling in love with her," Cassady said.

"If that's the case I'm truly sorry for your loss, but I understand it. She was a very lovely woman," Olivier said. "Can I ask you what she looked like? Many times, she told me she could be young and beautiful again, like when she made the movie."

"Yes, I have to say she was beautiful and young—exactly what she looked like in *Gone with the Wind*," Cassady said, glancing over to Brie Ann.

"She was amazingly beautiful," she said, agreeing.

"Thank God for that," Olivier choked out.

"Can you tell us anything more about what it was and how it works, and could she have come back?" Eleanor asked. Cassady leaned forward as if to say something and then sat back. Brie Ann put her hand on his shoulder.

"I naturally asked around to see if anyone else had any thoughts on this and a few things after her death, and even spent a few nights at Tickerage Mill myself, and then hired a man to stay for several weeks to see if anything happened; nothing did, and then Jack, her late husband, sold it and that was the end of it until now."

"That's all you know about it?" Cassady said. He kept the rest of his thoughts to himself. He sat back with a dejected look on his face. "Maybe this is the end."

"But this can't be the end. It can't. You have to know more, please!" Eleanor cried.

"Friends, I wish I could tell you more but I feel that after suppressing this for these last years," Olivier said dejectedly.

"I simply don't have more for you other than what this young man can tell us. It seems you've experienced it and somehow haven't succumbed to its compulsion, or coercion, perhaps?"

"I've tried to *not* think about it too much lately, but I have to admit it was some of the best times of my life and I'll remember it fondly forever. If I hadn't met Brie Ann, I'd probably have wanted to stay also, but at the same time I didn't have a Scarlett or a Vivien to pull me in. They actually offered me someone else," Cassady said in a long rush.

"Can I ask, or can you tell me who that might have been?" Olivier asked.

"Yes, it was Judy Garland."

"Oh my, dear boy, it seems you were wise enough to, as they say, dodge that bullet. I only met her once or twice, but it didn't look good from the outside. She seemed to have severe problems also. I think this is an extraordinary occurrence in all our lives."

"It didn't matter. It was almost after a time, like, they wanted Kyle more than me anyway. I had some feeling deep inside, like I knew it was wrong, but for the longest time I couldn't stop either," Cassady said.

"And Eleanor, you've been without your father for a much longer period of time, haven't you?" Olivier asked.

"Yes, he's been gone since the war, but I still haven't given up hope of contacting him. But Cassady, you have said many times Vivien was young, right?"

"Yes, the same age as she was during *Gone with the Wind*, as was Leslie. I thought she was even younger than that, the first time we saw her," Cassady said. "Judy Garland was the same age as she was in *The Wizard of Oz*, also."

"Pardon me for reiterating this point, but Vivien was the most beautiful thing you ever saw, wasn't she?" Olivier asked again.

Cassady blushed and looked down. Brie Ann smiled and leaned her head on his shoulder and whispered something no one else could hear.

"What?" Eleanor asked.

"She looked unbelievably beautiful," Brie Ann again said, looking at Olivier.

"Thank you for echoing that. I can never hear it too much. I'm happily married, however it still gives me chills thinking about the first time I saw her on stage in *The Happy Hypocrite*. Did you know they looked for over two years for a Scarlett and spent almost $100,000, and that was in the late 1930s? She secured the role from 1,400 other women. She was born to play Scarlett. She was not supposed to die to be her."

"I want my friend back," Cassady said.

"And I want my father back," Eleanor said.

"We'll tell you something that may or may not ease your suffering," Brie Ann said.

"Do we want to, really?" Cassady asked her.

"Tell us everything you know and help us understand," Eleanor said.

"It wasn't actually them," Cassady said. "At least, I don't really think so. It was some freakish unearthly occurrence."

"What do you mean?" Olivier asked, looking angry and his voice rising with every word. "Explain this to me."

"Explain it to me also," Eleanor said with the same incredulous timbre to her voice. "You've never whispered this to me, Brie Ann."

"I couldn't. I simply couldn't. I'm sorry, I had to wait for Cassady."

Cassady and Brie Ann knew they had to tell them the truth of what they experienced and what they believed the spirits in the Sift actually were. They looked at each other, understanding it was going to crush the memories Eleanor and Olivier were creating now.

"What we saw the last time before Kyle died was something horrific and terrifying but not them. It was something out of hell, not the malevolent spirits they first appeared like, but I don't know..." Brie Ann said.

"The last thing Scarlett said to me was 'Hell is empty and all the devils are here,'" Cassady said.

"That is decidedly something my Vivien would not say! At least we're dealing with educated devils. That's the first act of William Shakespeare's *The Tempest,* dear boy," Olivier said.

"What's it all mean?" Eleanor cried.

"I think it means that our friends here are surmising that they didn't, in fact, meet our loved ones, but something darker, ghastlier, and nastier," Olivier said.

"We think so also. If that's true, then our loved ones didn't become this by choice," Cassady said.

"Or, it's really not even them, but they were, maybe, appropriated by devils to spend time on the earth. That would make sense with what Big Sam said to us. He was trying to warn us," Brie Ann added.

"Big Sam from *Gone with the Wind*? He was there also?" Eleanor asked.

"Yes, he was. What did he say, Cassady?" Brie Ann asked.

"I'll never forget it. It was what a hippie on Venice Beach said to me. 'The cruelty of Satan, who seeks by all means to devour us, is overcome by watchfulness and faith.'"

"Once again a quote from literate ghosts, or as you say, hippies on the beach," Olivier said. "It's from 1 Peter 5. 'Satan is a lion, a stalker, looking for a way to exploit and destroy the next generation. Be sober, be vigilant; because your adversary the devil, as a roaring lion, walketh about, seeking whom he may devour.'"

"What does it mean?" Eleanor asked again.

"I think our very bright young lady here has come across the answer. It wasn't them. Perhaps they were stalked and taken, as your friend was," Olivier said. "For what purpose? We may never know or understand. But they were vessels in this supernatural or mystical, with some horrid overtones, with devilish intent, world. That's all I can surmise. Our loved ones aren't really part of this unless they agree to it somehow, but probably not without treachery or an incomplete willingness on their end. Do you agree?"

"I guess," Cassady said.

"I want to believe that my father didn't either know or understand what he was getting himself into," Eleanor said.

"They would never have participated, even in death, with a civilization that condoned and was part of slave trading and causing the anguish of millions of human beings," Brie Ann interjected. "We understood that from our conversation with Big Sam or Mr. Everett Brown."

"I want to believe that my father would never have agreed to that either," Eleanor said. "He told me he detested that part of the movie, and the part he had to play, acting like he missed the 'Old South.' He was a gentleman, but not a Southern slave trader."

"Kyle was pulled into it by Scarlett or Vivien. That's all," Cassady said. "Ashley, or Leslie, said they own his nephesh. What's that mean?"

"It's his soul, my dear friend. Vivien and Leslie may not have even participated in any part of this dreadfulness of taking your friend from you," Olivier said. "There is more to the world or universe than we can ever comprehend. Eleanor, I promise to keep in touch. Thank you, my young stalwart friends. You've helped me understand the impossible. With that I'll leave it. I absolutely have to be going now. I'm sorry I couldn't have been more help. Thank you, though, for this validation and help comprehending Vivien's last few years."

CHAPTER 35

The place still radiated in his soul. The dilapidated paint and structures remained in his memory and resided down in the depths of his heart. The eucalyptus trees would always sway in the slight breeze. The oaks would always create a dusky overhanging tunnel to stroll through. The stillness and quiet during the day and tranquility during the deep night would always be a private refuge in the midst of the insane life outside. The ending of their friendship didn't lessen the memories or their importance in his life. The passage of time only intensified the meaningfulness of those memories. His recollection of the Backlot was still wonderful and revered, because the friendship had been wonderful and revered.

Throughout their childhood, a freight train ran down the split center of Culver Boulevard from downtown Los Angeles to the beach city of Playa del Rey. The trains were never long. They only had four or five cars along with a caboose. Culver Boulevard and the train tracks might have seemed a superficial dividing line for the split street, but it was also a slight metaphorical actuality between the haves and have-nots in the west Los Angeles suburb of Culver City.

One of Cassady and Kyle's greatest interests was obviously

where the line split into Backlot 2 on the MGM Studio Backlots. Over the years, various friends and Cassady watched the trains slowly make their way down the tracks as they lumbered and clumped noisily along the ancient rails. They daily strolled the rails, balancing like trapeze artists, as they made their way home from school and, again, during summers and weekends, visiting other friends in their houses on the other side of the tracks. They had laid dozens of pennies on the rails over the years to flatten them.

One day walking along the tracks as a train rolled east slowly by, Kyle said, "Hey, let's hitch a ride."

It was a split-second decision, with no planning, no scheme, no strategy, and typically for them, no idea of where they would end up, or how they would get home.

"How?" Cassady yelled as they ran along beside the caboose.

"Up on the steps," Kyle answered, jumping on and pulling himself up. He reached down and pulled Cassady up.

They casually sat down and looked around as the train plodded through downtown Culver City. Cassady remembered waving to people in their cars and trying to act as if what they were doing was as natural for two young boys to do in 1969 as anything else during those years. That was the beauty of being Kyle's friend. He made it seem like what they did was as awesome during the occasions they did them, as they seemed now some years later. They waved, laughed, and smiled as people looked at them in wonderment. A few honked their horns at them and they responded, again, by vigorously waving back.

As they meandered out of Culver City and into greater Los Angeles, Cassady was sure he was the one who finally asked how far they were going to go and how long they going to stay on this adventure. Kyle's answer was a shrug that said, "Who cares? This is great." And it was. But after another ten or twenty minutes Cassady's concern was rewarded with a conductor or brakeman, probably wondering what all the horn honking was about, opening the caboose's back door and yelling.

"What the hell do you think you're doing? Get the hell off of here! Crazy kids."

The door actually opened out, so it practically forced them to jump off at that point anyway. Luckily, they were at an intersection where there was virtually no traffic, and they made a safe landing. They looked around and, not recognizing the neighborhood, had no choice but to begin walking back down the tracks until they got back home, several hours later. Once again, with Kyle, not really minding the walk at all. It was how he chose to remember Kyle. He'd hoped he'd never allow himself to forget him.

Several years passed and he heard the Backlot was being sold. MGM was selling off the land and bulldozing the old sets for developers to come in and build homes and condominiums. His senior year in high school, Cassady returned to the Backlot for the last time. He went by himself. It was dusk in April, not quite dark, and the Southern California weather was lovely. It was cool and sparkling after several recent rain showers. The bushes and shrubbery were green and the trees were tall and graceful. He didn't anticipate finding Kyle. He had given up on that notion. He had gone back several times after that fateful summer night and he knew Kyle was gone for good. The Sift was gone, as were Ashley and the beautiful Scarlett. He didn't quite understand where or why. He continued to feel guilty beyond belief. Maybe if he had been more persuasive or hard-nosed or hadn't spent so much time with Brie Ann. She was still his rock, and he still second-guessed himself.

Cassady had run the gamut of returning and going on in school, and then everyday life without Kyle and their routine. Brie Ann and he spent much of their time together, but it was hard at times to know what was real and what wasn't. They both hoped it would get better in time, and it was a bond they would always have together. She was starting college soon, but he was still unsure about what to do next. Cassady had become a pretty good runner and had some negligible offers to run at decent schools, but still felt he'd need a job; along with the training and working, it would be hard. He still wasn't as academically inclined as Brie Ann and didn't know if he would be able to hack it. While he was running all over Culver City, she had gotten into swimming and was going to UCLA on a scholarship.

"I wonder if there will be a time when I can forget about Kyle?" Cassady asked her one day.

"No, don't second-guess yourself. You aren't supposed to forget him. He was your best friend. I'm sure he hasn't forgotten about you," she answered. Brie Ann always knew what to say to calm him down.

"I know. Mostly I think, it's like he's living somewhere else and I haven't seen him in a while."

He walked by Eleanor's house. She had died early in January. After the small, lightly attended funeral, they both got called to a lawyer's office in the downtown Culver City office building. They had still visited her often after the city closed the small library annex. They felt like she had adopted them, in a sense. Her house became a second home, and she became someone they could always talk to. They talked about school, their future, books, and of course Leslie. Rarely about Kyle or Vivien. Eleanor heard from Laurence Olivier once in a while and told Brie Ann and Cassady about movies or plays he was in.

"Eleanor was very explicit in her will. I can read the legalese or tell you in a nutshell what she left you two," the lawyer said.

"You can summarize what the gist of it is. We weren't looking for anything from her," Brie Ann said. "This is a complete surprise to us."

"I know, young lady, she respected that. I had asked her one time if you had ever asked her for money or anything else," he said. "Do you know what she said?"

"No," they both answered together.

"She bit my head off and asked me if I had any friends and that she had made a couple late in life and to mind my own business. I was looking after her best interests, of course, but she still stood up for you and your friendship with her. She said you were her best library readers and she enjoyed your company. She didn't have any other family. She left you both, Cassady and Brie Ann, enough money for college and living expenses. Provided you major in something worthwhile, preferably as English majors, but actually there are no stipulations. It's a nice way of saying she wanted to help you out, since you neither have any real family money. Is that right?" he asked.

"Yes," they both answered together, both in shock with the present, but immediately understanding this was truly who Eleanor was.

This last time, Cassady climbed the fence and dropped down into the weeds behind the Southern mansion as he had hundreds of times. He paused as Kyle and he always did, before getting up and walking across the road to climb the scaffolding in the back of the mansion known as Tara. He went to walk around the Backlot. The unearthly spiritual connection was severed and, even as he felt certain uneasiness during the time he was walking near the mansions, European Village, lake, graveyard, and train station, he knew it was because of earthly fears, normal fears. It was because he was merely alone.

ACKNOWLEDGEMENTS

I would like to think all of my childhood/teenage friends and comrades who joined me in our adventures in the Backlots of MGM and Desilu Studios. We discovered and explored them together and it truly became our fantasy world. It could have only happened for a short period of time in one place: Culver City, California. I'd like to also thank the librarian in the small annex on Sepulveda, all those years ago, who helped turn me into a reader. The librarian at Howenstine High School, Suzan Brown, who had her student "readers" read the early manuscript drafts anonymously and comment and confirm the worthwhileness of continuing the effort. Meg Files, who gave me honest feedback through all those writing classes. And to the wonderful memory of Tempest Alabi-Isama, an amazing art teacher who enjoyed the story enough to paint the beautiful picture of Tara on the cover. I'd also like to thank Nick Courtright and the staff at Atmosphere Press for the opportunity to publish *Fedor* and now *Culver City*, with exceptional help from Bryce Wilson (editor), Amie Norris (editor), Ronaldo Alves (final cover), and many others.

I'd also like to think Cheryl Ann for supporting me, loving me, and finally having the patience to listen to the innumerable Culver City stories repeated ad nauseam.

ABOUT ATMOSPHERE PRESS

Atmosphere Press is an independent, full-service publisher for excellent books in all genres and for all audiences. Learn more about what we do at atmospherepress.com.

We encourage you to check out some of Atmosphere's latest releases, which are available at Amazon.com and via order from your local bookstore:

Dancing with David, a novel by Siegfried Johnson

The Friendship Quilts, a novel by June Calender

My Significant Nobody, a novel by Stevie D. Parker

Nine Days, a novel by Judy Lannon

Shining New Testament: The Cloning of Jay Christ, a novel by Cliff Williamson

Shadows of Robyst, a novel by K. E. Maroudas

Home Within a Landscape, a novel by Alexey L. Kovalev

Motherhood, a novel by Siamak Vakili

Death, The Pharmacist, a novel by D. Ike Horst

Mystery of the Lost Years, a novel by Bobby J. Bixler

Bone Deep Bonds, a novel by B. G. Arnold

Terriers in the Jungle, a novel by Georja Umano

Into the Emerald Dream, a novel by Autumn Allen

His Name Was Ellis, a novel by Joseph Libonati

The Cup, a novel by D. P. Hardwick

The Empathy Academy, a novel by Dustin Grinnell

Tholocco's Wake, a novel by W. W. VanOverbeke

Dying to Live, a novel by Barbara Macpherson Reyelts

Looking for Lawson, a novel by Mark Kirby